# Search for Lazarus

*Book Two of the Lazarus Trilogy*

## Johanna Ridenow

authorHOUSE®

*AuthorHouse™*
*1663 Liberty Drive*
*Bloomington, IN 47403*
*www.authorhouse.com*
*Phone: 1-800-839-8640*

*Published by AuthorHouse 5/2/2013*

*ISBN: 978-1-4817-3226-0 (sc)*
*ISBN: 978-1-4817-3225-3 (e)*

# CHAPTER I

## FROM BILOXI TO DENVER WITH LOVE

It was our last night on the road. Had it really been two weeks? That and a little more, which must have infuriated some people that were waiting for us at our destination to no end but delighted both Michael and I. A honeymoon should never be rushed, at least that was my feeling anyway. I had tried to warn Michael that somebody would be bugging us every day on his cell. Before we ever even hit the Mississippi river, Michael had put his phone away in our luggage in the back of my truck and just ignored it. If someone needed us our housemate Alison had my satellite phone number that worked no matter where I was in the country as long as there wasn't too much cloud cover.

Since Michael would still be sleeping for a few hours and I was more than awake at 3 a.m., I decided to go for a run. Denver was such a pretty city and had a very unusual quality to it. But every town or city that we had gone through on our cross-country journey had its own brand of uniqueness; some good and some not, but all different and memorable. Maybe it was looking at everything through the eyes of being in love that made the difference. A new and very passionate love that I hoped would take years if not decades to wane. I hoped it would be even longer before I lost my total fascination for the man sleeping peacefully in our hotel bed.

How had I been so lucky to warrant him? Somebody; somewhere must really like me and wanted what was the best for me. If I knew my late husband Rick it was probably him. It would be just like something he would do. Rick had been so selfless in most things, especially when it came to me, giving up his own life for me had only been the last of a

## ⋞ Johanna Ridenow ⋟

long line of things he sacrificed for me. Now I was bonded to someone else. A term that meant something much more than married and was difficult to put into words even in my own head. It was like he really was a piece of me.

I left a little note stuck on the pillow beside his head. It was difficult to leave him there unmolested. He was always handsome but never more so that when his dark brown hair was in curly disarray and his face relaxed so that the many worries we both carried with us every day were not there to crease his brow or make his jaw tense up. Small changes but I was sure my face reflected those same signs when things started to get too much for me. But he needed his sleep and I needed to get rid of some of this energy before I exploded. So I left him to his dreams and quietly left the hotel room.

Dressed in shorts and t-shirt, it was a little chilly this late at night but running always warmed me up and I would have to adapt to a colder climate than the sunny almost brutally hot Florida I had left just a few weeks ago. What I did wasn't jogging, it was running, almost a flat out sprint for a human and much faster than a nice easy jog. This never left me out of breath but I did notice the air difference at this altitude.

Running let me think of nothing or everything depending on my mood. Tonight it was an everything type of a run as I went over the last two weeks in my head.

Biloxi had been enlightening. Not for the gambling as it was for most people that came to that town. Ours had been truly enlightening in an information type way. I was surprised that Michael had come up with some very good questions concerning the obvious defection of our housemate and protector Gabriel. A man that was your best friend for decades didn't just try and steal your woman and betray you like Gabriel seemed to have done without some serious questions coming out.

The job of a protector for my kind was very serious and sometimes almost fanatical type of calling. Their job was the mental, emotional and physical welfare of their family group. Making ties to each person that lasted for a very long time. Many families moved from one house to another, gaining members or losing them as the size of the house and needs of the area dictated but most of the older members of the Resurrected group knew most of the other older members. With just a little under 400 people, our group of very special people in North America didn't leave many you didn't know unless they were so new you hadn't met them yet.

⋇ 2 ⋇

People like me. I was still relatively new to this life having only come back from the dead less than six months ago. It was still amazing that this entire subculture of our world had lived, loved, fought, worked and died without the rest of the world knowing we existed at all. Nohu's, short for normal humans weren't supposed to know of us. But Resurrected people had been around for over a thousand years maybe more since a lot of our history had suffered destruction just the same as normal human history had. Other than word of mouth, our true written history was only good over the last few hundred years and really accurate since the last world war. Manuscripts could be burned, destroyed, made unreadable due to time or just plain lost like anything else written down could.

It wasn't ancient history that had my mind whirling tonight though. A more current set of events had my attention as I ran through the quiet early morning streets of Denver. Gabriel's defection had been very public, too public. I had made a leap of faith when he used the name of a double agent from a James Bond book that we both knew very well as being a friend of mine. Had hoped that what I guessed was true and I took a chance when I fought him in front of an Aspanari agent that he had not betrayed his best friend. That it had been an elaborate game he was playing to get into our darker sides group in a way they would accept him and grant him access to things we could find out no other way.

I gave him his chance and he gave me mine. A chance to live another day for both of us had been our gifts to each other. I was a good fighter and with anyone else I could have won but Gabriel was better than good and I had realized I was over my head very quickly but he deliberately missed every chance I knew he saw to hurt me or kill me and in return I had waited until I saw the opportunity he gave me. A slip in blood already on the floor told me what he wanted and I acted the part of the lethal killer I could be, shoving my claw like nails under his ribs and up into his chest to almost rip his heart out. He had to trust me a lot for that to happen for two reasons. One, I could have ripped his heart clean out of his chest and I hadn't, making it sound when I explained it later that he was just to big to do that but my hand and arm can follow where my nails cut and I had let him know the chance he took as I gently tickled his still beating heart. But my nails usually had a poison like covering to them. A poison that stopped the rapid healing process that all protectors have. That day I had asked my nails to do something I had never done before, to take away that poison and leave them just as deadly in their sharpness but something my brother could recover from.

Now I knew that it had worked, Gabriel was still alive and Michael and I would have to wait until six months from August before we could do anything else to help him. While he sought information in the Aspanari camp, we would gather information and discretely ask questions in ours. That was all we could do for now. Something that Michael was much better suited for than I. I was an infiltrator, the first woman ever to have that calling and there hadn't been one since WWII. Even though my title bespoke of spy like abilities it was much more than that. I was something of legend already, much to my disgust. But since I couldn't stop it, I was determined to make the best use of it and control it as much as I could.

The Resurrected group had developed many problems in recent history and since members weren't slaves and could resign if disillusioned many had done just that. Michael and I wanted to stop the slide we had seen in our brothers and sisters, the slide into apathy. Until I came along even members of my own house had been like that to an extent. Going through the motions of living, existing. Having very little passion for what should have been a daily shot of adrenaline. Helping people, Nohu's and others of our kind, were why were back from the dead. Given a second chance on this world with gifts and abilities that made each one us very unique. Having the benefit of never growing old or getting sick and for me getting my youth back and looking and feeling like I did in my college days didn't hurt things in my opinion. Why didn't everybody feel just a passionately about their lives? That was what Michael and I had to find out. Try and fix as many of those problems as we could. Mostly, like my housemates, it was probably a matter of attitude. I was very good at making others questions how they thought of things. My absolutely odd way of looking at the world around me and unpredictable sense of humor had put all my new family on their toes from the beginning.

Michael had found that out on more than one occasion. Of course the most recent one I still had the results of bouncing around in the bed of the truck. Just how was I going to explain to someone why I had half dozen beat up platform and high-heeled mismatched shoes that were still tied together by a rope riding around back there? A practical joke that Alison and I had delivered a day before we left from Florida.

That's what my husband gets when he starts making comments like he's a storybook character. Cinderella was not something he had considered when he stated he had to be home by midnight once and it had taken me so long to deliver the punch line that he had forgotten all about it. But it had caused several strange looks and more than a few snickers from his pals at the fire station when he had tried to drive off in his jeep on his last paramedic shift and heard a very loud clunking noise coming from behind him. He came in dangling my gift in his outstretched arm with a very large happy grin. At least Michael understood my sense of humor most of the time. That one I had to explain though and even if he hadn't understood why, he had known who was responsible. He rarely got mad at some of the silly things I did and thought the whole thing was extremely funny and had laughed the entire drive home with a dozen shoes bouncing around behind him. Six hadn't made the entire journey and had been lost somewhere in the rural roads of Escambia County Florida. I could just image what someone would think when the rest of my joke was found some time in the future.

Our idyllic time alone was now at an end and we were arriving later today at the Resurrected headquarters in the mountains above Breckenridge, Colorado. We had spent most of the rest of our honeymoon the way most couples did, making love and getting to know each other better. The passionate love making still made me blush upon occasion but we fit together so well that it was hard to get embarrassed no matter what we discovered in each other to enjoy.

Michael and I had both been severely injured just a few short weeks before we left Florida. We had both healed, at least physically but Michael had required a transfusion of my blood to keep him alive. I had the same remarkable healing ability that all protector class people had, even better than the average one. My husband had come through a stabbing that should have killed him even better than before. It seems my healing ability wasn't the only thing my blood had given him. As we talked during our journey across the country, we discovered that he was developing abilities he had never had before.

When I started telling him about how sensitive my sense of smell was. That I could identify people just by the way they smelled to me, he had also noticed his sense of smell getting better. Not anything close to mine but it was an interesting development. Of course how was I supposed to know that he would find his particular aroma unusually funny? Why would anyone mind smelling like mint chocolate chip ice cream? I had thrown a pillow over his face to keep anyone else outside our rather poorly insulated hotel room from hearing his almost hysterical laughing. The resulting pillow fight that ensued sort of defeated the whole purpose of trying to keep him quiet.

That wasn't the first time we had to pay for the damages a hotel room had sustained because of our presence. The worst was a bed in St Louis. Excess adrenaline was the cause, or at least that is what I blamed it on in my head. That was the first time Michael and I noticed our crystals had unusual abilities. While I filled up with gas at a service station one late night, Michael had gone in to get some sodas and snacks. When the crystal under my shirt started throbbing my heart rate jumped sky high. My eyes sought Michael out immediately not understanding at that moment that he was the source of my panic. The store was being robbed. A masked man had a gun pointed at the terrified clerk and Michael was standing right there at the counter too.

Moving faster and quieter than I had ever moved in my life, I was through the door and had the robber on the floor before he had time to react to the chime announcing my entry. It had been rather easy for the police to accept that I was a black belt in several disciplines especially since it was more or less true. But people general accepted what we told them very easily. Part of our gift was our smell made Nohu's trust us. Other than some very deep thanks from the police and the very rattled clerk we got out of the whole thing much faster than any normal person would have been able to do.

Our nerves had been singing with so much energy that Michael and I had checked into the closest hotel we could find. Without even getting our luggage out of the truck, Michael had gathered me up in his arms and all but kicked the door to our room in. Our near brush with something that brutal had both of our emotions running even more passionately than normal. He had all but thrown me into the bed and followed so quickly that it had collapsed under the force. We hadn't really noticed that the mattress was lying on the floor. Not until we were breathlessly holding each other some hours later. I wasn't even sure how we had both ended up naked. My clothes were in tatters and pieces that started at the door and littered more than the floor. Parts of my bra had ended up draped across the TV set. Michael's weren't much better but at least he could go outside with just his jeans on.

The hotel manager had asked just two questions when I had very embarrassingly said we had to pay for some damages to the furniture in our room. Were we on our honeymoon and did we enjoy our stay? We had honestly answered yes to both of those questions. He had chuckled very knowingly at my vividly blushing face and Michael sheepish grin and said nothing else.

But Michael was discovering some very interesting things about having so much of my blood in his system. First was a very large increase in strength and endurance. We had at first thought that it would pass over time and some of it did but Michael was sure that he was much stronger than he had been before and I agreed. Then he noticed his hearing was more sensitive and eyesight better at see into any hazy distance. What other things he was able to do only time would tell but those things seemed to be the biggest changes. We had both decided that we would tell no one about these things and he had to try and act like everything was just the same.

I was going to be enough of a lab rat. If it was found out that large enough quantities of my blood could increase somebody else's physical abilities I'm not sure I would survive. That rotten husband of mine was all for just me being stuck with an endless amount of needles, zapped with multiple x-rays and have just about any test the medical and research people at our center could come up with. At times like that I had to wonder just whose side he was on.

My sense of direction had always been pretty good and was now even better but it would have been hard to get too lost in a city like Denver. As I continued my run I had almost come full circle. I was still a little amazed at how fast and far I could go as the circuit I took had me cover almost 20 miles. It was just a little harder to push myself at this altitude as I felt my lungs pulling in more oxygen to keep going than they usually did. My body would have to adapt to this change in living condition just like any Nohu did. Michael also was adjusting to the higher altitude and lower oxygen level and was sleeping a little more than normal for him. He had been rather tired last night when we pulled into our hotel room after catching a later dinner. Instead of the normal romantic night I had gotten very used to I got several yawns from my handsome husband.

He had fallen asleep before I even came out of the bathroom. His soft, even breathing had put me to sleep a lot sooner than was normal for me too. But still that pinging energy had woken me up in the very early morning hours and rather than disturb Michael I had decided to meet the day the same way I had several times before, by running.

I had never been much of runner before my change but now it was sometimes the only thing I could do that would take this edge off the restless energy that always seemed to be there. Combat training and love making were also good ways of decreasing my energy level. The combat training I would have plenty of in the days to come and hopefully it wouldn't be so bad that our lovemaking would suffer. I loved Michael too much for me not to show him at least once a day just how lucky I was to have him for a husband.

Most of Michael's old problems of self-confidence and jealousy had disappeared and he was happier than anyone had seen him. At least that is what our sister Alison claimed and since she dealt in matters of the heart for a living she should know. But I knew that he needed reinforcement of my love for him maybe not constantly but frequently. Those things that had been in his emotional make up for years just didn't vanish overnight and it would be silly to think that Michael was the completely well adjusted man he let most people see all the time.

There were still a few things that we needed to do today before we finished our trip. Stopping by one more bank to complete my hidden asset agenda, I would set this one up in both Michael's and my name and put the remaining money I had into it. Something easy for Raphael to find when he decided he didn't like my attitude and wanted to control me some how. That should be a rather enjoyable show. One thing about him, he was a predictable sort, if he didn't like something he wouldn't try anything slick or fancy. He would just make the biggest impact he could with the least effort. Taking away my money would be just something he would do to get me to behave if I started doing something that our reigning council member Phillip and he didn't approve of.

I didn't have to wait to get to my new home to know that I was going to upset the proverbial apple cart. I was going in there to do just that because right now that apple cart had a lot of rotten things in it and Michael and I needed to ferret out all those rotten spots and get rid of them. It was necessary to put things right because at the present, things were not very happy for most our Resurrected brothers and sisters.

As I finished up my run and came down the same street that had our small motel in it, I swung by the donut shop that I had noticed last night when we pulled in. Both of us had a sweet tooth so coffee, or in my case hot chocolate, and fresh donuts would definitely get that husband of mine out of bed.

A huge cup of nice black coffee and an equally large cup of hot chocolate and half dozen steamy donuts later and I was unlocking the door to our room trying to juggle everything without dropping it. I didn't even make into the room as a strong hand snaked out and drug me in.

At least I had enough forewarning that Michael was the one that grabbed me. I heard his beating heart and his breathing as he tried to surprise me when I came in. Good thing for him I didn't take his aggressive playing as an actual attack or it might have been a very bad thing.

Instead I just sort of giggled and managed to place the coffee and donuts on a nearby table before he picked me up and tossed me on the bed.

"Don't you want your breakfast?" I fussed at him.

"Definitely." He growled out and I knew it wasn't food that he was hungry for and those nice gooey donuts had lost all their appeal for me too.

By the time we even thought about food the coffee was ice cold and the donuts hard as bricks. Too bad they had smelled absolutely wonderful, of course nothing smelled as good to me as Michael did. Not even the real mint chocolate chip ice cream that was my absolute favorite came close to the way my nose perceived my husband. He still chuckled a little whenever we stopped by an ice cream store and I got a scoop of my favorite because he knew exactly what I was thinking of when I devoured my ice cream cone with an almost feral gleam in my eyes. If I ever wanted to just plain tease Michael I had figured out one surefire way to do it.

We had to hurry a little bit after our morning's activities and we packed up our stuff, threw the uneaten food away and checked out. Found the closest big bank we could. This would be something Raphael would have no problems locating when he went fishing. We wanted to throw him a nice juicy bone to keep him from looking too far into things.

Finally stopping for lunch at a nice steak house, we both fell on our food like we hadn't eaten in days. Michael wasn't yawning as much now and I think my body had almost adapted to the higher altitude. Less than a day and I could tell that my body temperature had risen to that of normal humans already. The waitress's hand, as she had accidentally brushed up against mine, had felt just about the same body temperature. Mine would stay that way now until actual winter came through, with its freezing cold temperatures and blizzards.

I had never really lived in the north before and was both looking forward to it and also not. The idea of being snowed in for days and weeks on end didn't have much appeal for me. Even if it did mean I could snuggle up with Michael under some covers and just hibernate until the spring thaw like a bear did. That might be nice for a few days but any more than that and my energy level would spiral right out sight and I would be literally bouncing off the walls.

Michael had finally convinced me to let him drive my truck over the last few days and I was still very nervously sitting in the passenger seat. Michael had his phobias and I had mine. At least I didn't freak out when I smelled fish anymore and this was really the last one that I had to work on. We went through the resort town of Breckenridge on our way up through steep mountain roads that lead to our center.

Everybody of course knew it existed and most thought it was a rehab facility for injured government employees. Rehab was indeed part of what they did here but it wasn't all and not even the biggest part. It did explain the several nerdy type people that were constantly seen coming and going. The few times people would stop by to check us out simply out of curiosity, they were given a tour of the most visible part of the center's top two floors. The other four stories that went deep underground nobody outside of us knew existed and remained a very guarded secret. They contained our research and training facilities, most of the garage and storage areas. Michael had of course been here several times in his long life and hoped it hadn't changed much in the last 6 years since he had paid his last visit here.

I gathered that about every 10 years or so they had a big shake up and reorganized everyone. Asking for requests for reassignments and such and general sending people where they hadn't been before or hadn't been in a long time. If we stayed longer than 10 years in any one place, people started noticing that we didn't age, unless you went to extraordinary lengths to pretend to age. Something Stephan our corporate lawyer and a few others did in order to work in their field for as long as possible uninterrupted.

So we were moved periodically to keep from being noticed as being different. Now I had to get used to the idea that I would only live in any location for about 10 years and then I would have to move again. That wasn't that upsetting to me. I had moved so many times as both a child because of my Dad and later as an adult with Rick's oh so many jobs that it had become old hat for me. I was really good at downsizing things to keep only what was important and could easily get rid of things that could be replaced that had little or no sentimental value.

So today as we pulled up out front of the two-story oddly shaped gray nondescript building it was with a sense of excitement, both good and bad that had my stomach tied in nervous knots. Michael looked over and couldn't help but notice how down right scared I was as he rolled his eyes and chuckled a little. "Maggie you go off to fight what you think are three Aspanari agents and a renegade protector with just Peter by your side without even flitching and this makes you almost want to hurl. You are absolutely green, did you know that?"

I made a rude noise in the back of my throat. "I am not going to throw up Michael." I growled. But he always seemed to know what to say to get me over something. That little blast of almost anger had been enough to jar me out of the case of nerves I had developed on our long drive up the mountains. I was glad that Michael had been at the wheel as we went around blind curves and passed by drop off cliffs that went down so far you couldn't see the bottom.

Was this what I had expected? I really wasn't sure what I had expected but this was definitely not it. It looked just so average, normal. Thinking back at how this place had been talked about constantly, especially when I had first started out this life had me thinking of it in extremely overrated almost impossible images of the center of all things in my new world. It was rather deflating in its ordinariness but I guess that had been the idea. Keep things subtle and something not worth talking about or even remembering very well.

Michael was already out of the truck and was holding my door open as I collected my thoughts. He smiled a little indulgently and all I wanted to do was smack him for his attitude of 'I know something you don't know' smugness. He gathered me up in a hug and kissed my forehead. "It'll be okay Maggie. I'm here and Anthony will be back in a few days and you already know Katherine and Joshua. Don't worry so much, everybody will be just as happy to meet you as we were when you came blowing into our lives so unexpectedly."

"Yeah like a freaking hurricane." I grumbled. But I shook off those depressing thoughts. This was what I had wanted wasn't it? To come here, get better training than the half way stuff that Anthony and I had cooked up on our own without a real clue what we were doing. I was lucky to not be dead now. What had we both been thinking? Of course PIB, my voice guide, hadn't left us with a lot of alternatives either. Still this was all a good thing. Stop being such a nervous Nelly and get on with it, I fussed at myself.

I plastered a nice fake smile on my face that would fool just about anybody but the man that had his arm wrapped around me almost protectively. How is it Michael always knew just when I needed his support and here he kept thinking his abilities as an empath weren't that good. He may not be able to fix a physical hurt like some of our kind could do but he had no problems fixing my emotional ones.

He opened up one of the double glass doors that entered into a nice, but not fancy lobby and was greeted by the pretty, of course young, receptionist. "Michael it is so great to see you again." She chirped. Her high-pitched voice was something I guess I would have to get used too.

"Hey, Rachael." Michael answered. Wasn't it just so annoying when you were the only one that didn't know who anybody was? I growled in my head. Okay, I filed her voice, name and face down in my head. Rachael, average height, sandy hair, blue eyes of course, high pitched voice and was annoyingly almost drooling over my husband. Jealousy was something I hadn't experienced much before and I had to remind myself that Michael had never found any of these women attractive before so why would he now. He was just the friendly type, still it made me wrap my arm around his waist and pull him just a little closer.

"This is my wife Gabriella Reynolds, I think you've been expecting us." Michael continued.

"Of course." Rachael gushed. "It is so nice to meet you. I was just so happy when I heard that Michael had finally found someone that he wanted to bond with. Felix and I were even happier when we found out that you were coming here for training. My husband works in the research department."

Great I thought. He'll be one of those with the needles chasing me around the building every time I blinked. "I look forward to meeting him." I smiled and nodded. Maybe I should ask Michael who the telepaths and emotional empaths were before things got much further along. I could fake a happy smile very well but that wouldn't fool someone that could read your thoughts or feelings like they could.

Michael at least wasn't that type of empath. I think if he were I wouldn't have found him quite so easy to love. It must be very difficult for someone like that. To find another that would put up with you picking the very thoughts out of their head or that could never be fooled into thinking you felt one way and when you didn't. Dishonesty wasn't something to have in a relationship but would Michael like to know right now just how grumpy I really was. Maybe, but it would be better if he didn't. It was just nerves and I knew it. So why should he suffer from my emotional roller coaster when only I could solve the problem. Having our heart spark bonding crystal issue was bad enough and we were both still dealing with everything that little hiccup had given us. But to have him be able to pick every single emotion out of my head was not a good thing in my opinion.

Michael and Rachael were playing a little catch up and I really couldn't blame them. They probably hadn't seen each other in at least six years. It would be that way for Michael with just about everyone here I realized so I better just smile, try and listen politely and pretend to be interested. Michael would have his hands full when Phillip started his show the infiltrator off to everybody and his brother. We both knew that was looming so delightfully on the horizon. I'm sure Michael wouldn't enjoy that any more than I was enjoying this. Of course I wasn't going to be too happy about it either.

It seemed Rachael wasn't always the receptionist. There were several that took that position as time from their normal duties allowed. Since Rachael was always available in the building because she was assigned to the medical research section also, she got the front desk more than all the others. She was that bubbly type that didn't seem to mind. After listening to her chat to Michael for a few minutes I knew I judged her incorrectly. She wasn't annoying just very outgoing and friendly and other than her voice being so high was someone I might actually like. Now why had I been so harsh to judge her like that? I knew I was on edge being in a new environment and we had been away from others of our kind for two weeks and now I was getting a huge dose of us and I wasn't sure I was ready for it but ready or not it was happening.

I didn't want to be rude but it seemed like Michael and Rachael were in no hurry to stop their conversation. Well fine, if they wanted to talk half the day away I could look around for a bit on my own. Michael was so involved he probably wouldn't notice if a hole opened up and swallowed me. Nix that thought I fussed at myself. This was like old home week for him and I have had him to myself for long enough. Time to share him with the rest of the world.

So I wandered down the hall by myself. I may be someone these people hadn't met before but everyone would know that I was one of them, my blues eyes and smell would tell them that. Having no idea where I was heading, I just followed the halls peering into any open door that I passed trying to identify familiar settings.

Okay, this floor may be more for show than most but it was certainly functional as I went by a very big gym with all types of athletic equipment in it, some even in use by men that were of the general body type that protectors were. I could also see a nice pool that had a gentle steam wafting up from it, heated I supposed and even though the building was at a comfortable temperature even an indoor pool would have to be heated all year long at this altitude. Of course, it was also being used as I could see physical therapists working with some people that had obvious injuries, missing limbs, burns and other things I guess weren't quiet so apparent. These people looked more like regular humans although they had our blue eyes and same pale skin for the Caucasian ones that marked them as also being my kind. I felt a little sorry for them. They didn't have the remarkable healing ability that I did. Maybe I wouldn't mind so much being a lab rat if it helped the less fortunate members of my extended family get better faster and maybe in the future have no lasting hurt at all.

I silently passed by the pool area and the gym finding myself at the end of the hall I turned the corner and went by the far side of the pool area. On the other side from it were more small office type rooms, some were exam rooms judging from the furniture in them but also regular offices with a few people on phones or typing diligently on the computer terminals. I went by so quietly they didn't even notice I was there. They looked so hard at work, so determined in whatever task they were at that I didn't want to disturb anyone.

Coming to the other end of this hall I turned another corner and found myself passing a very large dining area. In the back was something I was very used to but on a much smaller scale, the kitchen. Great at least I might feel a little more at home there. Someone was back there as I heard pots being clanged around and some general grousing, yeah and that somebody didn't sound very happy about something.

When I made my way around all the tables and chairs and finally entered the large galley type cooking area I saw the source of all the noise. One very angry little lady was taking out her frustrations as she was washing a huge pot. As it slipped out her grasped I caught it before it could make it to the ground, moving so quickly she had no clue how it didn't make the resounding noise she was obviously expecting.

My eyes caught her very surprised ones as I placed the big thing back up on the side of sink. "Would you like a hand?" I asked pleasantly. She was of course in her twenties physically but there was just something about the rest of her that made me think old, maybe from the tired look in her eyes.

"You're new." She commented. Of course someone that had been here for a while would know a newcomer.

"Yes, just got here today." I didn't give my name and she didn't ask for it. She didn't ask how I had managed to catch the pot before it hit the ground or why I would even offer assistance to someone they didn't know. She didn't seem to know really what to make of me but an offer of help was obviously something she got very rarely and wasn't about to pass up.

"If you want to help I was just starting dinner. How good are you in the kitchen? Can't use you if you're going to go slicing things off or burning yourself." With an attitude like that I could see why she was in here by herself but until Michael pulled himself away from all his old friends did I really have any thing else to do?

"Oh I'm passable in the kitchen. I don't think I'll go missing any body parts if you give me things to chop up." I smiled a little, I was almost as good as a food processor and came complete with my own set of nice little sharp knives.

She directed me to a hug stack of vegetables that she had set on the counter after washing them off. Popping out one of my nails to form a very sharp knife I started cutting away. I was done with the large stack and she never even realized she hadn't shown me where the necessary tools for the job were kept.

"Done already?" She asked me.

"Yup, all done." I smiled back. "Anything else you want cut up?" Since I had at least one claw already out I hated to waste it and grow another one if I could just do all of the slicing at one time. I tried to not run around with a dangerous thing like a six blade hanging off the end of my hand when there wasn't a need for it.

"Well if you feel up to it there are still the potatoes that need washing, peeling and slicing." My kitchen lady pointed to a big bin half full of spuds just waiting for someone to turn them into something edible.

"Sure, how many and how do you want them sliced?" I answered much to her surprise. Maybe by now most of those curious enough to wander in were ready to leave but I had spent more than my fair share of time in the kitchen and even though this one was a lot bigger than any I had worked in before a kitchen was a kitchen and things were done pretty much the same way everywhere.

"Oh around 40 or 50 would be good." Was the answer and the surprised look she got had her giggle a little bit. "Still want to work on those potatoes?" She chuckled again.

"Believe me until my husband gets done talking to all his old friends I really have nothing else to do but stand around and listen to stuff that I don't have a clue about. I would much rather be here and useful than that."

"Talking husband. Well that explains a bit. You may be in here until dinner is served at the rate most men yak and then they complain about our hen parties. If they ever listened to themselves I think most would fall over in a dead faint." Well that was more words I heard her speak in the last 30 minutes total. Yes I was right she was old and she had a slight accent that I just couldn't place. It was well hidden but to someone that was used to listening for that sort of thing I still noticed it. English maybe or Welsh but I had learned from Alison you never ask about things like that. It was rude. I could at least introduce myself since she seemed to be in no hurry to exchange names but I would at least like to tell Michael that I had met one person that I had something in common with.

"I'm Gabriella." Remembering to use my new name. That would take some getting used to but I was determined to keep it even though the reasons for my taking it had changed drastically.

"Oh, so that's who you are? Heard you were arriving sometime this week. Had this whole place just a buzzing for quite some time."

"Great." I groaned. "Just wonderful."

"I gather that isn't a good thing in your opinion."

"Would you like it?" I grumbled.

"Nope but considering what you are you had better get used to it. Jacob didn't much care for it either. But the poor dear didn't get a chance to enjoy any of the good stuff that comes from being famous. I was just so sorry to find out that somebody had killed that sweet man like they did."

My word she must be old, she had personally know our last protector or at least claimed she had and like me it seems he didn't much like all the legend crap that came along with this calling. Maybe it would help my new maybe friend to know something that not many else did.

"Well it might make you a little happier to know that the man that ordered his death is dead too. I took care of that little ferret personally."

Well that had certainly surprised her in a very good way. "Wonderful but if you don't want things to get out of hand too quickly you may not want to tell just everybody about that. To avenge Jacob like that would send some of these people around here into an absolute frenzy."

How could I have been so stupid? To go bragging almost when what I really wanted was to slide in under the radar as much as possible, at least in the beginning. Until I figured people out better I needed to keep the legend talk down to a minimum.

"Don't worry about it sweety." My new friend advised after seeing the expression on my face that I couldn't stop. "It's natural to be proud of something like that but I know these people around here better than just about anybody and believe me if you don't want to fall over someone every time you turn around you need to watch what you say. It will be bad enough anyway."

Proud. Was that what I had sounded like? Was I proud that I had killed someone, ripped their heart out and showed it to them as they died? I was many things but prideful for that act I was not. Maybe a little satisfied that Josef had received a fitting send off that was almost as violent as poor Jacob's had been but I hadn't known that he was responsible for that act when I had killed him. I had done it in self-defense because he already shot me once and was about to do it again and at that close of range I knew he wouldn't miss.

"Maggie." I heard Michael's voice calling.

"I'm sorry I guess I won't be able to help with those potatoes after all." I apologized to the wise lady that ran the kitchen.

"That's okay I'm used to doing it by myself."

"Well stop being used to it, plan on seeing a lot of me in the future. I like it here."

She didn't actually snort or laugh but I could tell she had been promised like that before and wouldn't be surprised if I never set foot in here again. Well she was the one in for a very good surprise or at least I hoped my presence would be a good thing. I had a feeling I could learn a lot from the kitchen lady and not just about cooking.

I followed Michael's voice back up the hall I had come down. He didn't look worried but he wasn't exactly happy that I had wandered away on my own. What did he think? I need a guide or guard or something. I may have been nervous to start out with but had a very good history of adapting quickly and easily. All I had to do was find one place I felt comfortable, a place to retreat to when I got stressed and I had already found it.

"Maggie." The almost relief I heard in his voice when he saw me was as much annoying as it was enjoyable. Now how was that possible? I was very pleased that he would be worried about finding me gone and just a little peeved that he didn't think I was capable of exploring my new, if temporary, home on my own. I felt a little bad for my childish thoughts earlier. Michael would have most definitely noticed if a hole had swallowed me.

"You were catching up with Rachael and I didn't want to interrupt." I started explaining. "I could tell you had a lot to say and I didn't like just standing around making you think you had to hurry up because I was waiting."

"So where did you disappear to?" Michael asked. Now that he had found me he was back to his smiling self. "One minute you were there and next poof. I still don't understand how you can move so silently. Did anybody else even see you?"

"Probably not. I tried not to disturb anyone. They are all so busy. I did find the kitchen though." I answered smiling.

Michael rolled his eyes a bit and chuckled. "Of course you did."

We went back up the hall a few feet to an elevator. "I got our room assignment." Michael said as he pressed the up button. "Rachael said we were lodged on the second floor."

"Second floor but aren't most people housed in the underground levels?" I was confused. Michael had briefly described the different levels of the center. First floor was receptionist, gym, pool, offices and dining facility. Second floor was executive offices, conferences rooms, council residence and VIP quarters. One floor down was the rest of the living quarters and the garage facility. Two down was the medical research area and labs and the surgery suite. Three had the combat training facility, armory and storage areas. Fourth sub level was almost all mechanical where the furnace, electrical system and mainframe computers were housed.

"Yes, but I guess Phillip wanted you to have the best." Michael answered. He could tell I wasn't as happy about this revelation as anyone had hoped for. "What's wrong Maggie, they just want you happy here. Is that a bad thing?"

Couldn't Michael see that the isolation that had separated Phillip and the rest of the council members from our family he was trying to pass on to me? I know he meant well, as did Michael. Everyone was just so worried that I wouldn't want to stay here when staying was the last thing I wanted no matter how nice my living area was. As soon as Michael and

I had tried to fix as much of our internal problems as we could and I had received the training I needed, we were leaving and we had until February to do it. Now to be separated by two floors from the rest of the people in the building was the last thing we needed. It would send the wrong message. I wanted and expected to be treated just like everybody else.

"Well maybe it won't be too bad." I answered. Quick to judge had already been a problem once for me today and I needed to at least take a look at what someone probably went to a great deal of effort to prepare for us.

As we exited the elevator, Michael turned left down the hall to the end and opened a part of large set of double doors. "I think this is it." He said as let me enter first.

I stopped dead in my tracks. "WOW." That summed up what we saw. It was indeed a living area but it was enormous. They're was a living room complete with high tech plasma TV and a stereo system that had so many buttons, dials and switches I was afraid to even touch it because I was sure I would break something. Tucked off to the side was a separate eating area and decent sized kitchen. In the other direction was the bedroom and I guess bathroom but what had our entire attention was the view. It was breath taking. A panoramic vista looking down the mountainside to the valley far below was what had both of us stopped after we barely made it into the room.

Was this normal for the VIPs? I had no idea but I didn't think so. "Michael, is this what you were expecting?" I asked, having to nudge him a little to get an answer.

"No. I mean I've only been up here a couple of times to see Phillip when we've both been here at the same time and I've been in the conference rooms on a few occasions. His apartment is nice but this is even larger and his doesn't have a kitchen in it either."

As we both looked over everything that had been done it became very obvious that there was a lot of time and effort made to make sure that the only reason I would have to leave this place was for training. The more I saw the more I just knew that even though it was very beautiful and had everything I could have wanted, I couldn't live here. It would very much put me in a different class than everyone else. The problem Phillip had was he didn't listen to the everyday people. Just like the rest of the council, they had isolated themselves so much from everyone that they didn't see enormous problems when everybody else seemed to be very much aware of them. But if anybody had figured out how to fix any of them they either weren't listened to or Phillip never heard about the problem or the answer. I didn't have any answers right now but sitting on my butt all by myself sure wasn't going to help. Both Michael and I needed to be in the thick of things. Hear everybody's problems and figure how to make it better and sitting up here like Rapunzel in her tower wasn't going to get it done.

I didn't even need to say anything to Michael. He knew it too. We turned around at the same time, went back out the door and closed it. "Let's see what else is available downstairs." Michael said.

"Let's." I agreed with a smile. Grandeur really didn't fit into his life style either. No matter how I was described later in this life I was not about to deliberately put myself on a pedestal to have people sort of worship me from two floors down. To have them almost afraid to talk to Michael or me sure wouldn't get us the information we needed to sort things out.

Rachael was a little flustered when Michael asked for the keys to whatever married couples suite was available in the lower level. "But don't you like your apartment?" She asked. "Is something wrong? Rafael was real specific about what you liked and didn't like and I thought we got everything just right."

How could I say what needed to be said without insulting someone. "No, Rachael." I explained trying to catch her eyes with mine so that she could see there was no anger or disappointment there. "It's very beautiful but I'm not here to be treated special. I'm just as much a worker bee as anyone else. I don't want to live away from everyone. I'm too used to just popping in across the hall and talking to a sister or sharing the kitchen with my family. Michael and I wouldn't be happy up there all by ourselves. I had looked forward to getting to know everyone here. I can't I do that if I'm isolated by two floors."

"But what are we going to do with it? Rafael will be really mad." Rachael was definitely worried that there would be repercussions directed at anybody and everybody that was involved in what seems to have been a very extensive remodeling job.

"Don't tell him. Why does he need to know where Michael and I are lodged? Do you usually advise Phillip's bodyguard where new people are housed?"

"No but sooner or later Phillip and Rafael will come by and see you aren't living where you should be." She argued. Still trying to convince me to live where I had absolutely no intentions of living.

"Where I should live is for me to decide isn't it? And when Rafael blows his cork, which I'm very sure he will do, tell him if he has a problem he can come talk to me. It won't be the first time I've told that man to get bent and I'm sure it won't be the last."

Rachael about choked on her tongue. Michael was very torn between losing his temper and laughing himself to pieces. He decided on a different option and went to Rachael's side of the desk. Looking over what I guessed were several keys, he took a set. "I think this will work just fine. I've been in this section several times when I was here last and it will be perfect."

We went back out the front door and Michael drove my truck around to the back section of the building. Underneath the kitchen area was a loading dock and a garage door that was standing open and waiting for us like we had been expected.

The underground parking garage was rather large but not nearly as big as I had thought it would be. There were several vehicles that were of the multi person type, min-vans, and small buses even. I guess most people that lived here didn't own their own vehicles. Well most Resurrected didn't anyway. The house owned them and they just had use of them for as long as they lived in that house. You leave, the vehicle stays and somebody else took over the use of it until it wore out and needed replacing.

As Michael found an open parking spot a man came out from a semi hidden office. He was sort of above average in the looks, not tall and not short with brown hair cut very short. It took him a minute but as soon as he recognized Michael at the wheel, his face lit up in a great big smile. "Michael. Son of a gun. We were wondering when you would show up."

"Hey Tim." Michael answered the friendly man that had his head half stuck in my window to shake Michael's hand. "This is Gabriella, my wife." I couldn't help but hear the pride that filled his voice when he claimed me.

Tim was not a stupid fellow and already come to that conclusion but what he said next didn't make him win any awards. "So this is our new infiltrator." From derisive tone in his voice it didn't really sound like a compliment.

Well I guess my arrival had been the subject of much discussion both good and bad. Maybe from all the preparations that had been done for me some people were feeling slighted. Well I couldn't change what happened before. From now on though that was something I had a lot of say in. "Is it okay if we park here?" I asked trying to start out on the right foot with him.

"It's open isn't it?" Tim sort of snorted. Michael may have been a favorite of this man but I sure wasn't, at least not yet. Time to start converting people and I had just found my first subject.

Michael got out and went over to a section nearer to the office and drug over a luggage cart. I guess there were people coming and going all the time here. People that had been injured and needed help getting used to their new condition. Others like me that were here for training. I'm sure even the medical personnel and research people moved upon occasion but it seemed that my friend in the kitchen and Rachael and husband Felix had been here for some time, over six years for the last two at least.

As we started unloading what we wanted out of the back of the truck it became apparent that one cart just wasn't going to be enough. Before I could grab another Tim was there. I knew he had been silently watching us the whole time. "Have a lot stuff." He stated. At least this time it wasn't nasty sounding, just an observation.

"Yeah, I guess most people fly in and we wanted a honeymoon and a chance to see more of the wonderful country before I started my training up here." I answered nicely.

"I see." He answered still in a noncommittal tone. "What's all the camping gear for? You can check that out from our stores any time you want to go hiking. Not to many like nature so there isn't much call for it."

"Maggie was worried that we would run into a blizzard before we got here." Michael chuckled. He had said I was going overboard with that part of preparedness but even PIB seemed to think it was a good idea.

Michael had used my nickname just like he always did and that had confused Tim to no end. "Um. Whose Maggie?"

"I am." I giggled a little. "It's my middle name. Michael needs to get in the habit of calling me by my first name or people are going to think he has two wives."

"Two!!" Michael all but yelled. "Two, Gabriella I have enough problems just putting up with one of you."

"Oh, you're complaining now. You didn't complain much when we were on the road every night and most mornings too." I chuckled completely forgetting that we had an audience. When Tim cleared his throat letting me know he was still there I turned a bright red. "Sorry." I murmured.

"No, its okay." Tim sort of chuckled. "It's nice seeing two people that enjoy each other as much as you seem to. I sort of miss that with my lady."

I didn't want to pry but he had opened up that can of worms so I asked exactly what I was thinking. "Why?" I questioned. But then I realized that simple question could be so misunderstood so I added what I really wanted to know. "Not why do you miss it. But why is it missing to start out with?"

"You know, when you've been with the same woman for a long time things just start falling into a routine. It gets a little tedious maybe. Work gets in the way and takes a higher priority a lot." He didn't seem to even know why his love life had flattened out but he was exploring the idea that maybe it wasn't too late to change that. "Any suggestions on what to do to about that?" Tim asked of Michael more than of me.

"A few." Michael answered with a nod. "Maybe we need to have a men's night and get a bunch of us old guys together and start swapping ideas. When was the last time you had a poker night and sat around drinking beer and telling stories?"

"It's been years Michael, years." Tim answered a little forlornly.

"Well you guys make your plans and I'll see what I can cook up for the ladies. If you think we are going to spend an entire evening cooped up in our own little private holes you're nuts. You get poker night and we get our type of get together."

"Sounds like a plan." Tim answered with a nod. "You know you aren't what I thought you would be like."

"Let me guess, you were expecting a Prima Donna that wanted to be waited on hand and foot and thought she was better than everybody else." I could be extremely blunt when I needed to be and from the look on his face I had been very accurate in my guess.

Tim nodded. "Just from all the preparations that Phillip and Rafael wanted for you, everybody was expecting something like that."

"We aren't staying in that stupid tower Tim. I'm not a princess and I don't like the idea of being treated different. So what, I have an unusual calling, big deal. Can anyone else do exactly what you do? And your lovely wife, what about her? Isn't she special with a talent nobody else has? We're all unique in our way. Why would that entitle me to special treatment for anything other than learning how to do my job and be of service? That's the only type of special treatment I want or expect from anybody."

"So if you're not staying in that ivory tower everybody spent to much time on where are you living?" He asked Michael as we finally unloaded the rest of our stuff from the truck.

We began pushing our luggage carts up the ramp and into the warren of halls that were well lit but still made me think of a cave from the lack of windows.

"Unless you have moved it's three doors down from you." Michael answered.

"Well I'll be. Neighbors. Now I would never have thought I would be getting new neighbors today." Tim chuckled. Yeah he was starting to warm up to me but I knew this was just the beginning of the attitude adjustment Michael and I would have to give everybody before we could get to work. That would just have to wait until we unpacked because you really can't change the world if you don't even know where your clean socks were.

As Michael unlocked the door to our suite I went in first and started throwing suitcases and boxes on the floor and bed. Tim helped and soon everything was off the luggage carts and he was maneuvering them back down the hall.

We started unpacking but there was something seriously missing. The room was just a little larger than the one I had back home so I knew everything would fit in just fine. It also had a computer terminal and TV set with the standard DVD player but there wasn't a stereo to be seen. How did these people live without music? Well my little portable stereo would work for a while but I might think about upgrading things. Especially if I was stuck in here for several days when a blizzard came roaring through.

Michael and I didn't need to talk much as we started unpacking. He had about as much clothes as I did and we had both made sure the new stuff fit like it was supposed to, opening up each box or bag and trying everything on. Now he took one chest of drawers and I took the other. We had all our clothes folded or hung up and the only thing that I needed to do was laundry. Michael still needed to take me on a tour but at least we could get a shower tonight and find nightclothes to sleep in. I still hadn't gone through all my lingerie on our honeymoon so maybe that would be a good way to break in our new place.

Looking over the nice room I knew I would be making changes to it. Not as many as what I done to mine back in Florida but a few bigger pictures and maybe upgrade the bedding would be nice. But this was Michael's room too and he had wanted no changes to his back home. Maybe he liked plain and was just too sweet to complain about what my room looked like. Not that it would have done him any good anyway.

"Would you like to add a few touches Michael?" I asked as he was coming back out of the bathroom. Well at least it wasn't like in some of the dorms that had community showers. I had absolutely hated those but could understand it was just easier to put in one or two big bathrooms than a whole lot of little ones.

"Sure. I liked what you did to your room." He answered. We had never really discussed that. Of all the things we had talked about that had never made it to the top of the list.

"Maybe this week we can get on line and order a few things. This is your place too you know." I wanted to let him know I wasn't going to just take over our space here. He needed to feel at home too.

"Army guy remember. Just as long as it's better than a cot and a scratchy blanket I think it's wonderful." He chuckled a little at his own past. A past so long gone it really had little to do with the man I married. Or did it? I had never asked what had caused his nightmare the first night we had spent together. He had never offered that information and with all the things we had gone through after that it hadn't been important enough. During our honeymoon the last thing I wanted to do was dredge up painful things. We had enough of those without me looking for more and we had been trying to enjoy ourselves. Now I had to wonder. Most of the trauma that was mental for us had to deal with our transition. My problems with fish had stemmed from just such a thing, as had Alicia's fear of knives after she was stabbed repeatedly and left for dead. Alison's night terrors were because somebody strangled her to death. But Peter's fear of snakes had been with him since early childhood.

Michael had a loathing of mud and he said himself that he had been on Normandy on D-Day. I knew history well enough to know that battle had been just as bloody as it was muddy, wet and cold. Could Michael have been one of those thousands of casualties that died that day? Was that why he freaked out so much because he had died in the mud and that was the last thing he felt as he left this world? I had to know, had to pry into my husband's life, something I tried not to do. If he wasn't willing to share I didn't want to know. But I had worked so hard on getting over my phobias and fears. Was there something I could do to help him?

"Michael." Calling his name always got his attention but he knew this was different, whether it was something in the tone of my voice or the look on my face or even my body posture that told him that I didn't know. But he knew that what I wanted wasn't something simple as he sat down on the bed to discuss whatever it was that had me saying his name. "Why do you hate mud?" I asked softly.

# CHAPTER 2

## MEET AND GREET

"Finally." Michael breathed out. "You are finally going to ask me that question I have been both wishing and dreading since we met."

The look on his face was both relieved and pained. I wasn't sure how he managed that but it was plainly there. "If you don't want to tell that's okay. If you would rather wait until it's a better time, I'll understand." I whispered. Why did I think I needed to open up this very painful can of worms? Couldn't I just leave this one thing alone and not poke at it with my curiosity stick like I did everything all the time.

"No." Michael shook his head. "This is as good a time as any." But he stopped and just couldn't continue.

Maybe if I sort of guessed it would help a little, maybe not but he said he wanted to tell me, he just couldn't get the words out. And for whatever reason I really needed to know this secret. Why? I had no idea but suddenly it was so very important.

"Were you killed on Normandy Beach Michael?" I asked softly. Reaching over to hold his hand, I don't think he even noticed I was there until I touched him.

"Sort of." He said. His voice had changed now. It no longer had that haunted quality to it, now there was nothing. No fear, no anger, nothing. "I didn't actually make it all the way onto the beach. A mortar round exploded right in front of me and killed me while I was still making it there. I thought at first that I had just been knocked out but when I couldn't move, even open my eyes I had assumed I was paralyzed but then the waves of pain started and I just wished I was unable to feel. I could still hear other men trying to get past me as a lay at the waters edge. Could feel the water as it washed up around me, then the pull as it went back out. The sound of the fighting got further and further away but the feel running passed me didn't slow down for what seemed like days."

"Finally, I guess things were calmed down enough that the morgue guys came through. There were so many dead they couldn't get everybody buried quickly and the stench was unbelievable. I got piled in with so many others that were waiting. The feel of other soldier's bodies as death worked its way through them was all around. Cold, so very cold and everybody was covered in mud and probably blood but to my hands and face it all felt the same, slimy, slippery and cold. I was actually happier when the heat of the burning fire was upon me at least that was warm, almost. But the freezing cold ones were just excruciating."

"I knew by then at least some of what had happened. I was dead as far as everybody else thought. There were few loved ones left behind to mourn me so that wasn't a big concern. My thoughts were very much centered on me. Was I really going to die waiting for somebody to figure out I wasn't already dead? I knew sooner or later that I would need water and food and I couldn't move to let anyone know I didn't belong where I was. Somewhere along the way the waves slowed down and where not so bad and I fell into an exhausted sleep. When I woke up I could move. I still had all the injuries I had to start out. There was still shrapnel in my chest and shoulder but I could yell, hell I could scream. I thought the guys still burying the dead where going to fall over with heart attacks. They were so amazed I was still alive. They threw me on a stretcher and rushed me to the closest aid station. That's were I met Phillip for the first time. He knew immediately what had happened, what I was. I realized later on that I was very lucky. Some of those that almost died in battle like me came around after they had been buried alive and had to dig and claw their way out. Whatever battle they were in had usually passed them by and they had to try and find help where they could."

"As bad as what I went through was at least I didn't have that. Phillip had been through many wars; many battles and he had seen a pattern that more resurrected happened during wartime than another other. So he pulled as many sensitive and medical people he could and placed them in aid stations as close to the front lines as possible and still be safe. He didn't want to endanger anyone either. He had an army surgeon's ranking of a colonel thanks to some of our very talented forgers and such so people listened to him. Because he knew so much and could pull people from the brink of death when it seemed like a lost cause he was treated with respect even by his peers."

I knew it would be a bad story but not this bad. So many of our resurrected had mental trauma from their transition I had to wonder why nobody addressed these issues when they first came across. Not everybody was as stupidly stubborn as I was. The idea of having anything control me like that drove me crazier than the phobia did. This was something that I would definitely have to discuss not just with Michael but also with other medical personnel that dealt with mental health. We had to have our version of psychologists or the like, maybe somebody that traveled like Anthony did was an option to consider, that is if we didn't have something like that already in place.

Right now Michael was just too upset for me to get into that. In the next few weeks it would be something I would bring up for us both to consider. If there was something already in place it didn't seem to be working like it should. There were just too many of us with problems that made things more difficult to live normal, well-adjusted lives. So if nothing was in place then we needed to put together some ideas, get the medical people to present them to Phillip and the council. It would look better coming from them anyway and I wouldn't know how to discuss mental health issues intelligently. Hell I had enough problems spelling psychologists without a dictionary.

As I held Michael in my arms for a while I was reminded of Alison and her night terrors. He was almost as stiff and unyielding in my embrace as she had been. Michael was wide-awake but I could tell his mind was far away in some very cold and scary place. I didn't think talking would help no matter what words of comfort I could offer. Words just weren't good enough now and showing physically that I loved him, I didn't think would be a good idea either. Michael had problems with being pitied even though I could never understand why he would think anyone would ever pity him to start out. Still if I tried to make love to him right now I knew in my heart he would accept it because he loved me but he wouldn't really enjoy it. His heart was somewhere else now too. With nothing else to do I started humming softly, some tune I pulled out of nothing. I wasn't even sure what it was I was humming until I heard Michael chuckling weakly.

"What?" I asked a little surprised by his reaction to my attempt at not going totally out of my skull because I didn't have anything to do but couldn't stand the idea of leaving him alone. Inactivity hadn't been a problem much for me, between loving Michael every chance I got, traveling and sightseeing over the past two weeks we had both been constantly on the go. Now was really the first time in a while when I was just lying around with nothing to do and not wanting to find something to keep my mind and body occupied.

"Your silly." He chuckled a little more but I felt him relax in my arms and kiss my face softly. "Thank you." Michael whispered against my cheek.

As I rubbed his back and caressed him gently in return it finally dawned on me why Michael had found my choice of songs so amusing. Where in the world had I pulled the Army anthem from I had no idea but I guess in some wacky recess of my brain it must have made sense. Unless PIB was starting to affect more than just my survival sense but it didn't seem like that is where it came from either.

Michael's stomach let a large snarl that made us both jump. "Wow." I snickered. "That's impressive."

"Dinner time." He said with a sheepish grin.

I wanted to say no kidding. That if I didn't find something for his stomach to devour it might eat me too but thought I might be pushing my luck. Michael usually got my sense of humor even sometimes when I didn't understand it myself. But wouldn't that be something I would have to reign in? Wasn't I supposed to be the mature, responsible person that people were supposed to look up to for inspiration and be a role model for others, something out of legend?

YUK!! I hated people that thought they were important but knew it was a necessary thing, to be someone that others would listen to for ideas. There were things that Michael and I knew needed doing but nobody else either had the position or the will to do it. Maybe I was thinking wrong? Maybe the reason I was chosen for this was because I was impulsive, emotional and willing to look like an idiot and maybe even have somebody laugh a little at me. I was mostly human still and humans made mistakes, fell on their faces and were far from perfect.

Why did I think I had to become perfect now? What would I be teaching and showing others if I lost myself in the process? Wouldn't I be showing them that being true wasn't worthwhile? That you should hide what you were to fit in? I would be setting myself up for some very big disappointments if I thought that or if allowed others to have that perception of me. I kept telling people I was just like they were when

I wasn't seeing in myself that those imperfections were just as much a necessity to keep me honest and human as those things about me that had been changed so that I could come back and fix the things that I knew in my heart were mine to fix. Anthony had said before that an infiltrator wasn't really a spy even though the name hinted at that. They were supposed to be all things that were needed when they were needed and right now a serious shake up, re-evaluation and maybe just not taking us so damn serious all the time was what was needed. It was something to try at lest and would let people know I wasn't just some Prima Donna as Tim said. Acting impulsive and joyful would certainly not be the norm if my family back home had been any indication of how most Resurrected where now. Well I had solved at least that small part of the world and I had done it because I was hot tempered, mouthy, silly and absolutely unpredictable. Why should I stop now?

So we went in search of food or at least that's what Michael and I knew we were starting out with but where we would end up was anybody's guess. We went up one floor as I figured out where the stairs were and went racing up them with Michael a half step behind. We came tearing out of the stairwell giggling like a pair of naughty children and had several people that were also going in the dining room looking at us with a mixture of humor, shock and maybe even disdain. The ones with smiling faces I smiled back at. The shocked ones I grinned even bigger for. The ones with disdainful looks I stopped, introduced myself, shook their hands and even gave a few happy hugs of greeting. Much to the complete humor of Michael as he was trying very hard to keep his laughter controlled to a few coughs and an escaped snicker or two.

We were very much the objects of quiet discussion, whispers and down right stares as we got in line with the rest for our dinner. Everything was being served sort of cafeteria style and the kitchen lady was hard pressed to keep tabs of everything. What, didn't she have any help? There seemed to be plenty of food it just seemed to have a lag in getting it up to the serving area. I nudged Michael in the ribs and nodded my head in the general direction of the kitchen. "How long has she been running things solo?" I asked quietly.

"What? Oh you mean Sue." Michael answered not really understanding where I was going or what I had in mind. "Quite a while I guess. Before you came along I never really thought about how everything made it out here. Never helped in a kitchen much either." As we both stood watching it was now quite apparent why she was in a bad mood a lot. She was beyond over worked and very much under appreciated. If nobody ever spelled her how did she get any time to do what she wanted?

I might not be able to fix everything today but I could sure lend a hand with this. Without saying anything I strode in the kitchen with Michael again being my shadow. It didn't take us long to figure out her system and we had everything back up to speed and things flowing in quick order. As the dinner crowd was for the most part eating quietly it was apparent that joy and laughter really didn't have much of a home here.

"This is just so sad." I mused sort of to myself but had Michael's attention very quickly.

"Sad, what's sad about everybody eating dinner?" He asked not seeing or hearing anything missing from the very subdued crowd.

"Where's the joking, talking, making plans for the evening or the weekend? All I hear anybody really talking about is work. There is almost nothing being said about personal stuff, no flirting between husbands and wives of things to look forward to tonight. Do you even see any of the single guys eyeing the single ladies with fun in mind? That's just depressing."

Michael watched and listened again. "You're right our house of five or six people make more noise during meal time than this room of almost 50 people. How did things get turned so upside down that work is all they think about?"

"I'm not sure but this right here is a place for us to start. Music would be a good idea, not loud but something to tap your foot to."

"Music?" Sue asked as she was starting on the clean up part. She hadn't even stopped to eat anything yet either.

"Not right yet you don't missy." Michael joked as he pulled a set of dirty plates out of her hands and put them on the counter. "Us hard working folks of the kitchen are going to sit down and eat too. Then we can all clean up. I think I can draft some help from all those that benefit from your hard work everyday to give you a break tonight. No dishes or pots for you."

"You rascal." Sue chuckled. "I see married life certainly has changed you." But she went along with him as we filled our plates and devoured the tasty meal that had been a choice of so many different things I didn't see how one woman managed to do it all by herself.

I sprinted down to our room and was back up with my little boom box and a selection of cd's, as Michael and I started on clean up. Tim and his lady Haley, a pretty woman almost his height with long blonde hair and oval shaped face and kind eyes joined us. And after a very hearty hug and an "I missed you" my very large lady protector Katherine tagged along too. Sue didn't really leave but she was delegated to watching supervisor as the five us went through the kitchen, scraping plates and loading the pair of huge dishwashers. Katherine and I tackled the big pots and pans, Haley and Tim cleaned up the dining room while Michael started putting away the few leftovers. This group could really pack away the food.

After we got done clean up Michael came up with a few ideas to give Sue some help. First put a couple of trash cans right by where the dirty dishes were stashed and have people clean their own plates off. Have a volunteer list for those that wanted to put time in the kitchen as helpers, dishwashers or the like. Just one day a week would be a big help or even one meal. I didn't think that would go over well for most people that thought working in the kitchen was boring and menial. Well it might be to some but I'm sure that we could change that attitude. So after dinner Sue, Michael and I sat down and started making some plans for some very needed upgrades for the dining room and kitchen. We all had some good ideas but we all knew it was just a start. The challenge at first would be to keep people from thinking we hadn't all gone of our rockers. Did I really care if some thought I was a little loopy? I was actually hoping for some of that reaction. It would beat zombie land anyway. You have to wake them up before you shake them up.

As Michael and I headed back down stairs for the night we were all but flying down the steps. When we closed the door to our suite we both were very happy about our first day here. As we got showers and ready for bed I came dancing out in one of the nightgowns that Michael hadn't seen yet. A rather frilly little see-through baby blue number that had Michael's eyes almost pop out of his head. "Do you like this one?" I asked teasingly as I crawled over the bed like a cat.

I was grabbed and pulled into a very passionate kiss as Michael growled possessively. It didn't take him long to show his appreciation of my wardrobe. But the extra clothing was soon gone leaving both of us as nature made us which was fine with me. Michael always looked unbelievably handsome but when he was like he was now he was all mine and I could love, kiss and caress him all I wanted. The sound of his heartbeat slowing into sleep lulled me into slumber too and I fell asleep with my husband holding me tightly against him.

When I woke it was a lot later than normal. I slept almost 5 hours this time. I got up and got dressed using only a night light's glow from the bathroom that must be in all rooms since without it we would have been in pitch black darkness.

As I left our room I really wasn't sure where I wanted to go or what I wanted to do. I left Michael a note that I would meet him for breakfast. Most everybody was still asleep. I wondered how many insomniacs like me were around or a graveyard shift that was working. I knew if anybody was up this time of night they wouldn't be hanging around in the cave like corridors of the housing section.

I hadn't made it down to the medical section or the training floor yet. Finding the stairwell from last night I went down one floor to the medical and research level. As I explored the entire floor I didn't find much activity. A few people in what seemed like the computer sections but they seemed so engrossed in whatever was on their monitors I doubted they would appreciate somebody just stepping in and starting up a conversation. This time of the night or early morning a strange voice might send them scrambling under their desks or I might have to peel them from the ceiling. That picture in my mind had me chuckling to myself silently.

One dark haired man in particular I thought might just be the nervous jumpy type from the way he sat with his back to the open doorway with his shoulders all hunched over. Just the body language alone made me think lonely, isolated. I stopped to watch silently as his hands flew over the keys. Then he would wait for results as information flashed across the screen.

After about an hour of watching him, he finally moved something besides his hands. He stretched and moved his head around like he had stiff neck.

"You know I was beginning to think you were a robot." I said as softly as I could.

Just like I thought he jumped out of his seat with an almost scream. "Good lord are you trying to scare people to death." Mr. Computer yelled.

"With your back to the door was there any other way of getting your attention?" I asked, again speaking as softly and quietly as I could. "At least I waited until you were done doing what ever you were doing."

"How long have you been there?" He asked. Realizing I must have been watching him silently for quite some time.

"Oh about an hour or so." I answered honestly.

"An hour. Why? Did you need something?" Now that he had gotten over his shock he was wondering why I was here in the wee hours of the morning. I also noticed he didn't ask who I was.

"I'm Gabriella." I said knowing he already knew that but it was a way of getting his name so that I could stop thinking of him as only Mr. Computer.

"I know." He answered simply. What? Didn't even give a name back in response like most would do. Jeez this was like pulling molars.

Well I guess tactful wasn't going to work so I went for just plain blunt and nosey. "And what is your name and what were you so busy with? It looked very important so I didn't want to interrupt."

"Oh, sorry." He answered with a shy drop to his head. He had very thick black hair that was a little shaggy and could use a good trim. Rather round face with a strong build to his body would have made me think he did something more physical than setting at a computer terminal all the time. "I'm Daniel."

"I really didn't mean to scare you Daniel." I apologized. "You just looked so intent that I was hoping to find out what you did?"

"Oh running programs and such. I developed the one that locates possible new people." Daniel said with a great deal of pride. Considering I knew next to nothing about computer programs and knew just enough to turn them on, surf the net, get email and general just play around I thought what he did was amazing.

"Wow. That's something." I agreed. He then went into a great explanation that I understand absolutely none of but tried to follow all the words that sounded normal but were being used in ways that left me speechless. I always considered computers to be things but the way he talked about his it was like that was his sister, girlfriend and mother all rolled into one.

"Daniel just how much time do you spend down here?" I asked a little worried. Was my new friend just like everybody else, lived to work? Again, I thought this was a little sad.

The way he looked at me let me know I had really hit the nail on the head. He spent almost every waking minute down here and had no social life and I don't think he even knew where to start to have one.

Realizing what time it was I had an inspired idea. "Is there anything you have to keep an eye for the next bit?"

"Um no. I guess not." He answered hesitantly. "Why?"

"Because you have been cooped up here too long tonight and you need a break." I answered with a smile and grabbed his hand. Daniel was rather shocked as I drug him from his office down the corridor and up three flights of stairs. I knew where east was and I knew were the best view was in the whole building for seeing a sunrise.

Michael had never locked the door back, just pulled it up and it was just before dawn as I ushered Daniel into what was supposed to be my living quarters. I had a better idea for it now. Phillip had wanted me to be isolated up here like royalty. Since it was supposed to be mine anyway wasn't it up to me how to use it? If I wanted to throw it open to anybody and everybody than shouldn't that be up to me? Well until Phillip got mad and took it away. Let him try. I'd give him a fight he wouldn't believe over this idea.

In all my exploring of the living area I had never once come across a community room. The only room that was big enough for everybody to meet was the dining room. This living room wouldn't hold everybody at once but it would handle at least half of us, maybe more if we wanted to be friendly. I had no problems with friendly. My personal space was almost none existent in the right situations.

As I watched the beautiful sunrise with my friend, I was laying out plans that would turn the stuffy people on their heads and make them spin around. But for us folks that thought living was more than a job it would be a wake up call. We all needed to find people and things we had in common. Families shared things. You didn't have to agree with them. You didn't even have to like them sometimes but the more you tried to understand others the more in common you found you had with them. And if you found you really had nothing in common with them or very little then you would know that too. Understand where they were coming from and why.

Daniel was just as moved at the sunrise as I usually was. Today my mind had been flying so fast that I barely noticed it. "That sure is some view." He admired looking all around. "Are we even supposed to up here?" He whispered to me.

"Sure. I was supposed to live here." I admitted.

"This is where you live?" He asked as he looked around more closely at the furnishing and all the extras that nobody else had.

"No." I snorted. "I said this is where I was supposed to live. But since I'm not going to let anyone treat me like something I'm not this is just unused space. Shouldn't it be used to benefit everybody?"

"So you want it deemed community property." Daniel nodded in agreement.

"Yes." I nodded. This would be a fight but wasn't that what I was here for? I don't think this is the kind of combat training Phillip and Rafael had in mind when they asked me to come here. Too bad this is the kind that I really loved. The physical stuff was great too but to address wrongs and set things right was more important than learning how to punch somebody better.

As the sun had risen and it was still rather early and I asked Daniel what he had planned. Since that turned out to be a very shy. "Not much." I drug him back down one flight of stairs and into the kitchen. I knew Sue would already be there starting on breakfast.

She was and was absolutely thrilled at having help. Daniel had no more clue of what happened in the kitchen than most of the people here did. He got a crash course from both of us and was soon beating eggs and chopping vegetables like a pro. I turned on some music and had it going with a nice steady uplifting group that most people liked. Well at least it had been a favorite at home anyway.

By the time the early breakfast crowd starting arriving at around 7:00 the food was all ready and waiting for them. Something I gathered surprised most of the people that were either night owls or the very early birds.

With people filing in to eat it gave me the opportunity to talk to more of them. Find out names and jobs. I got to meet the others in Daniel's graveyard computer group. Only three of them besides him and they seemed to be of the general mold he was; dedicated, hardworking and a little nerdy and shy. I guess geeks were the same no matter what. They would go off on tangents that made perfect sense to them but left me totally baffled. Well it seemed they did have a clicky little group but they were just so isolated amongst themselves that nobody else even paid attention to them. Just another cog in the machine like everybody seemed to be. The invisible cogs needed to start mounting some serious resistance to being ignored.

"Since you guys are up all night would you like to help out in the kitchen in the mornings before you go to bed?" I asked the surprised quartet.

"Kitchen, help in the kitchen?" The tall skinny guy named Simon asked amazed.

"Not all the time of course." I pestered. "Just every once in a while. Sue gets so overwhelmed sometimes and nobody seems to notice. I guess you guys would know exactly how that feels. People coming in and asking you to do the impossible and not caring how many programs you have to write or systems you have to hack in order to get what they want."

"Well that sure is true." The lone girl Brenda said. "Just last week, remember that request from medical that had us all crossing our eyes for two days."

"Yeah." Simon agreed. "That one was a killer. But I don't know anything about working in the kitchen."

"I didn't either." Daniel put in. "Not until this morning. It isn't that hard, just time consuming and it was sort of fun. Not like hacking into someplace that they think is unbreakable but still fun. But wouldn't it be better than staring at four walls until you wind down from watching the monitors every night?"

Well I had a champion of sorts in Daniel. He was of the very easygoing sort that was eager to please and I think he had already developed a sort of fascination for me. I just hoped that all the males here knew I was already spoken for.

Well speak of the devil and he appears, I thought with a smile. Michael had arrived and was looking just as handsome as last night. Well maybe not just as handsome, now he had his dark brown hair combed and was freshly shave and would smell like a mixture of his cologne and ice cream. I got all melty just watching him cross the room with his eyes fixed on me like I was the only person here.

I took me a few minutes to realize that Daniel had actually been talking and I had been so absorbed at watching my bond mate that I didn't even hear him. "I'm sorry, Daniel what did you say?"

"Do you think tomorrow we could all go and watch the sunrise?" He asked again. I guess my little experiment had paid off very well. Now I had four test subjects to work with.

"Sure but it depends on the weather too. Today was just the right amount of high clouds and nothing lower to interfere with the viewing." I had experienced enough very early mornings in recent memory to know now what made for a good sunrise and what didn't.

Michael had finally reached me after being stopped a few times by old friends that he hadn't had the opportunity to say hello to just yet. I was happy that he was re-establishing these ties. It was important for him to not wrap himself around me totally as he had a tendency to do. I would be busy some of the time, maybe even a lot of the time and he needed to have something else to do but work and watch what I did.

We were both trying to figure out what he was supposed to do while he was assigned here anyway. Phillip gave him no clue what, if any, duties he had other than keeping me on the straight and narrow. Michael was a sight empath and he might be able to help with the physical therapy and maybe even surgery but he didn't like the idea of putting himself under the thumb of a couple of the doctors that were in charge of the medical section. The term power struggle sort of came up and Michael lead me to believe that both of us would be having some serious confrontations with the heads of that department before too much longer.

Michael wrapped me up in a hug and kissed me gently, not the deep passionate kisses he was oh so good at. It was probably a good thing, we did have responsibilities and we weren't on our honeymoon anymore. "Have a good morning?" He asked smiling at my new friends to include them in his question. I had no idea if he knew any of them or not but it didn't matter we were all family it was just a matter of getting to know which ones you liked and which ones you didn't.

"Yes, Daniel and I took in a beautiful sunrise this morning upstairs. I think we figured out a better use for the ivory tower." I answered him happily. That brought a raised eyebrow but he would get the details later when we had a better chance to sit down and talk.

We both made a trip through the food line and smiled and waved at Sue very busily in the kitchen. She was ahead in her hectic schedule this morning thanks to Daniel and I helping out. A few little things made a big difference even if it was just a moral thing for her. It meant somebody noticed and somebody cared about what she did.

"Do you need anything for tonight or this weekend?" I asked quietly. The kitchen brigade had come up with some ideas for a few 'specials' tonight and also a bigger thing this weekend but Sue really hadn't been sure just what supplies she had on hand for some of it. The normal supply chain wouldn't work because she submitted to bulk suppliers on a biweekly basis. So it was off to town for Michael and I today and get whatever she needed. She did run out of things on occasion so this wasn't the first time somebody from here had to go to Breckinridge for stuff but it couldn't be done too much or the natives would realize there were a whole lot more people up here than was commonly believed.

Without saying anything she slipped me a folded piece of paper that I stuffed into my pants pocket and would look at it later. Michael and I finished our breakfast together listening and watching everybody as they came and went. Most were much more animated this morning as they geared up for another day of work. Even those people that were here for rehab seemed to be in good spirits. Still it hurt my heart to see those of us that had suffered injury and would never recover. The two with missing hands would be given the highest tech prosthetics that could be found and when they learned how to use them enough would go back out into the world and lead as normal lives as possible. The same with one that had suffered burns on his arms and chest. I wondered what more could be done for him. You could tell he had been handsome and he wasn't dealing well with his injuries.

Then there were the 10 or so protectors in training. Some must be very new to their size and strength judging by the way the walked almost hunched over from hitting their heads too many times when walking in low doorways that even this place had its fair share of. They also had a tendency to crush things Sue said when I found a few mangles pieces of silverware last night when we were doing dishes.

At least I hadn't had that big a growth spurt. I'm quite sure my awkward stage would have been even more entertaining than it had been had I sprouted up a foot instead of only three inches.

Just before Michael and I got up to leave I noticed a man approaching us and Michael let out a low groan. He had been one from last night that had a disdainful look on his face when we had come out of the stairwell laughing. "So when are you going to be down to see us Gabriella?" He said without even introducing himself. Like I was just supposed to know who he was. Maybe he had given me his name last night but I didn't think so.

"Excuse me?" I answered politely. His tone had been rather snooty, like he was asking because he was supposed to, not because he wanted to. "Where am I supposed to be going?" As far as I knew I had training with Joshua and Katherine this afternoon. Other than that my schedule was pretty open.

"You were supposed to be down in the lab first thing this morning but I guess nobody mentioned that you weren't supposed to eat before you had your blood drawn." Mr. Snooty said like I was an idiot or something.

He had a lot to learn about being nice to people. Maybe he thought he didn't have to be anymore. I stood up and Michael chuckled. He may not know what I was going to say, hell I didn't even know what I was saying until it came out of my mouth most of the time but he knew it wouldn't be sweet.

"First off you really should introduce yourself when you are trying to get some one's cooperation. Second, nobody even asked if I was willing to be a lab rat. It is my body we are talking about and I have the right to say no to anything I don't understand or agree to." I said it nicely with a smile on my face. But the smile didn't reach my eyes. I was pissed and anybody that knew me would know it too.

"But Phillip assured me you were willing to have a few samples taken." He said trying to pull out his little back up answer. Oh the council wants you to so you have to comply.

"So, did you ask me? No, not a word and a few samples means just that a few. Not a never-ending stream of needles and x-rays. I say what tests are allowed and if you don't explain them so that I can understand them you aren't getting them. If you can't ask and instead make it sound like an order you can just take all those tests and just stuff'm." Now the anger was coming out.

"You have to." He all but shouted back. "Rafael said you might be a little hesitant but that Michael could convince you of the necessity."

Michael stood up now too. "Paul, I don't think you get it. I don't work for you this time around. I'm a house leader now and have every bit as much authority as you do. I didn't resign my leadership to come up here with Gabriella, I kept it and she doesn't have to obey like a drone either. She's equal rank just like me. You want her to play nice. You want me to play nice then you had better start to also." Michael voice was ice cold. The voice I had heard before when he was really pissed but wouldn't show it.

"I see." Paul answered. He didn't say anything else but turned on his heel and left.

Those few people that were still in the dining room had either very pleased looks or extremely shocked ones but nobody looked angry about our confrontation. "So what's he going to do now?" I asked Michael.

"He'll run to Phillip and Rafael and they will either call us and ask us to behave or tell him too." Michael smiled. "If Phillip isn't totally stupid then I know what the answer is going to be."

"Yeah." I chuckled. Phillip and Rafael both knew I had a temper. That I was more or less just looking for an excuse to go home. They would tell Paul to play nice for a while anyway.

Now decision time. Should I go down to the lab and find out just what tests they wanted me to take. Lord I felt so torn. I knew that some of the things that my body did the medical and research people had never seen before but if I let them get away with thinking I was at their beck and call they would sample me into none existence.

No, don't give in just yet, I said to myself. I had made it a point that you should be asked to have bits and pieces of your body taken from you. It should be a choice everybody had but I didn't think it worked like that around here. Or at least not yet, but it was going to start. We weren't property and it should always be our decision, to allow that which is most sacred to be taken away and placed under a microscope or invaded by a machine's eyes to reveal what was special about us. Paul had to change. If not, well let's see how he liked intimidation. And I smiled that smile that I knew Michael wouldn't like. It wasn't a pretty smile, it was a smile that said bad things were coming better run, better hide. Yeah, Paul yanked the tiger's tail and got it's attention lets see how he liked my claws.

"You okay?" Michael asked. Trying to actually look me in the eyes. He was still a little angry too. We both sort of shook it off and decided we weren't going to let a petty tyrant ruin our day. He wasn't worth it.

"Yes. Just thinking what kind of reaction Paul's going to have when I give him a sample of my claws." I chuckled a little evilly.

"Can I please be there to watch?" Michael agreed with an equally devilish look.

"Of course, I have to have somebody smart to explain medical stuff to poor stupid me." I said sarcastically.

Michael just snorted. He knew I wasn't stupid. I didn't have the medical background he did or probably most of the medical staff around here but I wasn't some dumb newbie either. Did they need to know that? No, not yet. Playing stupid sometimes got some really good reactions from people. They dropped their guard more if they thought you didn't understand what was being said.

We headed downstairs to the garage after a brief stop in our room to pick up keys, wallet and purse. It helped to have money before you went shopping. I was more than a little surprised to find my truck surround by several of the protectors we had seen at breakfast when we came out into the big bay. Did I really want to know why they were looking at it with almost worship in their eyes? But my truck, please it was just a truck. There was not a thing odd or diffcrent about it. You couldn't even tell it had been shot and had blood all over it. Peter was a very good mechanic. I got a little misty eyed thinking about my family so far away. I missed them so much but I had work to do here and right in front of me was another very good place to start.

"Did somebody loose a contact lens or something?" I asked jokingly making 7 very large men jump a little in embarrassment.

"We didn't know you would be down here today." One of them said. It was so hard to tell them apart just yet. They were all of the same body type. Extremely tall, well muscled and when they moved you could tell they weren't used to how much their bodies had changed. I knew all about that but how could I tell them without making them feel even more uncomfortable about their changes than they all ready were.

"Why should you?" I smiled trying to get them to relax. These were the ones I would be working with during training. True I hoped to spend more time with Joshua and Katherine but it would be very selfish of me to take up all their time. These guys were just as important as I was. All the new kids could learn a lot from each other I was sure. "The bigger question I have is why are all of you?"

"We just wanted to see your truck." The only blonde out of the bunch said. I think he was a little more aggressive than the others. Why did I think that? Maybe because the rest wouldn't meet my eyes but he had no problems staring right into them.

"Sure it's a good truck but you guys might want something a little bigger when you get your next assignment. I don't have as long as legs as you do. Our protector had a big Ram that I fell out of the first time I road in it. Would have landed on my butt if somebody hadn't caught me." And I laughed at the memory with Michael joining in. Even though he hadn't actually witnessed he had heard all about it.

They all sort of took a step back mentally. What had they expected? That I would play up the legend. No, but I also wasn't going to be looked down on like the blonde was doing now. He wasn't impressed by me and at the moment that was okay. "What's your name?" I asked much to his surprise and everyone else's.

"Charles." He answered rather smugly. Like he was proud of his name. It was good a name but not something to write home about and as far as I could tell he wasn't either. "Why?"

Ah curiosity. Now that was a good thing. Something a lot of our family didn't have much any more. "Because I just wanted to know who I should ask for when Joshua wants me to pick a sparing partner when he's busy." I wasn't sure if this would scare him or not. It didn't. Charles was a little cocky. That too was a good thing. It was good to have confidence in your abilities as long as it didn't go to your head that is.

"Looking forward to it." He answered with a nod. Which got several looks of shock and a few murmurs of disapproval. Some didn't like that he was going toe to toe with me. That's okay I don't think Michael cared for it either, as I felt him shift protectively towards me. Time to leave before the testosterone started to get out of hand.

"Excuse me guys. But I have a few errands to run before I have training this afternoon. See you later." I expected to have to push my way through them but it was like Moses and the Red Sea and they just moved apart and let me pass.

Michael and I got out of the garage and down to the town on our scavenger mission but the whole time I was asking myself what I had in store for me this afternoon. I hadn't had to fight anybody but Gabriel. I didn't count Hans or Josef, those weren't fights, they were more like executions. So just how good was I? I had learned a lot in those frightening tenses minutes in the warehouse with Gabriel. Each second that had ticked by I could feel my reactions getting quicker. It had taken me a while to figure it out but now I realized that at the end I was as fast as he was. At the start he could have killed me at any time but not when we were done. He would have had problems then but it didn't matter anyway. He had been fighting to lose while I had been fighting to live. His life, my life, Anthony and Peter's, survival and the drive to protect those you loved were great motivators. Now I had to see if I remembered what he had almost died to show me.

# CHAPTER 3

## COMBAT

The training room was very large but didn't really look any different than what I had expected. I hoped that the walls were reinforced because the protectors were very large strong guys that could throw somebody right through a normal wall. Why was I worrying? Joshua and Katherine had been training people for a long time. I was just nervous. That was all. If somebody said boo I might just end up clinging to the ceiling myself. Why?

Did it matter to me if I made a fool of myself? Was that my problem? Getting too big for my britches that I didn't want to be seen as anything but perfect or at least better than all the other trainees here. Get a grip Maggie. I fussed at myself. You aren't supposed to know everything yet. I was here to learn not show off.

As the other guys started on exercises that I guess they had already been told to do Michael and I just sort of stood around looking stupid. I had convinced Michael he needed more than just the normal self-defense classes that he had along the way and both Joshua and Katherine agreed. He had a target on him too and if I didn't have to worry about him so much it would free me up to do what I needed to do. But Michael drew the line on guns. Joshua also trained people to use all matter of weapons that was why he was classified as a master protector. He knew it all and then some. How long had he be been doing this? I wondered. Protectors didn't age or scar so there was no way to tell and it felt invasive to ask but still I wondered 50 years, 75 or was it more. He didn't talk all that different than anybody else but we all adapted to the changes in speech that was currently acceptable.

Michael didn't sound almost 91 either. Every once in a while he would come out with something odd that would get a raised eyebrow from me but very rarely. We had to adapt well. We stood out enough without talking like we belonged in somebody's grandparent's age group.

Joshua showed up first but Katherine was only a few minutes later. Michael wasn't the only non-protector that was being trained today. It was a little sad that in this day and age everybody needed to be able to protect him or herself better. It was a sign of the times unfortunately. As Michael went to join the other normal Resurrected for his training with Joshua I got put in with mine. I didn't know most of their names but I picked up Charles very quickly. He was easy to spot with his blonde hair.

I watched silently for a few minutes as two of the protectors started a combat routine. One I had seen on video before. It was different in person. The vibrations through the floor had to be felt to really understand what was happening. Impressive was hardly the words, the new guys were already very fast but they would grow into their speed just like I had. It took a while to realize that your reaction time was just so much better. I remembered almost falling over my own two feet a few times until I got things down. Now I didn't do that anymore but as I watched my fellow classmates I started to pick out those that were very, very new and others that had been around a little while. Charles, it would seem, was one of those that had been here the longest. No wonder he was a little more aggressive, more confident.

"So, where did you want to start?" Katherine asked as she silently moved up beside me, still I knew she was there. "Do you know what they are doing?" Nodding to the others in my group that had already paired up for fight training.

"Yes, I've seen it before." I nodded. "I think I've seen most of the taped stuff that are in the archives." When I saw her eyebrow raised in question as to how I got those files, I just smiled and said a name. "Anthony."

"Ah, of course." Katherine said. You didn't need to say anything else. "So would you like to work with me on some of those moves?"

This is what I came for wasn't it? I nodded but I had to clarify a few things. "You're bigger than I am Katherine. I have to fight differently. You have more muscle mass than I do and much more strength. I have to be quicker than you, stay out of reach until I can either kill or disable you." I had never thought of pitting myself against my friend before but I had to. Stop looking at her as a sister and look at her for weakness.

Katherine had longer arms and legs than I did but was still smaller and shorter than Gabriel was. As we went to an unused part of the room everybody stopped what they were doing until Joshua barked and made them get back to work. Still I knew we were being watched. When Katherine swung her fist right at my head I forgot about everybody else. She was incredibly fast and quick too. Dodging and twisting away from her, I danced out of reach. She feinted quickly to the left but I could tell that it wasn't a committed move. Not enough of her weight was where it should be if she had planned on completely the kick she was telegraphing.

Whatever she thought I was going to do in defense wasn't what happened. I didn't defend I attacked. Dropping to the ground I kicked at her leg that had the most weight on it making her stumble briefly. She recovered quickly but not quick enough that I wasn't already on her with closed fist against her neck, knuckles up against the very large artery that I could feel beating. "Tag." I chuckled.

"Good Lord Maggie I didn't know you were that fast." Katherine grumped. She had underestimated me and I had to smile a little at that. Most big people didn't look at those smaller as a threat until confronted with the fact that smaller doesn't mean helpless.

The next few rounds we fought it was give and take. Sometimes I lost and ended up with my butt on the mats and others I was clinging to some part of Katherine like a monkey. Her leg, her back quite of few times but always where a major pulse point was or a large grouping of very important muscles. Something that if sliced open would be difficult if not impossible to work without or might drain a person of blood in just a few minutes. Katherine was trying to knock out, while I usually killed. For me going up against a protector there weren't a lot of options. I wish there were and maybe we could come up with some but right now it was all I knew. Kill and make sure they never threatened me or mine again.

Finally after about an hour Joshua called a halt to everything. Everybody was breathing rather heavily but me. Was I really just that much different than even my fellow protectors were? Somewhere I had already known that answer before I ever set foot in here today. Yes, I was that different. My very acute senses told me that before, now it was just showing in a more obvious way.

I both heard and smelled Michael as he cam up behind me. Felt his hand brush my back before it came to rest on my shoulder. Before I might have hurt him but I always knew where my other half was now. I had kept a sort of mental track of him the whole time I had been sparing with Katherine. How I did that I had no idea, it was sort of the way my hearing worked when I was asleep.

"Did you have fun?" He asked as he hugged me from behind, resting his chin on my shoulder.

"Yes. Katherine's great." I had enjoyed testing myself with her. She adapted quickly. Saw my weakness and had no problems pointing them out with a less than gentle tap to my stomach once that knocked the air out of me and if I had been anybody else would have broken a few ribs.

"You were very good for being the smallest and newest one." Michael said with a great deal of pride. It didn't even surprise me that he had been watching for at least part of the time.

"And you?" I had known where he was but hadn't watched. Had been more than a little busy trying to keep Katherine from removing my head from my shoulders most of the time.

"Not bad. Joshua said I should probably move into the more advanced classes next week." He said sounding a little surprised at that.

"Were you that good before?" I whispered. We both knew that Michael had changed because of my blood in his body but neither one of us was sure just how or how much. This was the first time he ever really tried anything highly physical with anyone but me. We had played around a few times while on the road especially after that incident with the robbery and I thought he was faster and stronger than before but wondered if it had been my imagination.

"No." He murmured. "Actually I pretty much stunk. Joshua is more than a little surprised too but he didn't ask why the big change. I'm not sure how I'm going to explain things if and when he does." We didn't want people to know how large amount of my blood changed him. One it would lead to Michael being a lab rat too but also wondering just how much blood I would be able to keep in my body. The research guys were out to get me to start out with why make it even more appealing to them.

"Blame it on hanging out with me." I suggested. That was about the best I could come up.

"Maggie love we've spent a lot of time rolling around on the floor and the bed but you weren't teaching me unarmed combat. You are right though nobody needs to know what we do behind closed doors." He chuckled suggestively. "Do you think I could get another lesson tonight?"

I whirled around in his arms so quickly that it used to almost scare him, now he had gotten used to how fast I was and was ready for my kiss as my fingers wound through his hair.

We both heard a voice clearing a throat. I knew it was Joshua wanting our attention but not wanting to intrude. He had always been very formal any time he had to talk to me. Not as formal as Phillip but almost as close. Maybe this was the only indication I would ever have when someone was so much older than the rest of us. I got the impression that Joshua was over 150 and maybe more than that. Why did I guess that? It was how courteous he was maybe or just the way he carried himself. Either way it didn't matter he was my teacher today and deserved respect for that position no matter his age.

"Joshua." I addressed him with a nod. We didn't apologize for our kiss, was it improper here, maybe, but I still wasn't sorry for it.

"Gabriella." Joshua said returning my nod. "You are much better than I had thought. I'm not sure why I was surprised. Anthony is not much of a fighter himself but he would certainly know when he sees something you did wrong."

"No kidding." I snorted, remembering all the hours we spent in the woods in Alabama training. Going over and over things until I was more than perfect. There were quite a few times I had been tempted to try out a technique on my teacher but Anthony was a tall skinny guy that would have problems fighting his way out of paper bag. We were so different but I loved him and couldn't wait for him to get back. It had been just a little over a month since I had seen him but I had missed him horribly.

"Since you and Michael will be together more than apart I thought it might be a good idea to see how you would fight together. It may be a little premature in things but Michael has surprisingly improved from six years ago."

The growl that escaped my lips surprised everyone, including me. I knew that it was a good idea. I knew sooner or later Michael and I would be thrown into a situation that would require us fighting together. It wasn't luck or fate it was just the way it was and we knew it. But I had come so close to losing him once that to have him threatened made me very defensive. Just from my reaction I knew this was not just a good idea but imperative. I had to know Michael could take care of himself or if he couldn't what I needed to do to keep him safe.

"Sorry Joshua." I apologized as my defensive stance relaxed. Boy, the hairs on my neck were standing up. I hadn't just been protective. I had been ready to attack and didn't even realize it. "You're right, I know that." I just didn't like it.

"So how are we supposed to do this?" Michael asked. I think he was more game than I was. When I looked at him a little closer I could tell he was eager for the chance to prove himself. Was it any wonder, we both knew that I was stronger, faster and much more lethal. But he was a man with all the male type desires of being stronger than his mate. Now I was even more worried. I didn't want him to look bad, would that inhibit me and make us both perform poorly. In a life and death situation I knew what my reaction would be. Kill what threatened us and it didn't matter how I did it and if a feeling got a little bruised along the way I really wouldn't care.

"Equal opponents. A protector for Gabriella and one of Michael's classmates from today as his target." Joshua explained. It seemed that this was something that Joshua had either planned out before or was very quick on his mental feet.

"All right, I guess." I answered still very apprehensive.

Michael smiled at me. "It's okay Maggie. What's the worst that can happen, we both end up on the floor. Big deal. I have had that happen plenty before."

Charles it seemed was my opponent much to his delight and a rather large man that I had seen in the same group, as Michael today was the other one.

"Well Gabriella we get to test each other quicker than what I had thought." Charles said with a very small inclination of is head. In dojo terms that meant he thought he was my equal at least.

Charles and his teammate would be the aggressors and Michael and I would be the defenders. What exactly did that mean? We would get attacked and have to defend ourselves. Real life scenario, kill before they killed you.

Without even talking about it Michael turned his back and pressed it up against me so that I could tell where he was without me having to think about. As Charles circled I moved and Michael moved with me. I had no idea how we did what we did but it was like we both thought the same thing at the same time.

I felt movement from Michael and a grunt that wasn't his voice and I knew his opponent had tried something and either been blocked or Michael had already landed a blow. Then my worry for Michael took a back seat in my head because Charles was in my face. Trying to land a blow to my chest. I danced away wrapping my hand around Michael's waist pulling him out of the way too. I didn't think, I just did it and Michael went along like he knew why I was doing it too.

We moved and circled and switched positions several times always trying to keep Charles in my field of vision and Michael safely away from him just like everyone thought we would. When I saw the same opening that Charles had given me a few times before, I was ready. "NOW." It wasn't a yell it was a hiss maybe or a heavy whisper. Something Michael would hear but his opponent wouldn't and it might even slip by Charles if he wasn't listening closely.

Sliding quickly in between his outstretched legs I grabbed Charles by his knees and yanked as hard as I could dropping him to his face. Michael had one of my nails placed at his throat before he could move. They hadn't noticed that I handed him one before we started this. It was the only way to prove we would have killed. I had his opponent on his back with my claws extended in his face before he could even blink. He had no idea that we were changing opponents. It was not something anyone would think of that's why we did it.

There was a bit of stunned silence then applause as I helped my second opponent up to his feet but to my surprise Michael didn't offer Charles a hand up. "I've had enough of this fun today." He said with a bit of growl and stalked out of the room. What in the hell was all that about? Michael was rarely moody anymore and he had been all for testing ourselves at the beginning.

Joshua raised an eyebrow but didn't comment on it but I left as soon as I could. I didn't even have to think about where my husband had disappeared to so abruptly. When I opened up the door to our room Michael was coming out of the bathroom. I didn't have to ask why he left. "I didn't want anybody to see this." He held up his hand from where my sharp nail had sliced his hand open and now was almost totally healed. Only a long pink scar was left and that too would be gone soon.

"You didn't think it would last this long Michael." I wondered out loud as I took his hand in mine to examine it better. "How deep was it?"

"About ¼ inch but I could feel it start to bleed and then stop. I could actually tell when the tissue started to mend itself." He didn't ask if that was the way it felt for me when I was injured, we both knew where his remarkable healing ability came from. His was just a lot slower. I would have healed that sort of thing in a matter of seconds but Michael took more like 30 minutes.

"Do you think it's permanent then?" We really weren't sure about any of this. Michael and I were very much in unknown, unexplored territory. None of the other infiltrators had been bonded, none had been women and as far as either one of us knew nobody had almost all their blood replaced by someone with a protector's healing ability. Was that the reason we almost thought the same thoughts sometimes, especially in stressful situations? There were just so many things that had happened to us that had changed us from what we had been. On top of all that we shared a heart spark. Which one or ones was responsible for what happened today?

"After this long probably. But still it shouldn't be something we rely on." He was very cautious and I could understand why. "Even this doesn't explain how we moved today. I have seen a few bonded people that took combat training together. A protector and his partner a few times and they had to work long and hard to understand what their other half was going to do. Today it was like I could feel what your fingertips were telling me to do before they pressed at all. I didn't even really think about it. I just knew."

"I know. How did we do what we did? Even though we said nothing I knew you understood what I wanted. When I pushed you that first time when Charles tried to hit me it was like you were already going the direction I wanted you to."

"I was." Michael marveled. "With your back up against mine I could feel every single muscle move and shift, could tell where you were heading before your fingers even started pushing were I was supposed to go."

"We won't be able to pull that same stunt again next time." I warned. That had been unexpected but when we had to practice again our opponents would be looking for something like that.

Michael had been through some of this before but I was still going through a severe adjustment phase. Everything was new to me including combat training. He knew most of the people here better than I did right now. "Joshua surprised us on purpose today just to see how well we communicated on an unconscious level." He said thoughtfully. "Now everybody knows we share a very strong bond. He may have expected some but I don't know if anybody other than a telepath would have read you like I did today or how you responded those few times that I need you to."

Whenever Michael had to move to avoid something or had attacked and then retreated I had either backpedaled or moved so that my back and his stayed in contact. Again, it wasn't something I thought about. How we managed to not fall all over our feet was a huge question?

"I'm surprised you and I didn't end up in big heap on the floor." I giggled a little. That would have been just perfect and would have been just what most had expected.

"Me too." Michael chuckled. "I think I would like to explore this more when we don't have an audience around. Maybe this morning when you wake up you can get me up too. We can get some extra practice in before everybody shows up Friday afternoon."

"Won't that make you too tired?" Last thing Michael needed was to be groggy during training practice. Good way to get something broken.

"No, remember Joshua said I should start taking the advanced classes next week. If I don't show up tomorrow nobody will think much of it. I'll just come back here if I'm tired and grab a nap."

"Oh, does that mean I can wake you up with a kiss afterwards?" I whispered.

"Well you could but I thought I was Prince Charming not Cinderella or Sleeping Beauty." He laughed, reminding me of the joke I had played on him a month ago.

Maybe not sleeping beauty but Michael was more than Prince Charming as I stared into his gorgeous blue eyes. He had the most wonderful thick black eyelashes that brought out their color. My hand reached up to caress his eyebrow and stroke down the side of his face. He leaned into my touch and I felt his hands go around my waist. We were almost half undressed and on the bed when someone knocked on our door.

"WHAT?!" Michael snarled out.

"I don't think they can hear you Michael, these rooms are really well made. Even I have problems hearing more than a few doors down." In my old home everything said I heard. I was used to the creaks and groans of the house and the subtle noises our housemates made in the night. Here it was almost like a tomb. Just one more thing that made me miss home.

I threw on my blouse without the bra. It would have been probably easier for Michael to answer the door but he was frustrated and pissed and wasn't about to get up for anybody. Right before I opened the door I knew who it was. "Hello Joshua." I said before I even had the door open enough to see him.

This was fun. The surprise on his face was something few if any people saw anymore. He recovered quickly and returned my greeting. "Gabriella. I just wanted to check on Michael. He left rather abruptly." Good excuse for an unannounced visit but I didn't think that was the entire reason he had for stopping by. He wouldn't have been the master protector that he was, the go to and know all about self-defense if he wasn't at least curious about our performance today.

"He's fine Joshua." I answered around the partially opened door but when I looked back at Michael he had recovered from his ill humor and already had his shirt back on and was setting up in a chair. He nodded that it was okay with him if Joshua stopped by for a visit.

7-foot tall people had to adjust in all matter of ways as he ducked more than his head to get in our door. "Is your doorway to your suite taller than most?" That was a little rude but I just couldn't help it.

"Yes. The protectors are usually housed in one area with the doors modified to accommodate our height and the furniture is much sturdier so that the new ones don't break things as easily." He smiled at that exchange. Maybe most people that weren't protectors didn't ask about that stuff. Me, I was just plain nosey enough to ask what ever was on my mind.

We tried to not pry and let Joshua get around to asking what both Michael and I knew he wanted to ask. He had a lot of problems asking questions. Finally after about 10 minutes of small talk I had enough evasiveness.

"Joshua you didn't come by to check on Michael or see how we were settling in. You could care less about our honeymoon and what we saw along the way. Now what did you really stop by for."

He backpedaled a little at my bluntness and Michael just coughed in his hand. He was used to me being direct when I had to be. Very few things were off limits for me. Personal things of course but this wasn't personal this was business.

"How did you do what you did today?" Joshua asked recovering well from his surprise. "I have had bonded couples that took training together before and I have never had one that worked that well together even after weeks and sometimes months. You knew every second where the other one was, were you were supposed to move to. Even Katherine and I don't work that well together. I trained her, I know how she thinks and how she will react to just about anything, still you might be able to give us a run for our money. Maybe not just yet but very soon you will be able to."

That surprised both Michael and me. We were good but not that good. I was fast for even a protector but when Katherine and I had spared today we had been pretty much equal. Michael was faster than a normal Resurrected but still much slower than a protector was. No way we could compete with our two teachers. "Stop blowing smoke up my skirt Joshua." I grumped. "Michael and I may be good but not that good and we probably never will be."

"You're talking about in the training room and I'm not." Joshua clarified. "I saw how many times you pulled up today with both Katherine and with Charles. They have no clue of course. You are very good at letting them think you couldn't just slice them open whenever you felt like it. Today when you slid under Charles's legs instead of letting Michael make the kill you could have just cut him open from the top of his thighs to his knees. I saw the few times you pulled back from hitting Katherine in the stomach and I know why. It brought back too many memories for you about Gabriel and Josef. You were afraid that you would not be able to hold back your claws and instinct to kill and you didn't want to risk that with a friend."

I sat down on the bed with a whoosh. "Yes, please don't tell her. I want to find ways of fighting that don't involve killing. That's all I know and it shouldn't be. Even a protector can be disabled enough to allow an escape and I need to know how to do that."

Joshua wasn't at all surprised by my admission but Michael was. "Why would you hold back like that?" Michael grumbled. I think he was a little pissed. Why? It was worth a little embarrassment on my part if it meant I could learn something less lethal. Didn't he understand that I hated to kill? All three times I had done that or almost done it was to protect myself. It had never been any glorious rescue that was being spread around now. That had been the results but at the moment all I had been interested was saving my own neck. I had sliced Hans open just like I could have Charles today and the results would have been the same, dead. Even without the poison on my claws it would have been bad and nobody can withstand having their heart ripped out of their chest, wonderful healing ability or no. I didn't need that special little additive on my claws for that. But couldn't there be other things I could do that would disable and not kill? Wasn't that why I had the poison on my claws to start out? That's what I thought, now I had to figure out how to use them that way, to damage and injure but not kill.

"It wasn't to make you feel better Michael." Joshua summarized. "You have become very good since your last visit. I would like to ask how but I think I'm looking at the reason sitting on the bed. I can tell there are things you are keeping secret and I can understand that. You aren't quite sure about any of us here and you have no reason to trust anybody after what Gabriel did."

Michael and I couldn't tell him that Gabriel hadn't defected but if Joshua was willing to accept that as the reason for our silence then I wasn't about to say something that would change his mind. I looked at Michael and he looked at me and shrugged. We trusted Joshua as much as anybody here but how much did we want to tell anybody?

While I tugged at the chain for my pendant, Michael knew exactly what I was asking. A heart spark could explain a lot of what we were able to do. Very few people had even heard of the phenomenon. He nodded silently and pulled his out at the same time I did.

"We aren't exactly sure Joshua but we think this is why we always know where the other is." Michael said. Placing his hands around the crystal so you could see the pulsing in the stone. Joshua's eyes flashed over to mine that I had exposed the same way. Anyone could tell they beat exactly at the same time.

"What is that?" He whispered. "I have never seen bonding crystals do that before."

"It's called a heart spark." Michael answered. "We didn't realize what it was at first either but then I remembered something Alison said about bonding crystals having unusual properties sometimes and then I realized what those little electric zaps Maggie and I had experienced were."

"Heart sparks." Joshua concluded. "And they let you know what?"

"Where ever he is I know." I answered. "The closer he is the easier it is. I never really lose track of him and he knows where I am too."

"Yes." Michael nodded. "When we first got here Maggie wandered off while I was talking and I lost sight of her. She had no idea the layout of the place, could have gone up, down or even outside but when I realized she wasn't standing right beside me, I knew she was on the same floor and not too far away. It was almost like following a blood hound."

"And you think this is how you did what you did today?" Joshua wondered.

"We were trying to figure all this out too when you stopped by." Michael explained. "Maggie and I aren't sure either but it's the only thing we could think of that would explain it. Was it just a one time thing that we can't rely on or will it get better, stronger as we figure out how to use it consciously instead of it being almost an instinctive reaction."

I had to smile at that. Michael was making it sound that this whole hour plus that was all we had been up to when in reality that part of our conversation had lasted only about 10 minutes tops. Joshua didn't need to know that. He was a single man and to have the fact that Michael and I enjoyed a very healthy sex life shoved in his face would be insensitive and maybe even a bit cruel.

Katherine and Joshua were working partners but nothing more than that. It had surprised me a little when I had noticed what was missing between them. They worked closely but there was no spark, no looks or touches that said they were anything but friends and really only working partners. Katherine and I had become not great friends but friends when she had spent those few weeks with us in Florida but Joshua although courteous never went the extra step to being a friend. That sort of saddened me. He always separated himself from everybody. That must be a very lonely way to live. I could understand the reason for that for most of his students, especially the new protectors. He had to be the strong rock type of person that nobody would even think about arguing with. But didn't he have anyone to be himself with, to share worries and laughter?

Why I did it I'm not sure but I went over to my teacher where he sat in a chair opposite Michael. Placing my hand on his shoulder I looked into his eyes. Even sitting down he was almost the same height I was. "You know it's okay if you show how much you worry about your students. It won't make you look weak, being human won't take away your Rock of Gibraltar status especially with me."

Joshua dropped his eyes but I could see the flash of emotion for a small second. He hid it well. My offer was unexpected but something he had probably needed for a while. Clearing his throat a little he didn't say anything about my comment. It would take a while for him to know that Michael and I kept our own council in most things. We shared things with others but discretion was of the utmost importance when you had a lot of secrets you were carrying around. Not only did Joshua have to prove to us that we could trust him but we had to prove the same. Still it was a start.

Our master protector was in a very good position to hear and know a great many things. He had been here for a very long time. Had seen people come and go and he had our very acute senses. If we could gain his confidence he could help us a lot. Joshua also had more than a little clout and that wouldn't hurt our agenda either.

As we finished up simple small talk about things, he was rather surprised with our dinner plans this evening. And of course he enjoyed what we had set up for this weekend. Joshua was a very private individual but he could tell that work wasn't the only thing that was needed in our world. He wasn't the creative or crazy person that I was. That was okay one of me was more than enough. Still he could see that there were things that had been missing from our fellow Resurrected but had been at a loss of what could be done. Like so many he had waited for somebody else to lead the way in making changes because he didn't know where or how to start. Neither did I really. Just jumping in and doing whatever occurred to me first when it came up was better than sitting on my hands doing nothing.

Joshua was all for the few changes we were making. We would see just how liberal his thinking was when more significant changes came about. What changes I had no idea but we needed more than just a few fun things to jump start this very subdued and apathetic group. I hoped it would be like a snowball rolling down hill. It started out small and slow but gained momentum and soon had a life of its own. That's what had happened at our home. Someone just needed to start the change with fresh eyes and ideas.

So we all left for dinner just a little earlier than normal. Michael and I had promised Sue we would help tonight. Joshua tagging along sort of surprised her but she gamely put him to work. At least this would show everybody else that nobody was above kitchen duty and Joshua was just sensitive enough to know that.

When people started wandering in the first thing that came to their attention were the large sombreros hanging on the doors of the dining room. Tonight was Mexican night. All manner of Hispanic dishes Sue had been preparing all afternoon. For those that didn't really care for the rather spicy fair there were a few leftovers from last night. I had downloaded Hispanic music and picked up a larger stereo system and Michael and I had strung speakers around the room so that you could hear the music everywhere. Not loud so that you could still talk and hold conversations but still the beat could be heard. It got the same mixed reactions as Michael and I did the first meal we had here when we came tearing out of the stairwell laughing. Most were pleased at the changes, some were a little apprehensive and a few were down right grumpy. Too bad but there were always a few rotten apples that tried to spoil everything for everybody else. Had I figured out what to do with those sour apples? Not yet but I would have to before too much longer.

As Michael, Sue, Joshua, Katherine and I kept the food supply going almost everybody seemed to be very enthusiastic about the different environment. The few actual Hispanic people we had in our group had a few improvements to recommend if we wanted to be more authentic. They were more thrilled than everyone else because even though we had no clue what we were really doing had tried to bring to light a very important part of a culture that was extremely important in the world and they could appreciate the effort that had been made.

At the entrance to the dining room we had set up a table with a ballot box so that people could write recommendations for next Thursday. What type of food and culture they wanted. We had several choices and people just had to circle the one they wanted or if they wanted one that Sue didn't feel comfortable making the food they would have to help out in the kitchen and show her how to cook what dishes went with that ethnicity.

Then there were the signs for poker night for the guys down here in the dinning room on Saturday night. For the ladies, we were having movie night and girls get together. Mine had a lot more area for flexibility and would be up on the second floor in the ivory tower. That, I was sure, would get a bunch of comments from everybody but the sour apple group most assuredly. Was I worried about that? Nope.

As dinner was devoured I could see a large change in how everybody was dealing with each other. The talk was much more animated and didn't just involve work tonight. True it had to do more with dinner but still it was an improvement over the workday that had been draining for everyone in some way or other. The spike in personal energy would come as soon as people started to figure out why they felt burnt out all the time.

We had much more help with clean up tonight than what anybody had expected. Several people, a few couples and singles stayed behind not wanting to leave the friendly, upbeat atmosphere. It wasn't a party but we still had fun doing dishes, cleaning tables and counting ballots for next Thursday. Well I guess Chinese was on the agenda but Italian had been a close second so maybe we would have two special nights next week. Sue had to cook anyway and it was actually easier to have all of one type of food than a rather large variety of several things.

"I don't think that place has had that much laughter in it in quite a while." Michael said as we finally made it to our rooms. He was right. Tonight the dining room had sounded more like I thought it should, with laughter and talking and people enjoying the closure of the day. Friday would go back to more normal but still I think the addition of some sort of soft music would go over well, at least for most people.

As we got ready for bed Michael reminded me that I had an undercover combat lesson I still needed to give. He should really watch how he phrases things but today showed me my husband was a lot more sturdy than what even I had guessed and as we played and wrestled on the bed and ended up with a thump on the floor I knew that even though I had landed right on top of him he wouldn't get hurt. After we made love Michael just pulled the covers off the bed and wrapped them around us and we fell asleep the same way we did every night, with his arms pulling me tightly against him and I could feel his strong heart beat against the side of my face. I always loved to hear his heart, remembering of the time when it had hiccupped and skipped and almost quit. Now just the beat of it let me know everything was all right. Maybe not perfect but as long as I had him everything else was workable.

The morning came early for me as it always did. Today we had an agenda though. Michael had still been adamant that I wake him when I got up. It wasn't that hard but I did get a growl the first time I tried. We had a bit of tug of war with the blankets but I finally had him up and moving. He was a little groggy as we made our way down the stairs to the training floor and I got the idea of getting a small coffee maker for our room just in case getting up before the crack of dawn was something that Michael did on a more regular basis. I avoided caffeine now. With the amount of energy running around my body adding a stimulant to the mix didn't sound like a good idea. Even though caffeine didn't have the effect it did on Nohus it still had some.

I was glad my night vision was very good. The lights were out on this level totally and only the glow from the stairwell illuminated the darkness. Michael stayed by the door and I went over to the switches and started flipping them on. Soon it was nice and bright just like yesterday.

As we began to play around with what we had done yesterday it became obvious to us that touch had played a very important key to how we did what we did. Not remaining in contact severely limited how we reacted to each other. This was something we would have to work on a lot more. In actual fighting it was sometimes very difficult to remain that close to each other. What if Michael and I were across the room from each other when something happened? As hard as we tried we really couldn't come up with any solution to our problem other than practicing just like another other couple would have to do.

So we would work out subtle signs and queues that would tell each other what the other needed or wanted until we could be closer. It would take time but still I felt like I was missing something very obvious. Like a huge sign that you never read because you looked right over it. I kept hearing PIB in my head whispering heart spark over and over again to point it was almost maddening. We figured out it was a heart spark already I thought at him loudly. Finally we both just shut up as I plopped down on the matt frustrated and grumpy.

"What's the matter Maggie?" Michael asked sitting down beside me. It was almost time for breakfast and now instead of food all I wanted was to go to the weight room and punch something.

"PIB." I huffed out letting all my frustration show. "He keeps repeating the same thing over and over and I know I'm missing something he's trying to tell me and I just can't figure it out."

Michael wanted to ask more but just then we were invaded by some of the new protectors and Katherine that had come in for some classes in basic fundamental training. I already knew this stuff and didn't want to hang around for it. These were the really, really new guys and they were the hardest for me to deal with. The ones with a little more experience didn't look at me with so much awe. It seemed that I had a very mixed reaction from my own people. Some wanted to prove they were better than me; others acted like I was a religious icon. Sooner or later they were going to figure out I was just me. What that meant, well I was still trying to figure that out for myself so why should they have answers I didn't.

We had friends waiting for us at the door to the dining room. My four computer people had caught the sunrise without me today and Daniel was wondering if he was in trouble. "Why? Did you break something?" I joked when he said were they had been this morning in a very subdued and worried voice.

"No." He whispered. "I just wasn't sure if we should go up there without you." I thought about that for a minute. Should I be upset? That was supposed to be my home but I had no intentions of using it for that but to just let anybody and everybody run through it didn't seem right either. Sue had control of the kitchen and dining room and nobody did anything unless they checked with her first. The same rules applied to the training room, the motor pool, the gym and pools. Everybody could use anything but you just needed to let a key person know you were. If something got messed up then they knew who to come to see to fix it. That kept everybody honest and responsible.

"I'll make up a schedule for stuff like that and post it on the door with a sign in sheet." For right now that was the best I could come up with. If it became a problem I might have to revisit it but not too many people were up at that time of the morning anyway so what was I getting my knickers in bind for anyway?

Sue had liked the idea of music in her dining room and had turned it on this morning already. This was an actual radio station that had news and weather along with a rather generic music family that wasn't doing much for waking people up but I understood what she had been trying to accomplish. Sue was getting what Michael and I were trying to do even though the over all goal had never been discussed she could see where this was heading. Make people more in touch with themselves and the world around them.

I knew on that first day I had met her that she was a very wise, smart lady. She heard a lot but was so much of the background nobody really noticed her. Those were the ones most people overlooked but were essential to making changes and keeping the cart rolling when you were busy trying to replace wheels and not have everything end up in a heap on the ground. Changes were sometimes a good thing but chaos was not.

Michael and I didn't need to help in the kitchen. Sue had more helpers now than what she knew what to do with. The four computer people but also a couple of those that had stayed last night for clean up. The newer ones didn't stay long because they did have daytime duties but the few minutes they spent in the kitchen were happy ones as everybody talked and laughed and shared experiences about last night but also about themselves.

This had been what I wanted. To get people to open up and share, to take the step out to get to know each other and who the person sitting right beside you every day was, what they thought and felt and wanted out of life. Find out that you had a lot more in common than what you ever thought. Everybody was different but in some ways most everybody was the same too. You would have thought that people that had lived side by side for years would know something about each other but it was like they were all meeting for the first time.

So what was I doing for the rest of Friday until my combat training class this afternoon? What had Michael decided he was doing? We hadn't been here that long and I hadn't been outside at all yet and was beginning to feel a little house bound. I still wasn't sure how I was going to deal with being snowed in for days or weeks at a time. I knew that Tim and a few others had snowplows and blowers and tried to keep the road down the mountain passable as much as possible. Still when winter finally set in I had better have a game plan on how to deal with all my extra energy or I would go crazy and probably take Michael right along with me.

"I want to explore this morning." I told Michael after we had finished breakfast. My previous bad mood forgotten as I got with the idea that I still had so much to learn and know about my new home. It was a temporary one but one I should get better acquainted with.

Michael gamely went with me for a walk around the building and the immediate grounds; I think he was happy to be outside in the fresh air, even if it was a little cloudy and overcast today. The clouds weren't the dark ominous ones that said bad weather was on the way but this was September and everybody knew that a storm or snow was now a daily possibility.

We did have a few weather sensitive people that were rather good at seeing long-term trends and they were calling for a late start to winter but once it got going it would be really bad. Lots of snow and bitter cold temperatures from the middle of November until probably March or April were in store for us this year. The ski slopes might be able to be kept open until practically the 4th of July. I had no intentions of being here that long but it did give Michael and I pause for thought. When we planned on leaving in February just how much trouble would we be getting into? Time for online shopping again I guess. Now snow chains and items that were self heating without flame were starting to sound like a good idea and Michael wasn't making so much fun of me for my buying splurge of heavy winter gear before we left sunny Florida.

As we wandered around the grounds I discovered something that nobody had mentioned before. Down the hill was a not so small mausoleum. I had to ask about that. It had never occurred to me to wonder what happened to us when we died. Of course somebody would have come up with a good plan for that. It was logical and made sense but seemed a little cold and unfeeling too. The crypt had the ashes of every single Resurrected that had died in the last century. All in neat little jars or urns that were lined up on shelf after shelf after shelf. What I thought was cold was there were no names, no dates, nothing to distinguish who anybody was. I could see it up to a point. But didn't like that so many had served and sacrificed so much and there was nothing personal of them at their final resting place.

It was too late to figure out who was who and it would be unfair to just memorialize the new people. I was very quiet and sort of lost in thought while Michael and I climbed and hiked around the rather rocky grounds.

When we got back in time for lunch Michael was starting to get worried about my silence. "You've been real quiet all morning." He said trying to catch my eyes so that he could maybe see what was wrong.

It hadn't bothered him to see all the remains of those that had died but had no record of their passing. He had probably seen worse in WWII. So many men had been killed and buried and little if any record had been able to be kept. I knew from history that there were still men that had fought on D-day that were still listed as MIA because nobody really knew what had happened to them. I found it very sad but that wasn't something I could do anything about. But this was family and they deserved better but what?

"Just thinking that our dead deserve something more than just an urn or a jar on a wall. In a hundred or two hundred years when my ashes join them I would like to think that somebody would like to know my name and when I died, maybe come and see me from time to time."

I could see the idea of my death upset Michael. I felt exactly the same way but if I were first and he second wouldn't he want some place to go and remember me. As excruciatingly painful as that idea was for me I think I would feel a little comforted if it turned out to be the opposite. His eyes got a little misty from the emotional content of our discussion and he shook his head like he just didn't want to think about it.

"I know." I choked out. "It's a hard subject but something we need to think about. Place ourselves in that position and try to imagine what we would want but also what would be fair. It is too late for those that are already there. I don't think we could ever match up who is where but better effort should be put forth from now on to keep track of things like that. And something needs to be done for our long dead and maybe not so long dead predecessors. I just can't figure out what." Leaving the biggest question that I had today. I was really good at finding things I didn't like but sometimes had no idea what to do about it. Before I had family that helped me out with things like that. Now all I had was Michael and it didn't seem fair to stick him with trying to find out all the answers to the weird questions I kept coming up with. I had no clue how to fix what was in my eyes wrong or at least not right why should he?

"You're right." He agreed, still sounding quite upset. "I never thought about it but if a close friend died today wouldn't I want to know which urn or jar was the only thing still on this earth that had some of them left. It would be better to visit there with a purpose of seeing just one than to see all of them lined up and no clue; which had been them. It would be impossible soon to tell unless something separated them. I think you might have stumbled on why everyone avoids that place. It's just so hard to see everybody and not be able to tell whom you knew and or didn't know. It never occurred to me that unless Joshua had kept track of things very closely he wouldn't even know where his Mary is now."

That more than floored me. Joshua had been married once. I don't know why it surprised me but it did but it also explained so much. If he had been in love with his wife as deeply as Michael was with me or I with him the idea of having another partner would never even be considered.

I guess Michael figured out that I hadn't known about that. Why did he keep thinking I knew everything he did? He was almost double my age and he always seemed to forget that I was the new kid on the block. "Info Michael." I pressed him as we made our way up to the dinning room for lunch. "You can't just lay a bombshell like that and not tell me more."

There was a long pause while we got our food and found an empty table. For once no one disturb us. Maybe others could tell we were talking about something that made us desire privacy. I would have picked up on the fact that I was sitting right next to Michael instead of across from him and our heads were so close together. The exchange between us was almost a murmur. He knew by now how good my hearing was and it was like he was almost whispering to himself.

"Mary was killed in an avalanche 8 maybe 10 years ago. She was one of our empaths, very good and extremely sensitive. I guess the accident was in an area were one had never happened before and nobody thought to warn her hiking party. Joshua wasn't with her that day and I think he blames himself for either not getting killed too or not being there to save her. She went out with a bunch of new protectors to get them used to their strengths and also how to depend on each other. Joshua and Mary trained the protectors together then. Showed them how to be the true protectors they are supposed to be. Not just the trained muscle that seems to be coming out of here now. I just don't think Katherine or Joshua know how to do the other side enough to show the new ones how they are supposed to be. They end up learning that side of the job on site and I sometimes I don't think that is enough, at least not for some of them."

So that explained why the new guys were more aggressive and less understanding than what Gabriel had been. I knew from talking to him that Gabriel was as old as Michael and had been around a while. Joshua and Mary would have trained him to be what a protector was supposed to be. I had been so lucky in the house I had ended up in and I realized that more and more every day. Most wouldn't agree with me right now if I said that out loud but I knew it. Now I had another riddle to solve.

"I know Joshua wouldn't want some one to replace Mary but couldn't another empath have sort of stepped into at least part of that role? We surely have enough here?"

"Not emotional empaths, Maggie." Michael said with a shake of his head. "We have plenty of physical types like me. That see or feel an injury or hurt but the ones that feel another's emotion have never been in that great a number and they suffer burn out quite easily, the same goes for the telepaths. Between burn out and death there are two maybe three that have any decent strength to their gift, a few more with lesser abilities that try their best but even combined they're not nearly enough to go around.

Something about that made my radar go off and I heard PIB sort of whisper. "See, see."

"Was it always that way?" I asked. "You know the history of our kind better than I do. But have emotional empaths always been so low in number compared to the rest of the other talents."

"No, not always." He admitted thoughtfully. "But lately there aren't very many that have come along and the ones that do get hurt and killed a lot more than other talents. I have started to wonder if they put themselves at risk more because of what they are. If they feel another's pain maybe they are easily distracted or not paying attention and have accidents easier than most."

That sounded good on the surface but if that were the case why was it just a more recent phenomenon. True it was a much more dangerous world than it had once been. "Have the other areas had a similar pattern of emotional empaths getting hurt and killed?"

Michael could see where this was going. If it were just the more industrial areas, the ones with the high crime rates or more dangerous living conditions then it would help to know that. Maybe a guard or something could be assigned to them to watch after them. But if it wasn't, and I was beginning to suspect it wasn't, then we needed to find out when this started and how long it had been going. More importantly why would just one element of our group be targeted like that? Were they a threat to the Aspanari and if so why? Too many questions but how to go about getting answers?

This also explained why so many of our family had mental issues. If emotional empaths that were able to help others with their problems had always been fairly limited and was in a severe state of decline than my plan of a roaming healer really wouldn't be a good idea. It would put those left at too much risk. Travel was always mildly chancy for anyone but for those precious few we had remaining, they needed to be safeguarded like they were the Hope Diamond and then some.

PIB was in my head again with a surprising suggestion that actually made sense. "Daniel?" He questioned softly. My voice guide was trying in his very limited way. We were both learning how the other thought but this morning had just been so frustrating that I had feared he might have just given up on me. I was glad he had the patience of the biblical Job when dealing with me.

"Maybe Daniel and his cronies could work up a computer program to research our concerns. See if there is reason to be worried or are we just getting paranoid in our old age." I suggested. Michael's eyes light up at that idea.

"You know that might work. When I was here last the computer section wasn't really as good as it is now. The only new addition has been Daniel so he must be very good at what he does."

"He said he wrote the program that targeted foundlings." I said remembering how proud he had been at that accomplishment.

As Michael and I batted around a few more questions and ideas I could tell it had been a very long day that started out way too early for him. The walk around outside and the food in his stomach was making him sleepy now as he yawned more than once. "Okay Prince Charming time for your nap." I chuckled as we both got up. I headed down to the training floor leaving my very tired husband in the stairwell at the housing floor with a kiss. How was I to know he would be starting his own investigations? I guess I didn't hold the patent on surprises or curiosity for that matter.

# CHAPTER 4

## CAN YOU HELP ME PLEASE?

*M*onday morning had me rising early as usual. Today I decided I wanted a swim. Making the opportunity to relax after the hectic pace Michael and I had this weekend. It had been fun, enlightening and exhausting in a lot of ways.

Friday had finished uneventful in some ways and not in others. Training had been just about the same as the day before with exception of no Michael there. I thought at first it was just because of his absence that I was better than the day before. But no, it was because I had gotten used to the way Katherine moved now and could anticipate her so much easier. Friday she had only scored two blows during the whole session, much to her total frustration. My senses were getting better at picking up the subtle hints that told me when she was moving and how.

After training I went back to our room thinking I was waking my husband up from a much needed nap and maybe get a little different time in bed with him but when I got there he wasn't where he was supposed to be. I had been so sure of where he was I hadn't thought about it really but the more I focused on his location I was feeling I had passed him by somewhere. I knew he wasn't on the training floor so I went back downstairs and found him in the computer section. Daniel and Brenda were also there. I wasn't sure if Michael pulled them out of bed or if they just sort of lived with their computer terminals attached to them in some way.

They were diligently working and discussing one of my requests. Finding out the names of all the Resurrected that had passed on in the last century or so. A list would be a good place to start but what to do with it after that? We were still deciding on the next step and hadn't come up with a firm decision yet.

Then they were going to do the more involved research project of when the emotional empath had started their decline, trends that covered all continents and regions. Michael was asking for everything they could dig up on the subject. I couldn't understand at first why Michael had become almost as obsessed with this idea as I was until I found out how he had gotten his promotion.

Why hadn't anyone ever mentioned that the entire house had burned down in Jacksonville some 8 years before? Most of the people inside had made it out except for the protector and the telepath that had been in charge. Now I was even more worried. There were a lot of things pointing to a real serious problem. A problem that nobody had looked into yet or maybe they had and it had ended up nowhere or maybe they just hadn't known how to look.

Daniel caught the implications very quickly. He was a good computer detective and if there were information out there to be found he would find it. He did tell us that sort of in depth search would take a while and would have to be as they could find the time among all the other things they had to do.

I gather the medical section kept them hopping and since ours was just a crazy and possibly very paranoid hunch I wasn't going to bitch at being put down the list some. Daniel wouldn't forget about it but did warn it may be a month or two before he had any conclusive proof one way or the other.

By the time Michael got to bed Friday night he was all but dragging. I felt bad about it a little but didn't blame myself too much. He had asked to be woken up that early and we had indeed learned a lot about each other. Saturday I let him sleep as long as possible and I had a bunch of stuff done before he thought about climbing out of bed. The morning was spent decorating and making a list of things we still needed for the festivities followed by a very quick trip down the mountain.

I spent the rest of the late afternoon and evening cooking in the kitchen I had never even set foot in before. I was glad I had bought mostly easily prepared things since whoever put that darned thing together had no clue what involved setting up a kitchen. I raided Sue a few times for a couple of baking sheets I needed with the promise I would bring them back when done and had everything ready for both Michael's poker night and my movie night. Light snacks and of course the ever present, just had to have, beer for the guys and wine coolers for the ladies. I kept several bottles of brew just in case some of us wanted that instead. If they guys wanted some wine I'm sure it could be arranged but I just couldn't see any of them going against the masculine tradition enough to ask. We also had lots of soda for those that didn't like the taste of alcohol at all.

Saturday evening had gone well for everybody. The guys had totally enjoyed their poker night and I think it would be a monthly thing. Some were all for every Saturday night but I had other plans for the dining room than poker. I was thinking about dancing and maybe a slide show presentation of pictures taken along the years. That was a big question, could we get enough people willing to submit things like that. How many actually took pictures to start out with. I thought it was a complete disaster to not take pictures of major events. It had surprised Michael to no end when I picked up a digital camera on our honeymoon to have visual memories of where we had been, what we saw and did along the way. Now all those pictures were downloaded and had been emailed home.

Michael and I checked our email every day, sometimes more than that. Keeping up with things in Florida and letting them know how things were progressing here. We didn't tell them everything but the fact that Michael and I were shaking things up well and proper was something that we weren't trying to keep a secret. If our emails were being monitored I didn't care. It helped a little to dispel the awful homesickness that we both had. We liked the center. Felt we were serving a purpose here but would be so happy when February got here. Of course that was never put down anywhere or told to anybody. The only ones that knew of those plans so far were Michael and I.

Saturday evening for me had been great. We picked a few romantic movies, had some nice music and a lot of laughs. Most of the women showed up, over 20 at least and even though Katherine had started out feeling very much out of place me sticking her as door greeter let everybody know just exactly how much I valued her presence. We made plans for other things, including some craft things that I thought maybe would be better thrown open for everybody. Come winter we might be trying to find things to occupy both body and mind in the limited space of the inside of this complex. Large though it may be at the present, just knowing that you either shouldn't or couldn't go outside for weeks on end had the tendency to make even the biggest spaces seem to close in on you.

How these people had managed to survive whole and mentally intact still sort of confused me. To be isolated for weeks and months at a time didn't seem to bother anybody until I brought it up and then it did. I began to wonder how high the suicide and the stupid accident rate climbed every winter and threw out the idea as being irrelevant. It wouldn't be that way much longer anyhow.

We had several women that were pretty creative with making quilts, knitting, crocheting and the like. Also a couple of painters that didn't mind showing what they could do and teaching any that wanted to see if they had the talent to put paint and brush to canvas. Me, if you wanted something that looked like a drunk monkey had slug paint on a canvas, just give me a brush with the idea of doing something pretty. Covering an entire wall with the same color was easy. Transfer what you see to where you're hand wants to put it was something I would never be able to do and I had great admiration for anyone that could.

As I lay in the pool and paddled around a bit I went over all that Michael and I had accomplished in just under a week. Things were starting out okay but had a long way to go. I could tell that most people just needed a rallying point and I guess that I was okay with being it. The snowball was starting to roll down hill.

My ivory tower sign up sheet was not exactly overflowing but had a lot less empty places on it than before. Every morning from just before sunrise to 30 minutes afterwards was reserved for morning wake up viewing. We had some of the women starting up classes, teaching those that wanted to learn how to quilt, crochet and cross-stitch. There was a shopping tripped planned for next Saturday to Denver to get things that might be needed by anybody that wanted to go. Most specifically hitting craft stores and the several malls that were everyone's favorite. I still had to arrange transportation as soon as I found how many people were game for a shopping trip. Until Saturday most people still weren't too sure what to make of me. Some of the single men might still be a little uninformed but at least the ladies knew me. Most seemed to like me but you really couldn't tell that right away. Only time would reveal how well my ideas had been received. Still it was a start.

So what did I want to do today? I pondered. Well I guess my pique had served its purpose and it was time to pay a visit to the medical people. Michael should probably be there for at least the first part. I had promised him that he could see the expression on Paul's face when I gave him a sample of my claws. I already knew what type of reaction I would get from that. Fear was the way most people reacted to them especially when I did it on purpose to scare. That might be a little mean but most definitely got whatever point I was making across. Usually don't mess with me was the message and six inch nails being shoved in your face was a real eye opener.

I was dressed in my standard blue jeans and t-shirts by the time Michael finally woke up and I waited patiently for him while he shaved and got ready for the morning. He seemed just as happy about our weekend as I was. By the time we made it to the medical floor it was starting to get its full complement of personnel. I had of course remembered to not eat anything for the blood tests. If I was going to do something I was going to do it right. Most of medical personnel really had no clue what to do when I just showed up at the door to the lab. Paul made a ready appearance, thinking he had finally won our contest of wills.

When they came after me with so many vials that I was wondering where the vampires were I had to say something. "Just exactly what is all this for?" The list was long and impressive and totally not something I was going along with. I didn't care to be part of the on going investigation of our sterility. Would they really want to know what I thought regarding that? And there were several others that Michael was sort of shaking his head about too.

We told them exactly which ones I was going to submit to and those that they could take and stuff. By the time we were done I still felt like a pin cushion and that I might just glow in the dark soon from all the x-rays, MRIs and cat scans they scheduled me for. The only thing they hadn't suggested was a mammogram. I guess since breast cancer was not something I would ever get even they weren't stupid enough to suggest something like that.

The biggest fit I had was when they told me my bonding crystal had to be removed. After a huge amount of growling, grumping and getting the general feeling like I was ripping off some very vital piece of myself I handed my crystal to Michael for safe keeping. The idea of anyone else even touching it sent me into a total panic. Something that totally confused everybody and made them just that much more curious about why I would have that strong of a reaction to something they considered just a piece of jewelry.

We did get even with Paul for his constant gloating presence. We were barely done with the blood tests and were heading over to the imaging department when I decided to be totally rotten. "Your lab people haven't asked for this yet but since you were standing around you would be a good person to leave a set with. You seem to want a sample of just about everything else." Giving no warning other than that I asked my claws to spring out. From my right hand the full six-inch nails came rippling out in his surprised face. I thought the man was going to faint and it was all Michael could do to not laugh out loud. When I asked them to they obligingly dropped off into my waiting left hand.

Michael was trying to maintain a straight face but even he had to have some fun at Paul's expense. "If you would like Gabriella can also give you a set that are curved and hooked. They make me think of something that you would see on a mountain lion or tiger maybe. You should see what they could do to a deer. The first time she brought back a kill some of it had to be turned into jerky because it was just in so many little pieces she just couldn't do anything else with it."

That was a total exaggeration but Paul wouldn't know that. I had been very good at killing things from the beginning and wasn't messy now unless I wanted to be. The effect was good but I had to wonder if maybe yanking his chain wasn't the way to win a friend. He was annoying and controlling but maybe I should take the time to figure out why. I was usually the one to ask that question and it bothered me that with him I hadn't.

Maybe Michael's already prejudiced attitude was the reason. He had many dealings with the head of the medical and research section and didn't like him. Before Michael met me he rarely asked why someone acted they way they did. Now he did, maybe not all the time but more than he used to. You can't fix it if you don't know how it's broke or whether or not that someone is worth the effort of trying to understand until you already did.

That was a very convoluted thought process that barely made sense to me. How was I going to explain it to Michael? Maybe this was one I would have to start out solo on and then get Michael on board when I understood our medical research leader a little better. But how to go about getting to know someone you really didn't like to start out with? I didn't have a clue at the moment but it seemed a much more important item on my agenda than it had been before.

The rest of the morning was spent getting all sorts of tests and scans run. I never thought of how a lab rat or animal specimen felt before but I was gaining a lot of sympathy for them every time somebody came after me with a different chart or new needle or some other way of taking a sample of me away and delving into what ever secret it had to tell.

I lost Michael about half way through all the tests because he had advanced self-defense training. It felt extremely odd to not have him beside me and that feeling was compounded by the fact that he had my bonding crystal with him. I had never realized until now just how comforting that little warm pulse felt until it wasn't there.

When lunchtime finally came I was as finished with the medical tests as I was going to get for the day. They may talk me into coming back but I had enough poking and prodding to last for some time. It wasn't even that hard to answer some questions with a slight understatement of my abilities when I was asked just how good my hearing was or some other ability I didn't think they needed to know. PIB didn't even have to influence me much anymore. By now I knew what should be kept to myself and what I was willing to share. Sooner or later I might be caught in not being entirely forthcoming but I didn't really care if I was caught or not. Did it really matter to me if I messed up some of their history records?

I didn't care to have all my abilities put down in writing for just anyone to look up. Remembering back to how easy it was for Anthony to access the records on Jacob and the training programs that Joshua gave made me realize just how compromising those records could be if they fell into the wrong hands. If I was going to one day go up against Aspanari I really didn't want everything I could to do to be recorded anywhere. Always have an ace up your sleeve was something I had learned from the Army Ranger survival guys. Never put out everything you knew to anybody and all those things that they had taught and my very paranoid little guiding voice were in agreement. Keep silent was still a mantra that I had in the back of my mind every time somebody asked me a question about what I could and couldn't do.

The same went for Michael now too. My blood had changed him very significantly and I was very sure this was something that both Joshua and Paul would find very interesting. But what I was sure of was that his abilities should be downplayed as much or more than mine. If people didn't know how keen his senses were now they would open up nearby him when they may not me. I was classified as a protector and everybody here knew what wonderful hearing they had. Quick reaction times and deadly fighting skills weren't much good if you couldn't tell where the danger was coming from in time to do anything about it. An accurately placed bullet could still kill me and I had to be aware of the situation almost all the time, especially away from the security of the center and its grounds.

Michael was having his own dilemma regarding his abilities. Unfortunately the best way for him to find out just how much better he was in a fight was to actual spar with someone. We didn't like exposing him that way and Michael and I were considering spending more time down on the training floor when no one was there to see what I could teach him. I knew how he thought but then we had the additional concern of his reactions to me. He could practically read my mind and it made us both wonder if he would be as good against someone he couldn't do that to. Going into a fight for your life when you were unsure of your own abilities was not something I wanted to do again. I had been very lucky the first time but didn't want to count on fortune smiling like that one me on an on going basis.

As Monday rolled into Tuesday I was still awake long after Michael had fallen asleep. Wondering where we were with things? For being here a week already things had progressed a lot further than I had thought but there were still as many questions we had to start with if not more. I wasn't sure where we stood on several things, Michael wasn't sure and I guess we would just have to go into the wait and see answer again. Something I absolutely hated, almost as much as waiting. They were sort of cousins both involving the passage of time to find a resolution to a problem.

But this week had a few good things that I had already decided on. Besides the shopping trip and the Chinese food night Tuesday, I had chosen Wednesday to celebrate Michael's birthday. Since that rotten husband of mine refused to tell me the exact date and even Daniel either wouldn't or couldn't tell me I was stuck. If Michael thought that would stop me he really didn't know me very well at all.

So I picked a date out of a hat and Wednesday was it. I had very elaborate plans for him that day and I had already let Joshua and Katherine know that Michael would not be attending any training what so ever. Sue had giggled like a high school girl when I asked her for help baking a small birthday cake. One we would fill with custard and make even more delicious than normal. My husband did have a sweet tooth and I planned on fulfilling every type of desire he could possibly have in mind.

I could barely wait and it would be very difficult to go through today without him noticing something. PIB came out with a touch, two words that sort of made sense to me in our normally odd way. "Acting training." He whispered in my head as I finished up my review of what I had ready and what I still needed to do.

It took me a few minutes to figure that out. Then I knew what he was saying. If I could keep Michael from realizing that I had something going then it would be good training for me because I needed to be able to do things like that. Not necessary to him but be able to perform a role in a very stressful situation. Now I had the how to do it. Make it feel like a test. Like when I had to play the hooker to get Anthony back.

That was another thing that should happen. I should be seeing my brother again. He had emailed me last week that he would be getting back this week some time but even he didn't know when. I gather some places in Asia weren't that reliable when it came to transportation. So it was again a waiting game. So many things were starting to involve the passage of time, some little, some not.

This morning I had coffee, bagels and juice ready for everyone at the sunrise gathering. Brenda was first with the rest of the computer crew not far behind. She was so different than most people thought she was. Kind, gentle and always wanting to help in anything I was trying to do. But work took up so much of her time and energy that she had very little left for herself let alone all the very odd things I came up with.

Still I knew if I asked she would be there for me just like Daniel and the other two fellows in the computer midnight lab. There were others that worked the day shift that I had met but for some reason I had more of an affinity for the graveyard shift guys. Maybe because they were the youngest, having been changed less than ten years, they seemed to catch all the stuff nobody else wanted to do. All the things that took a lot of thinking and time to accomplish and very few times did I ever hear anybody say thank you let alone what a great job they did.

That was something I was going to have to mention to Paul the next time I visited the medical section again. Something he had already been asking for. I gathered that my test results were a lot different than expected. Gee what a surprise. Now he had more specific test he wanted to run. It would involve pretty much the same thing on my end but what would happen to all the blood and images wouldn't be. And as far as my claws were concerned, Michael had been right. The lab guys were practically drooling over them. How many times can you make them before you can't any more? That was the most important one that I had no answer for. I had never tried to do it more than three or four. Why should I? But now even I was getting curious about my abilities and that was good thing. Shouldn't I know how far I could push things?

But this week was already full and I wasn't about to let Paul think I was at his beck and call. He would just have to wait until next Monday and when I told him that at breakfast Tuesday morning he nodded his head and almost smiled saying that would be excellent. This time I was the one that almost fainted. Paul had almost been pleasant.

Tuesday evening I picked at dinner. Chinese food was not my favorite, never had been but I wasn't about to say anything. It had been the first really big decision type thing that everybody had agreed on. I was just one of many and even though the atmosphere had been very enjoyable with all dragons on the wall the food still wasn't what I wanted. Sue had done an excellent job at egg rolls and sweet and sour pork, chicken and beef. The lo mien noodles had actually been pretty good but she had come up with things that I had no clue what it was. Maybe I was just not as adventurous in the food area as I thought because if I couldn't figure out what was in it I wasn't eating it. I knew that I would never get sick off of something that I ate any longer but old habits die-hard and in this instance it was in for a very long life.

If anybody else even noticed my lack of appetite they didn't say anything. I had managed to find enough stuff to fill me up so that I wouldn't keep Michael awake with a growling stomach but it would make me sleeping even more difficult. Between the excited expectation of celebrating his birthday tomorrow and being somewhat still hungry I didn't expect to sleep much. Thursday night would be better, that was Italian night and I promised to help with that.

After making love like we did almost every night, Michael fell asleep quickly and completely but I didn't. No surprise there. He was used to me prowling around half the night. Tonight it would be worse, a lot worse. Finally I knew if I didn't get out I would wake him up. Something wasn't exactly wrong but just not right and couldn't figure out what had me so on edge. Maybe some quiet private thinking would be good for a change.

I retreated like I had many times before to someplace I could look at the night sky and just leave my body behind. All night long my mind ranged out across the valley and mountains that were the amazing view I saw outside the window of my ivory tower. It wasn't exactly mine anymore but for tonight it was. I really didn't plan on thinking about anything really. Just like I had done once before when I had held Alison against me when she had her first night terror with me around I just sort of pulled up the mental oars and let my boat go down the river without guidance. Wherever my thoughts took me was fine tonight.

My first thoughts were of my family so far away in Florida. I remembered their smells. Peter all warm and fudgy smelling, almost Identical to his favorite desert, double chocolate cookies. Alicia and her spicy tangy flavor, like red licorice. Then there was my sister Alison and her subtle smell of flowers. When I had tried to describe her smell to Michael I really couldn't. It was like orchids but not and that was when I learned that Michael hadn't always lived in the U.S. He had spent time in South America and Europe too.

For several years Michael had found home too painful to be in and had traveled far and wide as a sort of teacher for others with gifts like his. I had never known that about my husband and was sort of surprised but he had lived so much longer than I had. Why didn't I consider that he would have done things and gone places that I could only dream about? He actually spoke or had at one time three different languages besides English.

My gift of languages was almost none existent but with Michael with me I didn't feel the need to learn French, Spanish or German. He already knew them. After Anya had acted the complete bimbo, Michael had left. Asked to be transferred as far as he could get. Phillip had been his finder just as Michael had found me. That made for a strong bond. Nobody knew exactly why but it was true. It made me wonder if he hadn't been the one would I have fallen in love with him so deeply and quickly. But that was useless speculation. Michael and I were bonded and only death would break that bond and I didn't think that would do it either.

My mind drifted to my missing brother also very far away and hopefully not in too much trouble, Gabriel. I missed him more than the others because I knew he was at risk and the rest of my family was safe. Away from me and all my enemies but protected with two guardians of their own. I knew that Duncan and Ezra took their responsibilities very seriously. They would guard my sisters and brother with their lives. I knew that dedicated mentality and even though had different ways to go about their duties it was the results that mattered.

But Gabriel was hopefully not in trouble but just his unknown status bothered me more and more everyday. If I could just know he was all right, just a hint like before with the picture and brief words that let me know he was still in the land of the living. He couldn't even know if I had received his message. The fact he put so much faith in me made me feel all-warm inside. He was handing me his very life asking me to come and get him when he wasn't even sure where he would be when February came around. He was with the Aspanari now and only the Power That Be would have any clue where he was, what he was doing or with whom.

I thought and missed and let time slip by. Maybe I even dozed sitting in a comfortable chair in the ivory tower staring into nothing. I heard a noise as the door to the stairwell opened and closed almost silently. At alert and fully awake in a second I knew who my very early morning visitor was and was very surprised. Sitting silently and totally still in the dark I let Paul come into the room without him even knowing I was there at all. My soft words made him jump and all but scream. "Good morning Paul." I said so softly that it shouldn't have the reaction it did. Maybe he was feeling guilty about something but now was the opportunity I had been looking for as circumstance put us both in an unexpected place at the same time.

"Do you always like to scare people?" He huffed as his heart rate came back down to a normal level.

I chuckled at that. "I have been accused of trying to give a few heart attacks before." I admitted. Something that made Paul almost smile again.

"I believe it even if we can't really get them you might just scare somebody into doing something that might get them hurt." He cautioned me sounding a little more like he usually did. He was once again the father figure that was always finding fault.

I smiled a bit but I had an answer that would turn him on his head. "No I would be able to stop any accident before it happened." I said confidently. "Any slip, trip, fall or even if someone dropped something I would be able to catch it before it broke."

He sort of sputtered at that. "Even Joshua isn't that fast."

Now I admitted what I hadn't ever told anyone but Michael before. "I am." Paul about fell on his tongue. I wouldn't admit to a lot but if I wanted Paul to open up I knew I had to first. "You should know that I wouldn't ever show all I can do to anyone Paul. There are too many things at risk. I have been cautioned to play things very close to the vest."

"By who, what things?" He asked. Not exactly quietly but he was perhaps beginning to see that I had reasons for doing all the odd things I had done since I got here and he was thinking in more terms than just work and obligations.

"There are things that I have seen, been shown and know that I can't say yet. Part of my job is and always will be to know more than others think I do. You have to in order to be a good spy. That's my calling Paul.

I am first and foremost an infiltrator. There is no war going on that we know of in the human world but can we say the same for ours? There are many things that I am here to fix that nobody other than Michael is aware of. Now the only question I have for you at the moment is, are you going to help me or hinder me? In the end it won't make any difference. The things that need to happen will but I would like to think that our chief medical officer would be in league to do the right and compassionate thing and not just be around to be an annoying pain in my ass."

Paul was sort of quiet for a few minutes. "I have never heard that I was a pain in the ass." He sort of huffed out.

"Then you haven't been listening very closely. Except for those that just want to climb the ladder you aren't looked at very kindly." Perhaps it was in Paul's case as it had been for Michael. Maybe he just didn't realize how he acted around people. How his words that were rather harsh and critical were just not considered before they came out. Maybe he was a nice, caring and compassionate doctor like I hoped he was.

I had revealed what seemed a lot to him but I hadn't, not really. I had told him what was blatantly obvious to almost every one already. That Michael and I were here to change things. I never gave him a clue what things. Whether all the wacky and weird things I was doing and getting others to was just part of my personality or was it something more. He couldn't tell the difference because even I couldn't because it was all rolled up in the entire goofy package of being me.

And that was the great part of all this. Being me was what I was supposed to be. PIB agreed that was why I had been brought back to start with, because I constantly thought outside the box. Because I did things not in an analytical cold way but a passionate from the heart way and this was what had been beaten out of just about everybody around. How it had happened or when it started I couldn't tell and I don't think anybody else could either. Was it a conspiracy or just the natural passage of time? Had this sort of thing happened before and a shake up been required? Nobody knew and I wasn't sure I would get those answers no matter what person I asked or what computer file I had Daniel look up.

What I did know was what I had to do now in this portion of time. I had to get the rest of the Resurrected on this continent happier about being what they were and what they did. Most of the ones here worked for Paul in some capacity of other. If I could change him even a little it would help a lot.

"I know you are the boss around here Paul and I'm sorry you and I maybe got off on the wrong foot but I don't respond well to a heavy hand. Most people don't like that sort of treatment either but they haven't said anything because they didn't have the authority to stand up to you. I do and I did. Besides totally pissing me off I was trying to make a point with you. A carrot will get you farther than a stick. It will make people loyal to you and loyal people will move heaven and earth for a good leader while someone seen as a dictator will be left to figure things out on his own because nobody will stand by his side."

"I can't change what I am." He grumped. Some people did just have a grumpy, snappy emotional make up. I had come across them before and in Paul's roll he had to be seen as the ultimate authority figure. In times of a crisis he needed to be listened to without question. I know that my standing up to him like I had hurt that authority but I couldn't see any other way of getting him to understand what I needed him to understand.

"You don't need change or at least not much." I said quietly, like I was perhaps thinking out loud. "Maybe if the changes were slight and gradual it would be better. Maybe just make those around wonder if they had totally misjudged you and just didn't see you in the right light. It would be great if they had one reassuring constant in their lives and you can be that. I will be turning things upside down and sideways on a rather regular basis. But it would be better to not be the arguer of change but the one that people went to that was the stable rock that didn't oppose change but allowed it to pass over and still remain true to what he was."

I knew Paul could do this or at least I hoped he could. Like I had told him changes would happen with his help or without it. I would either run him over, burry him and possibly destroy what authority he had or he could work with me and be the catalyst for change that everybody knew we needed. The choice was his.

He sat and thought silently for several minutes. I couldn't even read what he was thinking from his eyes or his face. He was the best poker player I had ever seen. Then he smiled a little. "I think I can do that. I have noticed that people aren't happy anymore. It took you pointing it out and making things different because it was such a slow process but even I haven't been happy for quite some time. But I don't know how to act differently. Maybe it is too late for me. I am just an old man that has forgotten how."

Paul sounded so lost this second I just wanted to hug him. "Well for one thing start out small. A thank you works wonders. And maybe if you didn't look down your nose at me whenever I do something oddly happy it might help some too." And I couldn't help but laugh at that and he chuckled a bit too.

"I think that much I can do." He was wondering if it was enough. What he didn't understand but he would was that change happened almost by itself when allowed. All you had to do was give that little push. When Paul started seeing how differently people acted around him then he would know what to do. If not well I could be the not so subtle guiding hand to get him back on course. He didn't need to be friends with those people that worked under him. As a matter of fact it was probably better if he wasn't. He should be looked at with a touch of awe because of his position and just like Joshua that mantel of authority was sometimes a very heavy burden. But there were others around that shared similar burdens and they needed to be the ones that Paul and Joshua turned to for help and an ear to listen.

I would be there but Tim was another. He hadn't seemed in charge of much but he was. He was the silent organizer of everything that happened. All the things and people that came and went in this place he had a hand in. All the repairs and building and maintenance he controlled and made sure that things were in place to happen when and, as they should. Then there was Sue in the kitchen. How long had she been watching and keeping her own silent council? It was past time for her to be included in the discussion of the board. I didn't want everyone to think that it was my way or the highway. Sooner or later I would be gone. Oh probably not forever but there was no way I was staying in one place for the rest of my life. That was the problem with the council. They were to out of touch with everybody, nobody argued with them, nobody pointed out when they maybe should reconsider an action or a policy. I had absolutely no problem if somebody said I was wrong but it was always nice if they had a reason for it.

That was the biggest thing I could see as the source of all the problems now. Nobody thought his or her opinions mattered. Well my opinion mattered to me. Others opinions mattered to me and I would be such a vocal, annoying pain that sooner or later everybody would listen. We would be the tide of inevitability. I had the clout to get a lot of attention, especially if I had almost everybody at the North American Center behind me. Even the overseas council members would notice that and if it didn't get Phillip's attention it meant he was dead from the neck up.

Paul had a lot to think about as he left Wednesday morning. I did too but they were much more enjoyable than his would be.

Bouncing into the kitchen I got Michael his breakfast ready and trotted down the stairs passing several of the early morning risers as they headed up. Most looked at me a little oddly but nobody really asked what I was up to. I wasn't sure how I would answer if they did. Would it be a good idea to say I was keeping my husband a very willing sexual prison for his birthday? That I would try and fulfill every fantasy his beating heart had ever had. No, probably not.

Michael was just waking up good as I came in the door trying to juggle the food tray. His eyes light up with both curiosity and hunger. But not the type of hunger I wanted. That would wait I had a plan that this was just beginning of. As Michael started eating the breakfast I brought I tore out the door and up the stairs again. Bringing back a large cooler I had bugged Tim for I had enough food for the entire day for both of us along with drinks and of course his cake. All of that would be kept nice and fresh, just waiting for when we got hungry. Last but not least I put a do not disturb sign on the door and closed it behind me.

"What are you up to?" Michael asked me very suspiciously. I smiled and disappeared into the bathroom. If he wasn't through with breakfast to bad, it was now time for the shower. We hadn't played like this a while. There just never seemed to be enough time when we were both wide-awake. I came out with no clothes on and pulled him bodily out of the bed. He could have fought me but he was more than amused at my actions so he gamely went along with whatever madness I was planning.

I pulled off his clothes he had put on just a few minutes before slowly enjoying everything as it was revealed, from the fine dust of hair on his chest to how it became thicker the lower it went. How wonderful and strong his shoulders were and the way his thighs and calves were tight cords of muscle. He wasn't built like a protector but that didn't mean Michael was weak, far, far from it.

He had always had a great body but over the last month that too had changed. Just as mine had when I went through my alterations, my blood had even altered him. Made him stronger, faster and much more of everything he had been before. He wasn't my equal in a lot of physical things but he was closer now than most were and like me you just didn't see it unless you knew what you were looking for. Now I loved all those things that had changed and all those things that hadn't.

Michael's laugh had always been able to melt me into my shoes. But the chuckles that were escaping him now made me burn and even though the water was running out of the showerhead as fast as it could I still felt like I was going to catch fire no matter how much liquid there was pouring over us.

His fingers never failed to turn me into a puddle of jell-o and this morning was no different. By the time we were finished in the shower there was probably no hot water for anybody else and for once I didn't care. Michael was very happy and was trying to get dressed again. Something that was so not happening today and he just couldn't understand why I kept pulling his underwear away when he tried to put them on. Finally he stopped being amused and got a little grumpy with me.

"Come on Maggie we have things to do today." He grumbled and I just smiled and danced away with his clothes.

"Not today Michael. Since you refused to tell me when you birthday really is I have picked today to celebrate it and you are going to stay just as you are all day. I think it is only fair to stay naked when you were born that way. Besides how can I do all the things I have planned if you have clothes on? They would get all messy." I said trying to sound innocent and maybe a little confused and not succeeding very well at all.

"It is not my birthday." My husband said still a little huffy. I just don't think he got it. Well he would. The clothes were tossed in the air and I was straddled around his waist and we landed with a soft thud on the floor. "Maggie!!!" Michael yelled. "What has gotten into you?" His only answer was a few giggles and my lips ran up his stomach. Now it was his turn to wiggle around and giggle a little. But he still hadn't figured out I wasn't joking about staying here all day.

One last time he tried to get dressed and I had had enough. He was not spoiling my birthday surprise for him. There was nothing more important today than showing him how much I loved him and all those important things that he thought were out there waiting to get done would just wait for 24 hours. Nobody would die and for those few that didn't already know about Michael's surprise would probably find out about it at breakfast this morning because for once Sue was all for spreading this type of gossip as far and wide as possible. She hoped it would make more married couples start to appreciate each other more. I agreed.

So when Michael had his shirt almost on I took the opportunity to show him just exactly what my claws could do as I shredded it like tissue paper and never gave him a single scratch. "And if the jeans don't get off right now they will end up the same way." I warned. I think it was at that point in time that he knew I was serious. Of course he did let me take the rest of his clothes back off and we had a small tug of war over his socks as he finally got into the mood of my birthday present. Socks were a lot more fun than what I had thought as we found some very interesting and odd things to do with his for a few minutes.

So for the rest of the day we laughed and talked and made love. We devoured every single bit of food in the cooler and he absolutely loved his cake but not all of that was eaten or at least not eaten the way most people did. That had to be followed by another shower because no matter how good you are some sticky things just refuse to go away with just a tongue to do the cleaning.

Of course we fell asleep a lot earlier than normal for both of us and I was up at just after midnight trying to figure out what to do to keep from bouncing off the walls. PIB didn't have any good suggestions and had been pleasantly quiet all day yesterday. I had noticed that when Michael and I spent time together that my voice guide either took a siesta or just plain bailed. I could almost always tell when he was active even when he wasn't actually talking. There was just this sense of other that was in my head. And as I left our apartment he was back. Not saying anything just of along for the ride.

The training floor was empty as was the gym, the lunch room and just about everything else tonight. Other than the graveyard crew nobody was up, nobody was doing anything. So I wandered up to the ivory tower. At least the view was nice there but I wasn't alone in my insomnia tonight. It wasn't Paul but it was a protector as I saw the image of a very large man play against the moonlight window.

He heard me as his head whipped around in surprise. "Oh it's just you." Charles growled. I smiled at that. Charles didn't like me much. Maybe it was my reputation or that Michael and I had won our contest the other day but he was showing his dislike for me very much this evening. I smiled at that. It was okay if someone didn't like me. I didn't expect everybody to like me but I did want to be treated with the same respect he would anybody else. That was just common decency. Well you get what you give.

"I'm sorry Charles I didn't think anybody would be up here this time of night. I have problems sleeping most of the time." I said pleasantly.

He answered me before he thought about it. "Me too. Especially the last week or so and I don't understand why."

Then he frowned a bit like he hadn't planned on revealing things like that to me.

"It's alright Charles we have all gone through periods of adjustment. What I think I missed the most when I went through mine was that I didn't have anybody to compare notes. Do you have any idea how confusing that was for me? I wondered several times if I just wasn't crazy. I envy you that you have others that are going through this very difficult transition to share things with. That you know you are not alone. I wish with all my heart that I had had that. But things are the way they are and wishing never got anybody much of anything."

He sort of humped and left without saying anything else to me. Well Charles was an odd one that was for sure. Quiet and moody, like a stream that moved quickly and had hidden currents and hazards. That was the impression I got of Charles' personality. I wasn't sure what his story was but time revealed as it wanted and now was not the time for Charles. Later was what I came up with. Sooner or later Charles and I would have our meeting of the minds. Like I thought before I didn't mind if he didn't like me. But I would at least like to know why. If it was because of what I was I couldn't help that. If it was because of how I acted I could try and find out what specifically it was that had offended and if it was just that he was a moody grumpy pain, well even those people had a reason for being the way they were.

So for the rest of the night I listened to rest of complex as it slept and started to wake but just before sunrise I went back down and woke my husband up. I think he was still a little spent from yesterday and that was okay too. Maybe we had gotten a little carried away but I didn't regret one kiss or single caress.

We went to breakfast together and we both got some good-natured ribbing about birthdays and surprises and the like. Michael had training this morning and mine was this afternoon. I finally got the chance to get with everybody and find out who was game for a road trip this weekend. I just hoped that Tim had enough buses and vans to get everybody to and from Denver. He was game for everything and smiled happily when he talked about how much Haley was looking forward to our outing.

All the women were going and of course for those that were bonded the spouses were coming along. I don't think most of the wives left the men with a whole lot of options or at least that was the impression I got. The single men didn't understand how important shopping was but there was a draw for them. If the few single women we had were going then they weren't going to be left behind.

About the only ones staying behind was Joshua, a few of the very new protectors because it wasn't safe for them to be out with anyone just yet and a couple of the rehab guys. I tried to convince them to come along but when they got very uncomfortable with my pressuring I knew I had stepped over the bounds. Instead I asked what hobbies they had. Did they like to read or take pictures? Something that would help take their minds off of the fact they weren't and never would be what they had been. You would think by now we would get used to things like that? Hadn't it happened to all of us already once? But I knew in my heart this was different. They didn't feel whole anymore and that was something we all needed to help them with. It wasn't just their bodies that had been damaged it was their spirits as well and that no amount of physical therapy would help.

So the trip was planned and I was a very happy camper by the time I left Michael after lunch for my afternoon training. I hadn't even bothered to find out what he was doing for the rest of the day. Of course he didn't always ask me either.

But today was a special day and I had no idea how special until I smelt him and heard him coming down the stairs. I didn't explain to Katherine why I left our sparing area so abruptly. Gave no reason for the almost insane giggle that escaped as I tore across the very large room just in time to grab Anthony as he came in the door. At least I had waited just long enough for him to be in the room where he landed on the mats that covered this entire floor and not the hard concrete that the stairs were made of as we both ended up tangled together.

I was kissing him all over his face and had him in such a hug he could barely breathe. He really didn't know how much I missed him but I think he figured it all out as all the noise behind us stopped. I didn't blush and wasn't embarrassed in the slightest. This was my brother and I had missed him and was happy he was home safe and sound. I never for one second thought that the way I had greeted him would be looked at any other way. Michael was chuckling right behind him as he stood in the open door. That rotten husband of mine must have known and not said a damn thing.

Helping my tall skinny friend up off the floor from where I had put him wasn't hard. Anthony still hadn't put on weight and I don't think he ever would. He ate like a horse but never gained an ounce. If I could pick somebody like Katherine up he was a piece of cake. All Anthony could do was laugh and hug me back, give me a kiss on the forehead.

"I missed you Ant." I said uselessly. "You were supposed to be back last week."

"Travel isn't as easy in some places as it is over here." He explained what I already knew. But now he had questions for me. "How have things been Maggie? Michael told me you have been doing a lot better in combat training since you got here. I guess I wasn't as good a teacher as we thought."

I rolled my eyes. "You kept me alive, kept both of us alive. What else is there? But if I don't get back to Katherine she will get mad at me. She is almost as annoying as you used to be."

As I went back to sparing with Katherine I had to really try and focus on what we were doing. Anthony's smell was a total distraction. I hadn't expected his cotton candy aroma to be here and it would take me a few minutes to adjust it out of my head. To focus on all those other things I hadn't had to worry about before. As the session ended I came to a conclusion today. Part of how I fought was subtle little smells that people all people put out. That would be something I would have to talk to both Michael and Anthony about and if they didn't have any decent answers I might have to go to Joshua and Katherine. I didn't like the last part but I had to get a handle on all I could do and how I did it.

I would try and keep most a secret or at least not widely known because both PIB and I were both coming up to the same conclusion and we didn't have to wait for Daniel's analysis to know something sinister was going on. I wasn't paranoid the last time I had these feelings and I didn't think I was this time either.

But all this would have to wait because I was going to enjoy my brother being home. I would enjoy going shopping with everybody this weekend and Monday was soon enough to deal with all the questions and problems that seemed to plague me every time I turned around.

I was wrong. Some things don't wait. Some things come up and smack you in the head because you didn't realize that people didn't always see things the same way you did and they have their own agendas. Friday was going to be fine but this weekend and next week would be the start of some very interesting changes. And this time I would be the one having to pedal like crazy to keep up with them.

# CHAPTER 5

## YOU ARE KIDDING RIGHT?

What was the phrase I wanted? The best laid plans of mice and men. That was what had happened to all of mine before the weekend even finished. I knew that Phillip and Rafael would have shown up sooner or later but why on the Saturday whenever everybody was gone?

This place must have felt like a tomb when he showed up. It was too bad that we didn't have cameras in place so that I could have seen his face. Of course, I had heard all about it when I got back with the rest from our excursion in Denver. All in all it had been great.

We got out and went shopping. Didn't get into trouble and had very few looks from anybody. Just a bunch of tourist types shopping and spending some money that had been the general impression we had given. Even the protectors, Katherine included had been subdued and tried to fly under every body's radar as much as their very large size and general imposing appearance allowed for. We even got Paul to dish out colored contact lens for those that didn't have any. Gave everybody some very much needed exposure to Nohus that hadn't had it much or at all.

Now we were all back and I was in deep trouble. Or that was what Rafael wanted me to think. I had back up though. Everybody that went was all for telling our resident council member what a good idea it had been. That it had been a very long time since anybody had even set foot out of the center and it was a much-needed break. Especially right before winter set in when people wouldn't be able to travel much or at all. Now we had things to do besides stare at the four walls and go batty.

At least all of Phillip's visitors hadn't come with him. He had come first to check things out. See how well I was adapting to my new environment. Like I really was some lab animal that everybody got to watch run through a maze. Did he have any idea how demeaning that whole attitude was? No but if I didn't calm him down Michael was about ready to tell him.

We were now in one of the conference rooms having a meeting. In other words I was away from most of my converted disciples and where he could chew me out in private. I didn't need others to fight my battles. That was one thing I had always been very good at. But if I didn't watch it Michael might just go from verbal sparing to a more physical type. I had never seen him this mad before. Not even when he was constantly getting pissed at me in our early days.

How could just a few months ago seem like early days? I thought with a smile.

"You find all of this amusing Gabriella?" Raphael growled. He had been doing most of the talking. Well actually accusing was a better word.

"Extremely." I chuckled. Much to his disgust but it did tone Michael's hostility down a notch or two because he knew I wasn't taking any of this very seriously. Why should he?

"You find it funny that you have destroyed decades of discipline on a whim." Phillip finally added.

"You can destroy nothing that does not have a weakness already. If it can be destroyed so easily then maybe it was all an illusion to start with. Or maybe it hasn't been destroyed at all just changed and made better." I answered him still smiling. "How could a simple shopping trip endanger anything? Nobody got in trouble and in a big city like Denver how could even our 40 people make a noticeable impact. What we spent wouldn't have even made a dent in any ones cash registers.

And that had been another sore subject. We had the balls to spend money. It was like these people here really were slaves and not entitled to anything that was not blessed by the masters. Screw that but I knew the general attitude I would be dealing with and I had arranged it with our five leaders that nobody had to use their money that was in very meager amounts and told everybody to get what they wanted and needed and it was a special pre holiday treat supplied by the center. Nobody but the five in charge knew it was my money we had spent. Debit cards had been given to Tim, Katherine and Sue. Michael and I had our own.

That was one less thing that anybody could complain about and if Phillip hadn't shown up like he had then he would have probably never found out about the trip at all. Well maybe a few months down the road somebody might have let it slip. Now it was just one more thing for those two to complain about.

First of course it had been the Ivory Tower. Well that had been resolved to my liking because neither one could really give me a good reason why it shouldn't be used like I was using it. The entire second floor should be open to everybody. It wasn't private property and other than Phillip and Rafael's quarters being off limits then why should things be kept like they were part of great secrecy? It made every one suspicious that things were going on that they weren't privy to. Of course there were research projects but day-to-day things should be out in the open. Did Rafael want people to think that they were a bunch of peons that were not smart enough to be told what was going on?

He didn't have an answer for that question either. I had reason for every single thing I had done since I got here and Phillip couldn't really argue with any of them. They had harmed none and actually made people smile. That was something that I don't think they had done in a very long time and even Rafael had mentioned seeing a difference in people's attitudes. I hoped he liked the change because I was just starting.

They couldn't complain I wasn't training, they couldn't say I wasn't cooperating with research and development. Maybe not as much as Paul wanted but I was even getting some unexpected support from him as he said he was satisfied with the visit I had already done and knew a good working relationship was just starting. Michael had almost fallen out of his chair when Phillip had repeated that piece of news.

He had looked at me and I just smiled and winked at my husband. So my late night talk with Paul was having an effect already. It wasn't great but better.

Now we had come full circle again and we were back discussing what was expected of me. I thought I had done pretty good but obviously there was much room for improvement, at least from Phillip's point of view. One thing that man should have figured out, if I go along with anything it means one of two things. I agree or I'm pretending to and I have my own agenda in mind. Now which one did they think I was doing now that I was just smiling and nodding the whole time as they told me what the next few days held for me?

Oh I didn't mind being put on display on Sunday. I didn't have anything much in mind anyway. Playing for a bit wouldn't hurt anything. Besides the more people I met the more people I could influence. But if Phillip thought for one second I was going to be all nice and complaint and show off on Monday at a special training session he was fruity.

I had training but if any of his little visitors walked into the training room and distracted someone and got someone hurt they would find out just how mad I could get. Fight training wasn't some sporting event like Phillip seemed to think and Rafael had been through enough of it he should know better and tell him. And just like I told Paul, if anybody thought I was showing all or even most of what I could do they were fruity too.

I was an infiltrator on a mission. Of course that was something else that Phillip and Rafael didn't know and I wasn't going to tell them. If they wanted to chalk up my general uncooperative attitude as the reason fine I didn't mind being marked as that at all. Time revealed all things and if I had any sense of the future I would have kicked myself at my own inability to see what had yet to be seen.

Now I had dinner to eat and a husband to love. Phillip and Rafael could just go leap for the rest of the evening. But even the normally happy dinnertime was disrupted as Sue was trying to make special food and get it up to the executive suite for our two special and annoying residents.

I about came unglued and I didn't care one bit that anybody heard my rant at the special treatment that wasn't just asked for but by now expected.

Sue had been doing what had been customary while Phillip was here but when she got ready to take it up I smiled suddenly and said she was busy and I would do it. She looked at me very suspiciously and Michael rolled his eyes. But I got my way. It was the last meal those two would get special delivery or at least the last meal that was edible anyway.

The next morning it was the same but this time I said I would cook for our distinguished residents and Sue knew I was up to something but left it all on my head as she just smiled and nodded again. By this time I found out from Michael all those things that somebody didn't like and made sure they were what I cooked. Eggs with peppers in them and half burnt toast, English muffins with so much cream cheese you couldn't find them anymore. The French toast had so many spices nobody would have been able to eat it and it smelled gross even to me. I even managed to sabotage the juice as I added so much water it would have been better just to have that.

Ten minutes after I delivered breakfast I had very mad Rafael at my elbow and everybody in the kitchen cleared the area because he was pissed and I wasn't far behind. "What was that shit you brought up this morning?" He snarled.

"Breakfast." I smiled pleasantly but just like before it didn't reach my eyes and he was starting to read me well enough to know I had done it on purpose.

"Nobody could eat that." He pointed out what I already knew.

"If you would rather choose what you eat instead of what is delivered special to your door than come down and get it yourself like everybody else does." I snarled back. Now we had an audience as just about the entire dinning room was either lined up at the food bar watching or in the room listening in some way.

"Security." He growled. "Phillip is council and needs to be protected at all times."

I laughed at that. "And you think you have to worry about us. We are all family. Are you going to look out there and tell me there is a brother or sister you don't trust? That Phillip has to worry about his own security in his own little fortress. You have over a dozen protectors and me besides Joshua and Katherine. Is there any place else that he would be better guarded than here in his own dining room surrounded by his own people?"

I had known before I had started this just where it would end up and I was right on target. How was Raphael going to say he didn't trust those people staring right at him? How would Phillip deal with the animosity it would start if he didn't resume taking his meals with the rest of us? Something I had thought he should do since I found out about it. No wonder he didn't understand us. He didn't even eat the same food in the same place as the rest of us did. All because somebody deemed us a hazard and I knew we weren't.

There would be hell to pay somewhere along the way but at lunch Phillip and Rafael were there right along with everybody else and nobody said anything off or did anything odd other than a few of those that I knew to be older members were happy to see their old friend again. Phillip too seemed to be happy with the change and totally ignored his bodyguard as he chatted up those same people that Rafael had insisted where dangerous.

Dinner changed again as all of Phillip's visitors made their appearance and I was expected to socialize with them. I did but that wasn't all of what I did. Michael and I had other duties too. We helped prepare food and had fun afterwards throwing wet dishrags at each other and in general acting like a bunch of very badly behaving teenagers. Something that got a few nasty looks from some of those important people that were here to see me in action.

I had gotten a few names this afternoon and knew they were all from the North American continent so I didn't have any problem pronouncing them at least. One woman, a pretty short blonde was an old friend of Michael's named Michelle. I had finally been introduced to one of the remaining strong emotional empaths we had left.

She was what I expected and yet somehow not. But after dinner she made an appearance at our room much to my surprise. Michael had been very happy to see his old friend again and the usual almost jealous reaction I had to that hadn't appeared like it usually did. At first I thought it was because I had finally gotten over all the insecurities I had that Michel had many more friends in our world than I did. But the more I was around her the more I realized it was Michelle that was the reason for my almost euphoric state.

I didn't know if it was something she did on purpose or not. How was I supposed to ask that sort of thing? Usually I was down right blunt when I wanted to know something but she was one of the last of our empaths and I didn't want to alienate her without a good reason. Besides I liked her.

She had noticed all the small changes that had happened since she had visited us last and was rather pleased with them. As she went over what she saw as different in her very quiet voice. "I was more than a little pleased to find you were not what Phillip has been saying you are." She told me looking directly in my eyes. That was another thing she had a habit of doing. Making sure you knew that she was talking directly at you and at that moment you felt you were the most important person in the world to her.

I smiled and Michael coughed and chuckled a bit. "Michelle you don't have to try so hard with Gabriella. She isn't that hard to get to know." The almost drug induced feeling of happiness lifted and I had an idea now what people felt like when they came down from a high of some type. It wasn't exactly feeling sad but just missing that extremely happy state.

I didn't exactly growl but I wasn't very happy that Michelle had not only manipulated me so well and easily but had felt the need to. "Please don't ever do that to me again." I grumped. "It isn't fair when you use your talent on someone and not warn them you are doing it. Don't you have a code of ethics or something that stops you from intruding when it isn't wanted?"

Michelle was sort of surprised at that. "No, not really. Personal judgment is considered good enough." I didn't like that answer and I think she could tell even if she wasn't the sensitive person she was.

"Not everyone has good judgment and everyone can misjudge things. If you don't have rules to double check yourself against then how are you going to ever know when you cross the line and do something wrong?" I didn't want to criticize but someone with her abilities or Phillip's could misuse them so easily. If they didn't have family around to remind them or if they didn't listen how could they be stopped if they started down the wrong road? How would they even know that they had erred to start with?

I had Michael and PIB to keep me straight and even without them I had a megaphone mouth conscience but what if you didn't have all that? What if all you had was a small almost silent conscience that some people seemed to have? Was that what caused some of the Resurrected to turn evil? Could some just not be aware of how much pain they caused? So many questions and no answers, well at least not yet. Maybe Gabriel would have some when we finally got him back in February.

Again I was reminded of how long just a few months could seem. I was sure that for him it would be even longer.

Michelle was giving me a very curious look. "What caused your worry level to spike so much just now?" She asked me.

Oh, boy. I would really have to watch that around her. Doing some very fast thinking I answered with a partial truth. Again I was glad that Stephan hadn't shown up with Phillip this weekend. I liked him but his truth seeing ability was something I wanted to stay as far away from as possible. "Just worried about all the new people I will be meeting in the next few months. I know I'm not what Phillip would like but I can't be other than what I am. To change everything about me to be what he wants would be living a lie and I won't do that for anyone. We should all take joy in what we are. To change and grow is important but to lose yourself in the process is not what anyone should be asked or expected to do."

I knew I answered her in a way that made her happy as I got hit with another wave of happiness. Maybe she just didn't realize that when she was happy she made others happy too. That might be something she had to consciously work at to control. If she got mad I didn't think I wanted to be around. That could be a really bad thing. But wasn't she pretty old? She should have better control of her talent than what I had been getting.

"Do others always respond to your emotions like that?" I asked. And she blushed a little.

"No." She looked at Michael and I followed her glance. He looked pleased but didn't seem to have the almost euphoric emotion that I was sometimes hit with.

Now I was the one getting more than a little mad and as that anger came over me all her influence just vanished. "Okay now would you please explain yourself." I growled.

Michelle didn't seem to want to but Michael knew enough or guessed enough. "Michelle's talent won't work if you don't let it. If you block it with an opposite emotion then what she wants then she can't affect you. I think she wanted to see just how much she could do. It was sort of a test."

Suddenly I wasn't very happy with my husband either. "I get enough of that shit from Paul and the rest of his department. I'm starting to think I'll glow in the dark and have no blood left. Then Phillip comes dragging all of you behind him. Asking me to do tricks and give performances like I'm either an oddity at the circus or some lab animal. Now you play let's see how giggly I can get Maggie. ENOUGH!!" By the time I was done I was pretty much yelling.

Michelle was staring at me in sort of wide-eyed amazement and Michael was looking none too pleased. That sort of did it for me. For once I had no remorse about getting angry. I was a person not some thing to be played with or displayed. My calling might be unusual, I might be unusual but that didn't change the facts, nobody should be treated like this.

I didn't say another word. I just left. If Michael wanted me I knew he could always find me but my angry switch had been flipped big time and I needed to get away from him and Michelle. The last thing I wanted right now was another of her happy pill hits. I had a right to feel mad and a right to be offended, I told myself as I retreated down to the lowest level of the complex. The maintenance section and all its depressing darkness fit my mood right now. I would run and stew and in general just be happy being mad.

By the time the lights came on in the morning I had sort of gotten over my pique. Oh it would be a sore subject for me for a while, especially with Michael. He had let Michelle experiment on me and hadn't warned me or tried to stop it. I thought he was supposed to be on my side? Why?? At this point I wasn't even sure I cared but I knew I should. This morning was Monday and that made me even less happy. I got to play lab rat and pincushion again.

I heard him as soon as he opened the door to the maintenance level. Some time in the night I had stopped running and was now just sitting on the floor in a corner looking just like what I was, sulking.

"Maggie." He said my name. It was sort of a question but also a statement, testing the waters to see how mad I still was.

"Yeah." I grumped back.

"Are you still mad?" He didn't sound like he was apologizing and seemed to be a little surprised that I was indeed still mad.

"Of course I am Michael." I said finally looking up. I had been sitting with my arms wrapped around my knees and my head sort of resting on top. "Why wouldn't I be? Aren't you supposed to be on my team? Not turn me over to be experimented on without telling me?" I knew he had to hear the hurt in my voice. That was one of the reasons I had gotten so mad. Michael had hurt me, not intentionally but still he had.

"I didn't think you would take it that way." He tried to explain what he had been thinking. "How can you have that kind of test if the subject knows they are being tested and how? When an empath tries his or her gift out on somebody new there is always a test period. Nobody responds the same way and Michelle wanted to find out how easily she could manipulate you." As soon as he said those last words I could see how what he said hit home. "Manipulate. Bulling, controlling, no wonder you went off. I never looked at it like that before but it is isn't it? An emotional control that you had no idea was being directed at you."

"Exactly, I don't care if it does screw up the test results. Nobody should be put through that sort of emotional roller coaster unless they truly have issues. Personal judgment my ass, if she either won't or can't control herself better or just plain wants to play hit the button, I think I have figured out how to make sure she stays out of my heart." I had been doing a lot of thinking about the few things that Michael had said last night.

Michelle's could only manipulate you if you were either ignorant and didn't know what to do to stop it. An opposite strong emotion would kill whatever she was trying to do. I had a plan now. One of the reasons she had such a strong affect on me was because I felt emotions strongly and easily. I didn't burry them down like most did. Oh I could control them no doubt, show only what I wanted seen. That had been something I had worked long and hard on the last several months but the emotions themselves were still there, all but one time.

As that night Michael had almost died came flooding back into my memory. The cold nothingness as I shut everything down so that I could think without distraction. But the gut wrenching fear when I had allowed it back out was worse than anything I had ever experienced before.

I was up and had Michael wrapped in a fierce hug, kissing him all over as much and as fast as I could. He had no idea what had triggered my change of emotion. One second I was mad, the next I was all over him. It took him a few minutes to respond but he did. Maybe it was because my anger last night had distressed him or it might have been just because I needed him this minute like I had never needed him before. For whatever reason he went along with my sudden passion without even seeming to consider that we were in the middle of the hallway in a public place. Granted a seldom used public place and we weren't even that close to the stairs. But none of that mattered until about 30 minutes later.

We both sort of giggled a little, embarrassed perhaps that we had lost total control of ourselves like we had. But we had harmed nothing and nobody would ever know. He didn't even really ask what had caused me to act so wantonly that I practically tore his clothes off and made love to him right then and there. I was glad because I didn't think I could really explain to myself and putting it into words, even for Michael, would have been almost impossible.

By this time breakfast would be just about over and I would be late for my lab appointment if we didn't get going. Michael as usual came with me. This was only the second time I had been a donor and I didn't trust Paul all that well yet.

Michael was skipping his combat training, which was fine with Joshua since he was ahead of most of the class anyway. My husband had increased his abilities by leaps and bounds since the last time he was here. Our training master still hadn't asked anything more. Hopefully he was still thinking I was the cause and in a way he was right it just wasn't my hands on training that was the reason.

We weren't sure but Michael was thinking that he had stopped changing now and I thought he was right too. It had taken me about three weeks to finish my physical changes and it was like Michael took about three or four times as long to do the same but once it was over that was it. Now it was just a process of him learning how to use his new body. Some things came rather easily to him but fighting had never been one of his loves. Now he didn't love it but he knew it was a necessary evil and he did show a certain amount of pride.

I was glad to have him with me all morning. Especially when I would have to take my crystal off during the x-rays and MRI's. With him just in the other room maybe I wouldn't feel so bad. The last time I was asked to take it off one of the technicians had actually reached out for it and a wave of nausea hit my stomach in warning. Nope, having somebody else handle it wouldn't be a good idea.

It was a good thing that Michael was there in medical with me this morning, because all hell broke loose at once. Joshua came charging in all but dragging a very pissed off Charles behind him. I didn't understand why either one of them would be here. Then things got even stranger as Katherine entered carrying a barely conscious Anthony in her arms.

My heart took a leap. "What in the hell happened?" I yelled as both Michael and I rushed over. Katherine looked just as mad as Joshua was.

Paul was right there looking Anthony over, as was Michael. I had never really found out Paul's talent but it must be something similar to Michael and Phillip's because they both had their heads together and started comparing notes of injuries.

"Slight concussion, a few cracked ribs but that left arm is a mess." Paul said. He didn't need an x-ray machine for him to know what was wrong. I wasn't sure why they kept putting me through them when all some of these guys here just had to look at you or touch you to know a lot more stuff than any machine could tell.

But for now that thought was cast aside as my friend groaned and tried to raise a hand to his head. "No moving now." Paul said sternly. "At least we aren't dealing with any neck fractures."

I had no idea what exactly had happened but since Anthony wasn't in any serious danger I was going to find out. Whirling around quickly I got a surprised sort of yip from Charles as I was in his face so fast he didn't know that I had moved. I had never actually done that before and even Joshua sort of jumped a little.

"What happened?" I snarled at all three of them.

"It was my fault, Maggie." Anthony said from the exam table. "I punched Charles first." Charles was nodding like that excused all of this.

"And that gave you the right to do harm to another?" I snapped in his face. "You are a protector. No matter what Anthony did it couldn't have hurt anything but your pride. How are you ever supposed to protect and serve your fellow Resurrected when you can't even control yourself? This is minor. What will happen when somebody gets in your face at a bar or out on the street and has a gun or knife and tries to kill you?"

I knew the answer before he said it. "I would kill them first."

That got an indrawn breath from both of his teachers. "No. We are stronger and faster than any human but we don't have to kill. It should never come to that." Joshua said.

"Gabriella killed, twice. Why does she get to do that and I don't?" He complained acting like I was above all the rules.

"I didn't have a choice then." I explained calming down. "I was confronted by an Aspanari assassin that was going to kill me. The second was a man that had a gun in my face and had already shot me once. If I had been better trained, if I would have seen a different way I would have taken it. Once a life it gone there is no getting it back Charles. It's gone and every chance that person ever had to do right, to help make up for the mistakes they had made is gone with them. That is something I will never stop regretting. That I robbed them of that chance to change."

I had never really told anybody how I felt about what had happened in Florida and it surprised everybody in the room except for Michael and Anthony. They knew me. Knew that what I had done still bothered me but right now that wasn't important. Getting Charles to see that killing wasn't the go to thing he seemed to think it was, now that was important.

"Charles what happened exactly?" I asked quietly. The fact that I wasn't as mad made him even more belligerent and defensive. Like it pissed him off that I had much more control over myself than he did, than he expected any one to.

"Anthony didn't like it when I asked him how good you were in bed?" He said with sneer in his voice. He was trying for insulting me and all I could do was laugh. Michael too couldn't help but chuckle at that thought. Everybody that knew us well knew exactly where everybody stood. Anthony was by brother and my friend. I was Michael's mate, exclusively just as he was mine. But Anthony was also Michael's friend. Charles could have just as easily asked Anthony how good Michael was in bed for all the difference it would have made to anyone.

"You find that Charles insults your honor humorous Gabriella." Joshua said. He was surprised and not very happy with any of this.

"He can't insult something he knows nothing about. And I don't think Anthony was defending my honor. He knows I am fully capable of doing that myself. Oh, don't worry Charlie and I here will have a discussion regarding this but it won't be today. It will be as and when I want. Anthony was pissed because Charles here insulted him, not me."

"Exactly." Anthony agreed from his position still on the table. That got a few surprised look from the three big protectors. They really didn't understand much of anything did they?

Katherine was just as much out touch with things as the two men. "But you have a very bad reputation Anthony. Everybody knows that you bother any woman around. Pinch and swat and annoy. You've even done it too me until I almost did what Charles did today." She said to him. Didn't she see one very big difference between her and I? Something I had noticed about Anthony that not many seemed to. Oh, he would flirt with any woman around but actually serious pursue he only targeted single women for that. As soon as I had married Michael I knew all the good natured flirting would be cut down to just about nothing. Anthony couldn't quite stop all of it. He did have a reputation to uphold too but to actually cross the line and have sex with a bonded woman was something he had never done.

He respected marriage and that is the reason he had never bonded himself. He knew he wasn't the type to stay faithful just to one woman.

"Maggie is married. She's my sister. I would never sleep with her. It would hurt Michael too much and I would never do that, never make anyone even think that. That's just wrong." Anthony said sounding still really pissed about everything.

I almost laughed out loud at all of this and wished once again for a video camera. One in the dining room this time as a replay of the events would have been very interesting to watch. I could just see it in my head when Anthony had enough of Charles's taunts and jabs that my tall skinny brother had punched him, probably right in the face. Anthony had studied with me but he just didn't have the co-ordination or muscle to be a good fighter. He was the smart guy, not the tough guy. That was for me and people like Charles here to do.

"Bet it shocked the shit of Chucky to have you try and punch him out." I chuckled as I left the three still very confused protectors and went back over to Anthony's side.

He smiled a rather strained smile and laughed a little too. "I just wish I could have left him with a little damage." He mumbled.

"Oh don't worry. He won't escape without some rather serious repercussions." I answered. Looking over at Joshua he nodded and between him and Katherine they sort of frog walked our problem child out the medical bay.

We would all sit down later when we had calmed down and decide what to do about Charles and others like him. He was the worst but he was far from being the only one that didn't limit themselves like I had expected a protector to do. Michael was right they were more like walking muscle than a true protector now. Something had to be done to change that but like a lot of problems I saw I didn't know just yet how to fix it.

As Anthony's arm was set and a cast put on it I was right there. I knew it had to hurt when Michael and Paul pulled the bones back the way they were supposed to go. That was one of the really serious drawbacks to being a Resurrected most drugs didn't work on us well. If it had been something really bad like surgery Paul had synthetic painkillers and some of the medical people could knock you out by manipulating blood flow to the brain but that was not done unless the need was dire. You just had to tough it out.

Luckily the ones that suffered the most damage were the same ones that healed so easily. Protectors were the ones in the front line of danger or they were supposed to be. Now that made me wonder how the three, no now it was four, Resurrected been injured so badly that they required rehab here? Where had their protectors been?

Sure unexpected things happened. Car accidents and just plain accidents but I had to wonder if the Protectors out there were slipping in doing their job. If they didn't care about their charges except as a job would they watch over them like they should? A Protector was supposed to almost love those he protected. That was also part of their job and for the last ten years or so what the center here had been putting out didn't do that part as well as those that had come before.

There were so many things that had changed in just the last decade. Things that even I, a newcomer, could see as being at least not good and possibly dangerous. Why hadn't somebody asked these questions before now? Was I just that nosey? Surely not but for whatever reason nothing had been done. Maybe problems had been fixed that were worse and nobody had thought these mattered and I was playing clean up but for some reason I didn't think so. I think this was reaching a point of no return and it wouldn't be much longer before something triggered an event that would destroy us.

I could see that happening too. When people got disillusioned and were unhappy for too long a lot of them left but for those that didn't for whatever reason leave things would get bad enough that somebody would go postal, maybe several at once. History showed us it could happen. All I had to do was look at our own Revolutionary War and Civil War to know that.

For now I would leave it alone as I held my friend's hand while my husband helped to fix a problem I had inadvertently caused. I knew exactly why Charles had said what he said. My greeting the other day had been a little over the top and if somebody wanted to find fault or see things for other than they were it would have given that somebody a perfect chance to cause trouble.

Charles was my devil's advocate or he seemed to be on the way to becoming one. The one that constantly pointed out how I was expecting different treatment or that I was failing in some way. Every time in training he always wanted to spar with me when Katherine or Joshua were busy. I knew I couldn't have their undivided attention and never expected it. But Charles was almost always in my face about something and never in a good way.

I had known from almost the beginning why he was like that. He liked me but felt threatened by me. If I were still unmarried then maybe things would have been different but he knew beyond all doubt that I loved my husband. He had to see it every second of the day whether I was with Michael or not our love was always with me. So that left him frustrated and angry and he didn't have the common sense or self understanding to see it for what it was, jealousy. Gabriel could have reacted the same way with more reason but he hadn't. Anthony could have too when I told him that I wouldn't love him other than the way a sister does. But neither had been petty like that. Now I had to find out what made our resident ass the way he was.

Perhaps Michelle could help a little or maybe it would take breaking down and asking Phillip to get a telepath in here. It would be better to do it without that. To get ole Chuck to open and figure out his problem with out that. Maybe I could help? I could annoy the hell out of just about anyone when I put a mind to it. I could also listen. Some of both would probably be needed now. I hadn't planned on filling Mary's long empty shoes and didn't know if I could but I had to try. There was no one else stepping up.

I would let things calm down for a week or two, maybe even longer. Make everyone think it had all blown over then I would cook up something that would put Chuck into a stressful enough tailspin that what ever pain he was harboring he would let loose without thinking. Take a big pot of water, add several metal things that bounced well, heat to boiling point, turn pot over and give good shake. Yeah that should make Chuck pretty much explode. Now I had to find out what would work for the bouncy things because I already knew how to heat him to the boiling point and the shaking wouldn't be hard either.

When I smiled that evil smile everybody around sort took a deep breath and a step back if they could. "Maggie, what are you thinking?" Michael asked me very worried. Yeah he knew that look but all it did was make me smile that much more.

"Me, nothing." I answered trying for innocent and even Paul wasn't fooled for a second.

"She's up to something." Paul said confidently. "Are we going to like it or not?"

I shrugged. "Depends on how you personally feel about exploding protectors." And my chuckle sort of made the hair on his arm stand on end as I saw him rub it without even noticing he did it. I didn't say anything else as I went back to finish up the blood work that I had left without a thought so many minutes ago.

I could hear him ask Michael if I was joking or not. He didn't get a verbal answer and I don't think my husband could really tell at that point either.

The rest of the morning I thought about my changed agenda and tried to work out something. I came up with a plan of sorts. It was in the infancy stage but it was a way to maybe get the protectors to work together better. To make them cooperate instead of always striving for individual achievements they needed to learn to work as a team or a pair even. To have to depend on another to get the job done, that was the one element I could see was really lacking in their training.

So as the morning progressed I was so lost in thought I didn't even realize that all the tests were over with. I hadn't gotten as upset this time and my nerves weren't frazzled into nothing. Michael had been right outside during the x-rays and MRI's. Being able to smell him so close and hearing his voice just on the other side of door had comforted me.

Now it was lunchtime and both Michael and I were starving. As we devoured our lunch Phillip and the rest of his entourage came in too and Michelle was with them. I didn't know if she had learned her lesson from last night but I had certainly learned mine. If she tried anything I was prepared. I waited for that almost euphoric feeling to come over me but it didn't. Instead I got grumpier and grumpier. It wasn't until I looked over at her rather pleased little smirk that I realized why.

Well two could play at this game I thought. She was now deliberately trying to provoke me, maybe wanting to show just how volatile I could be. It wasn't going to work. For her to affect me this way she had to be totaled focused on me. If I understood things right that meant she had to also be feeling what I felt in order to make sure that what she was doing was working.

Well my plan of getting angry again wouldn't work so I too changed tactics. I remembered every vivid detail of loving Michael just this morning. The strong almost over whelming feeling of desire and passion flooded my mind and heart as I went over every single second. Out of the corner of my eye I saw Michelle grab the table and turn absolutely scarlet. Before she could recover or pull her gift away I found another very strong memory of our time together and shot that at her for good measure.

She couldn't take it as she let out an almost moan as my desire for my husband found its way into her. What reaction she was having inside I had no idea but it wasn't one she was prepared for as she almost ran out of the room without saying anything to anybody.

As all my emotions were brought under control I started feeling a little bad. Michelle had been testing me for sure but I could have probably resolved our issues without resulting to what I did. It was because I didn't like how she did things but maybe nobody had pointed out how wrong it was before. When you had a lot of power you didn't always stop to think how that power should and should not be used. She had been around for quite a while and was one of the few remaining empaths we had. Michelle had probably been pretty catered to. Just like I would have been had I allowed it.

Maybe it was because I was so new to everything or maybe it was because I just looked at things differently but I could see how that kind of treatment was a bad thing if you wanted to keep your head on straight. I wasn't perfect. Heaven knows I had just sort of proved that to myself. I had over reacted and lashed out because I was pissed. Did I have reason for it? Without a doubt but that wasn't an excuse just a reason.

"Excuse me Michael." I said in his ear. "I need to apologize to someone."

He had witnessed some of what had happened. He wouldn't have known exactly what had transpired between Michelle and I but he knew something had. Given our history of just last night he had been watching for a problem today but had left it up to me. I sometimes wished he wouldn't have as much confidence in me as he did.

It wasn't that hard to follow Michelle's scent back to her room. It wasn't all that far away from mine really. She was sort of shocked when she answered my knock on her door. I tried to put how sorry I was as the only thing I was feeling. Could she turn off her gift like some could or was she always hit with other people's feeling even when she didn't want them?

"I'm sorry Michelle." I started. "That wasn't very nice of me. I sort of lashed back out because I didn't like what you were doing. It was a reason but still I should have found a better way than to make you get embarrassed especially in front a room full of people."

"Why?" She asked really studying my face. "I was messing you. Even after you asked me not to last night. I knew you wouldn't like it but I did it anyway. I'm not even sure why I couldn't resist the temptation."

So for the next 30 minutes we sat around and talked about things. I found out a lot about Michelle and never once did I feel something that was not of my own mind and heart. She did indeed feel the emotions of others all the time but she had some very good training and had learned to build walls around her talent. Something that she said the telepaths had to learn to do also. They had a school of sorts. Someplace very far away from everybody else, a very remote spot in the middle of Canada somewhere that allowed new people with that sort of gift to go and train and figure out how to withstand the pressures of being what they were.

I had wondered why didn't they have their school here with all the other Resurrected and that was exactly why they didn't. Too many people, a new telepath or empath was almost in a constant pain from the moment their gift manifested until they learned how to block out everybody else. That required as few as people around as possible. Usually there were other telepaths and empaths that knew how to block or stop their own thoughts and emotions there but right now that very isolated school was almost abandoned.

Even Michelle didn't understand why they had had so few of her type of Resurrected surface lately. They were beginning to wonder in the human stock from which we came was changing so that there was no one that could be brought back with those talents. Again I had to ask myself if that were it or if there was something we were missing. A key piece of information that we weren't privy to because both of those type talents were also not showing up worldwide. Even though I wasn't a genetics person I knew enough that an evolutionary change like the one Michelle suspected wasn't something that happened around the world all at once.

50 years ago there had been plenty of telepaths and empaths, Michelle said. Now it was like they were an endangered species. She was right but I didn't think it was a case of natural selection but a deliberate attack. I would wait for Daniel to confirm it but I was pretty sure what he would find already. The Aspanari or maybe somebody else was killing them off. Other than a spy they were the biggest chance of us finding out what they were up to. So it made sense. And then again there was that chance that Michelle was the one that was right and I was just paranoid. So I would wait. You would think by now I would be getting pretty good at it. I had learned that just because you were waiting for something didn't mean there weren't a lot of other things to do in the mean time.

For now I had a demonstration for Phillip and the rest of his cronies. Maybe I was being a little nasty with those thoughts. They had been brought here just for that. To see the new infiltrator in action but why did everybody assume it was a fight they needed to see. An infiltrator had a lot of other things they had to be able to do. First and foremost was to go where others didn't suspect they were. My calling or at least those few that had had it before me had indeed been spies. So why not show them what I could do when it came to that. I hadn't been practicing that much lately but I knew it was something I should work on more.

Today they would get a demonstration. I knew by now my limits when it came to changing myself. My face could look like almost anyone but I couldn't change my body structure much. I couldn't shrink my size to be Michelle's height or get a lot taller and look like Katherine. Oh sure I could put on their faces but everybody would known it wasn't them because I couldn't change the body to be a perfect copy. So I found somebody that was also going to the little demonstration today that was almost my size and we played switch. It required a little cooperation but Rachael didn't mind at all being part of the experiment.

So when I went in the door to the training room that had chairs and things all lined up nobody realized it wasn't Rachael at all. I didn't try and talk much because her voice was a little hard for me to imitate. Just smiling and nodding and walked by so many people that didn't have a

Search for Lazarus

clue I was the person they had all come to see. I had a little tube of lipstick with me and had rubbed it over my forefinger so that I could mark each person as I simply touched him or her on the back of the neck. They didn't understand what I was doing but they would know very soon.

Finally when the grumbling and growling got to be too much for Phillip he asked my husband where I was. Michael hadn't been told about any of this but I saw his eyes narrow as he focused on my location. "She's here but I just don't see her." He told Phillip and Rafael confidently.

It was time for the big reveal now. Rachael walking over to Michael was no big surprise. They knew each other rather well but her kissing him on the lips sure got a gasp out of everybody, especially Rachael's husband Felix who was also in attendance. "What are doing you Rach?" Felix hissed as he grabbed me and pulled me a way from an equally surprised Michael. Then everything clicked for my husband and he smiled and winked at me. He knew I wasn't Rachael and now everybody was going to know it too.

"That isn't Rachael." Michael told Felix. I got a very close look up and down by Rachael's husband. By now our little trio had a lot of attention.

"Sorry to worry you Felix." I said in my normal voice. My voice coming out of Rachael's face really surprised those that had no clue what was going on. Then I dropped all pretenses and the newest infiltrator was standing among all those that assembled to gawk at me.

I had never felt comfortable in front of crowds but this time I knew the role I had to play. It was me of a sort just not the me I liked all that much. The showman, the one that performed like a trained animal.

The ohs and ahs sort of spread around the room as they realized I had been in here a rather long time but my demonstration was also a warning. I called out in as loud of voice as I had. "Today wasn't just to show you that I could appear as almost anyone from someone you know to someone you have never met before it was also a way to make you realize that part of my job isn't to go around matching muscle to muscle in a fight. I was never supposed to be that type of resource."

That got a confused look from Phillip and Joshua both. Didn't they understand that yes I needed to be able to defend myself but that physical confrontation was a thing of last resort and unlike a protector it wasn't what I had been designed for.

"I am the one that goes in by themselves to rescue someone or when necessary to kill a single target without others knowing I am even there."

One of the visitors spoke up then. A man named Augustus that was the house leader from Chicago. A big burly man that must have been a medical in some fashion because only medicals could run a house, which again I thought, was extremely prejudice but that battle would wait for a different day. "The only thing you showed today was that you could walk around a crowded room." He sort of both sneered and grumped all at the same time.

Maybe some had heard about my claws and some hadn't but they were about to get a lesson on them either way. I walked up to him. "Check the back of your neck." As his hand came back with my lipstick on it he was surprised but still didn't understand the significant. I popped one long claw out and asked it to be as slender as it could possibly be. Now I had a six-inch long rather fat needle in his face. "Can you imagine what this would do inserted there?" He didn't have to imagine hard. Even a protector wouldn't survive something like that. I could severe the spinal chord from the rest of the body or destroy the brainstem itself. My biology wasn't as good as a medical person but it didn't need to be. It wasn't that hard to figure out if you killed the brain the body didn't take long in following it.

Everybody that didn't know me well that was close by took a giant step away from me, sometimes several steps away. I almost smiled at that. Before I had been an oddity to be talked about and looked at now I was a very dangerous person. This was a good thing in its way. Now others would listen to what I had to say, take what I thought seriously. Because whether they knew it or not I was very serious most of the time. I just didn't let most know it. You got better results when people didn't realize that the fun they were having was actually a lesson in life. I had learned that when I had tutored kids in school. The best results I had were when the child never knew they were being taught at all, that they had been having fun instead of learning and the great benefit to that is that you got to have fun too.

Today had been about learning. Learning that things aren't always what they seem. Both Michael and I had learned that a lot lately even when it came to our own bodies. Now it was something for everyone else to consider too. As I saw thinking and great deal of respect take away the fear that had been there. PIB was almost hopping around in my head in happiness. I wasn't sure what flipped his switch but I didn't always get the why of things from him right away. It took a while to figure him out most of the time. But for right now PIB, Michael and I were all happy with the way things were turning out.

When I looked over at all the protectors that had been there because Joshua had been thinking we were having a training demonstration I realized not everyone was a happy little camper. Charles and several others were not only unhappy they were mad.

Was it just because I stole their thunder today? This little meeting had been called because of me not them to start with. I hadn't asked for it but I wasn't about to turn down the chance to meet important members of our family. Changes happened best and easiest when you had those in charge in on it. I don't think the grumpy protectors were thinking that deeply though. They just saw the grandstanding. The performing circus act that I had done and didn't look any further.

I had been right in my evaluation of them. They looked no further than the end of their own noses and didn't try. I wasn't expecting them to be philosophers or anything but trying to see beyond the obvious was an ability they needed to develop. For some it was easy for others it took somebody they respected to show them how. I didn't have their respect much. YET. I would get it and I had the beginning stages of just how to do that already laid out. But I should have remembered what I had thought just this weekend and even a few times since then. My plans didn't always work out the way I wanted them too and sometimes an unexpected opportunity comes shooting out of nowhere. It may at first look like a problem but if you are smart and good enough you can use even the most threatening thing to your advantage. But only if you think really fast, have a lot of help and are very, very lucky.

# Chapter 6

## FIRST ATTEMPT DRUGS AND ALCOHOL

I was so bored. It was between breakfast and lunch and nobody needed me. I had already been down to medical this week to supply them with a 'few' more samples. Pretty soon I was going to run out. Just how many things could they find to run tests on? When Paul had even gone so far as to ask very nicely both Michael and me, I had to wonder what was up. Apparently just about everything about me was different and not just a little different either. They thought my white blood cells might hold answers for things like tissue regeneration for those of us that couldn't heal a cut in a few seconds but took more like a day or two.

Paul was gearing up big time and tried to talk me into really becoming a lab rat. He wanted to expose me to synthetic substances just to see if I had resistances that others didn't. Not for the first time did I tell him to get bent. It seemed that was a phrase I was using a lot lately, especially with people that thought they were in charge. Phillip, Rafael and now Paul were finding out I wasn't any easy person to control. But Paul had discovered one of my weaknesses, just tell me that a test or sample would maybe help someone that had no hope and I folded like a house of cards in a heavy wind. I wasn't even sure that all those blood samples were for what he said they were but I was never anemic or had any other deficiencies from all those things. Michael checked on the test reports enough to know that I was in beyond perfect health. I still didn't trust Paul and his bunch of cronies but if Michael was more or less okay with it then so was I.

Right now I was about to go out of my skull. I wanted to run but this area, although very beautiful wasn't really good for running. Hiking, climbing and the like It was great but the flat out running that I liked to do just wasn't possible. At least if there was an area good for that nearby I hadn't found it yet. I could go down to the maintenance level again and run there. That gloomy floor almost made me feel like a rat or bat; it was so dark and dismal. It was something I would no doubt be forced to use this winter when the snows got really deep but I was saving that for a last resort type thing. The pools were used right now for physical therapy, only a few patients were there but I didn't like nosing in like that. It was rude. The same thing with the gym and the tread mills, the new protectors still looked at me a little odd and running faster and longer than any two or three of them could do combined wouldn't help them accept me as just another trainee.

So what did that leave me to do this morning? Michael was down in the training room and I hated to distract people by hanging around when I didn't have a class myself. Joshua wanted to know if I wanted to help teach but I wasn't sure if I was up for that or how well that would be received either. Then I had an inspired thought. Michael and I kept our little room clean and orderly but there was another very large place that had been untouched by a caring hand for quite some time. I got together as many bottles of cleaning liquid I could scrap up from the supply closet that was located near the laundry room along with a bunch of rags and a broom and headed off down the hill.

The crypt type mausoleum hadn't been given a good cleaning or sprucing up in a very long time. I thought that it was long over due. As I cleaned each shelf I moved very carefully each urn or jar and placed it back exactly where it had been. The few stained glass windows were given a gentle washing and now glowed with beauty in the late morning sunshine. It was a pretty day with a few high clouds and cool temperatures that made manual labor a breeze even for a Nohu. Finally having all the cobwebs and other debris down at the lowest level I swept the beautiful marble floor, carefully trying to kick up as little dust as possible. By the time I got done every inch of the place was the way I thought it should be. It now reflected the care and respect I thought it should and would make those visiting a loved one maybe not enjoy it but at least not be ashamed of their final resting place.

I thought it appalling that it had not been given the attention it should have been. After all someday I would be here in some fashion and even if that wasn't in my mind I still didn't like that lack of respect those that came before us had previously received. Why did everybody just bury pain and their past away like it was a shameful thing? Was it shameful to love and then to feel sorrow when that loved one was no longer with you? Did it make you less because you still had human feelings and emotions? If human emotions were not important or essential to what we did now then why did we have them? You had to care, to love to do what we did. We weren't robots and I was some times very disgusted at the attitude that some people still had.

Closing the door gently behind me, I was very happy with how I had spent my morning and was unprepared when PIB screamed out in my head almost making me grab my ears because of how loud he had been. "Duck." He yelled. Maybe it was because of how loud his mental bellow had been or maybe because I was happily distracted that I didn't react quite as quickly as I otherwise would have. Soon I wasn't worried about anything but the burning pain in my left shoulder from the arrow that had pierced it. It would have probably gone straight through if I hadn't been almost against the granite wall. As it was the metal part was protruding from my back as I tried to pull the whole thing back out the way it had gone in. The damn thing was barbed or something because even more than gentle tugging couldn't dislodge it. Other than ripping it out I would have to wait until I got up to medical. I could tell my body was healing already and somebody would have to cut the damned thing out or maybe it would go out easier if it just kept going. But I couldn't reach that far back to do it and I couldn't get a good enough grip on the front part either. It was a lot more slippery than I thought an arrow shaft should be.

All this time I had my senses on high alert. Listening for the sound of another arrow or the smell of someone closing in on my location. It was close to hunting season for deer and maybe it had been an errant shot from a poor hunter but for some reason I didn't think so.

Suddenly I started feeling extremely odd, like the world around me just took a tilt off to the side. What was wrong with me? I had been hurt a lot worse than this little thing. But for every second that passed the fuzziness and just plain goofy disorientation got worse. My brain refused to work right. Somewhere in the part of my mind that was still working right it came up with the answer, very slowly as everything grew more and more disconnected I realized that the arrow had been drugged or poisoned in some way.

I don't know how far I made it back up the hill seeking help. Don't remember much of anything for the next few hours except flashes of disjointed memories of faces that made no sense and questions and words that made even less. My mind caught up with things all at once. I was lying on an examination table in medical and unable to move. Michael was in my face too holding me so tightly his fingers were digging into my cheeks. "Oww." I groaned out.

Michael could see the reason return to my eyes and relaxed slightly but still didn't turn me loose. "Maggie? You in there this time?" He asked me. The love and worry would have been hard to miss by anyone. Everything was still very fuzzy but some pieces were starting to come back now.

"What happened to me?"

"The arrow that shot you was coated in a very heavy dose of both PCP and LSD." Paul said coming where I could see him. He had a long set of scratches that went along the side of his face and down his neck. I knew beyond a shadow of a doubt what had caused his injuries, my claws. I felt horrible but also knew it could have been a whole lot worse.

My head was finally free enough to look around and see just what or maybe I should say whom was holding me on the table. Katherine and Joshua both had a leg each and two other big protectors I had seen in the beginner's class were on my arms. Just how bad had I gotten? My clothes were a mess, torn and bloody with very little left to my t-shirt at all and my jeans in not much better shape.

"I think I'm okay." I said. Did it sound as uncertain to everybody else as it did to me?

"Well at least she isn't cussing and yelling at us anymore." The one protector on my left arm said with a slight smile. Now I remembered his name, Bruce. At least I thought that was it. My long term memory was fine but stuff that had happened over the last few days were fuzzily starting to re-emerge from the fog but how had I been shot and where I had been when it happened I still couldn't dredge up.

As I was allowed to sit up on the table everybody else took a giant step back. They were afraid of me, of what I had done that I couldn't even remember. "What do you remember?" Michael asked me. He had been the only one that stayed right by my side.

"Nothing. Well not much. I'm not sure what day this is even. There seems to be gaps in my memory or at least I think there are." If you can't remember something was it even possible to know you that you didn't know?

"Maybe explaining what we know happened might jog her memory." Joshua suggested.

"That would be better than this giant hole I have right now." I agreed. Even if I never remembered I needed to know what I had done that the others had witnessed. What Paul had figured out had happened to me.

It came as no surprise that Michael started on the explanation first. Everybody else was still rather apprehensive. "When you didn't show up for lunch I started getting worried. Then when I knew you weren't even in the complex any more I went looking for you. Luckily Katherine noticed your absence too and went with me. I found you rather quickly but you barely knew who I was and Katherine you almost attacked on sight. As Katherine got more help I tried talking to you, trying to figure out what happened. I saw an arrow shaft still in your body but the front had been broken off and there wasn't much blood at all but the arrowhead was still in your back and protruding partially. I knew somebody had shot you."

Joshua took over the next part of the explanation. "By the time Katherine and I got to you the drugs had quite an effect on you. You were screaming about some one shooting you and giant fish that could walk trying to eat you and all manner of impossible things. It didn't take a medical person to know a drug induced hysteria starting. We got Paul down right away but even he hadn't seen anything quite like what you were going through or at least not recently."

"Living and working in the 70's gave me some clue as to what was happening." Paul started on his part of the story. "It had been so long that I had almost forgotten the effect that hallucinogenic drugs have on someone. You were so lost in your delusions you had no idea who much of anyone was at all. The only one that had any calming effect on you was Michael. If anyone else even got near you, well you weren't very keen about that idea." He said with a little bit of a chuckle.

Yeah I bet I was just sweet and gentle as wildcat set on fire. They still hadn't answered why I was outside by myself to start out with. I remembered my schedule and Michael's but still couldn't fathom what I had been up to.

"Where was I? Does anybody know what I was doing running around outside by myself? Could I have been attacked here in the complex and wandered outside?" I didn't like that possibility and maybe it was just a left over paranoid thought from the drugs I had been shot with.

"From where you were and a few other things we figured out you were cleaning the mausoleum." Katherine answered. She still looked more than a little frightened. Was it what I had tried to do in my drugged state that was the cause of her stress or was she simply still worried about me. I hoped it was the later but couldn't blame her for the other. In all the sparing we had done together in the weeks I had been here I had never really let loose with all I had. If I had felt threatened, I knew I would hold back nothing. I was just glad I hadn't hurt anybody worse than the small claw marks on Paul's face.

Then I realized I was missing someone very important in my life. If I was in trouble, Anthony wouldn't be far away and he was nowhere in sight. I frowned slightly trying to dredge up memories of faces that were distorted and terrifying even now. There was a memory of something that I hoped wasn't true but a total fabrication of my mind but somehow I knew it wasn't. "How bad did I hurt Anthony?" I whispered.

"See, I knew she would remember most of it." Paul said. He sounded maybe not pleased but unsurprised.

"Not really remember but if I'm here and he's not there has got to be a good reason." I answered, sounding very logical in my thought process.

"He got too close once and we only had you secured with straps then." Paul explained. "I had no idea that anybody your size could be that strong even with the delusions of PCP giving them extra strength. If Michael hadn't been here I'm not sure what we would have done to stop you. You were determined you were leaving and that you were in danger. The only reason you aren't running around loose is because you had to make sure Michael was safe too. You just wouldn't leave him and he wasn't going anywhere. That gave us the time to get some people in here that could keep both you and us safe."

I must have been a whirling terror right about then. "How bad did I hurt him and are there any other causalities? Other than that." I said pointing to Paul's face. "I am sorry Paul."

"Anthony's arm is rebroken and he has a few bumps and bruises but he will be just fine." Michael answered. "He doesn't blame you and neither does Paul."

Paul was nodding very enthusiastically. "I guess I gave you a lot of good information to study during all of this." I laughed a little weakly.

Paul turned first white then beet red. "I would never want something like this to happen to anyone, let alone as an experiment." He snarled. I hadn't even meant it that way really. But when you are at the constant receiving end of a stream of needles and x-rays and invasive questionnaires it was easy to think that he got off on delving into anything new and interesting.

Michael too came to a conclusion I would have with a little more time. "But weren't you asking Maggie to submit to just such a test. One that would expose her to synthetic substances to see her resistance." My husband's voice had more than a touch of anger in it.

"Not like this." Paul denied. "You are forever demanding to know what every test or examine we ask is for. I wasn't about to expose any piece of her to anything without permission. Do you really think that I would do something like that to Gabriella? Her body holds too many mysteries and possible answers to questions I had never even asked before. Besides being one of us, would I risk destroying someone that valuable, that special? Would I put in jeopardy the small amount of trust I have managed to get?"

"But you must admit that my reactions are something you are going to study." I stated. It wasn't a question. I knew Paul too well. He would never pass up this type of opportunity.

"Of course but besides putting you in extreme danger, there was just so much that we couldn't take advantage of because of how things transpired. So much information lost or compromised besides the very big hazard of you going totally psychotic and possibly killing quite of few people. Would I want that on my conscious? No amount of information is worth the price of a single life." He adamantly insisted.

Well some unusual insights had been revealed besides my having very little resistance to synthetic drugs just like the rest of our people. Paul, despite his cold demeanor, cared and worried about people. He wasn't as much of stuffy bird as he acted most of the time. He was passionate it just usually involved research and science. To me not the most pleasant way to spend my time but I could see how it would be a draw to somebody with his personality. The mindset of wanting everything perfect and every mystery solved. For Paul it was almost like an OCD type thing. And he had a real problem with those that didn't think like that.

But he was learning how to be a little more flexible in his thinking. Ever since our little talk that one late night I had noticed a small change in him. And the people that worked with him had noticed it too. With my hearing it wasn't impossible to pick up those discussions. In a big noisy room like the dining facility it was sometimes a challenge to focus on one conversation all the way across the room but I was getting better at it. Thankfully Michael knew what I was up to and when my mind was far away he would cover for me until I got back to the conversation I was supposed to be involved in. So far nobody had noticed what I was doing and I wanted to keep it that way.

For the next few days I was watched. I got to spend a goodly portion of it in the medical bay much to my disgust. The only one that really slept at all was Michael because he refused to leave my side. And I had to smile at my sleeping husband all curled up on one of the beds in medical. Even though I couldn't and wouldn't sleep much there it didn't seem to put a damper on him and I was glad I had a very high tolerance when it came to sleep deprivation, something that made the rest of the medical personnel even more curious about me. Like I needed another thing for them to poke and probe for.

I did manage to get Paul to let me out long enough to go see where I had been attacked. I knew my sense of smell and my eyesight was a lot better than any protector here. So I wanted to see if I could figure out what happened. Maybe seeing the area again would jog some memories for me.

It helped some. My memory of those things before the event came back pretty much the whole way but after I got shot was still a jumbled mess and I didn't think that would ever change. The bad thing about Joshua being so diligent was that after I had been contained and they knew I wasn't going to rip any body else up, he had sent most of our more experienced protectors down to that very area and along with Paul's people that were taking samples of anything and everything had contaminated the entire scene.

There were just so many scents that went in every direction and then doubling back over and over again. It was like the area had been walked over by a thousand people. Even with my nose I wasn't going to find a thing.

PIB wasn't any help either. He had no more of a clue who had attacked us than I did. And that fact wasn't very comforting. That someone had managed to take both of us unaware wasn't very good.

We all knew it wasn't an accident. A simple arrow used by any hunter would not have been dipped in PCP and LSD. But who would have known to use them? The drugs themselves were not that hard to obtain, at least according to Paul. How he knew I didn't have a clue but he sounded very sure of himself. We had a meeting to try and figure what had happened, why and who the culprit had been. Michael, Joshua, Katherine, Paul, Tim and Anthony were all there and even though I added a little insight because I remembered rather well what happened before the drugs kicked in nothing was resolved.

Very few things could even be determined and even fewer people ruled out as suspects. The arrow was a standard one that any bow could have shot. The drugs were unremarkable and ordinary and could be obtained from almost any street corner dealer. We were positive it was one of us. Nobody else would know where the mausoleum was and I had probably been followed in some way but I couldn't see how unless it was somebody very skilled in keeping silent.

To me that meant it was another protector or somebody that was used to being in the woods a great deal. Anthony would have even been a suspect if his arm hadn't been in a cast still. There were several people that hunted here. It was a sport and sometimes more than that as they bought in some very much needed food in the way of deer and other game. Sue never turned down anything somebody brought in and always gave good credit to whatever source it came from.

So where did that leave us for a suspect pool. Over 20 really and even some of the women used bows and hunted. Katherine didn't but some of the other women that had been assigned here a while had taken up the sport. I think they did it mostly to have something to do in the wintertime. Of course I could hunt and I didn't need a gun or bow and arrow to do it.

If I didn't have so much to do already and now had to worry about my safety whenever I stepped outside the door by myself I wouldn't mind bringing in a few deer myself. They would be more of challenge than those small things that were what Florida called deer. The ones I had seen around here were at least twice the size and just a little farther north there were elk and moose. Now that idea had my hunting instinct going a little fruity. Maybe the only difference the protectors that hadn't learned to control themselves was I had a bit more common sense. Right now wasn't the time to show off. I had done enough damage these past few days because of Phillip and all his visitors that most people were back to looking at me a little funny.

Had I choice in doing that? Not really but I had to ask myself if that wasn't the reason behind my attack. Maybe it was just someone trying to both show himself and me that I was still mortal and imperfect. If that was the case everybody in the whole complex knew how bad I had gotten. The looks now were even worse but there was a large amount of respect from the protectors that had tried to keep me contained. They had found out just exactly how bad I could get. And that had been without most of my brain being connected right.

I had watched the video of when they brought me into the exam room carried in between four protectors, struggling and screaming like I was mad. It was worse than Michael had told me. Worse than Joshua would admit but the camera had caught every rant and rave. How I totally destroyed the first exam room after I had been strapped down to a gurney and those nice restraining things hadn't lasted but a few seconds. I didn't even need my claws for that. I tore things from the walls and actually pulled the door off to get away from people I didn't recognize. Even Anthony had been a casualty as I literally threw him up against a wall when I broke free. It was only when Michael had been there that I had any type of control. That had only worked when he was close and if somebody else got to near us I would shove him behind me and snarl worse than any animal in the zoo. There was about 10 minutes of video from that room because I had thrown something into the camera at that point but it had been more than enough to scare the heck out of me. But it had also sort of impressed me. I had never dreamed I could do most of the stuff I did.

The second room's video was more or less boring except for a lot of very bad language on my part and a constant changing of the guard there really wasn't much to see. About 6 hours of me being held down and not being very happy about it. How they managed to get me on to a gurney again at all was still the subject of much discussion because nobody remembered it exactly the same way and Anthony had already been taken out of commission so I didn't even have his very accurate view point to go with. But one thing they all agreed with, it hadn't been easy or pretty and several of the protectors had suffered bumps, bruises and cuts along the way. At least I hadn't hurt anyone too bad.

Now I had to try and put things right. Get those people that were sort of afraid of me now to not be. Everyone knew that I had been drugged, that I hadn't been in my right mind but when protectors come out of someplace and they are pale and shaking because of you, well it sort of freaks the more normal of us quite a bit.

It would take time but I had high hopes that people wouldn't blanch when they turned around and I was there. It was maybe a good thing that by the time I was found that Phillip and all his entourage had been gone.

He hadn't even been told until everything was over with. An airplane isn't a very easy place to reach someone and Paul, Joshua and Michael had been too busy trying to keep me and everyone else safe to even worry about telling our council member what had happened until everything had calmed down.

Of course I had to talk to him. Reassure him that I was fine and that there seemed to be no lasting side effects from the drugs. PCP was bad but LSD was in some was worse. That drug could have reoccurring episodes that appeared for no reason at any time because it attached to a normal humans spinal chord. Now that was just one more thing I had to be worried about. Like I needed something else. But Paul said that was one good thing about being what we are. The initial reaction we had from synthetic drugs was just like any normal human but our bodies sort of flushed them out. As if we knew at some cellular level that this was not supposed to be there.

He thought that after the first episode that I wouldn't have much if any other reactions. But was he sure about that? Not at all, so I had been watched carefully just to be safe and I couldn't blame him. Didn't blame Michael or Joshua either for their constant presence. Now almost a week later I was allowed to run around without a chaperone and go back to my own room to sleep and relax I felt like a prisoner released from jail.

My energy level had been so bad I almost asked for something to calm me down but I knew that wouldn't be a good idea either. I had just had a shot, literally, of a synthetic drug in my system and didn't want something else in there. Besides wasn't I always harping at the new guys about self-control? So I sort of sat on my hands and tried to find something to keep me from going nuts. It wasn't easy. Michael knew what was wrong and why I was constantly nervous and fidgeting. It was like a very bad case of ADHD but Paul kept thinking it was a still a reaction from my attack. Should I have told him that my energy level was just that damned high? I didn't know but for some reason I thought not and Michael wasn't much help because for once he didn't have an opinion and told to make up my own mind. I had stuck my tongue out at him.

Now finally I was back in my room and got the chance to make some private phone calls and catch up on my emails. I hadn't felt right doing that while in the medical bay. There had been so many people hovering around me all the time. Now I called home and got an immediate relieved answer from my family there.

Michael had called Alison as soon as I got my head back on relatively straight. Had told her exactly what happened. She was all for coming up immediately but that would have served as much purpose as Phillip to come racing back. Of course Alicia and Peter weren't much better and have given me a very worried dressing down. I wasn't sure just what Michael had told them but it had been enough to worry all of them. Now that I had reassured my family in Florida, I was all for loving my husband until we both could do nothing but fall asleep in each other's arms.

Even though it was only early morning we both were for spending most of the day sequestered in our room but others had different things in mind. It was less than an hour before the first person knocked on our door. Michael's growl was almost scary. He didn't react well to being interrupted especially when it came to romance, well at the moment it had been about sex as he hadn't been very much into the foreplay and he all but jumped me as we closed the door behind us.

I knew what he liked but today it was as if he thought we had never been together before as he was very pointed with what he wanted and how. That was very different for him and after I had answered the door and told Katherine if she knew what was good for her she had better put the word out to leave us alone for the rest of the day, he all but threw me back on the bed.

He had been aggressive before but never like this. The first time when we had been together he had been very forceful but I had chalked it up to both of us being very sexually frustrated and maybe today was exactly the same reason, plus he had to have been worried. But today after we were done for a bit I had to ask him why he had acted that way but to also let him know I hadn't minded his change in tactics.

"You were very instructive today." I said in a joking manner. It wouldn't serve to have Michael thinking he had hurt my feelings. He hadn't been exactly demanding but he had been a lot more talkative today. As if he just couldn't shut up for some reason and his requests although not anything we hadn't done before was of the much more physical kind than he usually preferred.

He didn't blush exactly but I could tell that he was uncomfortable with something. I still could get embarrassed sometimes but it had been getting progressively less and less as time passed. Now it rarely happened. What was it that Michael had had running through his mind that he would react this way? He had never once been hesitant in talking about anything before.

"Yeah, I'm sorry." He said sort of avoiding my eyes. I didn't mind anything we did and knew him well enough by now that for him to have this reaction that something unusual was going on that I didn't understand.

"Why?" I asked. My curiosity was in high gear because I was sort of stumped. "You know we have done all of this before and I didn't mind the first time or the second, not even the 10 or 20 time, why would I mind anything we did today. Not to sound like you are boring because you most definitely are not, but we have done all of this a few times before so why would you be sorry for anything. I certainly enjoyed myself."

"But should you have?" He asked me much to my surprise. "No matter what anyone does to you, how powerful they are you can just take it. Ever since our first time together I have wondered if I hurt you in some way but you never once said anything like that. No matter what we do it's fine with you. How can you do that?" I wasn't sure but he sounded a little pissed.

I wasn't exactly mad at him but if he used our love making as part of an experiment, even if it was only for his personal knowledge, I wouldn't be very happy about it. "Were you actually trying to hurt me today Michael?"

"NO!!!" He yelled. "I guess I just realized from everything that happened the last few days that no matter what I do I really couldn't could I? It sort of pressed a few buttons both good and bad. I think I know why now."

I waited for him to continue. It was as patient as I could get which was to say not much.

"I have been watching and listening to everybody but most especially when you are sparing and I think I know why people have such odd reactions to you sometimes. There isn't any test I know of but I think you put out certain pheromones when you are aggressive. Most of the time it is real subtle but you seem to be more challenged with Katherine than with any of the men, even Joshua. I noticed that when you get done sparing you're more sexually attractive to me even if I wasn't around to watch you. And for the last few days I have been about going out of my mind. I couldn't quit figure it out but it is the only thing that makes sense. That is why all the men have problems fighting you. Protectors have a more pronounced sense of smell so they would be even more affected by it than others."

That made a weird kind of sense and I did have to work harder with Katherine than anybody else. And pheromones like Michael was talking about effected the subconscious almost and people had no clue about it unless they really thought about why they were reacting they way they were.

But I was getting something from PIB that said Michael had a good idea but had come to the wrong conclusion. He had been quiet for a while after my drugged state and other than to sort apologize for not communicating things fast enough hadn't said a whole lot. I had gotten used to him hanging around on the inside of my head that when he took a trip away I sort of missed his presence.

Oh, I knew why he did it sort of. He was a he and didn't want to join in when Michael and I were together and I didn't think that PIB was exactly human either and what two people did wasn't something he wanted to be around for. I appreciated him giving us that type of privacy. But now he was for him blabbing away. "Wrong. Danger attracts." He told me rather strongly.

I thought about that for a few seconds. Checking with him to make sure I understood what he was trying to tell me. I still had no idea why he could only give me a few words or hints at a time and had sort of given up that I would ever know all the reasons for all the things that had happened to me since I woke up from that car accident months ago. Just sort of went with the flow and my guide had helped me navigate some very treacherous waters. Not without a few bumps and even what could be seen as on overturned boat but we were getting better at our symbiotic relationship.

"PIB doesn't agree with you." I told Michael. He made of very unhappy face.

"Well what does all knowing PIB have to say." He grumped. "I would like to think there is a reason that almost every man around has the hots for you all the time. This hearing so good is driving me crazy."

So that was part of his problem today. He had been so close to so many people over the last few days and so many had been talking and discussing me that it was easy to see how he would feel a little slighted and also a little possessive. Our alone time had been nonexistent and I knew from past experience Michael didn't share me well with others in one very important way, sex. Even the idea of it sort of drove him a little loopy, maybe that was a reason I too was extremely sensitive about the subject.

"He doesn't think it's anything that exotic. Danger attracts some people." I said trying hard not to smile. Michael had said almost the same thing already. He had just come to the wrong conclusion. "Protectors are very big, very strong guys. Can you imagine how much they have to hold back so as to not hurt normal people, even normal us type people. I'm one of the few women any of them have ever seen they may not have to do that with and when we spar of course they hold back some because most were raised to not hurt a woman. But you must admit that my abilities would lead to a few fantasies and a whole lot of speculations and we haven't been at all discreet in the fact that we enjoy a very healthy sex life."

I could see Michael mull that over for a bit. "That might explain some of what I heard but why would it turn me on to see you like you were in the medical bay. Even though I was worried half out of my mind there was a part of me that found you almost erresitable. Why would I feel that way? I shouldn't have, I know. I buried it down so I didn't think about it but it was still there."

I had a pretty good idea why he felt that way. "You weren't wrong to be attracted to me, Michael." I could tell he didn't agree with me but he let me have my say. "Danger is always exciting in some way. That's the attraction behind scary movies and amusement park rides. It gives the illusion of danger without the real thing. You know I would never hurt you but to see me turned loose was exciting, it had to be. The adrenaline surge you felt when you saw what I could do, rip a steel door off its hinges and throw people around like they were nothing. Your heart over road your fear but you had to have been a little afraid, especially at first and you felt attracted to that danger and so did every other man there. Even Katherine if she would admit felt something, probably not attraction in a sexual way but if you asked her she would admit to being stoked because of it."

Michael nodded. "I remember a study once. Something stupid Gabriel sort of shoved at me about how if you wanted to increase the chances of a woman having sex with you take her to a scary movie and not a romantic one. But that is almost exactly what you are saying. That adrenaline from fear, even artificial fear, can lead to the urge to mate. Make it stronger almost to the point of overriding everything else."

I nodded. "And are you any different? And that is also why the protectors are more prone to it than other men. How often do they get afraid? How many people or things could really threaten them? I can and I do, every time I spar with one of them they know beyond a doubt now that I could kill them or injury them really bad. Can you imagine how stimulating that is to them? But being men they usually push that stimulation into what they know best, sex. Men think about sex almost 24/7. Women do too but not in the same way, I usually focus on just one but for a single man of which all our new protectors are they wouldn't focus on any one woman but any and all. I think they are all sort of like Anthony used to be and I am just a very convenient and rather obvious target, especially right now."

"I know from talking to Joshua, Gabriel and Peter that the first few months after you change it is even harder on them than most of us. They grow, get strong and fast. Some walk into door jambs and fall over their own feet because they aren't used to their own bodies and I know from man talk it isn't just their feet and hands that grow either." Michael said with a chuckle.

"My, my, no wonder Alicia is such a happy little camper." I snickered. It had been very obvious to me for a long time that Peter had nothing to be ashamed in the romance department. My room back home was right across the hall and even without that I heard almost everything that went on there anyway. Of course Alicia was a very eager mate and her small size didn't change the fact she was more than a match for Peter in every way.

"Yeah and why most of Alison's friends are protectors too." Michael chuckled. "She has always been a very sexual creature. Maybe in part to her calling, maybe not but I did notice that a lot of her friends are indeed protectors. They seem to stay single more than most of us do anyway. As you say it might be because they are worried about hurting a woman but when they know that one is capable of being with them, that know how to deal with their greater strength then yes they would be attracted to that, I know I would be if in their shoes."

Michael had finally calmed down some and was back to being the reasonable man I was used to dealing with. I had known that all of this had been just as much of a strain on him as it had been on me. How could it not be? Again I had to ask myself for the umpteenth time why? Why had this happened and who had done it?

Everybody that I knew here was a friend or I had thought they were until now. I had people like Charles and few other protectors that were questionable but they were more in your face aggressive and I didn't think could get this sneaky. This was down right dirty pool playing. Whoever did this, if they knew me well, hadn't been trying to kill me. Or at least I didn't think so. I was a protector and that meant I would have healed from that arrow unless it hit my heart or something else really important. I'm not sure even a strike to my liver or kidneys would kill me. That type of wound had been terminal for a few protectors over the years I had learned and again some had survived. It very much depended on how good their personal healing ability was and just like everything else about us no two of us healed the same rate or the same way.

So that meant I didn't go outside without somebody being with me. That made me pretty grumpy. I hadn't gone gallivanting all over the place before but now that I couldn't it made me chafe to do. Could I possibly get any more juvenile?

I smiled at that and Michael was curious about what had sparked my humor. "What has tickled your funny bone all of sudden?" He asked smiling too.

"Just realizing I can be just as stupidly irrational as our new protectors can be. Now that I'm not supposed to go outside it's all I can think about. I'm going to have to find a lot more things to keep me busy than before."

Michael sort laughed at that. "Well I do have a suggestion or two." I knew what his suggestions were going to be and didn't mind that type of very enjoyable distraction.

We didn't come out of our room for anything until dinnertime. Sue was so happy to see me she almost floored me with her hug. "Girl you scared me." She fussed.

I didn't remember her being in the medical section when I had my mental meltdown, well actually I don't really remember much of anybody. And she hadn't been by to see me when I had been down there during my observation period either. Now that I thought about it I had never seen her in any other part of the complex than the kitchen and housing. From just the way she sort of breathed through her nose when some of the medical personnel came through the food line I don't think she liked them much.

Paul wasn't the most popular person around and for some reason I had a feeling that they had butted heads a few times. Was I going to dig that up? Oh you bet I was but not now. I had enough to try and navigate through at the present. Their issue had been quietly stewing for a while or at least that was my impression. I couldn't see where it would hurt to have it stew a little longer. Funny how those things you don't think are that important, that couldn't possibly blow up in your face are the exact ones that do.

For right now all I was thinking about was food. I had my meals delivered to me while I had been in medical but eating hadn't been a huge draw for me. Now it was as the happy atmosphere of all the people I hadn't even known I missed was there to calm my very frazzled nerves.

I was beyond happy to be surrounded by people I knew and even some that I had grown to love. Anthony was all hugs and smiles as he sat down by my side. I wanted to apologize for hurting him but one look on his face and I knew how that conversation would go so I didn't bother. Shoving him with my shoulder and blowing him a kiss was all that was needed as he shoved me right back. He didn't hold grudges well to start with and with me, well I think I could have pulled his ears off and he wouldn't have cared.

But as dinner was eaten a lot of people stopped by to say they were happy to see me. That most had been worried about me. I felt things might get back to normal faster than I had thought. We still had to find out who it was that had shot me and why. There was a bigger more important issue sort of glaring me in the face at the moment. Charles was not a happy camper and a few of his fellow protectors were of the same attitude.

Why? Was it just that I had been such a terror that their fear had changed to anger. Michael had said that a lot of them had been more than a little attracted to me and we both knew that lust and passion could turn to anger and hate very easily. Was that their problem? Well some things I could do something about and others I couldn't and wouldn't. Even if I was still single I wasn't the type to go banging the entire team just to keep them happy.

Protectors were big boys and should learn to deal with upsetting things just like the rest of us did. Maybe because they had changed so much some of them didn't think the rules applied to them like it did for everybody else. They stayed pretty much together and even though rarely rude I could tell that some of the older ones sort of looked down their noses at the more normal of us. That had been part of the problem when Charles had gone after Anthony. I don't think that Charles really thought he would get into any trouble for anything he did.

Those same guys were in for very rude awakenings when they hit the real world and found out the medical people they sort of knew and presently looked down their noses at were actually higher in rank than they were. Just because they would probably never need the help of those same medical people didn't change the way our world was structured.

Charles and crew needed to learn they weren't the perfect specimens of Resurrected maleness they seemed to think they were. They also needed to learn to work together better. A few of them were not the typical alpha males that Charles was and they were doing better in my opinion in learning the subtleties that came with being a protector. But they were also catching a lot of ribbing from those same guys that they were weak or girly. All those things I had heard on more than one occasion down in the training room.

Charles hadn't even tried to keep his voice down last week when he had busted on the newest protector recruit Bruce. I liked Bruce because he tried to see more into what was being asked of him than just the brute force stuff. Recognizing that there was an easier way of doing things than figuratively taking a hammer to things when a press of a finger would work better.

I had an idea of how to teach a few of our more aggressive guys that they weren't all that a bag of chips. It may press a few buttons because I didn't think Charles was all that fond of dark and closed in places. I needed to talk to Joshua and find out how everybody had been killed when they changed. What was it that would probably trigger unconscious results when shoved in their face unexpectedly? I had found that was the easiest way to get a person to release all their fears, everything just came pouring out without them thinking and they would turn to a sympathetic ear then when they wouldn't any other time.

As I focused and listened to all the conversations across the room I heard my name called out pretty loudly. "Maggie you okay?" Katherine was asking. Maybe this wasn't the first time that she had said something to me and I hadn't answered.

I smiled at her. "Sure, sure. Just thinking that's all." And that had been the honest truth but now my mind had switched to my husband. Michael had been pretty good at letting me know when somebody had said something to me and I had missed it and this time he hadn't. Why? When I looked across the table his eyes were totally unfocused as if he too was lost in thought.

My hand caressed his. He looked into my eyes and his wasn't worried, happy or anything I had expected. They were sad and had a good amount of fear there too. His blue eyes had always been very expressive and I had been able to tell exactly what he was thinking a lot of the time. Tonight his emotions were not what I had thought they would be. Mostly happy to have me back whole and sane but a little worried because we didn't know who my attacker was or why.

But that wasn't what I was seeing and it wasn't what I getting through our heart spark, now I would have to find out why. We left as soon as we could. Claiming fatigue that most people accepted easily. For those that either knew or suspected that I had a very high energy level they left it alone too. It would come out if we wanted to share and if it wasn't their asking wouldn't get any answers any way.

We barely closed the door before Michael had his arms wrapped around me as he all but dropped us both to the floor. He had never just collapsed like this before and I was more than frightened. I could feel his heart pounding both from where his body was sealed against mine but also through my crystal as it all but hummed with emotional energy.

I couldn't even get any questions out. Michael was almost hysterical, mumbling and crying in my arms. Having no idea what had caused this I was sort of lost as to what to do. I guess this time I was the confused partner when emotional outbursts where what men usually complained about.

Finally I just picked him up in my arms and carried him to the bed. I was strong and if it surprised him he didn't show it. Cradling up against me I let him have a release as I tried to figure out what was the reason behind all this. His heart calmed and so did mine and I began to get an idea of what it was that had started all this.

The first thing that Michael wanted to do was love me. He wanted to reconfirm how we felt about each other. With all that had happened and all that he had overheard and experienced I understood it completely. But worry would have been there too. Something he had not expressed and now he was.

His crystal must have gone just as nuts as mine had a few minutes ago and I knew how terrifying it was when you realized that your bond partner was in danger and he had no idea where I was or what had happened. What feelings had he gotten through our shared heart spark? How bad had it been? He had totally downplayed how he had found me because as of this moment the only two people here that knew about our little crystal trick was Anthony and Joshua and now we were even more prone to keeping our extra abilities secret than we had before.

During all this I that I had gone totally insane and I was just really glad that Michael hadn't gone down that drugged induced rabbit hole with me. Having both of us in that condition wouldn't have been just double the trouble it would have shot it out the park.

Nobody would have been able to control me and I would have taken Michael with me in my drug-induced delusions. They may have actually had to kill us to keep us from harming others, both resurrected and Nohus because I would have stopped at nothing to get away from what my crazy brain thought of was a threat.

After many worried minutes Michael calmed down. His shuttering sobs stopped but the tight grip he had around me didn't loosen. I felt his heart slow even further and knew that he had cried himself into an exhausted state.

Part of me wanted and needed to stay with him. He hadn't really told me why he had reacted like he did but I was pretty sure I knew the reason. But there was a bigger part that couldn't be still for one more second. I had to do something. All the lovemaking had taken the nerve rattling edge off for a while but it was back again and it wouldn't let me just stay put.

I left Michael a very long and absolutely horribly handwritten note, telling him I wanted so much to stay with him but I couldn't. He would know why and hopefully he wouldn't be too mad at me for abandoning him.

When I left I still wasn't sure what I wanted to do. I had so many things running around my brain and it was just as energized as my body was. The pools were empty and since this was now a Friday night even the computer guys were not working. Everybody in the whole place was sound asleep except me.

I had to run but I didn't want to go down to the maintenance section. The outside called to me like a siren's song. I had stopped just inside of the lobby with my hands pressed against the glass door like a child looking at the candy in a store.

"Why not?" PIB's voice came to me. I was so shocked that he would tell me to do something that was dangerous. Or was it really? True I had been shot outside but he had warned me I just hadn't reacted fast enough. "Hamper you." He said again and that gave me a reason for my attack. I had never thought that my attack had been an attempt to kill me. But what if had been designed to cause fear. Have me and everyone else so worried that I was no longer able to function. Part of an infiltrator was sort of a solo thing. What if I couldn't or wouldn't do that any more?

I unlocked the door and took off at a dead run. Down the mountain road that Michael had driven us up several weeks ago. My feet were pounding a steady rhythm into the dirt and then later the pavement as I discovered the one place in my rocky home that I could run without falling off a cliff. Finally that pinging energy started to drain away. I still had plenty but now I might actually be able to keep from going crazy for a day or two. I might actually be happy with just combat practice and lovemaking. What in the hell was I going to do when winter came through? Maybe cross-country skiing might be an option. But something in the back of my brain told me I was going to have enough to keep me busy real soon. When the back part of your brain gives you messages you really needed to listen. Too bad the back part of my brain wasn't all that much better at forecasting the future in detail than the rest of me.

# Chapter 7

## REACHING OUT

Joshua had been all for my ideas. It was so much outside the box it wasn't funny but he thought it would work to shake the older protector trainees out of their idea that they were perfect and didn't need to learn any more. Joshua had held them back for a reason. He had told them it was because nobody had an opening at the moment but he had confided in Michael and I that it wasn't true. We had several openings.

Now that Joshua had sort of come on board he was telling me and Michael things that I hadn't known, that nobody but either Anthony or a computer detective like Daniel would have found. There were several protectors, mostly newer ones that had abandoned their charges and resigned. No warning, no reason but we had at least six in the last year to do just that. It had worried Joshua to no end as he was confronted with the fact that his training methods were just not enough to get the recruits up to the speed and abilities they needed. There were too many holes in their emotional make up. Again, there it was. The problem with people not being emotional healthy and that lead to all sorts of issues, some minor and others huge.

So what was my crazy idea? Well I wasn't about to take these unstable people out on a hike. That nutty, I wasn't. It might have been one of those that I was trying to help that had actually shot me. Was that fact lost on anyone? Not a bit. So we all agreed that my experiment would be done in the relative safety of the center.

Charles had been killed in a cave in at a mine in West Virginia. According to what the media and what little remained of his family he was the sole survivor of very bad accident. There had been four others that hadn't been so lucky. I could understand his issues. Men he worked with, men he had depended on and that had depended on him had died while he was still alive. Greatly changed from what he had been and that made the issue even worse. He was more than torn. Part of him must see himself as something wonderful to warrant this change while at the same time he had the typical survivors' guilt.

On the morning of my experiment Joshua drug Charles and Bruce out of bed at o'dark thirty with out any warning. Barely awake, neither was sure what was going on as they both showed up at the maintenance level. They were very surprised to see me waiting for them. I could hear the spike in Charles's heart rate and he must have thought for sure this was payback time. Even though I could see the almost cocky arrogance come across his face again it did little to squash the fear his heart was telling me he had.

I smiled a rather nasty smile. One of those that was not a happy one at all but pissed as hell. Now even Bruce was apprehensive as I saw him swallow nervously.

"Today is the first day of the rest of your life." I started. I wanted them both as scared as possible, to be totally out of their element with no clue what was really going to happen. "This is a special training session that I have made up just for you."

"What training?" Charles said. He was starting to sound a little worried now. "You aren't in charge of my training." He stated belligerently.

"Today she is." Joshua answered. "You haven't been doing as well as you should." He admitted and it sounded like he was really disappointed with everybody. "Now Gabriella is going to test you and if we find you less than what we think you should be… Well let's just say we might have a reason for a new urn or two to be in that mausoleum she has gotten all cleaned up."

Charles' eyes almost bugged out of his head at that little piece of news. Nobody had ever said what happened to a protector that failed to pass his classes. It had never been considered before. I knew of course but I wasn't about to tell either one of my test subjects that they were just held back until they got up to speed or were finally given an assignment with a very qualified protector and shown what was expected of a real honest to goodness protector that knew what he was doing. But they would also have very little if any responsibilities until they had improved. Nobody ever died because they were slow. Was I going to make them feel better by telling them that? No way

Joshua smiled a very wicked smile. For somebody that didn't do much acting he was really getting into the spirit, maybe because he too know how much was riding on this. "There have been a few times over the years that a protector trainee has not developed and had turned into menace instead. I am not about to turn somebody like you loose to hurt others. But Gabriella wanted one last chance for you Charles and she wanted a new guy that will be around for a while so that he can tell others what happened if things go south just what is at stake."

Nobody said anything. The silence was like a black hole sucking the air right out as both of them barely drew a breath.

"Follow me." I said. They did and for once Charles didn't have a cocky thing to say. We wound around and up and down the maintenance corridors. By now I knew them really well but other than a few tech people and Tim nobody came down here much and I thought that this was the first time either one of them had been here before.

We finally got to where I wanted to start the experiment and I told them what was going to happen. "This is the deal. Your whole reason for being is to keep your charges safe. That is your job. If you can't do that then you have no reason for being around. You may not like those that you are to protect and they may not like you, but that is irrelevant."

At this point Charles was tired of being lectured. He was tired of me being in his face about all his shortcomings, probably just as much as I was about him being in mine for exactly the same reasons. Oh, we were both aware of them how could we not be. So stage one was complete. We had the pot of water with all the little metal balls bouncing, now it was time to turn the temperature to the boiling point.

I didn't have to say it loud. Tim would be down at the entrance to the maintenance section standing right beside Joshua by now. "Kill it." And the lights went out and just as I had figured, Charles wigged.

The pitch-blackness didn't even let me see anything. Still I could tell just exactly where my two protectors were. I was better-equipped sense wise than either of them but there were two other things that made me better able to handle the situation we were in.

One, Anthony had been really good at training me in all sorts of ways that most people didn't think of. I had continued that training after my trip through the warehouse in Mobile when I realized there were times when you sight could tell you nothing but your ears and nose sure could. Those senses told you different things than what your eyes did. Things you would miss if you focused and used only one ability.

Two, I had known what was going to happen and had prepared myself for it. Was that cheating? Absolutely. But an instructor should know the conditions and situation of any test they were involved in and I had stepped into that role now.

Charles' heart rate went right through the roof and Bruce's wasn't too far behind. But over the next few seconds things changed. Bruce's started to calm down. He had been startled but was realizing that even though it was unexpected that he was in no real danger here.

On the other hand Charles had no such reaction. His heart rate and breath had continued to climb and he would soon pass out from sheer terror. Now was the time that was so pivotal. He had to see that he wasn't alone but he also had to be willing to reach out and ask for help. Help he would seek at no other time than this one.

When something terrifies you beyond reasoning is when you are at your most vulnerable. When things will change because there is no other choice.

"Charles." I said softly. Moving closer to him, I prepared myself in case he attacked out anger or fear. But he didn't he had dropped down on the floor and was huddled in as small a ball as possible.

My hand went and stroked his massive shoulder and he flinched but didn't pull away. "It's all right to be afraid." I continued gently. "We all have fears but also need to both face them and ask for help when we are confronted with something we know we cannot deal with."

"Oh God it is so dark here." He moaned. At least he was talking and hadn't gone all catatonic. That had worried me. I pulled him to me with both arms. At first he resisted but only at first. He needed to feel love and compassion. I think this was the one thing that had been missing in his life for a very long time, maybe even longer than his transition. Not everyone had the happy life I had been blessed with before I died and came back.

"And I am right here Charles. Bruce and I are both right here." I said as I held him. Bruce couldn't see any better than the rest but he had been listening to our murmured conversation and had found us in the dark. He was smart and thought things through well. Now he was kneeling beside me but was probably unsure just what was needed or what I wanted.

"What can I do?" He asked. Bruce was my type of protector. Even relatively untrained and unskilled, he had the mental and emotional skills needed to be a really good protector. He would be the nurturing type that was so needed, especially in the smaller houses when you only had one or two to keep a family whole and happy. He was loyal and dedicated and compassionate, all those things that Charles was not.

I couldn't ask Charles to be what he wasn't. That was like Phillip asking me to be nice and complaint. I never expected Charles to be that type of person. But he had to be aware of his own shortcomings. He was and he wasn't. He knew he had them. They had been pointed out enough from many people but he wouldn't really admit to them and he wouldn't ask for help. That was what needed to change.

"Nothing yet." I answered Bruce. "We are going to sit here and talk for a bit. We are going to close our eyes and listen to each other and forget all about where we are and what is around us and we are all going to know that we are not alone."

Charles was a little calmer but still wired. "What are we going to talk about? I just want to get out here." He said growling. Now he would get angry and I was ready for that.

"We can't yet."

"What are we waiting for? Tell them to turn the lights back on." He asked but it didn't sound quit as fearful and was heading towards pissed off fast.

"Not yet. And besides, I can't, everybody went to breakfast. They won't be back for a few hours at best."

That sent two stomachs snarling awake so much it was an audible reaction, which made me smile. One thing about protectors, they had one hell of an appetite. "I'm hungry. Food why did you mention food." Bruce fussed. He was just out of his growth spurt and was still getting used to his bigger size and his body was very much adding the muscle that his calling required therefore he ate like horse and then some.

"And you won't starve for missing breakfast. Right now your brother needs your help." I said sounding a little haughty. "I went without food for over a week, believe me a few hours might be annoying but nothing a double serving of lunch won't fix."

Bruce sort of flopped down right beside me, like a very large disgruntled child. He had been a full grown man before he was changed but now all the things he had been through had thrown him back into an almost adolescent type mentality sometimes. I understood that. He had been at the pinnacle of his life. 31 years old and unlike most protectors he hadn't been a cop or a soldier. Bruce had been a happily single guy working in the construction industry until an accident ended his life, sort of.

"So what are we talking about?" Bruce asked. It didn't take him long to get over his pique. His empty stomach now forgotten he was trying to get into whatever training this was. I noticed that about Bruce, no matter what it was he would give it a go, no matter if it were something he had never tried before, which right now was almost everything. I thought he would be a good one to augment Katherine and Joshua but it was probably too early to make that recommendation and it wasn't my decision anyway.

"Oh little of this and that." I answered trying to give both of the men the chance to say whatever was on their minds. "Anything you want to get off your chest maybe. Any questions you might have for each other or me. Then we can get into more serious stuff if we want or not."

"So this really isn't a dead man test is it?" Charles asked with a hiss.

"For you it is." I answered quickly. "This is the one thing that will determine how the rest of your life goes." He had to have heard the sincerity in my words because they were true. This was the last thing that Joshua was going to do before he turned Charles loose. By next week, maybe even tomorrow he would be gone to Chicago and the big house and the two waiting senior protectors that would take him under wing knowing full well what a loaded pistol he might turn out to be. But they needed help so desperately there. They had even lost a few protectors in the last two years. The violence and crime had gotten so bad there as it had in a lot of the big cities and even some of the smaller ones. Desperate people did stupid things and unfortunately our people always seemed to be put in the cross hairs. It was sort of in the job description of helping people to be in vulnerable positions. That was one of the reason we had protectors to start with. But things were getting hairy out there in the real world. A lot worse I was coming to find out than even I had guessed.

My little world before this hadn't really been touched much by all the bad things in this world. I had been sort of sheltered I was finding out and now thanks to my very improved hearing and my normal nosey ways I was getting my eyes opened a lot. There were so many things our people were being thrown into that they hadn't before or at least not to this extant. It was as if the whole world was being stretched and stretched like a rubber band until something broke.

The Resurrected were trying. We were busting our ass's trying but not getting anywhere and again I had to ask myself why. Why weren't they're more of us? Was it just that our ranks were depleted because so many had left? True there had been several deaths over the last decade. Very significant ones like a lot of emotional empaths and all but three of our telepaths. I think the only reason Stephan had survived all this was because he had been around a long time and he was near Phillip a lot and that guy watched out for his skin like it was a precious metal. And Stephan wasn't a true telepath either. He was a truth seeker not a mind reader and that may have been one of the things that had saved him.

I was seeing more and more that there was something going on and now I wasn't the only one. My questions had started others asking questions. Daniel had his nose to computer terminal almost nonstop for the last week. When I asked he barely answered. Something that was unusual for him because he was usually very talkative about what he was doing. Now nothing, like he was almost afraid of what he was finding. Even his other buddies on the graveyard shift didn't understand it because they were eyeing him up for a straight jacket according to Simon the other day at breakfast.

Shelving all those worries I made my mind come back to the here and now. Charles had calmed down some and was now leaning up against me and had my arms pulled around him like I was almost a blanket. He wasn't shaking anymore and seemed content to sit here in the dark and let me hold him.

"So what's going on in all those heads of yours?" I asked with an almost giggle. "I know you have questions about things. Who wouldn't? You are getting a free shot that most never get. Don't waste it."

If I wanted Charles and Bruce to open up about themselves and their problems I knew I had to go first. Be willing to answer things that hadn't been answered before. I would tell them what I could but there were some things that I couldn't and wouldn't reveal to anyone. I wouldn't lie but I didn't have to tell the whole truth either. Now I knew how a politician must feel, I thought to myself with silent chuckle. Well Anthony was getting more right by the hour. I was learning there were a lot of things to this job of mine that I never thought I would be asked to do. Holding hands or in this case bodies and training people that could bench press a Volvo had never in my wildest dreams been something I had thought I would be doing.

Bruce was first. He had a natural curiosity that was something most of the older members had lost. I hoped he kept it forever because it was bad when you stopped asking, why, what, when and more importantly why not.

"How do you grow you claws?" Well that wasn't one that I had expected but being that I was the only one to ever have that ability I could understand why it was a constant source of speculation from all of my sparing buddies. They had seen them a few times when I worked with Joshua and Katherine on something to see just how sharp, strong and resilient they were. The R&D guys weren't the only ones that were fascinated with them. My master protector and his protégé were too.

"I don't really know." I answered honestly but this got a snort from Charles like he thought I was holding back. "Really I don't. I have been asked that a bunch and all I can really say is that it is a like asking a muscle to move or when you flex your foot maybe. You think about it and it happens. Then when I don't need them any more I think go away and they fall off." That was the complete and honest truth and I felt pretty good that I could answer Bruce without trying to mince words.

"They are really something scary." Bruce admitted. "I wouldn't want you mad at me. Not ever, no matter how good I get I would never want to tangle with you and have you seriously try and take me out. You are as fast as Joshua is and he knows it too."

I laughed a little. "No I'm not." I denied. "He's the best." I knew if push came to shove I would have more than my hands full with Joshua. He was like Bruce Lee on steroids. Tall, lean lanky muscle that was a thousand times faster than any snake I had ever seen. In video even slowed down you could never really see Bruce Lee move and Joshua was like that but over 7 feet tall and had probably two lifetimes of experience to go along with it.

"Haven't you noticed that he won't spar with you anymore." Charles said. He was talking and his heart rate was almost normal now. Wondering if it was my presence or him closing his eyes but either way he was getting over his fear of the dark and closed spaces that had terrified just a few minutes ago. "Bruce is right and yet not. Joshua isn't afraid of you but he doesn't want to lose that image he has of being the best by having you knock him down a peg or two."

"Well I don't think I could." I said sighing. "I'm good and quick but he hasn't been around this long to be intimated by anyone. He should be looked at with a little awe shouldn't he? Because he has survived this long and knows so much and above all that he is willing to share what he knows. How many other people horde their knowledge like it was a precious treasure failing to realize that the treasure is worthless unless it is shared and experienced by as many as possible."

Bruce liked that and I could almost feel him smile from where he was sitting right beside me. Now it was Charles' turn as I felt him pull away from me a little.

"Why are you doing this?" That question was a lot more insightful than I had thought I would get out of him. I could deliberately misinterpret that question if I had a mind to be annoying but we both knew what why he was referring to.

"Because I hate waste." I answered simply. "You have so much potential, more maybe than even what your very lauded ego could come up with but you keep shooting yourself in the foot. You don't let your mind think things through and react from ego and emotion."

"But don't we have to react fast to keep somebody from getting hurt?" He snapped proving my point totally.

"Sometimes, but not most. On the street yes of course you have to be on high alert and react in a second but in the safety of family shouldn't you take that extra few seconds to try and see into things more. Ask why somebody did what they did or what might happen if you did what you were thinking about doing. How many of you're brothers and sisters would be hurt emotional by your words or actions?"

"I'm an only child." Charles snorted.

"Not any more you aren't." Bruce laughed. "I came from a real small family too. Just a sister that I haven't seen in years and my Mom can't stand the sight of me. When I woke up and then got sent here it was like I had this huge extended family I never knew I had. Everything felt just so right. Like I knew every face here without ever seeing them before."

"I don't even like most of the people here." Charles growled. "They are all just a bunch a complaining weaklings. So isolated here up in their little mountain retreat that they have no idea what is going on anywhere else. Other than that little outing we went on some of these people haven't been out of this building in months maybe years."

"And do you think that makes them happy? To be stuck in a rut. They have a reason maybe to complain don't they? Have any of them asked to be reassigned and been denied because they have been deemed too important to leave?" I shot back. "Have you tried to talk to any of the people that have been here a long time other than Joshua and Katherine? Found out why they are still here, whether it is something they want or not and if it is why they want to be here."

"No, I'm here to train not to be everybody's best friend." Charles answered and it was the typical answer I had sort of expected him to give.

"Not all training is in combat and protection Charles." I told him. "Protectors are more than just bodyguards you know. An internal problem can hurt a family unit more than any mugger with a gun could. Granted that may not be something you will ever be good at. Some people just aren't the touchy feely types but you need to be aware that it is a shortcoming and not look down your nose at others in your family that aren't what you are."

Bruce knew where I was going with this too. "I hate guns. Would never really want to train in how to use them but I understand that for some it is a total fascination. Like you and a few of the other guys that have been here a while that are down at the shooting range all the time. You get off on it and all I want to do is plug my ears and get away. But I also understand that sometimes having a gun or knife is what is needed to get the job done I just don't want to be the one to do it. I am very happy to leave that up to you."

I heard a giant growl from his stomach about that time. "Time for food maybe." I said with a chuckle.

"How, nobody has turned the lights back on?" He asked confused.

"And do you really need to see to find your way around?" I answered back throwing that exercise out for him to consider. Standing up and pulling on both their hands they may have been surprised that I knew exactly where they both were without any light at all.

"How can you find your way out of here without seeing a damned thing?" Charles asked. He wasn't mad for a change he was curious and maybe hoping I would fall on my ass trying to do something he didn't think could be done.

"Oh I'm not going to get us out of here you two are."

"No way." Charles shot back annoyed.

"Yes way. Think about it Charles. You can't see. What else have you got to work with? When you are confronted with something you don't have the answer for always think about alternatives. Look outside of the box and just remember sometimes when you hear hoof beats it really is a zebra and not a horse. Don't be afraid of taking a chance if you know that the normal answer isn't a very good one. I'm smaller than any protector and even most of the normal men here but I still hold my own because I do the unexpected." I knew that Charles was remembering the time Michael and I had bested him and his teammate during combat practice because we had done what nobody thought we would do, change opponents in the middle of the fight. So many things he had seen me do that were not what others did and everybody here knew I wasn't worried if it didn't turn out perfect. If I fell on my face I was okay with that too. You learned more about yourself and others when things went wrong than those that didn't.

"Well touch won't help." Bruce said. "All the walls feel the same, smooth except for when you hit a door and I didn't think to count how many doorways and corners we went by to get here."

Everybody just stopped talking at that point until Charles pointed out what I had already known. "The machinery down here just sort echoes everywhere I can't make out any differences in where it is coming from. It even feels like the constant droning is coming from the floors."

"So what does that leave you?"

"Smell." They both answered at the same time and heard them both inhale deeply.

"I smell oil and gasoline, metal, lots and lots of metal." Bruce said. But Charles had been around a lot longer and he had developed a lot of his senses that the new recruit hadn't yet and maybe never would. We were all different with different talents and abilities. I was noticing some things though. The best fighters also had the better sense of smell or at least that was my conclusion. Why? Maybe it helped to focus better; maybe it was something closer to what Michael had thought right after my little problem with a certain arrow. Maybe we picked up changes in smells like a shark did when it zoomed in on an injured fish? But for some I don't think it was a conscious ability, more something you did without even realizing you did it. I wasn't a R&D person but I knew my own abilities better than anyone and I knew that I could follow a person around a room, hall or building and tell you where they had lingered and when they speed up and if I knew them well enough I could even tell if they had been stressed by something because of how the sour smell of sweat changed the odor they left behind.

"Charles what do you think?" I asked.

"I think I can follow the way we came in here and get us back out. That's what I think." He said sounding more confident than I had heard him all morning. It wasn't cocky it was a realization that he could do something very few of us, even protectors could do."

"Do it." I said placing my hand on his shoulder and taking Bruce's and putting it on mine. We followed our combined scent and as soon as we came to a corner Charles hit a block that confused him for a minute until I explained what was the problem. "I doubled back a few times and crossed over the same corridors more than once." I felt him nod as he processed that and then took the route that I knew would get us back to main door the quickest. It wasn't that far really but they didn't know that when the lights had gone out. Now we walked slowly, using our hands against the wall as a way to judge where we were and were we were going.

It wasn't but a few minutes until I felt Charles run face first into the door and give a deep yip type sound that said he had smacked his nose flat into it. He had been steadily growing more confident and that made him get faster and a little reckless. I couldn't stop the little chuckle that escaped and didn't really try.

"Found something there?" I asked as I tried to not really laugh too much.

"Yeah the door's closed." He grumbled. "Who closed the freaking door?"

"Probably Joshua to keep us from hearing anything that would help us get back here." That hadn't really been part of the plan but I wasn't that surprised by it either. There was something else that would surprise my trainees. Charles yanked the door open and on the other side Joshua, Katherine and Tim were waiting and to my surprise so was my husband. I had known he was near but had been sort of focused on something besides him and didn't realize he was so close. I smiled and he returned it and I felt the nervousness he had tried to control fade quickly.

What we had done today had been a little dangerous but not that much but when you played with deadly things the unexpected happened. Charles was deadly of that nobody had any doubts. Now I could confirm what Joshua already suspected. Charles would be a decent protector especially in really dangerous situations but probably should have a chaperone for a bit. Until he saw how things in the real world worked. He wouldn't hesitate to step in front of danger not just because it was expected but also because he would relish the opportunity to beat the snot out of somebody.

Charles was more than capable in a lot of areas and I thought he would be pretty good in the bodyguard and escort type roles that a lot of our medical people needed in a very dangerous city like Chicago. Working in hospitals and clinics exposed our medicals to drug users and other desperate type people that had no morals about killing to get what they wanted.

He would also be a decent tracker if there was a need for it and now I thought he would jump at the chance to try things that would stretch his abilities in ways he may not have before. The protector trainee that had been a thorn in my side since I got here almost two months ago had grown up enough to be given what I called a journeyman assignment. Where he would go and learn in the real world and grow and hopefully become everything the Powers That Be had hoped he would when he was returned to this world.

I got a little misty eyed thinking I would no longer have my devil's advocate around anymore to point out all my shortcomings. As annoying, as he was Charles was probably somebody that I had needed to run into and I would miss him for making me always answer questions especially when I didn't want to. Now we would go and have a meeting and talk about what we found out. Charles would be there but Bruce wouldn't. The reason for that is Charles would probably never been seen by his fellow trainees here again. We wanted a little mystery to surround this trail by fire that would be different for every trainee that was sort of graduating.

Joshua and I had discussed this a lot. He agreed that we had no final exam before and that one was really needed. From now on, each trainee would have to face the one thing that they feared the most and also have to help another very young trainee survive the same thing. Teamwork was going to be pushed now more than it had been before. Our protectors were all big strong guys but out there even one really strong man sometimes wasn't enough. It was the last thing that Joshua could do to give them and their charges the best hope for survival. All touchy feely set aside, that was a protector's primary job. Keep us alive. Everything else, although needed and sometimes very important was extra and we all knew it.

Things were spiraling quickly. We all knew that too. To be happy was important, to be satisfied with what you were doing equally so but it all made no difference if you were dead. Dead in body, dead in spirit or soul, any of that can kill you. I felt like I was trying to paddle a boat up a waterfall. There was just so much and sometimes I just wanted to scream or cry at how much there was still to do. Michael and I had changed things. In some ways a lot and some not so much but there was a thousand times more left to do and I was running out of time. Nobody knew it but the two of us so nobody else could understand the almost frantic spin I was starting to display. Two months had already passed by and I still had so much that needed changing and instead of the list growing smaller it was even bigger than when I started.

The meeting went better than anybody expected. Charles had caught on to a lot of things that nobody had thought he had. Away from the rest of the trainees he didn't have to put on airs of being the oldest and most experienced. Didn't have to act all cocky to keep up his reputation. I really hated alpha male posturing and that had been the vast majority of what had caused Charles to act up. He had been expected to.

Now as we left the second floor conference room I was downright happy. That was until I hit the lunchroom and the complete yelling match that greeted us at the door. Just when we had one problem solved another one came roaring up to smack us in the face.

I had never heard Sue raise her voice to anyone. She was usually very calm and didn't get all snarly especially since she had been getting recognition and help in the kitchen. She had been a downright giggly schoolgirl lately. Now she was anything but giggly as her and Paul were facing off in front a very shocked lunch crowd her face red with anger as she stood across the counter glaring at our Resident Chief of Medicine.

I knew that there was animosity between our chef and some of the medical people but I had no idea it was Paul that was at the top of her 'I don't like you' list. Here I thought this could wait until things had settled down. Stupid me. We had to get this quieted down because Paul was just now starting to salvage his reputation from what I had done to it and the last thing it or him needed was the dressing down I could see Sue gearing up for.

Her words were coming out clipped and angry as an accent she must have worked long and hard to get rid of came out very strong. I had been right English and man was she pissed off.

"How can you possibly make such a selfish request?" She snarled at Paul across the counter that separated the prep area from the rest of the dinning hall. "She just got in last night."

"This isn't any of your business." Paul snapped back. "I'm in charge of running this facility not you. All you do is cook."

That was so not the thing for Paul to say if he wanted to calm things down. His 'I'm in charge' attitude wasn't helping to defuse the problem. The 'don't question me' way of handling things wasn't something he wanted to dish out at the moment. Sometimes those in charge had to explain why they wanted something the way they did and since I was totally clueless about the entire situation maybe I could get them both to say what was their problem.

"Can it both of you." I shouted. Something I also rarely did. "If you have problems that is fine but not here and not now. You will both meet me in my room after lunch." I said like a parent to two misbehaving children. Well if you act like you are four and having a temper tantrum than maybe treating you like that would make you realize it.

They both looked at me with more than a little shock. I gathered from the stunned silence nobody had talked to either one of them like that before. It was all I could do not to giggle because that wouldn't have helped matters either. When I turned around I could see the sparkle in Michael's eye as he too found the entire situation more than just a little funny.

Thinking about the whole thing quickly I could understand why it was sort of funny. I hadn't been here but a few months. Had been a Resurrected less than a year and I had stepped into a situation like I was the one in authority when really I wasn't. As usual though nobody else was doing a thing about it and that shouting match would have gone from bad to worse until somebody either said or did something totally stupid.

Paul would have dug his heels in and gotten even more stubborn than usual. Sue would have launched into orbit because she was being belittled and nobody likes it when that happens. Joshua had been there and so had Tim and a lot of other folks that I knew were twice my age and experience level. Why hadn't somebody said something? Was it just that they didn't know what to say? Or did it go deeper than that? Wonderful, marvelous, just what we needed. We were just starting to get things running better and something had set all this off. Well fine I was going to find out what had started this but also why it had all gone off like it had.

Lunch was more than subdued. No big surprise there at all. There were a few new additions to the hall that I hadn't seen before. Two men and one woman had been added to our ranks. From the way everybody talked to them I knew they had been here before. Sue had mentioned something about a 'her' just getting in last night. Logic told me the pretty lean blonde woman with very tired eyes and the lingering smell of ash was the source of this part of the problem.

Listening into that conversation I found out her name was Elizabeth. Her and her two male companions had just made it back in from the ranges. They were actually housed here but spent most of the summer and more gone. That was when pyrotechs were the busiest. Out and about trying to contain all the wild fires that sprung up every year. Now I understood the tired look and that subtle smell that I could pick up even from here.

I would love to know how they did what they did and maybe sometime in the near future I would be able to find out but today wasn't really about the pretty Elizabeth but my very good friend and our pain in the butt chief doctor.

It didn't take long for my room to be filled with very unhappy people. Maybe this would have been better up in one of the conference rooms but I hadn't expected for Joshua to come following behind Paul and Sue as they entered my room. Those two were still acting like siblings that wanted to be anywhere but where the other was.

I had wanted a relaxed atmosphere to talk and air things out but it was certainly not starting out that way at all. "Okay I'm here." Paul snapped. Telling me he hadn't liked my heavy handiness.

Sue on the other hand was obviously thinking that since I was her buddy that I would be all on her side and that Paul's goose was cooked. Wrong. I wanted to find out what was wrong and resolve it, not just gang up on somebody. Paul usually had a reason for the stuff he did. He wasn't very good at expressing the why of it but there was logic even if it was sort of callous.

"First of all I don't want to ever have something like that happen in front of everybody else again." I snapped back. This wasn't in my authority but couldn't they see it would tear this place apart like a civil war. "If you have issues fine but be adult about it. Take it someplace private and yell all you want but not in the middle of the dining hall especially when all and sundry are there."

Surprise wasn't all that surprising when they both sort of looked at me in shock. They really didn't know what to say. So with that big lull I plunged ahead. Let us get to the rat killing as John Wayne said in McClintock.

"Why is it so important for Elizabeth to pull receptionist duty the day after she gets back from being gone for months?" I asked and Paul almost fell over his tongue. "Why does anybody have to do it to start with? I have seen how many visitors we get and I think that is a totally useless way to spend the day."

"We have always had somebody to greet people." Paul answered back. I could tell he was confused at what I said and had no idea how I knew what I shouldn't have by all rights known. I hadn't been at breakfast this morning, hadn't been close enough to hear much of anything that he and his cronies had been talking about during lunch, or so he had assumed. He had been wrong.

"And if we kept the doors locked but the keys accessible why wouldn't a buzzer and an announcement speaker that calls into the first floor office area be just as good. I can see staffing it when we know we have visitors coming but all the time is a very inefficient use of someone's time."

"We can't just eliminate that position." Paul pressed.

"Why not?" Michael asked, speaking up for the first time since everybody got here. I knew he had my back but only because I was right. He would argue with me if I wasn't but I had watched his reaction during this first part and I could tell he liked the idea totally. "I have been here more times than my wife but she is right on. Maybe before when we first set things up it made sense. We had a lot of people come up because they were curious but that faded decades ago. We don't even get the health department up here very often and they always warn us before they come. Deliveries come on a very routine basis and know to come to the loading dock so who else is there?"

"But Phillip wants to make sure it is manned all day. He wasn't happy when I changed it so that we didn't have anybody on the weekends." Paul stated.

Okay now we were getting down to the rat of the situation, Phillip and his outdated ways of doing things. "And don't you run this place?" I asked him. "Not Phillip. Yes he is council but he can't just override you if you have a logical reason for it. Wouldn't he need a majority vote of the council to overrule a house leader's decision?"

That got a few more eyebrows raised. "Yeah I've been studying how things are supposed to work and the council or at least our representative here in North America has been making a lot of decisions he really doesn't have the authority to make. Pushing people into doing things that aren't his to push. I thought at first when I came on board that he was sort of a tyrant but tyrants only get away with it if you let them."

"Paul." Joshua said in his deep baritone voice, the one he used when he was trying to get a trainee's attention because they did something really stupid. "You have let him talk you into too many things that aren't good, especially lately. They may seem small but put all together they aren't. Curtailing trips of personnel because of work demands he caused. The extra reports of all sorts of things for no reason he can justify just because he can, sending you off on research projects that produce nothing over and over again. When are you going to stop it and get back to real work? Helping us and help the world. That is what we should be doing. How close were you to a preventive for aids five years ago? How close are you now? Still the same aren't you. Our blood may not help Nohus directly but you found ways to filter and adapt it that nobody else has."

Now I was surprised. A cure or at least prevention for aids would be a miracle and Paul had just let it slide. No wonder he was here and wanted every resource he could get, ones like me didn't come around every day. I felt a little bad for dragging me feet now. Here I had thought he was just a pain in the ass. Oh, he was but he had his reasons, big ones.

I could see the thought process almost like cogs in a machine as Paul thought quickly. "You are right, I have and Gabriella is right about the front desk too. Rachael could be used more down at the research center and anybody can answer the front door. So what if it takes a few minutes more? We don't like visitors anyway."

Well that solved that problem but not the reason all of this started anyway. Sue had been all over Paul because of Elizabeth. There was an emotional connection between those two that nobody could miss.

"And as far as our returned pyro's?" I asked. "Don't people coming in from weeks or months on the job deserve a little down time. Military people get leave for a few weeks when they return from being away from friends and family. Before they are expected to do anything more than get their head on straight. I mean don't they need some rest before they leave for the winter to help out down in like Australia or someplace like that?"

Confused silence ensued. What had I said that was wrong? Did our pyro just set out the southern droughts? I was starting to think so.

"We don't transfer people from one part of the world to the next unless the individual asks for a permanent one or something unusually happens, like a world war, at least not anymore." Michael said with a sad shake to his head.

"Excuse me?" I answered. That made no sense. We had so few people like Elizabeth and her fellows and I knew that some of the other talents were equally precious. Michael, himself had traveled all over the world training medicals. When had that stopped? Why would we hoard those gifts just for us? Weren't we supposed to be helping the entire world not just the North American part?

"Nobody sends their talents out anymore." Sue said. "I would give anything to use mine but there isn't a lot places for me to sniff out landmines and such. I thought about working with EOD but I would be pretty noticeable in a few short years. Most law enforcement that are into that are networked together, or so I am told. It would be pretty obvious that I didn't age."

"Well so what." I said sort of flabbergasted. I had no idea my friend had such an unusual talent. "Stephan and Phillip both have to fake aging, why not you. So every 40 years or so you have to go bury yourself for a bit, you would be at least using your talent for most of the time."

Sue blushed big time. "I guess I could but I came here with my mate. He was a pyro too and this is where they are stationed. I traveled with him sometimes but found it just easier to keep the home fire burning here. Nat didn't like me being in danger like that and if you don't have their gift it makes working the fire lines all that more perilous."

She had developed a really pained look. But she stopped talking suddenly and I knew why. She didn't want to talk about emotional things where so many people would hear her pain. Sue was easy going for the most part but she kept her private life to herself and I had never really taken the time to find out all about her past even if she had been willing to share it. What I got was mostly from intuition type leaps from small things she let slip. And the deeper the emotion the less likely a slip would happen.

I nodded my head at Michael and he knew what I wanted. The guys sort of disappeared out the door before Sue even noticed and we were alone. Now how to get her to tell me what had started all this? I had a few ideas and maybe if I guessed close enough it would get her to talk.

"Is that why you are so worried about Elizabeth? Nat's dead but he trained her or mentored her didn't he and you are afraid that something will happen to her too?" I asked trying to ferret out what this connection was.

"Yes." She said with a sigh and sort landed in a chair like a balloon that had suddenly lost all its air. "Actually Nat trained all of them."

I sat down beside her in the other chair. "Would you like to tell me what happened?" I asked gently. Losing a bond mate was almost impossibly painful to deal with. Some never recovered and most rarely found another to take the missing mate's place. There was just this huge aching hole that nobody else could fill. Almost as bad as an amputation and I guessed in a way it was an amputation of the heart and soul.

"He was serving in the war when I met him. Explosive sensitives and pyros get shoved into the same group a lot during a war. When things blow up fires get started. Nat and I worked together a lot. I would try and stop things from blowing as he turned the fires back. We kept many an ammo dump from going boom I can tell you." She said as she reminisced about the glory of days long gone, of working with the man that would become her bond mate and finding love and doing work that she was supposed to do.

"What happened to him?" I asked trying for all I was worth to not pry but needing to know. I couldn't help unless I understood things better. How had Nat died? From just the way things were said and not said it must have been rather recent. Within the last decade or so was my guess but with Sue being so damned close lipped about personal things it was really hard to tell.

"A fire got way out of control. Even a pyro can only do so much. Nat controlled fire by turning it back into itself so that it would burn out but if you have too much it is much more difficult." Sue said and it sounded like she was repeating something she had heard another say many times. A deeper voice seemed to emerge from her small frame. Usually she had a normal woman's voice but now it took on different inflections as if she was shadowing the ghost of her mate.

"Elizabeth was there as was Andrew and Jesse but even with all four of them together that big fire in Arizona was more than they could handle. Liz said they almost got it. She could feel it in her hands and then a sudden turn in the wind had it jump the lines almost like a living thing and it was on them in seconds. They lost so many that day, not just my Nat but a lot of smoke jumpers and firefighters too."

I remembered that fire or thought I knew the one she meant. Four years ago or was it five but I was right it hadn't been that long. Especially considering that she had been with her Nat for longer than I had been alive. I understood why she had stayed. It was where she still felt her Nat and could see what were essentially their kids when they came back from the fire lines. See that those he had trained and that he had most likely died saving. Feel better seeing first hand that they were safe and whole.

If Sue's Nat was like most Resurrected their personal safety was the lowest priority. Others were more important. Of course everybody had they're own way of looking at that but even stubborn and sometimes cold natured Paul had those tendencies. They just got a little warped at times. Why? I had no idea and at the moment didn't care.

So now what? I had as much of that story as I was probably going to get. Did it solve the issues of today? Not really. So change the subject and find out what had put a bug in her petticoat regarding Paul. There had to be something.

"Okay. I get that you were defending Elizabeth when she was to worn out to do it herself. But you have never pounced on anyone like that since I have been here. There have been plenty who deserved it just as much. Why Paul and why today in the middle of your own kitchen?"

I knew why the kitchen. That was her castle. Where she felt in charge. Besides how often did she ever leave it for long anyway?

"Because he's a git. Always pushing people around for no good reason other than he can. I'm surprised that Joshua is still friends with him at all. After all that has happened Paul is lucky to have his head still on his shoulders. But Joshua is right Phillip has been pushing us, all of us and for silly, stupid things. But it has been so gradual that I never really noticed until you came and starting pointing things out. Then it was like I was seeing a lot more that didn't set well."

"And since Phillip isn't here you snapped at the guy he left in charge." I nodded. That reaction was understandable but wrong. Paul was trying to change the way things worked some but he was like Phillip in that he wanted order and changes didn't usually come all neat and wrapped with a bow. Most of the time change sort brought a little chaos with it until the change was adapted to and the order of things reestablished.

Even my little scheme of voting on a menu twice a week had been a little chaotic at first but now two months later it was an established routine. The same people could be seen at sunrise in the ivory tower almost everyday and on the weekend there were more but at first it hadn't been accepted well.

The crafts were now so well established in everyone's lives that they had no clue how they had existed without them. I had seen so many of the women and even some of the men using the tower for meetings and such but just as much I had noticed an increase in visiting from room to room. The talk in the dining hall was a constant barrage of what everybody was doing and an exchange of ideas about anything and everything.

Poker night was once a month and the women had movie night and again it was like nobody knew why they hadn't done it before. Change happened and soon it was no longer change but routine.

But Phillip had routined everything into such rigidness that it was like being frozen. For the longest while nobody felt they could do other than what had been done. Now they knew better. Now they weren't afraid of stepping out and stepping up some. Oh did we have a ways to go? You bet, but zombie land was slowly waking up and even Paul was seeing the

benefits of it. He didn't exactly come out and say it to anyone but I would
get a small smile sometimes or a nod that let me know that he approved
of what he saw. And when he didn't understand something oddly weird
I did he would usually just shake his head slightly and walk away. Made
me think of a parent that was indulging a highly creative but totally odd
child maybe. I guess that sort of fit our relationship better than any other
description at the moment and it made me smile a bit.

"What's so funny?" Sue snapped. I had spaced for a minute as my
mind had reviewed everything and of course she hadn't been part of that
side trip.

"Just thinking how much things have changed in the last few months.
Do you really think that Paul hasn't noticed what we have been up to?
That he couldn't have made things almost impossible for me if he had a
mind too. He isn't good at expressing himself. I don't think he ever has
been or will be but it doesn't mean he doesn't care or want something
better. And doesn't there need to be somebody that sort of represents an
emotional Rock of Gibraltar? That is steady and reliable, something I am
so not."

"You're reliable." She said defending me. "We can always depend on
you to do what you say."

I nodded. "Yes but it is never what it is expected is it. Paul on the other
hand reacts the same in any given situation. You know what he is going to
do. He is predictable and people need that too. Stability is as important as
making improvements."

"You've talked to him about this?" Sue asked incredulously.

I nodded. "Sure I have. Not much but in the beginning right after I
got here sure I brought it up and we both agreed that it would be better if
he remained the stabilizing force especially since I was so not. It also keeps
me from going completely off the wall because I know he will slap me
down hard if I do something he thinks will hurt us."

"He would never….." Sue sputtered and I chuckled.

"No not physically and probably not in public either. He knows better
now, his reputation probably couldn't stand it. I have too many people on
my side and he wouldn't want to start what would be the same as a civil
war between us."

I could see when what I said hit home. That what she had done in the
lunchroom was almost as bad. She had been here a long time and now thanks
to me a lot of people looked up to her and appreciated her that hadn't before.

Sue didn't really know what to say at that point. She stumbled and stuttered a bit until she got herself together. "What can I do?" She asked very much embarrassed at the way she had acted. Did she have reason for acting like she did? Yes she did. But the way she did it was way out of line.

"Well apologizing in public would probably just make it worse. I think it would be better if I talked to Paul and sort of smoothed things over. Then the next time you see each other I want you to smile and be nice." She made a face at that as if she had swallowed a bug. "Come Sue he isn't that bad. Yeah he isn't my favorite person here either but he does good and you know it. You can't have been here this long and not see what he has done. Maybe not lately but I don't think you can put all of that at his feet."

"Yes. I just don't like his type. Never have." She grumbled. "But I guess if it is for the good everybody else I can be nice to the plunker."

I didn't think I was going to get a better offer. So one more problem was resolved and entire can of worms opened along the way. Why was Phillip sending Paul on all sorts of weird and unfruitful searches? Why was he interfering with the day to day running of a lot of the houses to start with? He had been doing that even with my house back in Florida. Being heavy handed and I was finding out it wasn't just because he didn't like not knowing what type of resource I was. It had made a sort of sense to me then but now I was starting to see a pattern that I liked even less than just a pain in the ass.

I would talk to Anthony when he got back from his current trip. See if the other council leaders were acting just as heavy handed or was it just ours. Daniel was still digging and the last time I checked with him he hadn't even bothered to look up.

So now what? I would have to make do with what I knew and that was enough. By the time that Phillip got back at Thanksgiving I was going to have a game plan in place. I was going to have so much damned information and statements that would show him that he was hurting more than helping. His antiquated way of doing things wasn't going to cut it anymore.

I would start with getting Michelle to pitch in. That wouldn't be hard. She had seen how much people needed help and weren't getting it. Michael wouldn't mind talking to her and seeing what they could work up together to get people some emotional help even if it meant doing it the old fashioned way. Hell I had done good and I didn't even know what I was doing half the time. All it might take is a caring heart and set of ears. Couldn't hurt could It?

By the time Thanksgiving rolled around and Phillip came back for the holiday's he was in for a ride and half. Well he was but he wasn't the only one.

# Chapter 8

## AVALANCHE

It was the Saturday before Thanksgiving and things weren't working out well at all. I had spent the last few weeks working on all sorts of things to show Phillip what could be done to fix some of the problems we all saw, to absolutely no avail.

Anthony had gotten back and left again and was due back again on Monday or so. He had confirmed my fears that our council leader wasn't the only one that was acting like a Napoleon. Not all but the fast majority of them were acting that way. They didn't seem to be listening to anyone either. It was scary the way that everything was going south at almost the exact same way all over the world. Even I could see a pattern forming. One I didn't like at all.

But it didn't do any good if nobody would listen. If those in charge wouldn't change what could I do? Start a revolution? I hoped like hell it didn't come to that. I had sort joked about starting a civil war and now I was coming to conclusion that that might be the only thing to wake everybody up. Problem with civil war was people died and we didn't have enough of us to the job as it was.

In the month that Phillip had been gone his little fortress had changed. Not the building but the people inside sure had. Paul was back to doing research. And that change made him almost perky. The others had stopped all the totally useless things that Phillip had sent them on and were doing what they felt they were supposed to do. Being lead by their hearts and not so much the directions of someone that had no clue what their talents and abilities really were.

The protectors had four more graduations. Trial by fire type graduations and the mystique behind that new tradition had started to grow. Now it was considered a right of passage as the myth and awe of what really happened was so clouded that nobody but Joshua, Katherine and I really knew the truth behind it all. It had been a challenge each time to find out what scared a trainee, what was their biggest weakness that hadn't been addressed yet. Now it was getting easier. What would happen when I left? I was sort of becoming not the boogeyman but somebody that even the protectors sort of looked at with awe. That part I hated. But I was also turning into the person they confided in when they had a problem or a question that their master protector didn't seem to be able to answer and that was a burden and a blessing all rolled into one.

I knew why it was turning out that way and the sooner I turned over that duty to another the happier I would be. But who else could do it? Well Joshua had better figure it out because I wasn't staying here forever and by now I think he had figured that out. Sooner or later I would have to get out and help others. I couldn't and wouldn't just stay here.

Oh, I was going to be put on display again sometime after Thanksgiving. Something that also disgusted me to no end but this time it was foreign guests. Some from all the different continents were coming to stare at the oddity. Could Phillip get any more insulting? Probably never occurred to him but I would make sure it did.

We had yet to receive a single response from all the plans and suggestions and a few down right threats that had been sent to Phillip this last month. Not a single word. I sent an entire list of suggestions from all the people here. Michael too along with Michelle had put forth what I thought was a great plan on using the few emotional empaths we had left and augmented by those that had a natural secondary talent for being good listeners that would help those that needed emotional counseling. They didn't even have to travel when people were more than willing to go to them. And what did we get for all our efforts? A big fat nothing.

I was pissed and about to start climbing the walls this Saturday before Thanksgiving. I guess that was one of the reasons that Michael insisted we get out. Something that almost everybody else had decided to do too. It was a beautiful day with temperatures in low 30's and even over that down in the lower part of the valley.

According to long-range weather forecasters and our own weather sensitive people this was about the last decent weekend we would have. After this month it was going to turn nasty. Snow, freezing temperatures and winter would be here for a very long time. It may not be this nice again until like July.

We had already made it some ways down the mountain trail. Taking our time and just enjoying the day and being out in the sunshine and fresh air. Michael and I holding hands and smiling at absolutely nothing, how could any day get better?

PIB yelled out in my head. His voice so loud I just knew Michael had to hear it too. "Look Up." He bellowed. My gaze didn't look skyward. Something in the way he said it had me looking toward the mountainside directly up slope from us. My sight saw a distant figure but with the amount of bulky clothing they had on I couldn't tell the size or even if it was a man or woman.

I didn't like the fact that whoever that was, was standing right on top of a huge snow pack. It was much too early for avalanche season. There just wasn't enough snow yet for it to be a problem. That's one of the reason's Michael and I had decided to go hiking. A lot of us had decided to do that this Saturday before the snows got so deep it was almost impossible to get anywhere without skis or snowmobiles and avalanche warnings were a daily worry. Grabbing Michael's arm I pointed to the distant figure. "Trouble." He didn't ask how I knew. By now he knew better.

We both heard the not so soft bang of an explosion. I didn't wait for the results. I knew what was coming next. Grabbing Michael by the hand, we ran. Maybe I could have made the distance if I had left him behind but we both knew that wasn't happening and he hadn't wasted his breath trying. He needed it for running.

Just before the ice and snow hit I grabbed Michael around the waist. Wrapping my body around his, we both curled in as tight a ball as we could. Locking my legs and arms around him to try and buffer as much of the impact for him as I could. I could heal much quicker than he could and his medical training could help me if was injured seriously enough to need it.

I knew it was going to be bad but even my imagination hadn't prepared me for the hit we took. Rolling end over end sometimes and at other times being bounced around like a ball at the worst, most painful tennis match in history. I couldn't even determine what was up and what was down anymore as our sliding and bouncing torment continued for what seemed like hours. I could tell our momentum was slowing and I thought good we were almost done with this as the snow flipped me one last time and I felt my left shoulder hit something hard and my shoulder blade snapped in two and my rotator cuff dislocated. I tried to scream but only managed to get snow in my mouth as I felt my tight grip loosen and Michael was torn away from me in the last few seconds of our snowy pain filled ride.

Which way was up and which down? My eyes were open but snow was everywhere, packed tightly around me. I could breath but it was difficult even for me. I kicked hard with a foot straight down and only found hardness; it was the same when I punched in front of me, it was a little softer but not much and I could dig into the snow with my fingers. My right arm shot straight up and my fingertips hit open air. YES!!!

I dug and kicked and pushed my way up less than two feet but it seemed like ten. It was like swimming through concrete. Soon I was on top of the packed snow. Looking around I couldn't see any sign of Michael. He must be buried close by but in which direction. I didn't have a lot of time. He could suffocate in just a few minutes.

Calm down Maggie, I said to myself. He's had as much or more cold weather training than you had. He'll know to not panic, to take shallow breaths and wait for me to find him. PIB, I called out in my head. Michael, help me find Michael. "Listen." Came his soft voice. The way that was said it didn't mean with my ears but I tried anyway, stretching out with every bit of my very sensitive hearing. Nothing.

Then I tried what I thought PIB really meant. I reached into my shirt and my hand wrapped around a crystal pendant, the mate to the one Michael worn under his shirt too. It had been our bonding presents to each other. Now they pulsed in time to our heartbeats. I focused on mine and listened. Not with my ears or even with my head but with my heart. Mine was beating at a frantic rate so I had no idea if Michael's was the cause of the tempo or not. I focused around the panic and did what Michael had said he did when I had been shot with the drug-laced arrow. I shut down every emotion but my love for him and reached out.

There it was like a brilliant light shining out from the gloom on a foggy night. Michael's heartbeat calling to mine, I followed the pulsing almost light. Our hearts had beat as one for months now. I followed where my heart lead, listened to its quiet, almost whispered voice. It knew where to find its other half. And then something PIB had pushed at me months ago finally clicked. This is what he had been trying to tell me when we had both gotten so frustrated when Michael and I had worked on combat training. The heart spark was good for more than just finding each other. I could feel everything he felt and could almost see through his eyes.

Stopping around five feet from the hole I had dug myself out of I dropped to my knees and started digging. My claws sprung out and that helped and I dug and clawed my way through the hard packed snow. I found a boot first, followed it to the leg it was attached to. I started to pull but he was wedged in too tight and he was almost upside down. Digging around him to loosen the snow I must have looked like a possessed dog trying to find a bone as the snow flew up over my head. Finally he was loose enough that my tugging on both his legs Michael came up out of his snow prison with an almost audible pop.

He was flushed and taking in huge gulps of air but otherwise he seemed fine. My shoulder blade had mended itself in the time it took me to dig my way out and find Michael. Before I had even given his foot the first yank it was fine. My rotator cuff needed help. It couldn't go back into place all by itself and even though I knew how, I hated to do something like that to myself.

But Michael was always a bigger priority than I was. "You okay?" I asked a little breathless.

He nodded. "Yeah. You?"

"I could us a little help." I didn't need to say more. His eyes skimming over my body, he quickly found the problem. "This is going to hurt." He warned me.

"Can't be any worse than having a bullet dug out of it." Our friend Anthony had to do that honor. That was the price he had to pay for me coming to rescue him when Aspanari agents decided they liked him and his computer a little too much.

Michael's hands grabbed my shoulder and with quick strong tug everything was back in place and would soon be working like always.

"You know the next time I get something broken or dislocated I wish it would pick a different section. My left shoulder is starting to feel picked on."

Michael snorted but didn't say anything. His eyes went up the mountainside that was now almost totally bare of snow. Mine followed but I couldn't see anything out of the ordinary from this distance either. "You know somebody just tried to kill us." He said. Michael rarely got mad anymore but there was more than anger in his words and in his heart. Not quite rage but something so close as to be a kissing cousin.

"Yes, somebody did." My voice was cold as ice just like my emotions. They went that way when I was beyond rage leaving me feeling nothing, only cold resolution and dedication to purpose. Somebody was in for a big surprise that we were alive. Revenge was not a thought I entertained but we needed to find out whom that someone was and why we had been targeted before they tried again. I was now very sure this was not an isolated incident. They would keep trying until they succeeded and it was a race now to see which one was not just the fastest but the smartest, the most cunning and maybe even the most cold hearted and calculating. I didn't like that aspect of me but I could do it but you have to be very careful when you start down that road because if you shut off all the good emotions for too long you can't always get them back. I had seen it when a few of my Army Ranger buddies came back from combat. Some were never the same after that experience.

By now the others that had gone off to hike on their own were arriving. That blast had to have been heard for miles. It must have echoed and reverberated up and down the valley and anybody around would have known that something really bad had happened.

Going through my memory quickly I tried to remember seeing anybody else down slope of us. My nose told me no, my ears said the same thing but until we had done a head count we wouldn't know for sure.

Some of the protectors arrived first. That was no surprise. They were faster and stronger than the more normal of us besides it was their job to go into danger. Bruce was there and Joshua and Katherine were hot on his heels. Then others from the medical section started showing up and everybody was just relieved that Michael and I were fine.

I tried to down play everything saying we had just caught the side of the avalanche and that seemed to calm everybody down. It wasn't even untrue. I didn't put in the part that we had run that far but when the explosion was triggered we were smack dab in the middle of the slope and if Michael hadn't been as fast as he was even I couldn't have dug either one of us out.

Joshua disappeared with Katherine by his side and I knew where they were going. Sure enough a few minutes later I could see two people standing on top of the outcropping where only snow had been before. When all the snow went down the hill any evidence would have gone with it. Smells, footprints, even residue of the explosive used would be spread out all up and down the slope I was now standing in the middle of. Even

I wouldn't find anything with all of this to go through. Maybe if I waited until the spring when the snow melted we might find something but I knew we didn't have that much time.

This was twice now that somebody had taken a pot shot at me. The first I don't think had been an attempt to kill just to slow me down or maybe change my attitude. Now it had turned deadly. Even if I hadn't been killed but Michael would have been, everybody knew how close we were. Michael's death would have been such a severe blow I wouldn't have recovered for a real long time.

But whoever this was couldn't have known about PIB. There were only three people here that knew about him, me, Michael and Anthony. I bet I was frustrating the hell out of somebody by getting warned just in the nick of time. This nasty little shit was getting on my nerves. He had endangered Michael and that was something nobody got to do and get away with. Michael and I had learned a lot in the last few weeks about how our abilities complimented each other. Did we have more to learn? Of course we did. But what we knew and with PIB's help it had been enough to keep both of us alive when I knew we shouldn't be.

I was coming to some conclusions about all this. Watching very carefully where everybody had come from and how long it took to get here I could rule a few people out this time that I couldn't before. Bruce was out, so was Joshua and Katherine. Were they had popped out at from the tree line it would be impossible to get there from the top of the mountain that fast even for me and I was faster and quicker than any of them.

Any of the medical people that had tried to render aid would be pulled from the list of possible suspects too. So now I had about 10 people that I could rule out as my nemesis. That still left a lot but it was a start.

Joshua still didn't like me gallivanting around by myself but PIB and I had resources he didn't know about. I nodded to Michael and as Joshua was trying to gather information from what everyone had seen and heard I moved further into the crowd and disappeared.

My master protector would probably give me one ass chewing when I showed back up but Michael would know if I ran into trouble or even if I found something that excited me a lot. My heart rate stayed the steady calm beat the whole time I climbed the mountainside. Scrambling hand over hand with my claws out I could go where mountain goats had problems and was standing just down a bit from where Joshua and Katherine had been not too long ago. What had taken them 10 or 15 minutes to reach I had done in less than 5.

I could track their smell back the way they had come and gone as their footprints also gave evidence of their route. But what I was looking for would have been earlier, not much but some. I started a spiral going out a little with each pass, further and further. Then I found what I had been looking for. Footprints, big ones so a man at least but the smell confused me. It was all wrong for one of us but it wasn't human either. Something else entirely, maybe what a hunter used to confuse their scent when they didn't want to spook their quarry. No wonder Joshua and Katherine had missed it. If I hadn't been so sensitive and so sure that I would find a trail I wouldn't have gone this far out to find where it started back up.

Well this was an ingenious devil that was for sure. Whoever this had been had never gone down the slope to find out if Michael or I had survived but headed straight back up the valley and the center complex. But he must have known that his trail might be found and that he might be tracked by somebody that had as keen a nose as a bloodhound did. As I followed further I found the heavy jacket buried in the snow right near one of the mountain trails and the tracks of a snowmobile where it had been parked and was now gone.

That little shit. Now I was really pissed. A few of us had gone out on snowmobiles this morning and everybody had taken the steeper mountain passes that had a lot of snow already for that sort of thing. It helped a bit because it would only be the half dozen of them that might be my culprit but this guy was smart. Suppose he rented one from down at the resort and then parked it here to use later or stole one even. That is what I would have done if I had been him.

He was good at preparing, really good. I underestimated him once but that wouldn't happen again. He thought like I did and that scared me even worse than I had been. Now my heart wasn't as calm as it had been before as I turned around and ran. Ran back to Michael and Joshua. Maybe my teacher was right? Maybe I did take chances I shouldn't? Here I was all alone again and if he was still hanging around I might just be in trouble because this guy didn't like taking the fight straight on but in ways you weren't expecting. But if I hadn't gone off I wouldn't know a lot I did now.

Now I knew that my enemy was one of us. Only another protector or somebody that was just as familiar with our abilities would know all that this person did. Even most of the medical people didn't know how sensitive our smell was and you would have to be able to fool yourself to make sure you could fool somebody else with the same ability. It would be the only way to be sure that what you were chancing your life on would work.

As I got closer I could smell Joshua's musky scent and Katherine's softer smell along with Michael's as they rushed to find me. I had hoped my almost panic Michael hadn't caught but I should have known better. We almost ran into each other as we all hit the same small clearing in between some trees.

Michael hadn't cared if he kept up with the two big protectors. He was breathing heavy but I could tell they hadn't had to slow up much as they had tried to find me. Later they would ask how he had done that but right now all they were thinking about was where I had disappeared to and what trouble I was in now.

"Gabriella have you lost your ever-loving mind." Joshua snapped out in his worry. It was all I could not to smile. We still weren't close friends but only a friend in danger would make Joshua loose that composure he always tried to maintain. "Michael said you were in trouble and took off so fast that I had problems catching him."

Those words hit home at about the same time I knew that we both had some serious explaining to do. Now I felt a little better about telling both of them some of our secrets. They still wouldn't get all of them but they needed to know more than they did or they couldn't help us. If I was going up against a fully trained rogue protector or heaven forbid an aware and cunning Aspanari assassin that had been hanging around undetected all this time I would need all the help I could get.

Joshua turned to stare at Michael with something close to accusation in his eyes. "How did you keep up with us? I was going pretty much flat out and I have longer legs than you do. How did you run that fast? Even taking into consideration adrenalin because you were worried about your wife it still doesn't explain what you were able to do."

I was impressed despite myself. Michael had changed a lot more than either one of us had really thought. This had shown it in a way neither one of us had thought of before. Me being in danger had dropped all of Michael's own self conceived notions about what he could and couldn't do. I could see it in his face. He had surprised himself too.

Michael didn't know what I had found. Didn't know that Joshua and Katherine were more or less on the good guy list that had previously only held three names on it. Before today the only ones I was absolutely positively sure I could trust was me, Michael and Anthony now I had at least two more and possibly 10.

But there was even a problem with those other 8 people. Could I put them in danger with my trust? Joshua and Katherine were more than capable. Bruce was still in training and wasn't experienced enough to defend himself against a trained assassin or a rogue protector and as far as the medical people was concerned, well they could be killed just as easily as any Nohus on the street if somebody wanted to.

Joshua was still waiting as Michael was deciding what I wanted said and what I didn't. He usually let me make those tough choices. Unless they were in his medical experience he let me be in charge. I smiled at him asking myself again how I had lucked out to have such a wonderful husband that didn't feel threatened by his wife being the one that had to be in control of things most of the time.

"Michael could run as fast as you because of the changes my blood did to him." I answered. That was one of those bombshell type answers that sort floored everybody for a few seconds. Now the questions would come pouring out. Before they could start I tried to answer as many as I could think they could ask.

"When I had to give Michael that much of my blood it not only healed him it changed him. More inside than out so that nobody really noticed it, not even him. The changes were sort of gradual so even we weren't sure what was happening until it just got too obvious. He can hear, smell and see about the same as a second rate protector. Strength and speed too seems to be about the same as what Peter has. I worked with him enough I should know."

"Holy shit." Katherine exclaimed. "When Paul finds out about this he is going to go nuts."

"No." Joshua said quietly. He had made the same leap that I had when it came to Michael's abilities. "Nobody can know about Michael. He's Gabriella's ace in the hole. Everybody, everybody thinks he is her weak link. That if something happened to him it would destroy her. It would but the task wouldn't be as easy as what everybody thinks it would. That is why he has been holding back in training lately. I couldn't understand how erratic he had gotten. Sometimes almost falling over his own two feet and now I know why. You realized you were being noticed and had to stop being so good but your own body was fighting against you."

Michael nodded. "It wasn't easy trying to be clumsy. Now I know some of what Maggie was going through a few months ago. I still don't know how she managed not to show more than the few small things she did."

Katherine was still pretty persistent though. "You really should tell at least Paul about this."

I shook my head. "Katherine, somebody just tried to kill me. They weren't trying to disable me or hem me in. I tracked them from just a bit away where they blew up the mountain. This person had large footprints, too big to be anything but a man. He knew enough about how a protector's sense of smell works that he could use something to disguise it so I couldn't tell who it was. Then he got on a snowmobile and disappeared. I couldn't track it. The skids mixed in with all the other traffic that has been all over this area today."

Joshua nodded understanding immediately what I hadn't said. "Paul went out on a snowmobile this morning. He would also know how most of our and your abilities work and how to disguise himself so that he couldn't be tracked."

"So far the only people I can rule out as suspects are 14 people. You, Katherine, Michael, Anthony, Bruce and the 8 medical people that showed up at the avalanche site. There are several more that are very unlikely just because they aren't physical enough to do what has been done easily."

"Yeah Sue, Haley, Rachael, Rebecca, Brenda and Simon are all too small to do what has been done. And others probably wouldn't have the knowledge. But are we sure this person is working on their own?" Joshua asked bringing up something that I had thought of and tried to dismiss.

"I hope they are working alone." I whispered. "If they aren't then I can't trust anybody and I am totally screwed."

"Isn't it bad enough to think we have one person that is a threat to her." Katherine growled. "What I want to know is why? All Gabriella has done was help people, make everybody happier about what they do. How is that a threat to anyone?"

Michael knew why. "It isn't what she has done it is what she could do, what she might do in the future. This person wants her out of the picture before she gets strong but he is already too late and he isn't worried about what she can do by herself. It is what she is getting others to do, work together and be a family. That is the biggest change I can see she is doing. Alone she is just one very strong and talented person. Even with me it isn't that big of a threat but people listen to her and they are changing because of that. She is the source of a virus that somebody wants to stop before it can spread."

I snorted at that. "Great I'm a disease now." Michael had broken the tension some doing what I usually do, saying something completely off the wall. It has often been said that married people start acting like each after being together for a long while. If it was this bad already what were we going to be like in 50 years? I had to laugh out loud at the image that came to my head. Michael and I almost like clones and unable to finish a sentence without each other. The giggles were still coming out when we got back up to the center. But they didn't last long after that.

Now everybody had heard what happened and Phillip and Rafael were livid that I had almost been killed. I was a valuable resource and shouldn't take chances like that. What I wanted to say was it was my life and I should have the choice on how it is lived. What I did say was actually much more tactful and very true. What type of resource was I if I couldn't step foot out the door on my own? I was supposed to be a spy or something like it. Granted that part wasn't needed now, or was it?

Maybe they sort of had a point. Maybe when I went out by myself from now I needed to look like somebody else, somebody that nobody would expect. I had come here to learn all the things that would make me a better infiltrator but everybody had been focusing on the combat part of my calling. That was important but was it the most important part? I was beginning to think that maybe I had a few things that I needed to teach myself now. With a little help from Michael and maybe a few lady friends like Haley and Rachael I knew I would be doing a lot more than combat training really, really soon.

Now I had to grow, now I had to change. Defending myself hadn't been all that I had come here to do to start with. I was the first female infiltrator ever so why not start using all of my abilities the way they should be used. Didn't Anthony once tell me that I was supposed to be all things as needed and I had seriously forgotten the one thing that I could do that nobody else could do, change?

Not even the medical people and archive monitors had asked what faces I had. Why? It wouldn't have done any good anyway. I didn't have but one face that I had put together other than looking like copy of Rachael.

I had a mission as the rest of Saturday came and dinner had me chatting up all the ladies I knew were interested in magazines and other things that had a big variety of celebrities and such.

Stopping by several suites on the way back to ours Michael had no clue why we were dragging back about 100 magazines. Things that I hadn't had much interest in before were now extremely important.

As soon as we were alone the questions started. "I know you have a reason for all of this." He started pointing to the mess all over the table and half the floor. "But throw me bone here love."

"Faces, Michael." I explained. "I need to see how faces are put together so that I can start working on mine."

He nodded and sort of smiled. "Do I get to see? Please don't think I am bored with you but I might like having a nice parade of pretty ladies in my bedroom." He said with a definite smirk. For his outrageous behavior I threw a pillow at him.

For about an hour I worked on my hair only. Making it grow was sort of like how I did my nails but getting rid of it was a lot harder. It had to be cut but I could grow it at the rate of about an inch ever 15 minutes. Focusing that hard on one thing for so long sort of fried my brain for a bit and didn't think I would be making my hair grow unless I had a real good reason.

By the time we got ready for bed I had figured out how to make my hair grow, get curly, straighten out and even get all frizzy like it was in the worst shape hair could get. I even had my hair get the texture of Katherine's. Now that was a challenge. I hadn't had to think about how different racial characters change things in a while. Now all those days of selling Avon and dealing with every manner of woman from the palest red headed to the darkest complexion African American came back to me.

"I knew there was a reason I was picked for this." I said sounding maybe a tad too smug. "There aren't too many men or women for that matter that know all the differences that make up each type of woman."

Michael nodded but as he had watched me change and made some very insightful suggestions he did bust my bubble totally. "But no matter what you look like you still smell like a Resurrected. If the Aspanari were expecting a spy they would immediately know what you were, maybe not who but what."

"Shit!!" I exclaimed. Why hadn't I thought of that? It should have been the first thing I thought of today after my nemesis had been so good at fooling even my nose. "I will see if I can change that." I grumbled to myself. But I had a feeling that it would be a lot more difficult than just focusing real hard to get the way I smelled to be different. Perfume wouldn't cover up everything. Not even if I put on so much it was a stinky cloud around me. It was just something embedded in us.

Maybe Paul, Daniel or Joshua would have some suggestions. I would have to be discrete with two of those but Joshua I could ask flat out and he would answer me if he had one and not really ask much. He knew I still had secrets. I think Michael and I had sort of pickled his brain today and he wouldn't be up to much more for a bit. Good thing too. I had so much going on that to have a nosey master protector nipping at my heels wasn't something I could handle. It didn't matter if I trusted him or not. Something he had said had put my radar on overdrive today.

Suppose it wasn't just one person that was causing me problems. Suppose it was two or more that was giving me grief? Now my paranoid voice was in complete panic and I was second guessing myself about everything and I was back to the attitude I had when I first got here. Trust Michael, Anthony some, PIB and myself always but everybody else had to be watched all the time. I had to figure out who I could trust and who I couldn't and fast or I was going to drive myself crazy.

So now what? How was I going to find out whom I could trust and whom I couldn't? PIB could only help me so much. I had sort of figured out he was good for safety things, keeping me alive and in one piece. He was comforting in an odd sort of way but wasn't infallible or perfect either, like there were things that he couldn't say. I had caught what I had thought was a hesitation sometimes when I asked certain questions. As if he was trying to find the best way to answer he could.

Again I had to ask myself the same question I had before. He wasn't human. That I knew. But what was he that he could hang around the inside of my head and give me pointers or suggestions, sometimes even commands really when he wasn't really there. Not in a touch it and feel it type there anyway.

If it weren't for the fact that other Resurrected had voice guides I would swear I had developed a split personality. PIB was a lot more active than other protectors and finders I had talked to before. Granted there were only a hand full of them in the world but I had tried to research the records to find them, contact them and find out how each one did what they did without giving away that I had one too. All had different answers and yet they were all the same. The voice guide did actually talk to them. A voice in their head that was much different than their own mental ramblings. So I guess what PIB and I did wasn't all that different than they were.

So what could I pull out of him? Unless it was a safety thing I had to let him know I wanted help, sometimes he would contribute on his but most of the time I had to ask and I had to be very careful how I asked and what I asked or I just plain didn't get anything out of him at all except of huff that sounded extremely frustrated.

I waited until Michael was asleep that night and I was up with my normal over the top energy level. This time I just wanted to beat something so I went to the gym put on some gloves and started pounding the heavy bags.

As my hands and feet started their own way of finding answers I started asking questions of my voice guide. "PIB can you help me? I'm really lost right now." I felt his presence get stronger. Then I hit a stonewall; I didn't even know what I wanted to ask. Maybe find out how much trouble I was in? "PIB how deep is the shit we are in right now?"

His voice was sort musing. Like he was thinking hard, about what I had no clue. "Deep." He answered.

"Can you tell me how many are causing me trouble?" And I got a flat nothing. Okay wrong question. So I started thinking what had been wrong about. To general maybe so I rephrased. "How many here in the complex that are a danger to me?" That would give me not just how many people were causing the problem but if it was an Aspanari or Resurrected.

Again I got nothing but silence. Well this was getting me exactly nowhere. Okay either I wasn't asking the right questions or just not in the right way. "Do you know who set the explosives today?"

"No. Couldn't tell."

Okay that meant he saw things from my point of view maybe. He was just more aware of things than I was. That certainly explained things. How when I was back in Florida he hadn't warned me about Anya and her fancy gun work. He hadn't know she would shoot so hadn't thought to warn me. Now anything that is different was pointed out if I didn't notice it. It wasn't always a hazard as I had already found out on a couple things but it was always something I hadn't paid attention to. I agreed with PIB on this completely. Just because you don't need a piece of information doesn't mean you shouldn't want to know. Some time in the future it may turn out to be really important.

So if he couldn't tell who it was, he wouldn't be able to tell whom I could trust and who was causing me problems. Well this was getting me absolutely nowhere. Then I had an idea. What if the culprit or culprits just thought I knew who they were? Michael, Anthony and I could spread little stories around and just see what was spread to whom. I had hearing off the charts and Michael was a lot better than anyone knew. We could listen, watch and with PIB helping out couldn't we find out at least who didn't like what was happening and maybe, just maybe, somebody would expose himself or herself because they thought I already knew and had nothing to lose. That could be a little dangerous but again Michael was better at defending himself than most knew and he was rarely alone anyway.

Anthony was the most to be put at risk. I would suggest that he keep close and not run around alone with anyone but me or Michael, Joshua or Katherine. Finally I knew I had to trust those two at least for the most part. This was too much, too important and way over my head to handle alone.

Now why didn't I try and include Phillip and Rafael in all of this planning? For so many reasons it wasn't even funny. They didn't like the way I did things to start with. Phillip wanted safe and predictable in just about anything. What I was going to do was so fluid it would by like trying to control a flood with two big paddles and kiddy pool.

I heard a chuckle in my head and knew PIB was still more than hanging around there and thought my evaluation was worth a laugh. I liked his mental laugh. It made me sort of warm inside and I couldn't help but smile. Yeah, smile now I thought coming down from that high way too fast. What I was planning wasn't just fluid. It was dangerous. It was shaking a big piece of red meat in front of a hungry tiger. The trouble was the person holding the bait was every bit as dangerous as the unknown tiger was. My combat training was more or less over with now. There was nothing else that either Katherine or Joshua could teach me. Even Michael had learned as much as he probably was going to there.

Now we had reached the point where we would do the other things that I had come here to do. Find out how everything had gone south. When it had started, how long and how bad was it really. Daniel had his more than the two months he had said he needed to play computer detective a lot more and it was time to start giving me answers. I had never been good finding out who the bad guy was before the end of the mystery story. Now I would have to be. Part of me knew it was necessary but part me didn't really want to know.

Ignorance was bliss but ignorance can also get you killed. Something that had almost happened to me today and it was a condition I couldn't let go on any longer. Too many people were at risk and the stakes were too high. No matter who was the culprit that had tried to kill Michael and I, it was information I had to find out. Even if it were somebody that I considered a friend and that knowledge would break my heart.

But I wasn't the only one with plans and schemes. So far by the grace of good fortune nobody had died, yet. How long would that good luck last? That wasn't up to me and even though my life would not be put in danger again while I was here I would find out that having somebody you loved killed in your stead was worse than facing death a thousand times.

# Chapter 9

## SPY WARE

It didn't take long for me to run my idea by everybody. Some were all for it as I could see plans forming behind Michael's eyes quickly. He was still extremely pissed at both of us almost being killed. The fact that I couldn't tell who it was had sent him into a brief tailspin. That man of mine kept putting me on a pedestal thinking that I could do just about anything, handle anything. It was like he had come to expect me to pull a rabbit out of my invisible hat all the time now. That was getting annoying.

How do you straighten somebody out that thinks you're perfect? Anthony knew better. Sometimes I thought he knew me better that my own mate did. Well he had trained me. But I had grown a lot since this past summer when we had played out in the woods in Alabama. Now that time almost had a nostalgic feel to it.

Joshua and Katherine were much more hesitant. I could understand that. But I was left with few options. Somebody was trying to kill me but what was even more disturbing was why? We all knew that somebody didn't like the changes that had been made. Thanks to Anthony's incessant chatter, those changes had been made known to others around the globe and were starting to have a ripple down effect even now.

That scared me. Especially since the only time Anthony had the extra security of his own protector was when he was traveling. Others wise Seth was somewhere else doing who knew what. How did Anthony rate someone like Seth to start with? He was a first class protector almost as old as Joshua was. Seth had said he might be able to help now and then but the truth was if Anthony wasn't gone then Seth was busy elsewhere. Right now Seth was in

Atlanta. That big house was having its fair share of problems too. He had his own feelings for that town having been a slave during the civil war and the plantation he had worked had not been far away from there but he roamed everywhere and wasn't really permanently assigned anywhere anymore.

It was amazing but the few times I had talked to him over the last few months he seemed to have no ill feelings from that time. I thought he was a very well spoken, well-adjusted man that was easy to be around. At a little over 6'6" he was everything a protector was supposed to be. He had the training and the experience needed to keep that walking recorder of ours safe from just about anything. And Anthony said he never ruffled any feathers no matter what culture they got sent to together. He was adaptable. Something not everyone could lay claim to.

Phillip had chosen well. I had never found out exactly how Phillip had met Seth. When or where their paths had crossed the first time. Right now that relationship didn't seem that important. But it did leave Anthony in very vulnerable position. All the protector trainees weren't up to the challenge. Joshua and Katherine were stretched enough as it was and I was chasing my tail and had a target already on my back.

So it was decided that he wouldn't have much part in my latest scheme. Something he didn't like at all. He would help plan. He would watch and listen but not have an active role in anything. And if any of us had a suspicion that he was actually in danger we were going to seal him in his room and not let him out. That part he didn't know about but I didn't care if I pissed him off. Keeping one of my best friends and a very loyal brother out of danger was more important than making him mad. Being mad you can get over. Being dead you can't.

So first thing Monday morning we started. Katherine and I had a whispered conversation in the breakfast room that wasn't that whispered. We made sure it was just loud enough to be over heard by a few people nearby. Talk of what had happened and that evidence had been found at the top of mountain. Evidence that even now Joshua had down in the training facility trying to determine where it originated from and anything else that might say who the culprit was.

Everybody already knew that it hadn't been a fluke. That it had been a deliberate attack. This made everybody in the whole place on edge and Rafael had once again insisted on separate meals for Phillip. I didn't argue this time. He was right to be worried. Somebody here wasn't what he or she seemed to be. But who and why were the questions?

I was surprised that Phillip and Rafael hadn't just left. Our council member's safety was of the utmost importance to his bodyguard and I could understand that. Maybe Phillip had put his foot down. Said they needed to stay around and find out what was going on? If so I wasn't sure that Phillip would like the answers any better than we were.

So we whispered and we let out just enough to make people think we almost had the answer. That we knew whom it was but were just waiting for all the facts to be double-checked. To accuse somebody of what was essentially murder wasn't to be done lightly.

By the end of the first day I wasn't surprised to have a lot of people stop by our suite to talk to us. To get a few more hints and some were even down right pushy.

Paul in particular was almost rude. Was extremely pissed off at not being in on the investigation. I wasn't about to tell him that he wasn't part of it because there really wasn't one to start with or that he was a chief suspect.

Rafael came and went away a very grumpy camper because we didn't tell him any more than anyone else. How could we? A secret only works when as few as people know about as possible. Besides, we all knew he would run straight to Phillip and Phillip being Phillip wouldn't like something this dangerously unpredictable.

Soon it was just us five in our room. Still crowded to an extent. But we thought things had quieted down for the night. It was past midnight and Anthony was almost asleep sitting up. His blue eyes almost closing now and then but the rest of us were wide-awake.

I felt a nudge in my head. PIB was trying to tell me something. Something about an odd sound or a vibration. I put my hand up for everybody to shut up and silence slithered into the room.

PIB was right. There was something new in the room. A vibration, a noise I could feel in the back of my jaw like a toothache that wasn't yet.

I followed that echo of an ache. Using PIB as guide for hot and cold I zeroed in on it. Finally there it was on the underside of the desk. A small little nub of thing that I would have never noticed had I not been looking for it. A bug, a listening device had been planted in my room. I know my face had to be positively scarlet.

Joshua was right there and his face was white as the snow I had been buried in this Saturday. Then he smiled. It wasn't a nice smile it was actually rather gruesome. What in the hell had he just thought of?

"You know Gabriella those tests you wanted run on you have turned out some interesting results. I haven't seen too many of us produce electromagnetic energy like you do. Maybe it has something to do with how you change. Do you think that might be it?"

I peddled quickly wondering where this was going. "Maybe."

Anthony wasn't close to being asleep anymore. "You know electromagnetic energy has some really weird effects on electrical things. It is probably a good thing you never tried to change your appearance when you were getting x-rayed. I don't think Paul would like to replace all his expensive lab equipment. You would probably burn it all out."

Then I knew why Joshua had said what he had. Anthony, my wonderful brother full of every tidbit of information showed me what I hadn't had the quickness of mind to figure out. I pulled the little bug from his hiding spot and popped into the small microwave I had gotten for popcorn and such.

It took about 30 seconds before it went poof and that irritating ache disappeared and I heard PIB give a sigh of relief. Then I took that little thing and put it right back where it had been.

Now if whoever it was that had planted it came back to check why it was no longer working it would seem as if it had reacted to me being close to it. Now that would drive that someone totally bonkers.

We didn't say anything else. Instead we all evacuated to someplace that probably wasn't bugged. The maintenance level, with all the machinery would be a difficult place to wire for sound.

"Okay." Michael started. "What was that thing?"

"Very high tech listen device." Joshua answered with snort of disgusted. "Somebody in this very place bugged your room."

"Well that narrows down the list of suspects doesn't it?" Katherine said with a nod. "Only about half the complex stopped by this evening at some point or other."

"I know which ones did and which ones didn't." Anthony chimed in. That was redundant, of course he would. It was what he did.

"Does this help us at all?" Michael asked. He looked sort of ill. The idea that if I hadn't found the damn thing that somebody could have listened in on our most intimate time together didn't sit well with him. I knew that look and it wasn't a happy one.

Joshua nodded again. "Yes, yes it does. I know who was at the site of the avalanche, whom we spread what rumors to and who showed up tonight. It does still leave several people on the suspect list but now you two know it wasn't us."

That leap of logic sort of escaped me for a second. Then I got it. Why would Joshua or Katherine feel the need to bug a meeting they were already part of? That meant it had to be somebody else. There was no way that anybody could have known I would find it. It was by lucky chance and having PIB around that had revealed it. My voice guide was still something that those two didn't know about.

Closer, we were getting closer.

Over the next few days the visitations waxed and then waned and everyday a new listening device would be found and disposed of the same way. Joshua never asked how I found them. Maybe he too could detect their slightly irritating pulse. I didn't ask him. I didn't really care.

For once my brain was on nervous overload and when it came time to sleep my body went along with it. Trying to hide from what it didn't want to accept. That somebody here was a spy. Somebody, a friend most likely, had tried to kill me.

Soon it came down just a hand full of people but to my surprise Paul wasn't one of them. He had stopped by the first night but hadn't after that. Maybe Joshua had been right. Maybe there was more than one and we had more problems than any of us wanted to admit.

We let things die down and the visitations stopped. Of course we didn't stop meeting. Didn't stop discussing things. But those also morphed and changed as theories were laid and found to have merit or dismissed. Finally we came to the conclusion that this was getting us absolutely nowhere.

Who ever this was either knew or had guessed accurately that we had no evidence and didn't know anything. Couldn't prove anything and we had been doing a very elaborate game of fishing.

Maybe because they were confident enough in their abilities to know they had left nothing to find. But then why try and listen. Maybe at first it had been to find out what we knew or maybe it was to find out what we ourselves were planning.

I thought more and more that was it. It wasn't what we knew that was trying to be found out but what we were planning. What schemes I was going to turn loose next.

Somebody hadn't liked the few changes that had been set in motion and they were afraid I would do more. They were right. I was starting to see a pattern as clear as jigsaw puzzle with just one missing piece. It all made perfect sense.

There was an Aspanari spy in our midst. How he had come to be here I didn't know. Did he have somebody to help him? Again same answer but I was sure of one thing. That this person wasn't going to give up. Wasn't going to stop because he was found out. Oh he would, or they would hide but if confronted they would go down fighting.

That is what I knew Gabriel would do. It is what I would do if I felt I was on the right side. I would lie. I would kill too. Because I would feel that what I was doing was right. It had happened already. Granted for a very obvious reason that was still by my side in all things. I had killed to save Anthony. Maybe that was the difference between them and me?

I did things because I loved. Why did they do what they did? That mystery of motivation was what we had to discover. When we did, well then we would have who was responsible. Until then we were shooting in the dark.

So it was back to playing detective again. It was back to making plans that upset the apple cart. If the spy didn't like the changes already made what would they do if something really big wasn't just suggested but forced.

Michael and I started planning quickly. Gathering our forces. Getting everything in order. We would have everything together in a matter of days. The best way to upset this apple cart big time was to challenge the council head on. Starting with our resident one here in North America.

The pyros were needed in Australia. The fires for their summer had already started. They were anxious to go. Wanting to be needed instead of sitting on their butts all winter doing gopher work. Why?

Sue had been doing her own research and had asked for a transfer to one of the houses to be assigned to a police force. It had already been denied. Twice. Why?

Joshua had been told that the graduation ritual was dangerous and to stop it. Didn't he have final authority on the training of his students? That little email almost sent him flying up to the Phillip's room.

We finally got him to calm down. There were a lot of things that were getting ready to blow. It was like that pot again with all the metal things bouncing around in the boiling hot water. It was almost time to turn it upside down and give a good shake. Almost, almost.

As Thanksgiving finally arrived and the winter storms came with it everybody in the whole building was on pins and needles. We could all feel that sense of impending change or was it doom. I knew we wouldn't make it to Christmas before things blew. You just couldn't contain that amount of pressure for that long.

We waited. We did nothing for a week just to see if somebody else would stir the pot. Maybe, hoping that would make us less responsible for the chaos that would follow. We were right in a way and we were wrong too.

Everybody was responsible in some fashion. By neglect and withdraw things had deteriorated. Over time people stopped caring about themselves, their work, their lives even.

When that happens the change that follows isn't nice. It isn't easy. It is difficult and painful and sometimes explosive.

Things started out that first day of our first time of chaos almost simply. Daniel had finally come up for air during Thanksgiving. Had said he had some results he wanted to share. They weren't what I thought they were going to be.

When we went to see him down in the computer lab he had somebody new there. She was a little thing. Only around 5 feet or so with auburn hair and pretty round face. She was supposed to have been here for Thanksgiving but holiday travel and the winter storms had delayed her.

Sara was one of the few metal manipulators we had. She molded metal by simply touching it. Her hands making it almost melt as she drew images into sold blocks by just running her fingers over it. She could take a whole piece of metal and join it, shape it into anything she wanted.

Now she had a present for me and everybody else. As we trudged through the snow and ice down the mountain to the mausoleum I had thought Daniel was mental. But as soon as I saw the door I knew he wasn't. One big marble door now sported a beautiful bronze panel with all the names of every single resurrected that had been placed there.

No dates, no last names just the first and their talent if available. Some were so old that I guess not much could be found out. But I knew that the best most thorough research that was possible had been done to find out who was in there.

On the second door was another panel of unadorned bronze. This would be similar engraved when somebody new passed on. Sara said that from now on the urns would have the name of the person that resided there. It wasn't perfect and it wasn't exactly fair to those that had gone before but it was the best we could do and I thought their souls would rest a little easier now. I know mine did.

The artwork on the panels was amazing. Sara was very talented as ivy and vines circled and wound there way around and up and down the sides. For having no colors it was like those vines and leaves were almost alive and moving. How she did it I didn't know but it was beyond beautiful.

With so many compliments Sara shyly accepted them with a blush and a quiet "I am glad you like it."

"Where have you been all this time?" I asked with a smile. This woman was amazing and totally not appreciated. Well I guess most of us weren't. Judging from the sort of surprised face she got as I kept telling her how great this all was.

"Really it's nothing." She answered finally.

"I didn't even know were to start." I told her. "What you and Daniel and the others have done was right a wrong that nobody even noticed. And you did it with style and taste. It is not nothing."

For now I was happy. It would be fleeting I knew but this was just what we all needed to let go of that feeling of the world ending. It gave all a sense of perspective. Some day we would be here too. It reminded us that even though we were different. We were special. We were also mortal. We would die. There was nothing better to get your feet back on the ground than to realize that you would be dead some day.

The rest of the day should have gone simply. I was happy and so was most everybody else in the building. But leave it up to our resident councilman to throw a wrench in things again. Visitors. Of course most other countries didn't celebrate Thanksgiving. But the weather had turned ugly and Tim and a few others were having a devil of time keeping the roads even marginally clear for traffic.

European this time as other languages that I had heard but didn't know flowed down the corridors to caress my ears. The French I got and the German too. But the others were unknown. So what did Phillip plan this time? I didn't feel up to what I had done the last time. These past few weeks had frazzled almost every nerve I had.

Waiting had never been a good thing for me. It was worse when you were waiting for something bad to happen. It was like we were all stuck in the waiting room of hospital for the bad news and I had a few nightmares of when both my parents died.

My Dad of throat cancer and my mom because she just couldn't live without him and had decided to slowly wither away. But just like last time, I had somebody that loved me to stand beside me, to be there through it all. If not for Michael I would have probably gone insane or at least pulled the trigger on things early. Before we were ready.

This time I didn't mind a combat lesson. The idea of testing my abilities against the bigger guys was a way for me to blow off some steam and some of the newer guys still needed to be reminded that smaller didn't mean less dangerous.

Oh, some had seen me in action with Katherine and Joshua a few times but I had stopped challenging them right around the time Charles left and actually my combat lessons had sort of disappeared pretty much altogether over the last month. Those older guys that had also been cocky had had their trail by fire and were gone. Most greatly improved now that they weren't the senior class and had gone back to the new guys as soon as they hit their first duty assignments. Real world will do that to you.

So the newer trainees that were left hadn't really seen me grow. Didn't know all the things I could do. Hell I didn't think that two or three of the really new ones had even seen my claws yet. They were about to.

Wednesday after Thanksgiving arrived and it was time for my demonstration. It wasn't hard to put the new guys on the mats. I was small, quick and knew how to move against somebody that was two or three times my size. The new guys moved a little clumsy still not used to their bodies completely. The more experienced ones were more trouble, especially my buddy Bruce.

He had finally fleshed out as much as he was going to and he was shaped like a shorter version of Joshua. At right around 6'8" he was now all wiry, lethal muscle, Bruce was somebody to watch out for. Quick as well as strong, he had been training more and more with Joshua and I could see how all those same ways of not just moving but thinking were being absorbed by a sponge like Bruce.

But when Joshua asked for volunteers he was one that wouldn't step forward. I wasn't sure why. He would have given me a good go and I liked a challenge. Did I always win in our little mock combat sessions against the protectors? No but I always gave as good as I got and if I wasn't playing and was doing this for real I wouldn't keep my nails short.

By the end of the session I had been knocked on my butt only twice. Of course the six other guys had all been sent to the showers with bruised egos and a few scratches that would take time to heal because I hadn't asked my nails to not mark them up.

The visitors were all sort of hushed and murmuring to themselves when I finally got finished. The demonstration was all that Phillip had wanted. I could see the glow of satisfaction on his face.

Yup, this is my girl and see what she can do. If he could have managed to put a stamp on my forehead with something close to a license plate or legal ownership he would have. Well I could play nice when I choose to and I wanted to win as many of these people over to my corner as possible. So let them think what they wanted for now.

As the day went by I talked and listened and found out that even though these were all house leaders from Europe none were council, which sort of surprised me. But they too were noticing things. The five co-conspirators, as I had started to think of our group, were busy asking questions. Like what type of help could you use? Did you have extra talent that you might be willing to lend out? How about people that weren't being used because their gifts were no longer needed and were now just flotsam of days gone by?

There would always be some of those. That had a necessary talent once but time and technology had made their gift useless. What was being done with those people? We started to find out that the European house leaders where having the exact same problems we were.

Not enough cooperation from house to house and almost none from one section of the world to the next. Even ideas weren't being passed along. Some of the house leaders were taking back our ideas. The trial by fire was a big hit for their training facility in Sweden and would be suggested by the medical in charge of that house as soon as she got back.

To my surprise that little lady was nothing like Paul. She was a sight empath like Michael but the way she carried herself and the way she talked let me know she valued herself more than my husband did even now. But she was friendly and agreeable and listened well to those around her. She gave merit to others idea's. It wasn't until after they left that I found out she had just taken over. Her predecessor had just up and disappeared one day two years ago and nobody had found out what happened to him.

Okay. Now if that didn't point out to something really sinister I don't know what did. Chief medical officers just didn't up and vanish. What was even more worrisome to Michael was the medicals that were left behind weren't nearly as strong or gifted as what had been before. All the really good ones were dead or missing. Just like almost all the telepaths and empaths. If Daniel hadn't come to this same conclusion I was going to be really disappointed in him.

In Europe it had gotten so bad that some of houses were under the direction of an older other type talent. At least they hadn't put all their eggs in one basket but made it a joint leadership between a senior protector and somebody with a different outlook of things. It was almost that bad here that was why Phillip had almost forced Michael to take on the responsibility. There just weren't that many medicals of any type left.

But at least they had kept the dual guardianship going. I could see giving any one-person free reign was not smart. We had been shown that with the council. Now it was time to show it to Phillip.

We decided to wait until the visitors left. Maybe that was a mistake but we didn't like to air out dirty laundry that way. Family was one thing but telling our leader he was an insensitive ass really wasn't a good idea in front people that I considered cousins at best.

I finally got the chance to talk to Daniel and he had concluded a lot of the same things I had. He looked crestfallen when I didn't act surprised with what he had to tell us. That the medicals were being systematically killed or removed in some fashion and it wasn't just here either. It was all over the world.

I hadn't known that for sure but with what I had just learned from our European cousins it didn't surprise me. It hadn't all started at the same time exactly. The more remote regions actually had more casualties than the more civilized and that made no sense to Daniel at all. Until I pointed out that remote usually meant accidents could be arranged easier and communications itself were not as good as in other places.

Hell it took Anthony two weeks to get home from that remote training facility in Vietnam this fall. Again I was glad that he had his own protector on jaunts like that and I shivered when I thought of all the times he had traveled more or less alone to places that bad and maybe worse. Now he didn't have to. If Seth couldn't protect him nobody could.

Daniel went over a lot of what he found but he said he still had a few more things to check before he gave me everything. I tried and tried to get him to give me a hint of what it was but he was stubborn. The one thing that froze me to the bone was when he said he didn't like making unsubstantiated accusations.

What in the world had he meant by that? It couldn't be about my avalanche incident. I knew if he had a clue who had done that he would have been beating on my door immediately and to hell if it put somebody on the spot and turned out to be wrong. A life wasn't something to be played with. He and I and most everybody here felt the same way.

So now what?

Michael and I geared up for battle but things like that never turn out like you think they should. We were going to confront our council member and find out why he hadn't answered us with the suggestions we made. Why he had turned down almost every single application for transfer for the last two years. That was another nice little tidbit that Daniel had given me for our war of against apathy.

No wonder so many people were up and quitting. They were literally stuck in a rut with no hope of things changing until the big shuffle. But that time was almost here and nothing seemed to be in the works to move people around like it was normally done. No requests from the admin people going out to find out preferences of where people wanted to go. When I asked Raul who was in charge of personnel, he said that it didn't matter because he had been told just to use what he already had on file because nobody was going anywhere until things settled down some. A big shuffle now would put new people in unfamiliar situations.

I could see that to an extant but this couldn't go on for too much longer. People were going to notice that we weren't aging. Ten years was about the max we could play that game and not be found out. Some of my Florida family had been in state for 7 and change, almost 10 already for Peter and Alicia. Granted they had been in the house in Jacksonville before it burned down and the few survivors that wanted to stick around had been relocated to the outskirts of Pensacola where it was deemed safer but even they couldn't stay around much longer.

We had to start moving people and soon. Did Phillip want to increase our risk of exposure? Didn't he care at least that much. Granted maybe a different way of shuffling would be better. Send a few and not move whole houses at one time like had been the tradition. Always have some of the old crew there until the new ones settled in. Hadn't anybody thought of that? That had actually happened with Alicia and Peter once when they had stumbled into some mob type dealings in New York that even they couldn't get themselves out of. But they had been moved when nobody else was. That sort of thing had been done before when unusual circumstances occurred. Why not on a larger scale?

I had thought it before and I was again. Change was needed but chaos was not. Now we were almost to the point that chaos was all there was left because people just weren't going to take it anymore. That feeling of doom came crashing down on my head so hard and fast my knees almost buckled, as I had to steady myself against the wall.

Raul looked at me with worry. "What's wrong Gabriella?" He asked reaching out to me to offer a steadying hand.

I shook my head. "Nothing, everything." That answer wasn't much help but he seemed to understand it all to easily.

"Yes, I have noticed it too." He said his Spanish accent coming out strongly. "I have known Phillip for decades, been in this position and seen four transitions but never anything like this. There is something wrong but I can't figure out what. I am afraid."

"Me too." Admitting when you didn't have all the answers wasn't wrong or foolish. "I don't know what is wrong or how to fix it but doing nothing isn't going to work either." I said. I shook myself and stood as tall as my 5'9" frame would allow. "Time to do it."

I had done all the waiting, research and beating around the bush as I was going to. It was time, time and past time.

I found Michael, Katherine and Joshua all in the dining hall, as it was almost lunchtime. "Sorry guys but food will have to wait." I told them. "We have to go slay a dragon in his cave."

The look on their faces was a mixture of surprise, relief and almost anticipation. We had tried every avenue we could without it coming to this. Joshua and Michael both had tried to see Phillip in the last week and they could never seem to find a free time. Rafael kept greeting them at the door and the excuses ranged from sleeping because of late night conference call, on a call or some other type of political nonsense that they just gave up.

This time I wasn't going away. This time we were going to demand answers. We may not have elected Phillip but by golly he had to be answerable for his actions or inactions. Was it my right to force it? Definitely. Why? Because I said so and for once I didn't need any other reason.

# Chapter 10

## CONFRONTATIONS

Rafael answered the door. We had expected that. He told us Phillip wasn't available. I got into his face as much as our height difference allowed. Of course me being smaller never made a difference to me any more. Now I understood exactly what Rick's sister Laura had meant. When everybody is bigger it is only a matter of what angle you have to look up. More and more I was starting to appreciate her attitude.

"I don't care if he is taking a shit at the moment." I stated bluntly my language making his eyes get round and sort of bug out a little. Being small also had its advantages as I slipped right under his one outstretched arm quickly.

"Phillip, we really need a few words with you." I yelled out. My voice carried pretty well when I wanted it to.

In a jiffy he was there, all happy smiles like he hadn't a care in the world. Well goody for him. His attitude made me even madder than I had been before. "What do you need Gabriella?"

"We want to know why you didn't answer our emails." I snapped.

Now Phillip's face was confused, very confused. "What emails. I haven't had but a few in the last few weeks. I was starting to think that nobody liked me any more."

That sounded really genuine. "We sent you over a hundred this week alone." Michael answered for me. "Ideas of making changes for the better. How to augment our dwindling medical staff to keep them from burn out and ideas how to make things run smoother."

"WHAT!??" Phillip said shaking his head and looking at Rafael. "Did you get anything like that?"

Rafael shook his head too. "No. I was wondering the same thing you were Phillip. But I thought it was maybe just the holidays and people were busy doing their own thing." He said that like that was something new that he didn't really like. How much can be carried in the tone of words was amazing when you really listened.

"You never got them?" Joshua said sounding very worried. "Then where did they go? Some were even answered and it made us think that you just didn't care about anything anymore."

"Rafael you need to get to the bottom of this." Phillip said quickly. "It sounds like somebody has compromised our secure system."

"Maybe. I will find out. I might need help though. I had no clue this was going on." He said with a strained voice.

Without thinking anything of it I opened my mouth and started the whole avalanche again. "You know Daniel is the best guy we've got. I'm sure he wouldn't mind helping you. He has been a big help to me over the last few months."

I was so proud of my friend. He had helped me out with so many little and not so little things that I wanted to prove to others how good he was. Let his light shine as much as possible. The graveyard shift didn't really let that happen much.

Rafael left promising that he would get help. We knew he was good but it seemed that whoever had hacked into our system was better than he was. Nobody had a clue it had even happened so I didn't understand why Rafael was blaming himself for anything.

"This isn't good." Phillip said. Well that was sort of a redundant statement. I had begun to think that it was somebody here that had been the source of my problem but maybe it wasn't or not completely and that gave me hope. Maybe I had been totally wrong and it wasn't a friend that had been trying to kill me.

Somebody that lived in the complex could have only bugged my room but our computer system could have been compromised from anywhere. Maybe those two incidents were completely separate? Maybe the person that bugged my room was somebody that just wanted to know what was happening. Simple nosey curiosity wasn't something that could be totally ruled out as my heart tried to grab what hope it could.

Something about all this wasn't sitting right though. I could hear PIB mulling things over in my head. He wasn't talking exactly but I had gotten used to him and knew when he was thinking. Then I got an insight all by my lonesome.

"Why did you turn down Sue's transfer request?" I blurted out. She hadn't applied by email but had sent up an actual paper request with one of their many meals and had received a denial the same way. That couldn't be blamed on a computer glitch.

"What transfer?" Phillip asked and then all the little puzzle pieces came together at exactly the same time.

I knew and my face turned white and my breath went out at the same time PIB screamed out in my head RAFAEL.

Tearing out the door so fast I left everybody behind I hoped like hell I was fast enough. I wasn't.

I could hear the pounding of running feet follow me and my named yelled out a few times but it did nothing to slow me down as I flew down the steps to the medical and computer floor.

Of course nobody was there. Everybody was at lunch as I raced down the maze of corridors using my claws to dig into to the walls a few times to keep from sliding out of control as I rounded corners.

I hadn't lost the rest of them because I could still hear them but the distance between us was growing. Daniel's office wasn't empty. I hadn't expected it to be. But what I found my brain just wouldn't accept at first.

Daniel was sitting in his chair in front of his terminal with his head totally wrong on top of his shoulders. I heard Rafael behind me and ducked quickly going into a shoulder roll to keep away from his grab. There was a whoosh of his hand missing where I had been but a second ago. But I was already gone.

Now Joshua and Katherine were rounding the corner and Rafael seemed to be trapped. If that was truly the case why was he sort of half smiling? His face taking on an almost sneer.

"Why Rafael?" Joshua asked. I hadn't bothered. I knew why.

"He's Aspanari." I answered for him. All those little puzzle pieces had fit together in such a way that no other answer was possible.

Somebody had sent Gabriel on a mission into the Aspanari camp. He had thought, as had I, that is was Phillip. But now I knew it wasn't. Gabriel must have been real close to stumbling onto Rafael's secret so he had to be gotten out of the way.

That game should have also bought Anthony and his computer with him but I had totally thrown a monkey wrench into things because Rafael had no idea I would come along. I had not only gotten Anthony back but had killed Josef too. So Rafael and his buddies had adapted.

They may have actually planned to kill Gabriel at that time. I had upset their apple cart big time and they had gone through with the game Rafael, Josef and Anya had started.

Gabriel had been alive in August. Was he still? I didn't know and I probably wouldn't get a straight answer out of Rafael.

Now all four that I had left behind had arrived, Phillip being the last. He may be over 200 years old be he didn't show it. The only thing that had slowed him down was the fact he was not a protector.

Rafael was surrounded but still dangerous. I could see the cogs in his head whirling. His eyes narrowed and I knew he had made a plan and I braced myself for his attack.

It came but not my way. In less than a blink of an eye he had Michael by the throat. How he managed to get by Joshua was beyond me. Maybe because we all just knew he would try and take me on.

I was the one that had turned everything upside. But he was to smart for that. He knew he would have a tough go. So he went for what he thought was my most vulnerable side.

What he didn't know and nobody but the five of us did was that Michael was a lot more than he seemed. But even with Michael's increased speed and strength he couldn't take on somebody like Rafael. Especially the way he had his arm in an almost choke hold around my husband's neck. Michael's body firmly shifted in front of him.

Joshua and Katherine were frozen. Indecision clearly etched on their faces. Phillip looked totally in shock as who knew what was going through his mind because he too seemed unable to move an inch.

Michael's eyes grabbed mine and it was like I could almost read his thoughts. His eyes nodded in ways his head could not and even though he really had no clue what I was going to do he was prepared for whatever it was.

In a flash on inspired lunacy I tried something I had never even dreamed of before. I slung my hand out as I ordered my nails to grow and at the same time asked them to go away. I wasn't sure it would work. Wasn't sure what would happen but had a pretty good idea.

Just as I had thought my nails shot out literally. Flying daggers of over 4 inches long that flew through the air without guidance once gone. Three found they're way to my target. One hit a glass partition shattering it on impact and one buried its way into Michael's left shoulder.

Rafael bellowed in pain as one of my claws hit the nerve bundle in his left shoulder. Unable to keep the grip on Michael he let him go. If only for an instant, Michael was free.

My husband's time in the combat sessions hadn't been wasted. He slammed his elbow into Rafael's midsection and dropped down to floor. Now Rafael was exposed but not for long. He was down the hall so fast he was a blur even to me.

He would have to go up and Joshua and Katherine were after him. I knew that Michael was hurt. One of my flying claws had landed where I hadn't planned. Well planning at all hadn't been in my head. It had been a crazy; think outside the box idea that I knew Rafael wouldn't be expecting, especially with Michael right in front of him.

I hadn't asked the nails to take away their poison. The one that stopped a protector from healing, so neither Michael nor Rafael had any protection from their impact.

Michael was still lying on the floor. He wasn't groaning or complaining but I could tell that he was in a lot of pain. How did I know? I could feel it like a bad echo of heat radiating in my own shoulder at exactly the same spot.

As I kneeled by his side I could have cared less what was happening with Rafael. If Joshua and Katherine had managed to catch him wasn't important. Phillip had at least lost the frozen disbelief as he too tried to help Michael.

"It's okay." He murmured as he pulled out the nail that had almost disappeared in the muscle of my husband's shoulder.

Michael hissed for a second but his eyes never left mine. There wasn't a single bit of accusation there only love. "Thank you." He told me. His voice much stronger than I thought it should be.

"Sorry, love. But I didn't know what else to do." I told him uselessly. He knew that already. He had either seen or I had told him every single bit of my training and that hadn't been on the list.

"Very creative." Phillip agreed as his hands put pressure on Michael's shoulder. "I'm not sure that Rafael will fair well with his. If he even gets away from Joshua. Which I doubt."

I nodded in agreement. Joshua's face had been one of pure rage and betrayal. If he did manage to get Rafael I wasn't sure just how alive he was going to be by the end of it. The idea that Rafael might just end up dead didn't upset me at all. But I knew it should. There were still so many questions and without him alive to answer them we may never get them all.

Phillip's healing hands worked their magic on Michael and I knew he would be fine. The poison from my one claw didn't seem to be affected by Phillip's gift. That was another thing we had never thought to check out in these past few months. Would a healer be able to treat something that my poisonous claws had caused? Phillip obviously could, as I saw the bleeding slow down and then stop. Could feel the deep burn in my own shoulder lesson to a dull ache.

At least I hadn't broken anything. Bones were harder for Phillip to fix, muscle and tissue were more his forte. Maybe that was why he didn't go into orthopedics but stayed in more traditional surgery. You can't perform miracles as easy if you weren't in life and death situations and Phillip's ego sort of needed that. And metal was draining for him almost to the point of being dangerous. Phillip may be a naïve pain in the ass but he did give his all when the situation called for it. Like mine had several months back.

Joshua and Katherine still hadn't made it back yet and I wasn't sure if that was good or bad. But I had another obligation that made my eyes burn as they began to tear. Daniel. Michael was in the best of hands but I had to make sure that what I saw before was true. My heart and my head had refused to accept it at first.

As I came around in front of him I already knew the answer I didn't want to accept. Daniel's neck was broken; from the looks of it he hadn't suffered at all. His eyes wide-open, hands still on his one true love of a keyboard. He had died somewhere he had loved to be doing something he loved to do. How many of us get to say that? Not many.

It did nothing to lessen the guilt I felt. I had caused this. Well maybe not entirely but if I hadn't opened up my mouth like I had would Rafael had taken the time to kill my computer investigator? Or would he have just left and disappeared?

All of this left me angry and confused. Why didn't Rafael just leave to start with? He had to have known that we would discover the truth about him. Maybe not as quickly as we did but he had to have known he wouldn't be able to hide what had happened forever. We would have put the puzzle pieces together sooner or later. Was Daniel's death just a way of delaying things for just a little bit longer? Or was it something else, something bigger? My gut told me it wasn't quite so simple. There had been that information that Daniel wouldn't divulge. Could that be part of my missing answers?

I gently moved Daniel's body out of the way, pushing the chair he was still sitting in and tried to get the computer to come up but I couldn't. Techie things weren't my strong suit but even I knew how to turn a computer on and use it. Now there was nothing. No little cursor, just a totally blank screen that was as dead as its operator was.

Well this would take more than what I could do. Now both Phillip and Michael were standing at the entrance to Daniel's office/cubicle. Both looked as upset as I felt.

"I don't understand this." Phillip said. His voice coming out sort of shocky, which I guess was to be expected. Neither Michael nor he had needed to check Daniel over. Medical people certainly had one up on me when it came to being able to tell when somebody was dead.

"What don't you understand Phillip." Michael snapped. "Rafael was a spy and he had been a snake in the grass for a long time. He had been quietly sabotaging things around here for a while. Gaining more control over you and things for the last 10 years."

"Why didn't I see it?" Phillip was working real hard to figure out all of this. I sort of had a little sympathy for him. Was it his fault that Rafael had been so good at isolating him? Yes and no. He had played up to Phillip's ego and most people didn't have a problem being treated special.

Then there were weird people like me that absolutely hated it. Of course I hadn't been pushed and prodded to accept by somebody that they trusted either. If Michael had pushed me into taking all the special treatment that I had been offered saying it was my due or that it would be harmful in some way, would I have had the strength of will to refuse? I didn't know and that made it easier to see things from Phillip's point of view.

"Just give him a little time Michael." I said gently. "It has been quite a shock and he hasn't been digging into things like we have for the last few months. He has no clue what all we have discovered."

"But he should have." Michael grumbled.

"He will. Why don't you take him back upstairs and start with all the things we found out. Grab a couple of the older protector trainees just in case Rafael manages to get back in or never left." I suggested. One thing I didn't suggest was which ones. Having Daniel get killed because I had said how good he was had taught me a lesson. Never expose your helpers to anyone on purpose. You should be willing to take the heat for your own ideas. So which ever ones Michael chooses would be up to him and chance and that was as good as that was going to get.

It didn't take long to have a bunch of people down here in the computer lab. A lot more than I thought needed to be here. The entire computer techs were here, even the day and night shift ones. Paul and his medical group came and took Daniel away and would determine cause of death. Like that was a huge unknown question with his head half turned around on his neck. That was a callous thought if I ever had one but I couldn't help it.

I knew what had killed him. Rafael's big hands around his neck and head. And someday I hoped to return the compliment if Joshua or Katherine didn't beat me to it.

Finally about an hour later our head protector returned. He was still pissed and would probably remain that way for a long time. Rafael had escaped.

It had taken this long to figure out not just that he was gone but how he had done it. That masking agent had been used again. I knew whoever I was being plagued with was a good planner and wasn't really that surprised that Rafael had gotten away.

Joshua really hated to explain why he hadn't caught his prey. "He went back up the stairs to his room but with that damned spray he let loose in the stair well I couldn't tell where he went. By the time we checked all the doors and knew from the lack of tracks in the fresh snow that he hadn't gone out that way a lot of time had passed."

I nodded. Yeah, doing the unexpected had been Rafael's calling card from the beginning. But if he went up to the second floor how did he get away? "Joshua you don't mean to tell me he jumped out the window?" I asked because I just couldn't see any other way for him to be gone.

"Not exactly." Katherine growled. She was really pissed off too. "He had a rope and climbed down the cliff face. Must have been rather dicey going since the wind on that side has picked up and the snow is coming down a lot harder than it was."

"I hope he freezes." I snapped. I knew he wouldn't. He would have thought about something like this happening or he wouldn't have stashed an escape rope long enough to reach the base of the cliff. That was almost of four-story drop from the second level. Well one thing he hadn't planned on was having my nails in his shoulder and part of his chest. If he took the time to take them out he would be bleeding pretty freely. If not he would have to deal with them impeding the natural way his body moved.

"We wanted you to go out with us to track him." Joshua admitted to my surprise. "You have better senses than I do and you think like he does too."

I hissed at that but couldn't deny it. For several months now I had been training myself to think outside the box even more than I had before. Especially when it came to causing trouble for us. You can't take precautions if you don't know what might happen.

"Yeah. Okay." I nodded. But I wasn't about to let the rest of the people here fend for themselves. Granted we had almost a dozen protector trainees in residence but how much good would most of them be against somebody like Rafael and they couldn't be everywhere.

"We need to find Tim before we leave." I said as I turned and wove my way through all the people that were still milling about the computer section.

"Okay." Joshua said but he didn't understand why I would delay even those few seconds.

"He needs to lock this place down." I told him. "Nobody in nobody out but us three. I want this place so closed not even a real rat could sneak in."

"Rafael won't come back here." He said sounding a lot more confident than I felt.

"Humor me." How long would it take to tell him all my worries and fears? A lot more time than we wanted to take right now. If we stood any chance at all in finding even what direction Rafael went, if he had anybody helping, we had to move.

We found Tim in the garage bay already closing up the big roll up doors. The weather was turning nasty but not that bad. He spotted us as soon as we emerged from the corridor. "Don't want that sneaky bastard getting back in when I ain't looking."

I smiled a small smile. Tim wasn't interested in catching anybody. All he wanted was to keep his Haley safe. Keep us safe. "Lock this place up. Every door, every window, vent, nook or cranny, secure it. If you need more people draft em." I told him as I followed Joshua and Katherine out the side door and slammed it behind me.

Tim hadn't asked how we would get back in and neither did anybody else. I wasn't interested at the moment on getting back in. Just finding that snake or at least get an idea where he had gone was the only thing on my mind.

It took longer than I liked getting down the side of the hill to where Rafael repelled too. Slipping and sliding a bit in the fresh snow, I was once again glad I had claws that could dig through wood and even loose dirt easily. My footing was usually very sure but today I was trying to go so fast I ended up on my butt more than once, snagging trees to keep from going end over end. Something that would have made many people laugh but not the two I had with me. Because Katherine was in just as much a hurry that she wiped out and almost started her own avalanche of snow and rocks. If Joshua hadn't been as fast as he was we would have been digging her out at the bottom of the steep hill.

Finally, we were down and we all took a minute to catch our breath and our senses as we looked up the vertical wall almost 40 feet of solid granite. I could see the rope still dangling from what must be a broken window. Those up there didn't open up for air but were completely for show.

There was broken glass under foot now but even I couldn't tell by the feel only the way it refracted differently in the sporadic shafts of light that broke through the clouds.

That would help and hurt, the changing light might hit something just right but I couldn't trust it to show me everything I needed to see. But there was somebody else in my head that missed nothing. No matter how small, PIB saw it. How he did that was still a mystery. Did he use my eyes to see through or something else? I knew I wouldn't get an answer so didn't even try.

The tracks weren't hard to find. Rafael had hit and hit pretty hard judging from the deep impressions in the snow. A few what seemed to both Joshua and Katherine as stumbles as he left the shelter of the cliff face and then there was nothing.

"WHAT THE HELL." Joshua fumed as he scanned the area trying to pick up what wasn't there. The footprints in the snow had stopped.

I tried to find them too, looking closely for the faintest disturbance. Tried to see if I could follow his scent. His was musky one a little bit like Gabriel's was but sweeter less woodsy. Always reminded me of stale candy bars in a locker room. That should have told me that he couldn't be trusted I thought with a silent chuckle. But what I came up with made no sense until a little whispered voice told me what I had missed. "UP." PIB said.

And there on the side of the tree were scrap marks going up and up and up. I was scrambling up that damned tree before Joshua even had a clue why. Then I heard his snarl and they were climbing too. It was more difficult for them since they had to actually use the available branches and I didn't. When I got to the top I half expected to find Rafael there.

What was waiting for us again told me how wonderful he was at planning. Ropes were strung from one tree to the next, to the next. An entire pathway high up in the trees so that he could move around up here and nobody would have a clue he was here or had passed by. His scent would have never reached the ground for most and even a really sensitive protector would have taken it for an old trail since it would have been so faint.

"That little shit." I growled. Not for the first time though I had to admire his ingenuity and planning. One part of the pathway went down the mountain. The other went up.

"Which way?" Katherine asked both Joshua and me.

We both answered at the same time. "Up." I said.

Joshua said. "Down hill."

He was expecting that Rafael would do the predictable thing and that is one thing I had learned about him. Never expect the normal from him. Even hurt and on the run he would never do what somebody else would do.

Every superhero had their arch nemesis. Well I wasn't a superhero but I sure had found my arch nemesis and he had been living right under my nose for months and I never really had a clue.

I think Daniel might have but then again if he had why would he be alone with him? Probably because he just couldn't conceive of why anyone would want to hurt him. He had known Rafael longer than I had been a Resurrected so why would he really think he was a danger? Had probably been alone with him plenty of times before even.

We took our separate paths and for the first part of the airborne trek I could see Katherine looking back over her shoulder at me a couple of times. As if to make sure I was okay. Then the branches and pine needles got in the way and they were lost from sight.

I had no idea how long their path would go but mine only went less than ¼ of mile and then I understood why nobody had been able to follow the trail of the person that had shot me. It ended up just a few yards from the mausoleum.

As I scrambled down the tree I half hoped to find Rafael laid up here. He would still put up one hell of fight and wouldn't take kindly to being taken prisoner. He may not give me any options but to kill him. But all my halfhearted wishing went nowhere.

He was already gone. Too much time had passed. I could tell from the smell though that he was still bleeding as I found several discarded bloody rags, torn up pieces of clothing that he had tried to bandage himself with.

Maybe he had heard us going down the hill. It wasn't that far away and I knew I would have. I said a thank you prayer that Tim had been on top of the game. He would have secured the complex so much that other than busting in the glass door in the lobby Rafael wouldn't get back in.

That would attract way too much attention and I'm sure that the others would have thought about that too. So he would be on foot. And then I heard it, the not to distant sound of a snowmobile starting up.

As I ran and clambered back up the hill I knew I would be too late. I was. Even as fast as I was I couldn't out run a snowmobile at full throttle and I could see where the tracks lead, right down the mountain. There were a few others out here to use but I didn't have the keys and picking locks is a lot different than hotwiring a machine.

The Army Ranger guys would never show me how to do that. Thought it would be too much of a temptation for a half grown kid to go joy riding. Why the B&E idea didn't bother them I never figured out.

So I was standing there figuratively with my hat in my hand. Rafael was gone. I couldn't catch him at the moment. That still left me with a lot to do, more than I wanted. Pick up the pieces. Find out why everything had happened and what could be done to salvage as much as possible.

Waiting for Joshua and Katherine at the base of the cliff, I tried to figure out all those questions and only ended up frustrating myself. When they finally got back over 30 minutes later I was getting cold and had already gotten way beyond grumpy.

Hearing and smelling them before I saw them, I stopped my pacing that had practically worn a channel in the snow down to earth below.

"Nothing." Joshua told me. Well I would have been surprised if he had actually found something. Rafael may be a Professor Moriarty type personality but even he couldn't be in two places at once.

"No he took off on one of the snowmobiles right after we split up." I told them. That got a complete tirade of cussing from both of them. That sort of cracked me up. Not that I hadn't done more or less the same thing when I had been alone and waiting for them. By now I had gotten over most of the anger and hit the frustration and was in the general mood of just wait until I get my hands on him.

I knew I would. Stubbornness was an admiring trait sometimes and I had it from my Irish mother in spades. Sooner or later I was going to get Rafael. I had no idea how at the moment but that did nothing to stop the determination that flushed my mind.

But I put those feelings aside for right now. We had other things to do that required all the brains I had. Like honoring a fallen brother. Finding out why he had been killed. Then dealing with whatever that brought to light. I knew the next few days were going to be a roller coaster of emotions. Feeling PIB presence in my head let me know that just like always I didn't have to face any of this alone. Thank the heavens for family. I wouldn't know what to do without mine.

The rope was now missing from the cliff face. I wasn't sure who had removed it but it was a smart move on their part. Wishing for once to actually have a telepathic mate I tried to come up with how to get back in. Tim knew this place inside and out and if he decided to lock down the complex a mosquito would have had trouble getting in. We were a lot bigger than a mosquito.

Well there were locks I might be able to pick but the big roll up doors in the cargo area dropped down and were pinned at the base and sides from the inside. It was the same with the side door; it had a bar that slides across. This place had been designed to keep people out when those inside didn't want them in. I had once joked with Phillip that he had a fortress. Now I was one of those stuck on the outside wanting to get in.

The weather was getting worse now and night wouldn't be too far away and the temperature would really drop then. Of course we could survive some cold as our body temperature rose quickly to offset the fact that nobody had even thought about coats or cold weather gear before we ran off.

Time to get inside. I looked up and thought about trying to scale the cliff but knew that this almost solid block of rock was more than what I could dig into. The cargo area wasn't happening because there were no locks for me to pick, so that left the front door.

I didn't say anything to the others as we started the trek around the complex. It was on exactly the opposite side and faced almost due west. We found out that the wind was being blown with almost gale force as we rounded the corner and got hit with it almost head on.

We didn't try and talk, just trudged through the almost blizzard conditions as I tried to think of warm thoughts. By the time we reached the front door my teeth were chattering. The wind was pulling any body heat I had right out of me.

Thankfully the front door had standard locks that I would have had open in just a minute or two but with my shaking hands and shivering body it took a lot longer than that. About the time Joshua was about to crash the door in I got it and we both fell in on top of each other.

Sheez he was a lot heavier than he looked. But seven-foot men no matter how much bulk was still a lot to have land right on top as the door blew open from the snarling wind.

We managed to get the door closed and relocked without anybody appearing. As the warmth spread quickly through us, I could see that the others were wondering just exactly what I was. "Where is everybody?" Katherine asked.

I didn't have a clue either. Could we have been so absorbed in finding the obvious mole that we overlooked someone that was also waiting to strike? Maybe we had done all this for nothing and some or all of our family was dead. No that wasn't possible if Michael had been hurt or killed I would know it as my still rather cold hand wrapped around my bonding crystal. It was warm and alive and pulsing.

"I don't know where everybody is but Michael is still up on the second floor." I said confidently. "And isn't any more scared or mad than he was when we left a few hours ago."

Joshua's eyebrow went up and I could see Katherine trying to make sense of that news but didn't even have enough information to ask questions. Off we went in search of my missing husband.

As soon as we reached the stairwell we realized why nobody was around. The entire ground floor was abandoned and the stairwell door was blocked and the elevator turned off. Well when I had told Tim to secure this place he really took it to heart. Things couldn't stay this way for long. The kitchen was on this floor and people needed to eat sooner or later. But that left us in a lurch for the moment.

"At least we are warm." Katherine commented when we couldn't get anywhere in trying to find out what was going on.

"Just so." Joshua agreed. "But there are questions that need answering and we aren't any closer to finding out why Daniel is dead than before."

I plopped down on floor with a huff. "I know. I just don't understand it. Why didn't Rafael just leave and save his own skin. He had no way of knowing when we would figure it all out. I mean he must have known at that point that somebody would but why not just leave then and get a head start on everybody."

Joshua shrugged his big shoulders and Katherine looked as bewildered as I felt. Well this was getting us absolutely nowhere and I refused to sit on my butt and do nothing. We couldn't go up or down. The phones weren't even working on this floor. It was like we were in an alternate dimension or something.

I got up from the floor. "Well I am not going to do nothing. Sooner or later the rest of the building will have to show up. They can't go without food forever."

"And you can cook." Katherine laughed. That deep throaty laugh that made her face light up when she knew she had caught something before most did.

Joshua chuckled and off the three of us went to the kitchen. I had somehow lost track of time or really even the day of the week it was in all of this. Had that ever really happened to me before? Trying to go back in my head a ways I knew if it did I couldn't remember when except for that time in Florida when I had tried to die because I thought Michael didn't want me, didn't love me.

The sadness of that moment flowed over me and tears sprung in my eyes. "What's wrong Gabriella?" Joshua asked when he noticed the sniffles I had weren't because of the onions that Katherine had been chopping. "I know you blame yourself for Daniel but it wasn't your fault."

Totally misunderstanding why I was upset he had actually made the situation worse. Now the guilt I felt over exposing my brother to Rafael's hands hit me hard and I started to cry in earnest. Only a few minutes later and the smell of mint chocolate chip ice cream and a few other familiar scents caressed my nose and knew that Michael was on the way with reinforcements.

He didn't call my name, my pain and sadness had called him better than any phone could and he knew exactly where I was. I smiled at him from across the countertop that separated the kitchen from the dinning hall and it was like it always was when I saw him. Everything was suddenly better. Not perfect and with all the same problems we had had but I knew that together we would find a way.

Phillip had joined him along with about half the protector trainees along with Sue and Paul. Joshua was briefing them on what we had found out and the fact that Rafael had indeed gotten away.

What had worried me about him not leaving right away still nagged me and now another thing had been added. Why hadn't Rafael just hiked it down the hill to town? Surely he had reserves stashed there of money and things. I mean I would have if I had been him. So why hang out in a place he might be discovered until he heard us searching for him? Why did he keep cutting things so close?

Had he been waiting until our guard was down so that he could sneak back in and cause more problems? Maybe kill more people too? Something about that scenario didn't sit right. No, he had done plenty of damage and if something had kept him here it wasn't because he was trying to cause more. He had killed Daniel because he was worried that Daniel had found something or would and he wanted him out of the way because obviously he hadn't told me or anybody else. If Daniel had, Rafael wouldn't have gotten a foot in his escape.

That meant that he might have been getting back in because he left something he didn't want found. Some damning piece of evidence but not something that would condemn him but somebody else, maybe a lot of some bodies.

Now a plan was forming in my brain. "Paul did you make that masking agent for Rafael?" I knew he didn't. Joshua had described it to him when I had my attack to see what type of reaction he had. It was one of curiosity and confusion. He had no idea that was even possible. We had at that time no samples but maybe now we did.

"No of course not. Joshua told me what happened on the ridge and how you smelled something that confused even your nose. Yours is the most sensitive I have ever come across, if you couldn't make heads or tails of it most of us wouldn't have even known what it was."

"Can you search Rafael's room and see if there is any more there. If there is can you make more of it?"

Paul nodded. "If there is I will figure it out." Most people would have said they would try but Paul was one of those type people that didn't try, he did. No matter what it took or whom he had to keep up all night or all week it would happen. I smiled. He may have personality issues but putting your money on him was the safest bet I could think of.

Okay. First issue tackled. I wanted some of that masking agent. Something Michael had brought up weeks ago. I may be able to change what I looked like but I was still recognized as Resurrected and no matter what I tried I couldn't change the way I smelled or at least not totally but maybe if Paul figured out how that masking agent worked I could get some help there too.

Now the more pressing issue of why hadn't Rafael just left. The gig as they say was up so what had he been protecting, hiding. That was a two-fold question. Obviously it had to have something to do with Daniel's computer because that had been wrecked pretty well on the quick look I had been able to get.

"Has anybody had a chance to look at what was wrong with Daniel's computer?" I asked to everybody assembled. Michael looked confused and so did everybody else. Well I was dealing with a bunch of highly trained muscle for the most part but some of these had been cops and soldiers so why hadn't they thought to investigate?

I snorted. "Gee what happened during your transition? Did your brain get dumped like a computer and you don't remember what you were?" Asking the few closest to me that I knew for a fact had been beat cops, one in Atlanta, and one in Baltimore. Both almost killed in the line of duty. It had been so easy to make them disappear. I wondered for a second what story the recruiters came up with but it was always something that made perfect sense given the situation.

Now I could see things start to click behind their eyes and the talk went quickly into what I couldn't follow. I wasn't trained in forensics but I think these guys were barking up the wrong tree and I didn't want to waste time on things we already knew.

"We know who killed Daniel." I said stopping their animated discussion that had drawn just about everybody else in immediately. "I caught him. If you want to verify it was Rafael fine, we can do that later, but right now we need to find out why. Why not just leave? Why kill Daniel when that put him in danger with the delay? What was it that he was afraid Daniel would know or find out? Why sabotage his computer? He was in a hurry, had no chance to go back to his room for any length of time. Did he leave any evidence behind that might help us?"

I was putting to words all my thoughts I had had in the last few hours. Things that obviously Joshua had thought of too. He was nodding his head in agreement.

So it was decided that those protector trainees that had investigative experience would team up with the computer people. Try and track down what Daniel had been working on. Others would go through Rafael's room with a fine toothcomb and find what was left behind. Maybe something written down, a plan or agenda of some type or a contact list even. It would be well hidden because Rafael was beyond computer savvy and didn't think inside the box much either.

I couldn't help and I knew I would only get in the way so I let them do what detectives and investigators have done in some way or other for centuries. Investigate, snoop, ask questions and draw conclusions. With Joshua to help organize and find out who had what detailed background the dining hall was soon very empty, with only Philip, Sue, Michael and I left.

Phillip was still looking a little numb and I could understand that. Michael wasn't. My husband only wanted to stay as close to me as possible. My fear and anger had probably been very frustrating for him. He knew I was as safe as possible with Joshua and Katherine and that he couldn't have helped much. Could probably pretty much track me or at least could tell when I was outside or inside if he focused on his crystal. But all of this had drained him, the injury my claw had caused and Daniel's death and having to deal with a very surprised and upset Phillip must have fried just about every nerve he had on top of me being away from him which he never liked much to start with. Now that I was safe and everybody was doing other things I could tell he just wanted to be near me.

This wasn't the time for sex. We both knew it but the holding of my hand and gentle caress was enough to have him sort of smiling in a few minutes.

Phillip clearing his throat brought us both back to the situation at hand. "I don't know whether to thank you all for this or not." He said.

"You should kiss their asses." Sue snapped. "If they hadn't done all they did how much worse would it have gotten? And you were totally clueless. All of you on the council were. Thinking just because you were older than most of us you were infallible and nobody could do anything better than you."

WOW. I was sort of shocked too. Sue saw a lot but rarely said anything. I knew it but now she had not just stepped up to the plate she had hit a line drive right at the pitcher on purpose. And it had hit Phillip right between the eyes.

She wasn't finished either as she kept going. "Gabriella and Michael have done things in the last few months that should have never fallen to them to do. We are all to blame in one way or another. We have all gotten complacent and stuck in the way things have been. It took her pointing it out to me but she was right. I haven't been happy for a very long time and I should have done something about it before. Should have come straight to either you or Raul and asked for reassignment but I didn't. My fault but the rest of this mess isn't my fault and now you need to do exactly what should have been done before. Find out how Rafael got in here and see if there are more of his type around."

I could see where this was going and had to stop it before it snowballed into a worse disaster than the one we were dealing with. "NO!!!"

"What? No? We need to be secure." Phillip said whipping his head around to stare at me in anger.

"You don't want to turn this into a witch hunt either. Yes, we need to investigate but to make everybody suspect would destroy us worse than what Rafael has already done."

Michael wasn't very happy with my evaluation either. "But Phillip is right. We need to see if there are others that can hurt us."

"Yes we do." I agreed. "But in the right way. Not by turning loose on everybody at once on a paranoid vendetta. Most people here are very loyal and wouldn't hurt anybody. That's why they are still here. If they were disillusioned enough they would have already left. How many have we lost in the last 10 years? Plenty. The ones that stayed are probably the most loyal we have."

"Or they are here for another purpose." Phillip snapped again.

"Possibly a few and maybe none at all. Isn't it possible that Rafael was the only one? Of course it is. What little help he may have gotten he could have received from unwitting hands. If you are going to crucify people for being ignorant you might as well join them Phillip."

"Then what would you suggest? We need to make sure our house is clean." He was listening but still not happy. I couldn't blame him for that either. But couldn't he see that to go and pull a Spanish Inquisition would do more harm than good no matter how many Aspanari spies we had.

"First we let the investigators do their thing. Who knows what they may find. It may solve all our problems or it may change the questions we have completely. Let it take the time it needs to take. We have a few other things to take care of in the mean time." Everybody got what I was saying without saying. Daniel. He should be mourned and honored for the fallen hero he was.

"Yes." Phillip agreed sadly. "Daniel paid a price I never want anyone to pay."

"Sweet boy. Never had a clue what he was getting into." Sue chimed in. That made me feel guilty but not as much as it would have even an hour ago.

No, Daniel had known a lot more than even I did. I didn't know what that was but Daniel was good at ferreting things out in a computer but did he also put things together as well in the real world. He lived and breathed in cyber space. He was home there and this one just didn't fit him as well or was I wrong? He knew that there was something going on, something dark and sinister. We had discussed it and he had wanted to be absolutely sure before he turned loose whatever it was he had discovered.

Thinking harder on that subject I realized that it wasn't ignorance that had lead him into what happened or even naivety. He had realized, even before I did, what kind of repercussions an Aspanari spy in our midst would cause. He had wanted to be sure before you pointed fingers, maybe he even suspected Rafael and that was why he put himself in that position. To find out once and for all if it was true. He might have deliberately put himself at risk to give him the chance to prove himself friend or foe in the only way that would eliminate any doubts.

Daniel had sacrificed himself. Not on purpose I was sure but I was also pretty sure that he hadn't done it because he was clueless or stupid. That wasn't the Daniel I knew, not at all.

We fixed dinner, it would be rather late but I think most people's hunger would be severely diminished tonight. Only four of us but Phillip gamely put on an apron and pitched in to help and when everybody came rolling up when Joshua had Tim give the all clear they were even more subdued than I thought they would be.

There were several noticeable absences, the computer geeks and all but two of the protectors were not at dinner and the mood was so subdued it was quieter than the mausoleum down the hill was.

Nobody talked much and when they did it was with quiet whispers and more than a few sniffles could be heard in the room all during dinner. Everybody left as soon as possible, all wanting to keep to their own thoughts.

The four of us waited. Waited for what Joshua and the others would find out. Waited also to see if we could help. It would be a long sleepless night but for the life of me I couldn't see doing anything else. Finally at around dawn I had had enough of staring at ceiling and floor tiles to last a lifetime or at least a normal human one.

Getting up without saying anything to anybody, I realized that two of us had fallen asleep. Phillip was with his head thrown back sitting in a chair. I was surprised he hadn't snored. Sue was curled up in corner with her chin resting on her knees. Maybe I should have woken them up to go to bed but I couldn't force myself. At least this way they had a little peace, a little chance to hide from all of this.

Having Daniel die like he had would hurt everybody. We were all so close now and that was one of the bad things about what had happened since I got here. Now when somebody was lost it made the parting all that much harder, a lot harder to take than it had been.

Michael looked at me. Maybe he was hoping I heard something he hadn't. I shook my head. "Just can't sit any longer. My butt is numb." So was just about every other emotion I had at the moment too.

He nodded and went back to staring at nothing, lost in his own thoughts, his heart as heavy as mine was right now.

I wandered away aimlessly. Went by the workout room and pools and the lobby with its windows fogged up from the cold. At least the snow had stopped for the time being. Oh it would be back again in a day or so according to the weather people.

I hadn't checked out anything but the first floor since all this had started and I soon found myself on the second and could easily hear the conversations of the people in Rafael's room, still very much in the investigative mode. There was no place for me there and would just be a distraction.

As the sun came up I found myself in the ivory tower again. Someplace I thought was very appropriate. It was a chance to say a private goodbye to a friend in a place he had loved at a time of day he would have enjoyed too. I put on some music for company. Something I hadn't done in what seemed like months. For so long music had been one of my constant companions and I had missed it and hadn't realized how much had changed in my life in the last few weeks alone.

I had been so busy trying to fix things that I had forgotten that I need to stay healthy mentally too or I wasn't good for much. Things like that are so easy to put aside when your world was being turned every which way but right.

A song came on just as the sun broke through the clouds and came streaming in the window to land straight in my face. It was like the world was saying hello as those same words came across the speakers. Hello World by Lady Antebellum was so right for the moment, sad and inspirational and moving.

Daniel's scent had been just as unique as he was, a mixture of fresh linen drying on a line and some tropical scent like mangos but yet not. Suddenly it filled my nose and I knew he was there. Not in body but in spirit. My knees hit the floor as I realized this would be the last chance I ever had in this earth to feel my friend. Trying to say what couldn't be said in a hundred years in just seconds I knew time was a fleeting thing and that smell was just gone.

I tried to reach for it but you can't grab something that is not really there no matter that I had claws that could make a hole in almost solid rock. You can't catch the wind or a departing spirit of a friend that was saying goodbye.

When I got up from the floor I realized I was no longer alone. Several of the computer people, including Brenda and Simon along with a few of the protectors were standing in the doorway with Michael.

I didn't know what to say, so I said nothing as I wiped away the tears on my face. Didn't apologize because showing what you felt is never wrong, possibly inappropriate or uncomfortable but never wrong.

There was a look in their eyes that I didn't understand, one of amazement and wonder. Could they have seen what I only felt? I guess I would have to ask my husband later because one thing I did know. Answers had been found.

# Chapter II

## RATS IN THE CORN CRIB

J had been right, there were answers but those answers brought out even more questions than we had before. The computer geeks turned loose en masse was beyond a force to be reckoned with. Along with those protector trainees that had been investigators in some capacity in their former lives, they had turned Rafael's room upside and inside out.

They had found plenty of that masking agent for Paul to play with and our chief medical officer was down in the lab with a gaggle of his people taking it apart to see how to put it back together. I was positive that when I had to go up against the Aspanari again I would have my own version of it to help me slide into their presence without being known for what I was.

Joshua and the chief of the computer section, a man named William, had come up with a lot of things that had scared all of us to the bone. Daniel had been a lot smarter than Rafael had given him credit for. He had more than left breadcrumbs for someone to follow and figure out what he had discovered even with his own computer totally destroyed.

Most of the time Daniel kept his work on his own server until he turned the completed work over to his boss. The rest of the computer people were similarly like-minded. Sort of on the paranoid side they didn't like somebody looking over their shoulder until the work they had taken on was complete and ready. But this time Daniel had put an encrypted file that was updated on a daily basis on the internal servers. Something almost everybody had access to so who would look for something that was a secret work project where just about anybody could find it? That was why Rafael hadn't discovered it. Daniel had mailed it back to himself everyday. William had been impressed and said it was a simply elegant plan.

There was plenty of evidence according to the computer people that somebody had been monitoring computer activity and it was no wonder that Rafael had targeted Daniel. He would have known who was looking into what and would have probably killed him even if I hadn't said how much help he had been to me. The computer guys had torn through Rafael's own personal computer and discovered an email system set up completely separate from everything else.

I would have thought that would have given us all the evidence we would have needed of conspiracies and who was involved. But Rafael was a smart SOB. He had written a program that deleted all incoming mail within just a few hours of being opened and read automatically. The only thing remaining was what had come in since he left. It wasn't a whole lot but fortunately it did have a few things we could use.

There was an email that could have only come from Anya, which sent my heart into complete freefall. From the way it was phrased Gabriel was still with her and still very much alive. It never mentioned him by name and the email didn't really identify the sender in any way but just from the way it was worded it was the only thing that made sense to me. Michael agreed.

Of course this caused all sorts of problems because nobody but the two of us had a clue that Gabriel hadn't defected like it had been reported. That he had thought that Phillip had sent him on a mission to find out what was going on with the Aspanari.

Phillip of course wanted to hear nothing about it. From his point of view I could understand it. He had his hands full already and that little wrinkle wasn't something he wanted or needed to worry about.

It was taking all he could do to handle the bigger picture. Even though there was no evidence from Rafael's computer to confirm it, Daniel had painted a very good picture of a very intricate and deadly conspiracy. A conspiracy that showed that there was a least one spy tied to every single center that were disrupting everything and had been for a very long time.

He had compiled a very compressive list of deaths of our medicals along with the telepaths and empaths. When it had started increasing, where and how they had died even. It clearly showed that those that had died or disappeared had been linked to a systematic plan to weaken us targeting the strongest and most pivotal people first and working down the list from there.

The destruction of the empaths in particular was a really bad thing. They helped everybody not just the Nohus. I could see how just one death had changed a lot around here. Mary's had changed the way the protectors were trained and now they weren't as effective as the older ones were. Joshua about came unglued when Daniel most specifically made a good argument that her death had been caused by the same person that had almost killed me. The circumstances had been almost identical. I had noticed the similarities too but said nothing because I didn't have any proof, just hunches. And Daniel to had no proof but his hunches sure were scary in their accuracy.

Now Joshua had even more incentive to find and kill Rafael. But for now he, Paul and Phillip had their hands full. Those three along with every other section chief were even now compiling their own list. List of people to be questioned and investigated and our resident over reacting council member had already asked the last of the telepaths to come running.

The Spanish Inquisition was starting and I couldn't do a damn thing to stop it. I had tried. Argued until I was blue in the face almost literally but nobody would listen. Finally I had met a stonewall of resistance. Phillip was bound and determined to get to the bottom of this. No matter if it drove a few people off. In his opinion those that left were already guilty and he would shed no tears over them.

I almost told him to get bent and walk off right then and there but when I looked at Michael and how he too just didn't seem to understand how these actions would hurt us more in the long run than any information we garnered could, I knew I was in the minority. Actually standing on my lonely only was more the truth.

Could I be wrong? Yes, but I didn't think so. I knew how I would react if I were accused, brought in for questioning just because I happened to get transferred at the right time or if by chance I had been in the wrong place at the wrong time or had the wrong attitude. Yeah I could see me being accused of that last one real easy.

Phillip had also been on a teleconference with all the other council members and recommending exactly the same thing be done there. If this wasn't a Titanic type disaster I didn't know what one was. I had once said something about starting a snowball rolling down hill. Little did I know that the one that came from my wanting to find out why nobody was happy any more would turn brother against brother. It had taken a life of its own and I could do nothing.

Nothing but shake my head and try and contain the damage as much as possible. But when I kept arguing against all the paranoid actions I finally got told to essentially go to my room and let the grown ups deal with the problems.

I left the second floor conference room in complete disgust. I had tried but now there was nothing I could do. Nobody was willing to listen.

When I finally hit my room I slammed the door so hard it almost broke as I heard the wood splinter a bit in the frame. It didn't dampen my anger and when I heard a knock on the door a few minutes later I almost screamed in my frustration.

"WHAT!!!" I bellowed as I opened the door to find Anthony standing on the other side.

Anybody else might have been a little shocked, maybe even a tad afraid. Not him, not my brother but he did look worried.

"I know what happened with Gabriel, he never was a traitor was he?" He said without so much as a bit of warning.

"No." I snorted. Well finally somebody besides Michael and me were championing him.

"All of this made me review what happened in Mobile a little closer. It finally dawned on me that the friend he mentioned was something more than just remorse. I researched that name Vesper Lynd, found it as a character in a spy novel and I knew it couldn't have been a coincidence. But I really didn't know what he was trying to tell you, that he wasn't the traitor he was pretending to be. You both should have gotten academy awards for that performance." He said nodding his head in appreciation of what we had to do to get Gabriel into the Aspanari camp. That he put it together at all with the little bit of information he had was amazing.

"For all the fat good it did." I fumed. "They knew he wasn't a spy. That he was just trying to find out the way they worked. I'm really surprised he is still alive."

"I know. Why would Anya keep him around? She has to know that he will come back to us as soon as he gets something concrete. Something he feels will fulfill his obligations."

I kept forgetting that Anthony knew everybody. That he remembered not just who they were but what their personalities were like. And he didn't even know about that nice little picture with the message on the back asking me to come and get him in February.

Now with Rafael gone I think that time frame just got moved up. Gabriel wasn't going to find out anything Anya didn't want him to know. From what I had been able to understand of her personality she was probably dangling things just mess with his head. She was the queen of manipulation.

Maybe that was the reason Gabe was still alive to start with. A new toy that she could play with, somebody she could try and turn inside out like she had Michael. I didn't think she would get as far with Gabriel but he might just be smart enough to go along to see what it might get him.

From the message that I had thought Anya had sent Rafael she was a little frustrated that she wasn't getting the responses she wanted but she also hadn't given up on the plan either. I could just imagine how badly she wanted to mess with Gabriel, if for no other reason than he was Michael's best friend. If she were the manipulative woman I took her for that would have been like giving cream to a cat. Something she couldn't resist if she tried.

But now Rafael wasn't stuck here in hiding. He was out and about in the world. Granted he was injured but sooner or later he would heal. I knew when I gave a lethal blow and when I didn't. His would bleed and hurt and maybe even damage some tendons for a bit but he would survive what my three claws had done to him. Then he would be looking to catch up with Anya and her group and I had no doubt that when he did he would kill Gabriel no matter how much Anya might not like that idea.

I had tried to do what I thought was right here and nobody would listen to me. Not even my own husband, which totally pissed me off. Well if I couldn't do any good here I could certainly find somebody that needed help. Gabriel, my brother, was in trouble. A lot more trouble than even he probably realized.

There was an outstanding obligation that I had and now I had absolutely no reason to stay here. I was just annoying the hell out of everybody. Even though I had caused all this to come to light now it was like I was just in the way.

Maybe it was a bit of a pique I was feeling, actually I knew it was but it did nothing to take away the urgency I felt when I thought of my brother. Something that had fallen by the wayside as others and I dug into things and found out how deeply all these problems went.

Anthony had been quietly standing while my mind went on its trip, his eyes never leaving my face. I was getting no argument from PIB that this was wrong. He didn't seem to have an opinion at all which really wasn't that surprising. When I got a head of steam going on something he usually just shut up and let me either do good or fall on my face. Which this one would turn out to be was anybody's guess.

Now a plan was forming in my head. I would need things and I would need help. I was no good at finding people other than my own husband or somebody that I could literally sniff out. Gabriel's location was a mystery to me. That meant I had to make a call to Florida. Explain a few things that nobody down there knew.

I would get a little anger but I also knew there would be relief. Relief that Gabriel our friend, protector and brother hadn't let us down like I had made everybody think he had. The price of secrecy was high but I did what I thought was best. Alison in particular would be relieved and happy, maybe not at first but when it all sunk in she would be happy. She had known Gabriel forever and what she thought had happened had hurt her a lot more than she tried to show.

"I need to leave." I blurted out and Anthony did a sort of double take.

"We need you here." He shot back.

I shook my head. "Nobody is listening. I am just beating my head against a brick wall with Phillip and everybody else. They are going to do exactly what they want and I can't stop them. But Gabriel's situation I can do something about."

He mulled that over for a second or two and nodded his head. "Yes. I can understand how you feel. I'll come too." He offered.

"No, they will need you here. You may be able to talk some sense into them from a logic stand point when appealing to their emotions hasn't worked."

Our walking recorder was the best at doing that. Taking all the things he saw and heard and finding the patterns in them. Maybe Anthony would see how horrible this could turn out if I just stopped nagging him about it. He had been all for the Spanish Inquisition too.

He shook his head. "You know I don't agree with you about that."

"I know you don't now but you will. When you start seeing people leaving in droves you will know I was right. Maybe I'm wrong. I hope I am but with all the work overload and the other things that have been going on I have a feeling this is going to be the straw that broke the camel."

"No, I don't think so. What you have done has pulled us all tighter. Nobody will leave now no matter what type of questioning they have to go through and we really need to be sure who is loyal and who isn't."

I wasn't going to argue with him anymore. We had already been over this so many times I would remember until I died, I shrugged it all off. This had been the reaction I had gotten for the last day and change. There is a point in time when you realize that what you want isn't going to happen and when you reach it you have a decision to make, to keep fighting an impossible battle or withdraw with dignity. I had made mine. I may be the first to bail but I wouldn't be the last. One good thing was that I wasn't resigning. I was just going off to fix a problem that I knew I could do something about.

It didn't matter if not too many other people deemed it an important problem. I knew it was. Yes, Gabriel was just one person but we all made up the whole and anytime you lost one it diminished those that were left. We had so few of us that to lose even one now hurt.

So I was going and that was that. If Michael wanted to come too he could. I wasn't sure if he would or not. This facture between us was the tip of the iceberg in my opinion. It showed how much people were not willing to listen and I was just as guilty as they were because I too thought they were wrong. So instead of continuing to argue I would leave. Find something else that I might be able to do good with.

For the moment I could completely understand why so many people had abandoned the cause. If they felt they were wasting their time and potential then why not see what they could do on their own. I had an advantage over them though. I could leave because I wasn't assigned to this place to start with and lucky because there was absolutely no regulation that said how long it had to take to get to where you were going. The higher ups hadn't made one for that yet but if I kept pushing things they probably would. By that time it would be too late at least for this trip.

Anthony had taken only a few seconds to absorb all this and then he was right there pitching in. "Okay. You are going. I'm not happy about it but I can tell by that look on your face that I won't change your mind. What can I do to help?"

"Go down to medical and see how they are progressing with the masking agent. I think I will be needing that before all this is done." Everything else I thought I might need I could get myself. Right now I didn't want to butt heads with Paul. He was a great guy in his own right but his personality and mine had never gotten along easily. Now with all that was going on he would be totally in that mode that was really good for doing his job and absolutely not what I had the patience to deal with.

Anthony nodded and left without another word. Now I started to pack. All those things that I brought were coming back with me. The few things that I had purchased while here I would leave. If Michael decided not to come with me he would probably be able to use them. It made my heart even heavier to think that we would be apart but I had been shoved in a position that I didn't feel I had many choices. This was the only thing that I could do and feel right about myself.

I couldn't change what everybody else was doing. But I couldn't stand by while they could possibly destroy what was left of us either. The best thing I could do was leave for a bit then if things did go really bad they might be willing to listen to reason. If things didn't go as horribly wrong as I had a feeling they might then I would be doing a job that needed doing and I wouldn't be an annoying thorn in the side for everybody.

Nodding to myself as the last of my suitcases was packed, I knew I had made the right choice. Going down to the cargo dock, I grabbed one of the luggage carts and was back to my room in just a few minutes. When I rounded the last corner I was sort of surprised to find my husband leaning up against our door.

He wasn't happy. His handsome face a mask of pain and disappointment. He had seen the luggage cart I was pushing in front of me. Did he really think I would leave without letting him know? Without giving him the chance to come with me? From the look on his face that was exactly what he thought.

"Why?" Was the only thing he asked. Which why I wasn't sure. Why leave, why not say something to him because I knew that was what he was thinking. Why give up and run away because that is what I was doing in a sense.

"I wasn't going to leave without telling you." I answered him. That issue was far more important than anything else.

"But you don't want me to come with you. You have been upset with me for days because I don't agree with you." Michael sounded so disappointed. I wasn't sure why and this heart spark thing right now was more of a pain in the ass than a help. I could feel what emotions he had but not tell why he had them. And like now when a lot of strong emotions were running around in his heart it was hard for me to make sense of any of it.

I wasn't a trained empath and I didn't want to be. That had been a talent that I hadn't wanted when I first heard about them. Now I was what I was and had that gift rolled into too. I couldn't help but sigh.

Everything had gone straight down hill from the moment Daniel had died. I had studied history and knew that sometimes it wasn't a huge thing that started a war or a disaster but something small. Not that I considered his death a small thing but in the giant scheme of things it was. Now that spark had ignited a fire, the blaze of which was impossible to contain.

This was why he had been so hesitant in revealing what he had discovered. Maybe if he hadn't died like he had, we could have worked things out with more discretion but I had forced things because I hadn't known what I was doing and now everybody was paying the price.

Looking at my husband's face I could still see the pain there as easily as I could feel it echoed in my own heart. "No, I want you to come with me. But I wasn't sure you would. Gabriel is in trouble. I know it and I'm going to go get him before Rafael can find him and kill him or before he can convince Anya he needs to die."

"Okay." He answered. He didn't say anything else. Just opened up the door and started packing too.

I was surprised and yet not. Getting on the phone I made a call I needed to make and was ready for another bout of anger.

This time I didn't get any. A little confusion but no anger at all and other than a direct order from my sister Alison that if I ever did something like that again she was going to come unglued on my head because one free pass was all anybody got that was it.

It would take them a few days to wrap things up but I had help coming. The best help I could have asked for, the rest of my family. Not that the people here I hadn't grown close to because I had but those three down in Florida, plus Gabriel, Anthony and of course Michael would always be the ones I knew I could depend on and that I would turn to when I wanted answers that I knew I could trust, good or bad.

We would meet up in St. Louis. Not my favorite city but it was sort of in the middle and we could decide where we needed to go from there. Peter wanted to spend time with that picture I had been sent and see if

Alicia could zone on the ring that Gabriel had on. If she could then it would be easy to find him. If not, well that would certainly complicate things. But I knew Peter and his little redheaded wife had found people with a lot less information. It was only a matter of time.

Michael was packed and ready to go by the time I got off the phone. He helped me load everything onto the luggage cart and started pushing. Never once did he look back and I could feel things start to change in his heart and mine. We were once again a united pair on a mission and I had to smile a bit. Was it going to always be our fate to be the ones to go out on limb? Probably, the way I did things I just couldn't see it changing. I thought outside the box, been given a job that sort made sure I was doing things without the support of a lot of people and sometimes none at all. Most people didn't understand so that meant I had to do the slightly and sometimes not so slightly weird things that were unpredictable to get the job done.

We put everything in the back of my truck except for one suitcase a piece with our heavy winter clothes in them and my laptop and the sat phone I hadn't had to use since we got here.

Then we went in search of all of our camping gear that Tim had stashed with all the ones the center had. That took longer than packing did. It was everywhere and I had problems figuring out which was actually mine. In the end it didn't matter whether I got the exact stuff I came in with as long as I got the same type of stuff then nobody could bitch about it.

Michael hadn't complained this time when I told him we needed to be well prepared before we left. This was dead winter even though the calendar technically said it was fall it wasn't. Not here. And I had about frozen my ass off when I went out searching for Rafael just the other day. I wasn't about to go off without thinking things through this time.

We were packed and almost ready to go. Now we had to say goodbye. Something I hated doing but also knew I had to do. I hoped everybody had gotten so used to me doing odd things that they would take it in stride now.

I was wrong.

Phillip about came unglued. If I thought he had been mad at me the last few days this was nothing compared to the tirade I got when I told him of my worries about Gabriel and that I personally needed to go get him.

"No, you are not going." He said sounding just like a dictator. It was all I could do not to stick my tongue out at him. I knew he had to see how pissed I was getting and just what that could mean.

"Why are you so worried about Gabriel anyway?" Joshua asked. He didn't want me going anywhere either. What made it worse is that he really didn't buy that Gabriel had been mislead into leaving us. He still thought exactly what I had tried my damnedest to make them all believe. But Gabriel hadn't betrayed us in general and Michael and I in particular, it had been a ruse to get him where he thought he needed to be.

"Because he is trouble." Michael answered for me. Once again it was us against the world and I shot him a look of gratitude.

Phillip didn't understand what it meant to be family. Then something that I had totally missed came roaring in my head. "If Stephan were in trouble like that you would move heaven and earth to help him." Stephan had been Phillip's friend for at least 3 normal lifetimes or more if I added things up right.

Phillip blushed and looked away from me quickly. I had no idea what I had stepped into when I brought up Stephan but it was a strong, guilty something.

"What happened between you two?" I probed deeper. I hadn't seen Stephan since he had come down to Florida to bring Anthony. Stephan was a truth seer, a more generic and limited form of an empath or telepath, some of both but not really either one.

Why hadn't Stephan seen what was going on with Rafael? Was he in on all this and Phillip just didn't want to admit how deeply he had been played? Was that it? Was that why he didn't want to believe that Gabriel could still be on our side, because his own best friend had let him down?

Something about that didn't ring true. Stephan had known that I wasn't what I was pretending to be but he had said nothing. He could have totally blown my story if he had wanted to. Warned Rafael that I was something to be watched out for and they might have just changed their plans totally. But Rafael had no more clue I was an infiltrator than anybody else had. Nobody knew because I had listened to PIB and was grateful I had obeyed his warnings even though at the time I thought he was an annoying pain in the butt for all his worry.

"Rafael set him up didn't he?" I said as I jumped to the only conclusion that fit the situation. Rafael had known that sooner or later Stephan would figure out what he was. He had probably kept as much physical distance from him as possible but as things came to a head in Florida he didn't have that luxury any more and he had caused a falling out between the two friends.

It would have also made Phillip more vulnerable to manipulation without Stephan to be a reality check. Stephan was out in the real world a lot and because of his talent would have been hard to fool. Maybe Stephan had known something was up with Rafael but had given him the benefit of the doubt just like he had me. But if something had happened to him then Phillip would have done just what I said, used every resource to find out what happened and why.

That would have been something that Rafael wouldn't chance. To have Phillip turn out every resource to find out why somebody he cared about had died or disappeared. So Rafael had caused a distancing instead, something that nobody would look into much not even Phillip.

"He turned me against him." Phillip whispered. "And I had no idea. None at all." Guilt was the main reason Phillip was reacting as he was. Why he was now refusing to listen to anybody that didn't agree with him completely and absolutely. It just reinforced the idea that it would be better if I left. This attitude wasn't something I could deal with and I knew that only more hard feelings would be the result if I stayed.

But I couldn't go against orders totally so I played the only card I had to play. "I am leaving Phillip and since my transfer here was only temporary to start with you can't stop me. Michael and I are going home to Florida."

He knew what I wasn't saying. That the route and the time it took would be dictated by where Gabriel was and how hard it would be to find him.

Joshua really wasn't happy about it either. "Absolutely not or at least not right now. There is big storm coming. The weather sensitives have been having a fit for a week regarding this one."

"All the more reason to get going before we get snowed in for a month." I snapped back. "I will not stand by and have somebody I love die because I was too chicken shit to brave a little snow and ice."

There were more arguments coming but I more or less just tuned them out. I could be stubborn too. I was going as soon as I could get out the door and nobody was stopping me. Trying for as polite as I possibly could I stood my ground and pretended to listen even though everybody there knew nothing could sway me.

It took another hour before both Joshua and Phillip ran out of words. Phillip had tried to order me not to leave but he couldn't. Joshua couldn't stop me because both he and I knew that all my combat training had been completed weeks ago and I had been utilized more as another instructor for the last month or more. There was no logical reason they could give me to stay and that was it.

I didn't even have to go to medical to get some of that masking agent. Anthony was leaning up against my truck as Michael and I came into the cargo bay. He had a small package in his hand and he looked totally delighted with himself.

Michael started chuckling as soon as he got a good look at his face. "So why do you look like that cat that ate the canary?" He asked with a big smile on his face too.

"Because Paul didn't want to let any of this go so I snitched his first batch when he wasn't looking and I took some of the original too just in case he isn't as good as he thinks he is." Anthony chortled.

"But he is isn't he?" I asked. I had gotten to about 5 feet of him when I realized I didn't smell his cotton candy scent. "You just had to go and try some on me before I left didn't you?" Typical Anthony always pushing things, he had been like that since I met him and I loved him more because he was sort of like me. Always trying to annoy people because it upset the apple cart.

Anthony just threw his head back and laughed. As I focused on the smell in the bay I also knew this was not the same thing that I had encountered at the avalanche sight either. This was just different enough that it totally colored Anthony's smell. Paul had outdone himself. He had made it so that you couldn't even tell what we were or that we were there at all.

I couldn't smell me, Michael or Anthony at all. In fact it had a slightly sour smell, the same thing you got when a Nohu had been around. Now how Paul had done that I didn't know, didn't want to know and at the moment could care less. I would take his hard work and run. Anthony could fend for himself. What could Paul do anyway? Not much other than get mad and chew him out. If he even figured out where it went and didn't blame me to start with. And I didn't have any problem with it if he did.

I hugged my skinny brother tightly to me and looked into his blue eyes. "You keep them straight okay, handsome." I said as a few tears welled up in my eyes.

"Not as good as you could do but I understand why you have to go. It's who you are just as you came after me. You have to do the same for Gabriel." Anthony said with a nod. He got me. Not many did but Anthony understood me down to the core.

Michael gave him a pat on the shoulder and we were out of there. Tim was now opening and closing the door and nothing stayed open. Just a little bit of added security that I know would get more as he figured out what worked and what he needed to change because he wasn't the trusting soul I had first come across in September.

We had had our own version of 9/11 now. Had been attacked at our most guarded and trusted center and that had shaken us badly. Could we come back stronger now because of it or would it tear us apart? Only time would tell but I knew one way or the other I would be back. No matter what happened, whether I was quick enough and lucky enough to get Gabriel and bring him back here or not. I had to come back. To either pick up the pieces or say I was wrong but for right now I was gone.

I had never driven in snow and ice and it was slick as anything all the way down the mountain road. Letting Michael drive had been a real smart thing. Even though it had been awhile for him too his time in New York and Chicago were experiences that I didn't have.

Watching everything he did I saw how he slowed the truck using the automatic shift as a way to make the engine slow us down instead of using the brakes. He never even got out of second gear the whole way down the road and it was a long slow process until we hit the paved part and then it got better.

Down in Breckinridge the roads were more or less clear and we would make decent time. It wouldn't be long now before I was with the rest of my family I thought with relief.

"You know I wish I had been able to find Katherine before I left to say goodbye." I mentioned to Michael when we had both drawn in a deep breath from the tension that had filled us the whole way down the mountain. I had managed to find just about everybody else for a quick bye and most didn't seem to be all that surprised that I was taking off. Maybe they thought I was on a mission, which was sort of true.

He nodded. "Yeah me too. I was surprised she didn't try and argue you out of leaving too."

I snorted at that. Because Katherine knew better, she knew it wouldn't do any good. But I hadn't expected her to just go off and sulk either. When something strange happens that isn't the norm for a personality I would have thought by now I would have started to question why.

# Chapter 12

## WHITE OUT

We were stuck. Well and truly stuck. In a freaking snow bank in the middle of absolute nowhere. At least Michael wasn't blaming me. He had been driving but even with my reaction time I wouldn't have done anything different. How could anybody see that silver mini van turned sideways in the road with about half its butt sticking out? More than enough to block part of the road but not any of the reflective part that would show it for what it was. A vehicle, not more of the never ending white.

Michael had put us in a skid that reminded me so much of my accident this past spring I couldn't help but scream. This was the last time I was ever riding in the passenger seat. Now three times bad things had happened when I was there and I wasn't going to go for four. My husband could just deal with it because this time I wasn't budging on my paranoia.

I grabbed my coat as I shoved my door open just to get hit with a huge gust of wind. Shrugging into it quickly I was glad this one had a hood on it as I pulled the heavy gloves out of the pockets and onto my hands.

That silver van had looked so much like the one I had bought for Alison I had briefly wondered if chance would have had us on the same road at the same time. But no it was only a superficial resemblance. This one was older and had gone through a lot. Even in the fading light of very early dusk it wasn't hard to see that the tires were pretty worn and should have been replaced some miles ago.

I hoped that who ever the occupants were had gotten a ride already to someplace nice and warm. Michael and I could wait it out in our truck. We had things to keep us warm and food and water and when the storm cleared I could call for help. Get a wrecker to pull us out of the ditch because I didn't happen to have three or so big protectors to pick it up and get it out. So we were stuck and I ground my teeth a bit in frustration.

Maybe I should have waited, I thought belated. Listened to Joshua's warnings about how bad it was going to get. But as usual I was eager to get going and didn't listen.

I looked at Michael over top the cab of my truck. "I'm sorry we didn't wait."

He shrugged. "Why, you had no way of knowing that some idiot would be sideways in the road." That was nice but I had been the one to push us and now we weren't going anywhere.

But as usual Michael was always the understanding husband and that sort of made it worse. "Why don't you ever get pissed at me?" I asked. It came out sort of grumpy because even though I valued his love and support it sort of made me feel I was taking his good humor for granted sometimes.

He sort of gave me a look that I had no idea what it meant and the shared feelings I got didn't make any sense to me either. It was sort of humor mixed with something I couldn't quite understand and the closest thing I could come up with was awe. Why would Michael be in awe of me?

"Your kidding right?" I asked. This made no sense at all. But quite a bit lately didn't really make sense to me anyway so why should my husband be any different. "Why you think all this is funny I sort of get but why should you be surprised at anything I do anymore?" I used surprised because awe or something close to it just wouldn't come out of my mouth.

"Oh you surprise me Maggie. You have from the first but the more I'm around you the more amazing you are."

I shook my head. "Yeah right, I get us stuck in the middle of nowhere. How amazing is that?"

"I was driving not you."

"And I made us leave even when everybody else said it was a bad idea. Not just because of the mission but because of the weather and I just didn't listen."

"Because you are worried about Gabriel." Michael answered back. Well this was getting me nowhere. It really wasn't even answering my question about why he felt something towards me that made no sense probably because I wasn't even asking the question I wanted answered to start with.

"Michael why am I getting something that is close to awe from you? Have I done something recently that has caused this?" I tried to look over everything that had happened in the last few days, the last few weeks and even though it had been frustrating in the extreme all those events we had tackled as a whole and I hadn't done anything more than I had before so why all of a sudden was my husband acting so weird?

"You don't have any idea do you?" Michael chuckled. "When you turned around that morning and saw us I knew you couldn't have or you wouldn't be so calm. But you still don't have any clue what a miracle we saw."

What in the heck was he talking about? What morning? What miracle? "What are you talking about Michael? You aren't making any sense."

"You still don't realize it do you? I should have never doubted you for a second after that morning in the ivory tower and I'm sorry that I disagreed with you at all about anything."

Something he said clicked. Ivory tower in the morning, was that when I had said goodbye to Daniel? I had known something wonderful had occurred but had no idea that the people standing in the door had been able to see anything at all and I had sort of just shoved it away because it wasn't something I wanted to share with anybody. That had been private and I hadn't even told Michael about it. Mainly because I had been damned busy with trying to stop everybody from going stupidly nuts.

"What did you see?" Now that I knew he and the others had seen something I had to wonder just what. A ghost or some type of apparition was what I would have thought of but what ever it was hadn't scared anybody. What ever it was couldn't have looked much like Daniel because Brenda and Simon would have freaked out if it had.

"You glowed and it was like you sprouted wings and halo." Michael said his voice once again filling with awe as his eyes lost focus on the here and now and was back in that moment. "I had no idea that I was bonded to an angel."

I almost fell over laughing. Angel? Me? Oh, I was nice some of the time but angelic? Please. I was so far from that category it wasn't funny. When I could contain the humor I wasn't surprised that Michael hadn't shared it.

"Why don't you believe me?" He asked sounding more than a little miffed.

"Oh, I believe you saw something alright but why you and the others would jump to that conclusion is beyond me. What you must have seen was Daniel. I was saying goodbye and part of him must have been hanging around still and wanted to say goodbye too. That's what you saw. His spirit. Believe me it wasn't me. I'm not saint like in the least."

Michael mulled that over for a second and he nodded. "Doesn't change what we saw. You think it was Daniel. I think it was you. Maybe we can agree it was something special and leave it at that."

Stubborn. Why was I not surprised? It would take somebody equally stubborn to put up with me and I couldn't help but laugh a bit. But he was right when you deal with spiritual things it was hard to get somebody to change their minds. If he were convinced it was something about me no amount of arguing would get him to think differently. He would have to change that attitude all on his little lonesome.

As I started around the back part of the truck I ran smack dab into a smell like it was a wall. KATHERINE. What was her scent doing all over my truck? It hadn't been there when we left. I would have picked it up. But now here it was and not some faint after market scent but the real strong deal. That meant only one thing. She was here too.

Michael had no clue why I dropped the tailgate down or why I was crawling inside the very dark interior. I didn't make it far when I came face to face with her. The back of me hanging out of the truck must have been rather funny sight for Michael since I heard him snickering before he asked what was going on. "What's up Maggie? Getting cold already?"

"No I'm dragging our stowaway out so that she can help get us out of here." I answered back. I could see relatively well even in the dark cramped space the truck bed was with the top all nice and secured. She wasn't the least bit remorseful and was smiling right back in my face.

"You know you are in so much trouble." I told her as I started backing out and she started scrunching forward.

"Yeah. Joshua is going to be really pissed." She said back. That sent me for a loop. For the first few seconds after I knew she was with us I had thought our protector instructor had told her to come along and keep Michael and me out of trouble. Now I find out that he didn't ask her to come and didn't even know she was gone.

Well crap. I was going to get blamed for a lot of things when I got back to the center. Whenever that happened to be but I had a lot of explaining to do when I did. First I left and I really shouldn't have. We took some experimental medical research product that nobody gave us permission to test. My Florida family was on the way to meet us without anybody's say so except their house leader Michael, of course all three of them had carte blanche travel ability because of their job so they could go were ever they wanted as long as it was job related. This was technically okay but how much heat would we all get when this was through? We all knew that none wasn't a possibility but so far what we had done wasn't against anything in the rulebooks. Yet. But Katherine had tagged along with out permission, in military terms that would have been considered AWOL.

We had bent every rule backwards, sideways and inside out but technically hadn't broken any of them with the exception of Katherine. She would get into trouble but how much I didn't know. Joshua would have to decide that.

I shook my head as I finally reached my feet and grabbed Katherine's outstretched hand and gave a good tug pulling her out too. "How in the hell did you fit in there?" Michael asked with eyes a little bugged out. "Maggie had that thing pretty stuffed."

It had been awhile since I saw a black person blush but contrary to prejudicial belief they can indeed turn red. Katherine's normal tones had taken on the typical darker tint that someone with her skin tones did when embarrassed. "Anthony and I sort dumped some of the stuff we didn't think was needed." She said with a shrug.

Well double crap. I had no idea what they had thought wasn't needed but I was sure it would be now. Katherine, Michael and I might be able to get this truck out of here but even with all three of us it wasn't a for sure thing. If we had to spend the night it was going to be cold and cramped and uncomfortable.

"What stayed behind?" I asked sort of numbly.

"Just some of the bulky things." Katherine answered and I knew just what those bulky things had been. Our artic tent and two sleeping bags along with some of the food boxes. I knew that our suitcases would have stayed because Katherine wouldn't see them as being not needed. I just hoped she brought some clothes too. But considering it was a spur of the moment thing I kind of doubted it.

"Did you bring a coat?" Michael asked as he eyed her up and down. She was in the typical protector training gear they wore most of the time in the center. Sweats and cross-trainers, nothing heavier and jeans and t-shirts were only worn when then ventured out of the complex. The medical guys had their own type of garb and were typical of hospital staff everywhere. As for the rest of us we got to wear what ever we damned well pleased. I had spent plenty of time in sweats and just as much in jeans and t-shirts.

Now both Michael and I were in heavy jeans and insulated shirts along with our winter coats and gloves. I was toasty warm and I don't think by body temperature had to rise much to compensate for anything yet.

Michael was a little smaller than Katherine was but maybe some of his sweatshirts could be stretched to fit. A few layers of those and she should be okay except for her feet and those I couldn't do anything about. 6 foot plus women usually had bigger feet than a 5'9" one did and Katherine's were pretty sizeable. Maybe once again we could snitch something from Michael's suite case. It wouldn't be stylish but if it kept her from freezing I didn't think Katherine would care. She was not the prissy type.

I crawled back into the cab of the truck and had Michael's suite case open when I heard a voice I didn't know. Almost banging my head to see where the unknown man's voice was coming from. "You guys alright there?" He said with a very distinct accent. It was southern, very, very southern.

Michael was all smiles as he tried to calm the flustered man down. "We are fine. We didn't realize anybody was in that van. Didn't even see it until it was almost too late."

The man blushed and looked very uncomfortable. "Sorry, not used to snow and ice. Shouda listened to my lady when she tried to tell me it was gettin' too bad to drive. I just didn't want to stop someplace we didn't know." I tried to understand why he would drive with bald tired when he had a wife in the car too.

Well we had done the same thing hadn't we? So I shouldn't judge him. He had overestimated his abilities and underestimated the storm. Now we were all stuck in the same place.

Michael was doing the normal things we all did. Making the Nohu feel at ease. I could almost see when he got close enough to us that our scent relaxed him. That he trusted us for no good reason at all. We were strangers that could have been a threat to him and his wife but now it was just like we were friends that he didn't even know he had.

He smiled deeply and stuck out his hand, bare without gloves for Michael to shake. He had to be really cold. His clothing was not designed for this weather. He had a decent coat but no hood to it and no snow boots either as his rather worn tennis shoes showed through their coating of snow.

Michael had returned the gesture. He had also evaluated everything just like I had and was now shepherding the man back to his van and his waiting wife. "Come on let's get out of this wind. I'm sure your wife must be worried in there all by herself."

"Oh she has the youngins to keep her company." The man continued as he allowed Michael to follow him to the van.

"Kids?" I whispered. Well that certainly complicated things more. Katherine looked at me and I looked at her. This was quite a mess we had found ourselves in. First things first though, Katherine wouldn't be much help to anybody in her state of dress. I pulled out two heavy sweatshirts and a hoodie that would help some against the wind. It wasn't like what I had on but anything would be better than what she had now.

Tossing them to her, I went to rooting in the back of the truck for Michael's other suite case. Luckily it had been pushed pretty much to the tailgate. I was sort of surprised that Katherine hadn't given a good yip when we went off the road. Maybe she had and I had been to busy screaming myself to have heard her.

I found a pair of hiking boots that I thought might fit. As it turned out Michael's foot was just a smidge bigger than hers but that was good because we added a couple pair of socks and soon she was maybe not dressed for a blizzard but she wouldn't freeze her butt off if she had spend a little time in the snow either.

Now that we were as set as we were going to get, I started looking over what I had still in my truck. I had been right. The sleeping bags were gone as was the tent. Some of the food packets had managed to stay but the bulk of it was as AWOL as Katherine was. We had plenty of warmer weather clothes which could be layered, if necessary, to help fight off the cold. There were even some heat packs for hands and feet that would be really useful.

At least she hadn't chunked Michael's medic bag. I would have been pissed if that had been left behind. You don't come across those things in a department store and it would have been damned hard to replace no matter how much money I had.

I was sitting on the tailgate holding out the last boot for Katherine to put on. As I looked over the scene before me something really started to bother me. Granted the chances of somebody else coming down this road in the south ranges of Colorado were slim and none but two of us had already. What if somebody else did?

In the total darkness that was almost here nobody would be able to see that van until they were right on top of it. Michael had better than average eyesight and it had been marginally daylight and he had almost hit it too.

My truck was pretty safe having coming to rest all the way off the road and nose down in a ditch. It wasn't going anywhere without a lot of help. I just hoped it hadn't scraped up the underside too much. I hated to get a new one when this one wasn't even a year old yet. Besides it had sentimental value.

But that van was still in the road enough to get hit. It had gone off on the side that was sort going up hill not down. Maybe between Katherine, Michael and I we could get it going again. Maybe not but it was worth a shot. Even if we couldn't get it all the way free we had to get it more off the road than it was. The snow was coming down in earnest now and if it weren't for the fact that Katherine and I both had very abnormal eyesight I wouldn't be able to see a foot in front of me as it was I was having problems just seeing across the road.

"We need to get the van moved at least enough to keep it from getting hit if another car comes down the road."

"Do you think that is likely?" Katherine asked as I saw her blink several times to get the snow out of her long eyelashes. That was one of the things about Katherine that had always made me think of her as beautiful. She was big and strong as most of the guys were but her hair was always done up in pretty tight beaded braids that coiled and looped. I had no idea how she did it and had never asked but Katherine was a sight worth seeing. When we had gone out shopping that one day she had garnered her fair share of looks from men that might have wanted to strike up an acquaintance with her. Most hadn't even gotten a word in. She could give that withering 'why are you annoying me' look better than anybody I had ever met. Of course she could give you a look that said I'm going to take you apart before you sneeze too.

I nodded. "We did, didn't we?" Getting up I wasn't sure just how we were going get the job done but we would. There wasn't any alternative.

We went around to the passenger side of van and knocked. I didn't want to scare everybody in there. Kids frightened easy to start with and they were stranded in the middle of nowhere, cold and probably hungry too. That was one thing I remembered very vividly about my mentoring days. Young people were always hungry, worse than newly transitioned protectors in that respect.

The door slid open and it was the man from before, his face still with that goofy sort of look that we could make some people have. All happy smiles without a care in the world type face. Yeah Michael was really good at having that affect on people. "Come on in ladies. Y'all must be freezing out there." He said to us giving me a hand and then Katherine. She had to duck a lot to fit into cargo compartment of the van.

"WOW." I heard a small voice from behind us. And in the dimness of van's internal light I could see two children, a boy and a girl sitting in the back with a woman. It was all I could do not to groan and I could feel Katherine stiffen beside me too.

The woman wasn't just pregnant; she was very, very pregnant. As in going to go into delivery any time now. Michael had his work cut out for him. I hoped this wasn't his first time in this situation but I could feel from the crystal at my chest the anxiousness he was feeling. His face was the masked of unconcerned friendliness. I just didn't see how he managed that. My face couldn't be nearly worry free and neither was Katherine's.

We needed to try and get these people unstuck and to a hospital. I didn't bother to care which child had said the wow. Whether that wow was directed at me, which I doubted, or more likely at Katherine because she was certainly a surprise, we had things to do before the weather got worse.

"Michael would you like to give us a hand, maybe between the three of us we can get them going again." I told him as he nodded.

The man didn't seem to keen on that idea. "We ain't gonna just leave you nice folks out in the middle of blizzard."

"Oh you won't." I said quickly. "We will catch a ride into the next town and get a wrecker to come out and get my truck free."

He nodded and climbed into the front seat so that with our help we might get this thing going again.

I dodged over to my truck and grabbed some kitty litter and a collapsible shovel. The kitty litter was for traction, the shovel for Katherine or Michael because I didn't need one. Grabbing the pair of flashlights from my glove box, I tossed the shovel and one of the lights to Katherine as we made our way back to the van.

I remembered just barely in time to take my gloves off before I asked my claws to come out to play and as they did I directed them to curve and flatten out some so that they were like a bunch of mini shovels at the end of my hands.

"Never saw you do that with them before." Katherine said as she was eyeing my claws." I smiled a bit. Did she really think that she knew everything I could do? That wouldn't have been that smart of me and PIB chuckled softly in my head.

"Good girl." He chortled. Yeah, I learned paranoia from him very well. Never show your hand to anybody was something I had also learned from the Army Ranger guys too. Keep an ace up your sleeve always.

Michael and I got one side of the back of the van and Katherine took the other. Together Michael and I might be able to offset Katherine's brut strength but I doubted it. She was one strong lady. The van was in pretty deep, almost up passed the top of the hubcap on one tire in particular and the more I looked at it the less likely it seemed that we could get it free.

Katherine managed to find a lot of loose sticks and we thought that might help some as I spread the kitty litter down in front of the tires in the hopes that the tires might be able to grab it for some traction. But even with all three of us pushing as hard as we could it didn't budge much. We did manage to get the one wheel on the back left side of van to dig some since it was partially on the road but the van was front wheel drive and those two were the ones in the snow the deepest so it really didn't do anything but make the van spin off the road more.

Finally after about 30 minutes we had it off the road as much as we could and it wasn't going anywhere any more than my truck was. We were both well and truly stuck. I could call for help as soon as the weather cleared but even my sat phone wouldn't work in this blizzard. So we would all just have to wait it out and I said a small prayer that the lady in the van wasn't as far along in her pregnancy as I thought she was.

We all piled back in and I got introduced to KW, short for Kevin Wayne. He was the husband with the sandy brown hair and warm brown eyes. His wife was Martha Sue and the two children were Billy Joe and Mary Anne. I really wished somebody would explain to me why a lot of southern people had to have two names tied together like Siamese twins. I had been exposed to that a lot and nobody had been able to make sense of it before and I didn't really ask about it now. Still it was a mystery I would like solved someday but I knew today wasn't the one.

I had been very right in my estimation of Martha Sue's condition. Michael had been so busy trying to get the van moveable again that he hadn't said much and that alone made me more nervous about our situation.

We had passed a town some miles back. Around 12 or 15 if I remembered right. According to the map the next town was about the same to the south of us. There were a few to the east of us but that would require either hiking, skis or a snowmobile to reach. And those weren't happening right now.

So what options did we have then? Not many, especially when I felt my husband's nerves start to twang like an over tightened guitar string. I knew that he was getting more and more nervous as each second went by.

I didn't ask why. I knew why as he just refused to look towards the back part of the van much at all. And this also told me that this was probably Michael's first solo delivery. There wasn't much I could help with. I hadn't had a kid of my own and neither had Katherine as far as I knew. So we had no more experienced in childbirth than a new cab driver in New York City with very unusual fare. Which was to say none what so ever.

"GET HELP." I heard PIB fuss at me.

I fussed back. "The telephone won't work dippy."

"Not phone. YOU." He shot back quickly.

Then I knew what he wanted me to do and he was right. If I stayed on the road the snow wasn't very deep there and I could run all the way back to the town we had just left in less than an hour. If the weather were nicer I would even enjoy it.

Leaning over so Michael could hear me I told him my plan and he nodded. "Yeah you better Maggie. Martha Sue is already in the early stages of labor. I don't need to examine her to know it. If she doesn't deliver by morning I will be very surprised."

I knew things were bad and wasn't really even that surprised. Katherine would want to go too but I could actually run faster than she could. How that was possible even Joshua didn't know and had scratched his head constantly when my treadmill times had come back off the charts. My shorter legs should have limited the speed I could go but I guess somebody forgot to tell them that.

Now I was beginning to see how Ezekiel had managed to run across France in a day. That might still be beyond me but it wasn't as impossible as I had once thought it was.

I motioned for Katherine to follow me. She had heard my husband's and my whispered conversation even though nobody else in the van had. She would want to go too. But we both knew that was a bad idea. She wasn't dressed for this weather and even though we had a natural tolerance for cold weather and she even more than most because of what she was she shouldn't take that kind of chance.

When Katherine decided to throw her lot in with mine she became my responsibility. I hadn't asked her to but I knew why she did it. She was my friend and a friend wouldn't ask another to risk herself without good cause. This wasn't the time or place for that sort of heroics.

"I'm going for help." I told her as soon as we closed the door behind us. "You are going to stay and help Michael as much as you can."

She blanched and turned as white as her skin tone allowed for which was sort of a weird kind of gray that I had never really seen before. "But I don't know anything about babies." She groaned.

"And you don't have to. Michael will handle that. All I need for you to do is keep everybody safe, warm and here. Don't let anybody wander off. Keep the kids entertained if you can and if you have to sit on KW so that he doesn't panic and cause Michael more trouble."

I could see how, even though he tried not to show it, that Kevin Wayne was holding on to things by a very little thread. He needed a steady set of nerves besides Michael because my husband was probably going to get real busy, very quickly.

Katherine nodded and some of her normal color returned but she still looked unsteady. Giving her something to do would be good. The two kids hadn't said anything yet about being bored, scared, hungry or cold but it would only be a matter of time before any and all of these things would surface. The sooner we cut off those complaints the easier it would go. I had some food. Not the greatest but if you were hungry it would work. Power bars had chocolate in some of them and I had an affinity for those type anyway.

I did have a pair of blankets in the cab of the truck just in case and I was glad now that I put them there on a whim. Grabbing those, I sort of laid them out in tailgate of my truck. I went through everything that was in there. Sifting, sorting and trying to remember what I had put in there that was still there. It was better in some ways and worse in others.

We had about two dozen power bars left in a small box at the very front of the truck bed. It had been sort of squashed flat, probably by Katherine's feet. Those went on the blanket along with the hand warmers and some of my nice fuzzy socks that I ran around in when I didn't like putting up with cold stone floors at the center. Actually I just played around with them sliding around on the floor acting like Tom Cruise in Risky Business. Something Michael had found funny in the extreme. At least I never wiped out like I would have in my human days.

There was also a camping kit that had a small pot and sterno packs that either Katherine or Michael could use to melt snow for water. I had no idea if all those stupid movies I had seen growing up were true or not but in just about every delivery sequence somebody was running around trying to boil water. So I figured what the heck it couldn't hurt. Yeah I know real life and movie fiction were light years apart but I didn't really have much more to go on. I wasn't a medical and didn't want to be.

There wasn't much more left in the truck that I thought was useable. Some how my stupid practical joke shoes were still in there and I thought belatedly if Anthony and Katherine had to chunk something why couldn't they have made the list and a few more of the emergency type things have stayed. I shrugged and wrapped up the few meager things that were useful in this situation and handed them to Katherine.

She still didn't like that I was heading out on my own. "I should go with you." She complained.

"No, you are needed here. You are a protector, do your job. I'm an infiltrator remember. I supposed to go off on my own a lot. Time for me to do my job too."

"But what if you get lost, get hurt or something."

"I may not be able to find help or even the next town if it gets much worse." I admitted. "But I can always find my way back." I said as I fingered the slight lump under my coat that you couldn't see. I would always be able to find Michael. No matter where he was that heart spark of ours was like a homing beacon for an airplane and it would draw me in no matter how dark and cold it was.

"That is something you will have to explain one day." She said nodding. "I have known you two share something almost creepy but you have never said what it is. Joshua knows, I think, but he won't turn loose a confidence no matter what so I have never asked."

I felt bad a little for not telling my friend things that others knew. Why had I kept things so close to the vest with a friend like that? Probably because until Rafael had been discovered I really hadn't been totally sure who was friend and who wasn't. And the old adage that the less people that knew about a secret the less likely it was to get out had been in play too. If I had been all blabby about things then how long before somebody I trusted had let something slip even if they hadn't meant to. And Rafael had been smart, cunning and noticed even the littlest things.

Again, I was reminded that he was more like me than I wanted to think about. But now he was on is own or at least I hoped he was. He could have friends though and I should take that into consideration. I did, so why shouldn't he. Just because he was on the other side of our war didn't mean that he wouldn't have allies at least and family at best.

That was for another time and I had enough to worry about as it was right now. Katherine took the bundle and headed back to the van. I took off at a fast trot. Testing out the footing on the road to make sure it didn't have an under cover of ice. Not so far, it was all just snow. Thick and wet and a little slippery so I wouldn't be able to go all out. The flashlight didn't help at all and just hit the falling snowflakes at weird angles that shot back into my face unexpectedly. Finally I just turned it off, found the very side of the road where the gravel and pavement met and started moving.

My ability to judge distances was totally off because even though I knew I was on the road it seemed like I had been running for hours. I didn't have a watch so had no way to tell time. I usually didn't have a problem with it but tonight I sure did.

I could feel the anxiousness from Michael go up not a lot but enough to know that things at his end were progressing not in the way we wanted but that we had known would. So far panic wasn't there. Just a growing concern and worry, probably some for me too. But he would know that I was safe because he wouldn't be getting any unusual feedback.

The snow fell, the wind blew and the night and the road before me continued on and on and on. Finally in what seemed like days I saw a soft glow in the distance and passed a road sign that said I had reached the city limits.

Thankfully the police station was on the main drag. Of course with a town this small there weren't that many side streets to start with.

Going in I was hit with a blast of warm air that felt tropical to my half frozen face. The desk guy's eyes almost bugged of his head. "You okay there miss?" He said getting up from his desk quickly and coming to my side.

I had to stop for a second and realize what I must look like. Covered in snow and ice and probably looking half froze I must have scared him pretty good.

"I'm fine but my truck went off the road a few miles up the road." I told him.

He nodded. "Bad weather out there. You should have stayed with your vehicle though. It was dangerous to walk all that way. You could have gotten lost. Good thing you made it because they are calling for white out conditions and nobody is going to be moving for the rest of the night if they have any sense."

My heart did a hiccup. I had known it was bad but not that bad. White out conditions was something I had been briefed on in my cold weather training. Along with the fact that not everything froze at 32 degrees like most people thought, running water didn't and was very much determined by mineral content and how fast it was moving. So just because a river or stream looked frozen over and the temperature was 30 degrees didn't mean the ice on top, possibly covered in snow would hold a person's weight. Salt water didn't freeze until 28 or lower and would suck the warmth out of anybody in just a few minutes. We could die from hypothermia just like anybody else.

"But I have friends that I left there and another van is stranded too. It has a very pregnant woman in it that I don't think has a lot of time." The deputy's eyes sort of bugged again.

"Well shit. That ain't good." He said and I thought gee, really? What a news flash to me.

"I know that's why I came. Do you think you could rally up the troops? We could certainly use some good Samaritans right now."

By now I was close enough to him that even with the heavy clothes I had on he had caught my smell and though his training said that this wasn't a good idea he was thinking maybe he should go against it and get people out of the warmth and into the cold.

He picked up the phone and started dialing. "Hey chief, I have a lady here that needs us to go and rescue her friends."

I heard the other half of that conversation and it consisted of the chief not caring if it was the governor of the state that was stranded. He wasn't sending people out until morning and maybe not then. The weather conditions were just that bad. If it weren't for my eyesight I wouldn't have been able to see but a few inches in front of my face and even for me a few feet was the best I could do.

I understood why nobody would drive in this weather but I wasn't going to sit on my butt and wait it out here either. They had their job and I had mine.

When the deputy hung up he didn't look happy at all. "I'm sorry miss but the chief won't authorize anybody to go out in this weather." He did indeed look very sorry as he told me what I had overheard on the phone. Most people couldn't hear that well so he was expecting an argument. I wasn't about to disappoint him.

Just as I was about to open my mouth my crystal almost jumped out of my shirt. That flash of beyond panic had me drop to one knee with the force and I knew beyond a shadow of a doubt something was very, very wrong.

How was I going to explain to the kind Deputy that I would have to leave? He was even now looking at me with more than concern as he helped me back up to my feet. My hands were shaking and there must have been panic in my eyes too.

I had to get help coming but I couldn't stay to do it. Michael needed me. I didn't know what was wrong but my heart wouldn't let me stay here one more second.

Grabbing a piece of paper from a nearby desk I wrote down the location to best of my memory and shoved into the Deputy's hands. He looked more confused than anything. "This is where we will be." I said as I flew out the door.

As fast as I could move it would seem that I had literally disappeared as in a puff of smoke. It would probably be more like a snowy puff but I was gone I didn't even hear him if he did say something to try and stop what was to him a suicidal type decision.

This time I wasn't nearly as careful where my feet were going and I did stumble a few times as the snow on the road got heavier and thicker than it was before. The swirling mass of white was before me and behind me but Michael's heart called to mine and I knew right where I was going even if I couldn't see an inch. Which was almost the truth. That frantic beat making me try and move faster than was possible for even me.

If I thought the run going to town had been slow, the run back was even worse. The Deputy had been right. The white out that the weather had been teasing us with for the last few hours hit with a vengeance as a gust of more than gale force hit me and all but knocked me down. At least I was going with the wind and not against it like I had been heading to town.

The snow had changed too and wasn't the heavy wet flakes of before but little stingy pellets that seemed more ice balls than snowflakes. I could feel them hitting the back of my coat and hood and my legs although in heavy denim were beyond cold. The material had been frozen stiff and it made moving all that more difficult.

At first what I heard I mistook for the wind but as I got closer and knew that Michael and the others were only a couple of hundred yards in front me I realized the noise I was hearing wasn't the wind. The howling was coming from throats, a lot of them joined in unison. The unison of a pack of wolves that were working as a team to eliminate a target and that target was standing on top of the mini van, Katherine was in a world of trouble.

# Chapter 13

## FRIENDS, ENEMIES OR SOMETHING ELSE?

I charged forward without even really thinking about it. This isn't what I was actually trained for. My combat training had been against two legged adversaries not four but my claws tore through my gloves and into the first wolf as I got to it. Its scream of pain did nothing to slow me down. I didn't even ask myself why they were attacking us when all the things that Anthony and I had found out said this could never happen.

It didn't matter what the other guides had experienced. This was real and happening. A pack of at least a dozen wolves had surrounded the van and it didn't seem to matter to them at all that the weather was crap. Their fur coated in ice making them look more like hounds from a frozen hell than animals that were intelligent and the family oriented creatures I had read about so many times.

All of this was sort of going through a separate part of my brain as I tore up the next wolf. Its bloody cough made me feel a little sad as it landed at my feet with its throat ripped open. I just didn't understand any of this. They weren't starving because these guys were strong, well fed and very fit. Not a single one that I could see looked diseased or unwell. All were in fine form as they tried to jump up the side of the van only to get clunked in the head with one of those shoes that I had wished hadn't made the trip. Now I was betting that Katherine was very happy she had them.

Three wolves were down with their skulls looking a little dented. Katherine may not like guns much but she was pretty lethal with platform shoes. If we survived this I was going to give her one hell of a ribbing.

I heard a loud snarl from behind me just as something very heavy landed on my back and I felt my coat get ripped open by long claws. It would take a second to catch the wind that had been knocked out of me as the impact with the ground left me breathless. I didn't get it.

Fire tore through my back as claws once again racked down. With my coat in shreds there was nothing to stop the second onslaught. I couldn't think for a second how a wolf could be so heavy that I would have problems raising my self up or how their claws could rip the fabric of a very heavy coat as easily as melted butter.

There was a snarl that would never come out of a wolf's throat by my right ear. A sound that I had heard before in the big cat houses at the many zoos I had visited over the years and I knew that what I had on my back wasn't a wolf.

Using my speed that even a big cat would have problems matching, I flipped over taking the mountain lion's jaws in my hands. Digging my claws into the side of its face as it had delivered his into my back it jumped back surprise showing clearly in its animal face.

Humans weren't supposed to be able to do that. I could read that thought in its fuzzy brain as easily as if it had spoken out loud. The wolves were still giving Katherine fits but she was holding her own. I had know idea how she learned to use a rope like a whip or whether it was inspired out of desperation but I heard the rope crack like a gunshot over and over again.

My attention was more on the big cat that was bleeding but still very lethal as it looked me over from head to toe. I saw it zoom in on my hands and my own set of claws. Ones that were just as long and as deadly as its' were.

On top of the snow and ice there was the strong smell of animals but now mixed with that was the smell of home. That warm wrap yourself up in front of a fire hot chocolate smell that I knew immediately.

I knew where Michael and Katherine were and had easily identified their individual smells. This was different. It had the smell of home but along with it was a wild smell that I knew and yet didn't, like a den or a cave but stronger, infinitely stronger.

That leap of knowing what should have been impossible to know came upon me. The crazy think outside the box idea that would have occurred to few because most wouldn't accept it as a possibility but the facts added up no other way. As Einstein once said 'if you rule out the impossible, the improbable however unlikely is the only thing left.' I wasn't sure if that was the exact quote but what I came up with however improbable left no other answer that was even possible.

Wolves and mountain lions were not like sharks. They never hunted together and usually avoided each other at all costs. That meant these predators were being guided, directed and that sudden smell of home told me it wasn't just possible but more than probable. We had a Resurrected out there that was controlling things. I hoped I wouldn't have to kill them.

Aspanari were our enemy but I wanted to make peace with them if possible and killing every single one I came across didn't seem like a great way to do that. The Resurrected were too few and too fractured that we needed our darker brothers and sisters. The world couldn't stand much more of what was happening unless we stopped our stupidity and intervened and soon. That was why we were here and I didn't care about opposing ideology and the way we did things. We had to reach a common ground before it was too late.

There would be casualties I was sure. Some of us no matter what side would refuse to give, to try and see another's point of view. Then there were those that had done their level best to destroy anything and everything. And that just wouldn't work any more. We had to work together before our society as whole reach a point of no return.

I wanted to yell out for that gifted person to come and talk but the wind was so bad that whoever it was would never hear me. Katherine was behind me still in combat mode as I tried my best to look non-threatening. I let my claws fall off and the mountain lion in front of me took a step forward. Unsure just what had happened it was cautious but still more than wanting to take my throat out.

Sliding one claw out of my gloved hand. I wagged that forefinger with its claw back and forth. "No, no nice kitty. Don't play with me. You will lose." I said to it. I had no idea if the person directing them communicated with the animals or just gave them a mission and turned them loose. I was hoping for a bond of some type. Something that I could reach through these four-legged lethal emissaries to the person calling the shots.

The cat stopped its forward motion and cocked its head sideways. Like it was thinking or listening to something I couldn't hear. Then it did what I had hoped it would. It sat down. Behind me the growling and snarling came to an abrupt halt and even through the screaming wind I could hear the silence.

I chanced a look behind me and just like the great cat; the wolves were on their haunches sitting down. Some I think had a confused look on their face but the howling terrors were gone and in their place were big fuzzy looking almost dogs, still with there coating of ice and snow mixed with blood. Katherine had been damned accurate with her rope whip and the wolves had several pieces of fur missing and a few bloody muzzles too.

Katherine looked at me like I was something she had never seen before. I didn't even want to know what she was thinking right now. She didn't have the sense of smell I did and didn't jump to wild, crazy ideas. The only explanation in her mind right now as to why all the fighting had stopped so abruptly was what she could see and that was me.

I didn't need any more stories going on about me. There were enough already. Hopefully I could convince her to keep her mouth shut when she realized that I hadn't done anything but extend a hand of peace to one of our own. A lost one of our own, a misguided and forgotten brother or sister but hopefully not anymore.

Now that I had more than a second to look at my Amazon sister, she appeared to be an ice-covered snow bound Statue of Liberty. Flashlight swinging every which way trying to notice any little twitch from the wolves that seemed to surround the entire van, she was more than a little ice covered herself.

I couldn't help but chuckle at the image but a larger gesture of trust was needed now. Doing something that Joshua would have my head for; I turned my back on the enemy and joined my sister on top of the van. At least this close we stood a chance at talking and might actually be able to understand each other.

There were so many questions that I had but right now she needed to know there was a gifted person behind this attack. It wasn't just the wilderness out to get us. "There is an Aspanari directing them." I started quickly.

Her eyes narrowed and I knew what she was thinking. Let me at them and they won't last long. "No Katherine. The wolves stopped because whoever that is told them to. Undirected do you really want to take the chance on what they would do?"

"But they have been harassing us for the last hour." She growled out low. I didn't tell her I already knew when the trouble started so I just nodded.

"And if they would have really wanted to they could have killed you already." I wasn't exactly sure of that but there were more than a dozen wolves I had counted when I first arrived on the scene. Some had been on the other side of the van. Most likely to keep the people in the van where they were. If they had really tried those on that side could have leaped up to where Katherine stood. I don't think she had considered that.

But she was right too. What they had done was harass more than anything and considering the retaliation that Katherine had inflicted I was surprised that things hadn't skyrocketed out of total control. The wolves had been hurt, some killed and in a pack type mentality that would cause one of two things, turn tail and run or attack in mass to get rid of the threat. They had done neither. They had stood their ground and made sure nobody went anywhere.

Why? Why had that been the choice? Why not kill everybody here or leave us alone. Why corral us into a van that wasn't going anywhere to start with?

Then I knew the answer. Me. I had been the reason. This person had either been watching or having us watched. Had done absolutely nothing as long as we didn't endanger ourselves. But then I took off on my own for town and I bet I had been followed in some way to make sure that I wouldn't get into trouble.

But I hadn't. I had reached help and our guardian angel had wanted to make sure that nobody else would try anything that they deemed pretty darned stupid.

The cat had been sent because I had been more of a threat than Katherine with her tossing shoes had been. I was an unknown and obviously very capable individual that was very dangerous. The cat had been trying to injure me so that I wouldn't be able to do more damage to his other fuzzy friends.

If I remember how most big cats hunted, they usually attacked from behind to surprise their prey. Then they tried for the neck and head. Mine hadn't. My kitty had just given me one hell of a good scratching. Something that wouldn't have been life threatening to anybody but sure did hurt and would have disabled a normal person for several days or weeks. Thanks to my healing ability I was fine if very cold because my coat was a tattered mess.

Now what I asked myself? Did I want to stay up here on top of the van, putting more dents into an already dented roof? Did I want to be out in the cold and snow and wind for who knows how long? No, I didn't but did Katherine or I have any other options. I agreed with her. We both wanted to be out here so that we could see trouble coming and have a chance to battle it without involving anybody else.

The Nohus didn't need to see it. How could anybody possibly explain what Katherine could do to start with, and me, I didn't even want to think about what they would make of my finger nail claws. Besides Michael would be busy and didn't need the distraction either. We had to try a keep as much of this away from them as possible.

Thankfully the storm and darkness had been so much that they couldn't have seen anything. Only heard and that would have been frightening all by itself. I could only guess what they had heard and felt and imagined in there. Katherine would have shaken the hell out of things as she jumped around up on top but how much could we contribute to the wind. Hopefully a lot of it, the same for the howling noises. Luckily people believed our concocted stories rather readily. I think most people didn't want to see or believe there was more than what they knew and accepted as being real.

The Resurrected were real but not to Nohus and that is how it had to stay. So we would mislead and distract and even lie to keep their world the nice safe little place they had come to know. And the idea of being out here fighting wolves and mountain lions was less terrifying to me than being in Michael's shoes right now. I wouldn't want to be responsible for two lives like he had to be. Being in charge of me was as much as I could handle. Did that make me a coward? Absolutely, cluck, cluck, cluck, I should change my name to Maggie the chicken.

I caught movement out of the corner of my eye, down by my truck. Focusing as hard as I could through the blowing snow pellets I knew I saw something move but even I couldn't tell what it was.

The nice kitty got up and went to where I saw the disturbance in the swirling white and dark. Then what ever it was got closer and my eyes got as bugged out as the Deputy I had left a brief time ago. It was a person. I couldn't tell whether it was a man or a woman because of the heavy coat and hood they had on and it wasn't abnormally tall, not that that made any difference when you had women that were stacked like my friend was. But what had surprised me was they were escorted by two of biggest grizzly bears I had ever seen.

Katherine let out an oath that told me she too had seen them and it wasn't just my very over active imagination. I waited before I moved even a breath. Waited until the entourage was so close to the van that even Katherine could smell them for what they were. "Us, that's one of us." She whispered to me. "That must be what has been causing problems." I could hear the tone in her voice change quickly from one of surprise to one of anger.

"Yes and they could cause us a lot more so cool your jets. If we play nice maybe they will too. We didn't plan on being here and maybe we can just get our vehicles out of here and leave them in peace."

"But they are Aspanari, like you said. They must be."

I regretted jumping to a conclusion without any facts to back it up. "Why? Why not an independent? Just think. Alone with a gift I have never heard of, they might not even be aware of what they are."

That part did make sense. Most Aspanari were like us as far as anybody knew. Family groups or their version of it were how they lived. Alone did make me think this was someone that had resigned from us or had never been part of our family to start with.

Alison had been on her own for decades. Until chance and luck had her stumble across another of us and it was only then that she discovered what she was and that she wasn't alone. Of course that had been a very long time ago, when transportation wasn't quite as easy as it was now. But couldn't it still be possible?

Katherine was calming down. I could hear it in her breathing and see it in the lessening of the tension in her body when I glanced her way. She nodded. "Yes that is possible. I just jumped to the conclusion that they must be hostile."

I smiled at that. Well hadn't I done the same thing at first and she had been trained to do just what she had done. Think of everything as a threat until proven otherwise. Her job was to protect others at all cost and if you didn't look at things like it was dangerous you would let your guard down when you shouldn't. Sometimes I probably didn't do enough of that but so far I had been lucky. Between my instincts of friend and foe and PIB warning me of trouble it wasn't just luck that had kept me alive when I probably shouldn't be.

Waving at the hooded person, I wasn't sure what to do next. I didn't want to just jump down in the middle of that mess. A pack of wolves, one mountain lion and a pair of very nasty looking bears was not something you walked into without a few qualms.

Maybe that person could guess why I did nothing but stand and stare at them or maybe they too didn't have a clue what to do either but a stalemate wasn't the answer to anything. She dropped her hood and I could finally see it was a woman that we were dealing with.

Around my height with a solid build of around 150 pounds or so, maybe less because the bulky clothing was probably deceptive with an oval face, high cheekbones and strawberry blonde hair pulled back very tightly but was probably at least shoulder length or longer. She was nice looking but not drop dead gorgeous like Alison was.

This helped but I still wasn't too keen on getting in the middle of those nice predators. I was a good fighter but against those odds I would be turned into kibble in about a minute or less.

Instead of getting all the way down I opted for a safer avenue. I slide down the windshield and sat on hood. Katherine hissed in fear. Michael would be having a cow about now since my crystal had to be twanging every bit as much as his had early. Actually we were both bouncing off of each other so much I'm not sure just where the fear was actually coming from.

I reached into my coat and tried to send back at him that it would be okay but a lie doesn't translate worth beans when you are dealing with something that sees directly into the heart and I knew it had helped not one bit.

But our lady visitor took my gesture for exactly what I had hoped. Let's talk but you will have to meet me half way. She nodded and took the five or six steps necessary to be right beside the van.

I saw the split second that her nose hit my scent. I knew then that she knew not just what we were but what she was too. That answered some questions and raised others. "Hi." I said loudly.

The wind was still howling around and it would be difficult to hear well. Even if she couldn't hear me I had said that one word as clearly as I could and anybody would be able to lip-read it.

"Aspanari." She hissed and her eyes narrowed and her group of fuzzy friends all stood up at once and did their version of growling.

"No, Resurrected." I said shaking my head. "We are transferring and our house leader is with us. We didn't mean to infringe on your territory."

She nodded and everything calmed down. I could have just lied through my teeth but she took me at my word and most people that are liars themselves don't trust easily. The fact that she trusted made me feel better about her.

Her hand ran up my leg and I jumped a little, startled. Katherine did her own version of a growl. I held up my hand to tell her it was okay.

This lady was one of us and I think I knew what she was and how she had ended up being here. I didn't know everything but I could guess quite a bit.

"How long?" I asked and tried to put as much sympathy in my eyes and voice as I could. My partially gloved hand stroked her hair and down the side of her face. She breathed in deeply, leaning into it. Like she smelted something that was beyond wonderful and I knew I had guessed right about part of it.

She had been on her own for a very long time. Now that she had that smell of home she was almost rolling in it like a dog would do when it found something very appealing to play with. I smiled at that because most of the time the stuff they found great stunk like mad. Hopefully my smell was just a little bit better than something that had been dead for two weeks.

I slid off the hood of the van and gathered her in my arms without even thinking about it. PIB was in my head sighing like he too had just found a long lost friend. He picked something out of my head that I hadn't heard said aloud in over 30 years. "Lambkin." He whispered. It had been my grandmother's phrase for me when I had been a child and had been scared or unsure of myself.

"You aren't alone any more." I said with my mouth to her ear. You could feel the shaking even through the heavy coats we both wore and the wind that was gusting around us was nothing. It took me more than a few minutes to notice that the wind had died down and my legs weren't so cold any more.

I was surrounded on all side by the pressing of warm bodies as they too rubbed up against us and the cat was almost purring himself silly while the bears rumbled a sound that made me think of total contentment.

Katherine was probably having a seizure on top of the van right now but at the moment I didn't care. This woman was a sister that had been abandoned or had been allowed to leave and then shut out for it. Had been alone for quite some time if I had to make a guess. And she was an empath or a telepath. Maybe her gift didn't work with humans or at least it didn't seem so. I had met both of those types before and what she did seem to work with animals only or at least that was my guess.

"What's your name sister?" I asked gently as I pulled away from her embrace slowly.

"Jerri." She said as she wiped at her eyes quickly.

"Hi Jerri." I answered back smiling. "I'm Gabriella or Maggie. I answer to either one so take your pick."

She smiled back. "I like Maggie. That other is a mouthful."

I nodded. I didn't care what she called me as long as enemy wasn't it. She had a very powerful gift and to just let it wallow in nowhere wasn't something I liked. Really I couldn't do a damned thing about it at the moment except find out what had happened and why. Maybe get some cooperation out of her. But rest assured as soon as I completed my mission with getting Gabriel this was one I would come back for also.

Katherine wasn't too keen on it when I told her to come down but she did. Thankfully our closeness had overridden the natural protector sense of kicking everything's ass when you don't know what else to do. Then she was in the thick of things too standing right by my side.

Jerri was a strong woman as she gazed up unafraid at my big friend. Of course when you have a lot of deadly friends of your own backing you up I could imagine it is a lot easier to be brave.

I was still freezing cold but I wasn't about to go into the van dragging all of my sort of fuzzy friends with me and Jerri didn't seem to be to inclined to get anybody out of my way.

Michael's crystal jumped but it wasn't panic this time. It was wonder and awe and pride. Then we all heard the unmistakable sound of a baby crying and I knew what had happened. Martha Sue had just had her baby and it sounded loud and totally pissed off. Something I could understand. If you were nice and warm and then got shoved into a totally cold and different place that you had never seen before you wouldn't be too happy about it either.

Actually something just like that had happened to all of us Resurrected. Different circumstances but we had all been essentially born again back into this world to live a life few ever get the chance to live. Now I had things to do and this snow wasn't going to last forever and I needed to get my head back on my mission.

First Gabriel, then pick up the pieces of a very broken society and try and put it all back together again. I had started with the Resurrected but now I could see that my group wasn't all I had to worry about.

The Resurrected were afraid of the Aspanari, almost to the point of paranoid panic. If Jerri was any sample of what the Independents were like then they weren't too keen about our dark brothers and sisters either. But I knew the Aspanari had talents that we needed. Maybe not all of them but probably a lot and like the one that had sabotaged that bridge in Michigan it would be better to have them as a friend and not a foe.

Could I do that? Did I want to? For some that hadn't wronged me and mine possibly but for those that had hurt for revenge or anger or just because it was in their nature to do so, then no I didn't want them. But did that give me the right to do what my heart was telling me to do? Kill them? Even most societies frowned on the death penalty. But was there any other option? Did we have prisons? Somehow I didn't think so. So what did that leave us with?

These weren't decision I could make on my own but I knew I had to start somewhere. And standing in front of me was a really good place.

"We have to complete a mission that may take a while." I told Jerri. "We have a brother that is in more trouble than he knows and I have to try and help him before it is too late."

She nodded. "I haven't had family in so long I wouldn't even know how to act." She sounded so forlorn and I wanted to do something to change that but right now all I could do was make a promise.

"You will. I promise that you will. I don't have the power to change things right now but something has to be done. Nobody should be left alone if they don't want it that way."

"I did at first." Jerri said. "I left, oh heavens it must be forty years ago or more, because nobody considered what I did as being important. I was given stupid things to do and everybody thought I was a freak. Telepathy with animals, what good is that?" I could hear the hurt from those long ago words that must have been thrown at her time and again.

"Well I think your gift is amazing and so are you. And whoever said that was an idiot."

"I don't know who said it first but when I complained to our council member he didn't understand why I was upset. He thought my gift was worthless too."

I gritted my teeth and I could feel Katherine probably doing something about the same. "Phillip is a bozo that is most likely getting a hefty eye opener even as we speak."

Her eyes flew open as she heard that name and I thought I had screwed up royally by bringing him up.

"You are coming from the Center?" Jerri asked making sure that she had understood everything correctly.

"Yup, just left and then we hit this wonderful weather. Almost hit that van and ended up in a ditch. Had a pregnant women, a frantic father and two kids all thrown into the mix just for fun."

My sense of humor coming out to play mostly because I had almost reached that overstressed point and I was starting to get a little punchy.

She chuckled at how I put all that. "Yes and then I complicated things even worse didn't I?" I don't think she was really apologizing. Just admitting to making a very weird situation all the stranger.

Katherine chuckled too. "Like you could possibly know what we were, what Gabriella was." And I had to smile up at her. She was trying to see things through different eyes and I squeezed her hand to let her know that I appreciated the effort it took to think differently than she had been trained to do for years and years.

My large lady protector looked down at me and smiled too. "I didn't know what to make of her when I first met her either. Still don't most of the time. But I have learned to never underestimate her. When she thinks she can do something she does it. If she says something is wrong it usually is even if at first you don't see it that way. I have never had the pleasure of meeting an infiltrator before but I doubt that even the few we have had before were like her." I could see the surprise in Jerri's face when that phrase came out and I elbowed Katherine in the ribs.

"Cut it out." I complained. "You know how much I hate that title." And she did too. I mean yes that was what I was supposed to be but did it have to have so much awe and mystery surrounding it. I wasn't really all that different than anybody else. We all had gifts that were unusual, even Nohus did, we were all in our own way special. I would never get used to that reaction and I wished I could reclassify myself but I didn't think anybody would let me get away with it.

Too many people just loved the idea that there was another person around to save the day. Like I was some sort of superhero and I literally snorted at the idea. Right, I couldn't fly worth beans and looked really dorky in a tights and a cape. Maybe when Halloween came back around I could dress up as something totally ridiculous and even things out a bit.

Jerri had been listening to both of us and was pretty good at reading faces. Of course mine had never been a poker one to start with unless I really worked at it so she shouldn't have any problems. "What do you find so amusing?" She asked raising an eyebrow as her curiosity showed.

Katherine rolled her eyes and sort of groaned. "Anything, everything. With Gabriella there is no telling."

I answered her. "I think next Halloween I will dress up as an M&M candy and make Peter's entire month."

That got a sort of mixed reaction from everybody and I wasn't sure just were we going to go from here. Then the door to the van slid open and my husband's mint ice cream scent slammed into my nose.

I was over the hood of the van and by his side before he could get both feet out the door. It barely registered that I had vaulted over a bunch of wolves to do it either. He didn't have to ask a thing as I started jabbering away so fast and low he had problems following. Finally he put his hand on my mouth. "Maggie give me a minute would you?" He said smiling at me.

It was so easy for me to forget that he had had his hands full, literally, for the last bit of time. Delivering a baby, especially in these conditions, had to be taxing and nerve wracking. I blushed up to hairline. "Sorry. I forgot what you were dealing with." I admitted, totally embarrassed that I could do something like that.

"It's all right. I knew you were busy too." He said still smiling. Michael was usually pretty easy going but there was something to this happiness that was beyond the norm even for him. I felt through our crystals and knew what it was. He was Jonesed big time on what he had done and I couldn't blame him one bit. Delivering a new life into this world must be the biggest high a medical could possibly have. To me it was even more amazing than saving a life. That life was already here but this was a whole new beginning as the cycle of life renewed again.

"And you brought a baby into this world." I had no idea how to congratulate him. He hadn't done it alone of course. Martha Sue had carried it and KW had sort of been on the making of it but my bond mate had brought it healthy and alive into this world and that should be recognized. How do you say good job for something like that? I high fived him because I just couldn't think of anything else.

I guess that was good with him as his hand slapped mine and held it up above our heads for a few brief seconds. The joy was there for anyone to see on his face as a glow from inside made his face shine. "A fine baby boy, healthy even if a littler early. And if you ask me looks so much like his father that I think KW has been cloned." He laughed. I couldn't help but smile too.

The constant pinging happiness was starting to wane just a bit. I could see Michael look over my shoulder and across the short hood of the mini van. His eyes sort of getting large and I didn't need to turn around and look to know what he saw.

Jerri and her entourage was truly a sight. Michael may not even see the wolves but the bears were enough to make an impression all on their lonesome.

"You have been busy." He said in a horse whisper.

I took his hand and sort of pushed my way through the fuzzy warm bodies of three of the wolves. But they parted ground easily enough and we were standing in front our new friend.

"Jerri this is our house leader, Michael." Technically Michael and I were equal and he wasn't Katherine's house leader at all but she didn't need to know that. What I was trying to show her was that I hadn't lied to her. That we were being transferred and on a mission to get somebody that was in danger and that Michael was deserving of all the respect that came with the title of being in charge of a house.

This was something that if she had lived as a Resurrected for any length of time was sort of ingrained in you. Being in an infiltrator or a protector or even a finder like Peter was got you help but a house leader got more than that. They got the bend over backwards, what can I do to help reaction that we really needed right now.

Suddenly a huge wolf jumped up and placed his big paws on Michael's shoulders. Staring at him eye to eye almost knocked him down. My claws started to come out. But the wolf wasn't growling, was making no aggressive sounds and was sort of looking him up and down as if trying to place him or evaluate him in some way.

"Ah, so you are the other one we saw before." Jerri said in what sounded like relief.

I was scrambling trying to make sense of what that meant. Michael was now staring back at the wolf and tracing the identifying markings on its face with a finger as if he recognized them.

Katherine had backed up to stand by Michael and was gazing down at the big wolf too. "So you are the one that started all this." She said surprisingly to the wolf.

For once I had no clue what was going on. Somebody figured out that I was the odd girl out and would like a little info and everybody started talking at once.

Michael started. "While you were gone one of the kids saw something staring at them from outside a side window. Then they were both screaming about monsters and werewolves and just wouldn't shut up."

"I thought it was just the storm that had shaken them up." Katherine added.

"Yeah and your ghost stories really helped keep them calm." Michael snorted. I knew what Katherine had been doing what I said, but ghost stories? Really?

Jerri added her own part. "One of my wolves found the van earlier and was coming back to check on it. See if the people had been rescued or not. We try not to be seen or get involved unless we have to. Most people freak when they see a wolf or a bear so we have learned to keep a low profile. Then he picked up your scent that lead away from the van and I knew that was trouble brewing because most people would get lost about 5 feet away from their cars. He wanted to see if anybody was left here to worry about. I wasn't sure just what we would have done if we had to search for lost people. That doesn't work out very good most of the time." She sighed and sort of rolled her eyes a bit.

And of course the wolf didn't know I was Resurrected. Hadn't thought that the unusually, highly enticing and easily traced scent would be one like his long time friend that could share his thoughts. Maybe as far as a wolf thought there was only one like her. I had no idea what a wolf thought and just like a human-to-human telepath didn't really want to know what was going on in a fuzzy brain.

Everything sort of clicked in place then. "And when you knew there was more here you just wanted to make sure nobody else wandered off. You didn't know I had already made it safe to the next town or that I would come back with or without help."

I had no idea what type of stories Katherine had been telling but even a fairy tale would have started those kids imagination going and then looking out into the darkness to see a giant wolf face staring back would have been enough to scare me. I could only imagine what they had thought.

Then Katherine had for better or worse bailed out of the van to see what in the hell was truly going on. She had been pretty ice covered herself when I had first caught a glimpse of her so she had probably been up there either looking for trouble or looking for me for quite bit.

When the wolves had shown up they may not have even been aggressive at first but she had taken it as an attack rather than a guardianship and gone on the defensive, pummeling the wolves with first shoes and then that rope of hers.

I realized then that Michael had more medical work he needed to do. Could a human sight empath see what was wrong with a wolf? The only way to find out was to try. We had accidently caused pain and death and we needed to do what we could to fix it.

For the next bit of time we all played Dr. Dolittle. Patching up injured wolves and mourning the one that I had killed. The second even though very badly cut up Michael thought would pull through. Katherine surprisingly had a very steady hand and was great at stitching things up. Me on the other hand was only good at putting on antibiotic cream, cleaning wounds and tying bandages. My stiches looked like a poor excuse for a Frankenstein movie. And luckily the knocks to the head that Katherine had delivered would heal with time and that no brain damage had been caused. The wolves came through it with a very healthy respect for women's shoes according to Jerri, which made everybody laugh.

Soon everybody had left the area except for Jerri and her one big wolf friend. Even the bears and the mountain lion had left. It had been amazing to pet them and consider them as a sort of friend even though I couldn't really understand a single rumble or purr I sort of told myself I did. Maybe they weren't that much different than us I thought to myself as the last tail swished out of sight.

Who was I kidding? They were different; it was only because of Jerri's influence that made them so human like. Away from her they would be just like any other wild animal and although because of what I was I didn't have to worry about them harming me I would be foolish to think that they weren't dangerous. Wild things were unpredictable and you were stupid not to know that you can never take the wild out of them completely.

We waited until dawn started to belatedly arrive. The storm had died down to almost nothing during the night but the overcastting made the sun's arrival almost impossible to see. It began as a lessening in the darkness that I knew nobody but the four of us could detect. Jerri noticed it but only because she could see through wolf eyes when she chose. Her own were unable to tell that dawn had arrived. The people in the van had stayed put. Michael had checked on them from time to time to make sure that all was well. Had concocted the craziest story that I was sure nobody would swallow but somehow they did and now they were waiting for the promised tow trucks to arrive and get everybody going again.

Of course they would be heading straight to the closest hospital, wherever that happened to be. We would be heading to St. Louis and Jerri would be heading back to her lonely cabin in the woods.

I knew approximately where it was and if I had Peter with me was positive that we could find her when the time came. There still was no firm answer on what we could do for her but I refused to accept that the answer would be nothing.

Then help started showing up. When I could hear vehicles not too far away I knew it was time to start with the goodbyes. It was difficult for Jerri to leave. I could see it even though she tried not to show it and there was nothing I could do but hug her and make the same promise. This time she would not be forgotten and left alone because she was different.

I knew that Jerri would be useful in the future. How, I wasn't sure but I was coming to get her even if her talent would have been, as needed as making light puppets on the ceiling. It was wrong to abandon anyone and everyone was important and should be made to feel as such. That was one thing that Phillip and I had disagreed upon from the first.

He felt that he should be able to use anybody like a tool and if you didn't fit into his agenda then he tried to reshape you until you did. I refused to be reshaped and I had no problem beating the hole to accommodate the square pegs because us weird pegs were people too.

But that was a fight for another day.

# Chapter 14

## FAMILY REUNION.

It took us almost a day to get out of the snow of Colorado and I was never so happy to see the desert terrain of New Mexico in all my life. We had tried to take the more southern route in an attempt to out race the storm we knew was coming and had ended up smack dab in the middle of it. But the delay I hoped would prove worthwhile. We had gained a new sister. A lost sister named Jerri and I would be back to get her as soon I got my brother out of the hot water he was in.

Now that I was actually going it was all I could think about. And the restless energy almost drove everybody crazy because sitting still in the back seat of the truck was almost impossible. Soon I was making Katherine and Michael almost twitch as much as I was.

When tiredness and cramped driving conditions forced us to stop for the night once I about went crazy. All night long all I could do was pace out front of the hotel room while Katherine and Michael slept. I felt like a century on guard duty with nothing to guard against.

Nobody knew what we were here. There was no sense of our kind anywhere around the small town we stopped at in the panhandle of Oklahoma. The closest family group that I knew of was in Dallas but we hadn't bothered to call them to let them know we were passing through. This was sort of secret mission and the less people that knew where we were the better. Besides nobody could order us anywhere if they couldn't find us. And we weren't going to hang around long enough for anybody to zero in to start with.

When the arches of St. Louis came into view and I was so glad I wasn't driving right then. My truck engine would have never survived and the police would have probably been a little pissed too. As it was when we pulled into the hotel we had stayed at once before in September I about shot out of the truck.

I knew they weren't here yet but I had hoped they would be. We had heard absolutely nothing from Alison or Peter or Alicia at all. No word that they had closed up shops and were able to get away without Duncan or Ezra stopping them. I didn't think those two would stand a chance when Alison got a head of steam going but they were pretty big guys. But other than keeping my two sisters and one brother prisoner what could they do? And that was against every rule we had. Still if those two had word from Phillip that somebody needed to be investigated then they might try.

As low down as Phillip could get I wouldn't put it pasted him trying something like that just to prove to me who was still in charge. I had seen the boss's job and even though he may not realize it, I didn't want it. He could keep all the stress and problems. I had had more than what I wanted of that sort of trouble and if I could manage the rest of my days of not having to deal with it again I would be very happy. But I also knew that was very unrealistic. I was needed as a sanity check and even though I didn't always act like I had all eight oars in the water I was saner than anybody else I had left behind right now

A fact that scared me more than just a little, everybody had collectively lost their marbles, including my husband for a time. I still think he agreed that we needed to investigate and interrogate anybody and everybody down to the cleaning lady in the hospital Phillip did surgery in last month.

My very different opinion had been for discrete and quiet. Only bring out the big guns when needed. Not brain scan everybody and his brother as a loyalty check. Our three remaining telepaths and four emotional empaths were nice people or at least I thought so but to be given such a horrid task as this was unfair and with the paranoia they would be getting from everybody that was in charge it wouldn't be long before they started seeing problems where there weren't any or hadn't been until they started doing their witch hunt.

But nobody wanted to listen to me. Nobody could see why this would be a problem and that everybody would just roll over and allow their own private and personal thoughts and feelings to be torn into for no reason other than those in charge thought they had the right to do it. It was worse than having the police raid a house without a warrant or due cause. This was raiding yourself at the most basic level there was.

And Phillip and the rest of the council just didn't understand why I thought this was wrong. I guess the old saying about power was correct. Absolute power corrupts absolutely and the council had been gaining power more and more over the years and now they thought they could pretty much do whatever they wanted and nobody had the right to challenge them.

Guess what? They were wrong. Somebody would. If I were right there would most likely be lots of some bodies.

Right now I would leave it alone because I had other things that were more urgent. Time would tell who was right and who was wrong. That was the great thing about time. You didn't have to do a thing except sit back and enjoy the fireworks. And I wouldn't even tell Phillip I told you so, well maybe a little.

We got three rooms in the hopes that the rest of our family would be here soon. But after another day came and went and no word I thought my phone was broke. Michael finally called home to see if they had left and didn't even get an answer, just the machine with Alison's voice asking to leave a message. Her cell phone had been disconnected for some reason when I tried to reach her and we had no more idea what was going on than we had when we were stranded in the middle of nowhere. Of course when Michael's cell bit the dust I just knew that it was Phillip trying to cause us as much trouble as he possibly could. He still couldn't be happy about my leaving like I had and maybe by now things had already started to fall apart.

Then finally on a very dreary cold Wednesday afternoon there was a knock on our hotel room door. I didn't need to answer to know who was on the other side. Their smell came wafting in almost before the knocking and I was throwing open that door so fast it banged into the wall with crack.

It didn't matter to me if I broke it. Alison was almost bowled over and if it weren't for Peter standing right behind her we would have both ended up on the pavement. As it was she was sandwiched in between us.

Peter's long arms squeezed us both for a few seconds until he let go one side and Alicia was there too. If anybody had asked me how we managed a group hug like that I could never have explained.

Other bodies joined in and I knew that Michael was there as well as Katherine, which sort of surprised me. I hadn't thought she had grown that close to the others in my house.

"Gabriella was really getting worried." She said as I felt her take a step back.

I didn't care for the first few seconds why it took them almost another three days after we got here to arrive. But when we finally got everything unloaded from the van I started wanting answers.

Our adventures, which had started out as something worth telling, was now very much secondary on my agenda. Why did it take almost a week to make what should have been a two day trip at most. Even if they had hit some of the bad weather we had why this long. We had tried to chill as much as possible thinking that a case for Peter and Alicia had arisen that they just couldn't say no to. A missing child had been my guess and I knew Peter would never turn down something like that.

But now seeing how tired and haggard they all three were, I was beginning to think that it had been something else entirely.

"What took so long?" I asked as I helped Alison throw her last suitcase on the bed. I hoped she didn't mind sharing with Katherine. She just looked happy to be here.

"Oh Lord, everything." She said with sigh. Flopping down on the bed she looked really worn out and I thought maybe that the explanations could wait.

"Never mind. You can tell me about when you get some sleep." I told her as I tried to leave. Her hand grabbed mine and pulled me back.

"No. It is alright but if one more thing had happened on the way here I would have gone crazy." I waited patiently for her to continue. It wasn't hard. She was fighting sleep and if whatever she had to say made it easier to rest I could listen.

"Well I'm glad you are here. I was starting to worry. You could have called and let me know that you guys were on the way." I hadn't understood that. Why no word? I had gone over so many scenarios in my head that I had about driven myself crazy too.

With no cell phones it might have been difficult but Alison had my number and it still worked just fine. I don't think that Phillip had even known I had it.

I was partially right. "I have no idea what you started but the shit rolled down hill pretty quick right after you called." Alison started and even though I could tell she was exhausted it didn't slow her down as anger gave her the strength to let me know what happened.

But the part that she thought I was responsible sort of pissed me off. "I didn't start a damned thing. I just found out stuff that was already there." I snapped back at her. The last thing I wanted was a fight with Alison but I wasn't going to let her blame me for things that I had tried really hard to have not happen. That was like putting salt in wound right now.

She looked at me and could see the anger and frustration there all too easily. She wasn't an empath exactly but she was a sensitive, which was one stage down from what a true empath was and even though she couldn't affect a mood she did feel it, read it, see it. Why that made her in the medical/other category was a sore spot with both of us because I thought she was totally awesome.

Alison patted my hand. "I know you didn't do it on purpose." But that phrase didn't help one bit and I growled down deep and she could see that I wasn't happy about the entire situation. "Maybe if I explained you will understand?" I nodded and let her tell her story but I really didn't see how I could be held responsible for much of anything that had happened.

"Right after you called, it couldn't have been more than an hour or two when we had a hiccup in power. When Duncan went to check on what had happened, he saw that we had lost power and that the back up generator had kicked on. As he checked everything over we found out that we had lost everything, power, phones, Internet, even the satellite was out. Ezra was sure that the end of the world had started."

I chuckled at that. That was Ezra for sure. He had sort of thought the world was going to end in like 1970 something and that we were all living on borrowed time. I hadn't been able to get why he felt that way but it he was sort of the dark gloomy type so maybe he didn't need a reason.

"We called to find out what had happened just to get told it wasn't area wide just us. It confused the heck out the customer service reps but they all had orders to cancel for non payment but the customer service guys could plainly see we weren't delinquent."

"Rafael." I said spitting out his name. "He hacked into those places and deliberately shut you down just to annoy the piss out of me."

"Oh, not just us. He managed to do that to just about every house all over the country. Then he hit the cell phones too and we are still working on getting that straightened out because he didn't set up things to cancel for non-payment. This time it was a customer request and we had to pay deposits again to get them reactivated and he managed to freeze all our bank accounts too."

Now I was livid. Rafael had singled handedly managed to cripple just about every single house in North America at the same time. If the Aspanari didn't do something pretty major it would be a wasted opportunity.

I knew that Ezra and Duncan would be just fine until things got straightened out but it was a pain in the ass for them to have to deal with. "Did you call the Center? See if the computer guys could fix things or at least trace it to find where Rafael is?" Alison was a smart cookie but this was so unexpected would she have thought to ask for help.

"Sure I did. First thing I did luckily before the cell phone disaster. You were already gone by then and everything there was in such turmoil I was lucky I managed to get to talk to anybody. That's how I found out that everybody had been just as fortunate as we were. They hadn't managed to trace it yet but they were working on it. But I guess Phillip was practically ranting about waging war and that everybody was a spy."

I groaned and knew that this little thing from Rafael had been the straw with the camel and Phillip was beyond paranoid if such a state exists. But he would not be happy until he found more spies even if he had to get false confessions from them or make people think they were when they really had done nothing wrong.

Rolling my eyes I knew this wasn't the entire story and I was right. "Ok what happened next?"

"Maybe we should have stayed and made sure everything got put back together but from what I heard from the Center it seemed like Ezra was right for once and the world really was ending. I wanted us to be away from there and out of communication before Phillip or somebody ordered a total lock down, no travel anywhere. That hasn't happened in a long time but I can see where it might be asked for now."

I didn't even know that was possible but why not. The Resurrected had been around a very long time and had to deal with all sorts of problems surely they would have a course laid out to deal with emergencies. Plagues and virus, natural disaster and even manmade ones would have all been thought of. Just look how our country had changed things since 9-11 and we had been dealing with disasters and problems for a lot longer than that.

I nodded. "Yeah Phillip has really lost it." This hadn't been my fault but I had been responsible. If I had stayed maybe I could have calmed things down. But no he wouldn't be in any better mood to listen to me after all this than he had been before and I was just kidding myself that I had that type of influence.

"So you left but why did it take so long to get here after that?" From the way she was telling things that should have only delayed them a day or so not almost four.

"I wrecked the van." Alison said turning totally crimson. I didn't want to laugh or get mad either. Things happened especially when you were under a lot stress. You got distracted easy and didn't always pay attention as well as you usually did.

"But it's okay now right? Nobody got hurt and you can drive it right?"

"Peter had to pull the back fender out a bit and since we were sort of short on cash we had to do a little extra work to pay for the repairs. But its okay and we are here and ready to help."

All this came spilling out at mach speed. Alison never liked the idea of letting anybody down. I would bet it would be a cold day in Hawaii before she got behind the wheel of that van again. That was okay Peter and Katherine had better reaction times and I knew they wouldn't mind being behind the wheel.

I didn't ask what happened. It didn't matter. Didn't matter if Alison had been the cause of the accident or not. They were here and that was all that was important.

"No problem. You got things handled and you are here. Now we are together. You guys need to rest up a bit, get something good to eat because tomorrow morning we are going hunting."

I left Alison curled up around a pillow and out like a light about 15 minutes later. After all the adrenalin had finally worn off she was exhausted. Figuring how empty her stomach must be she might sleep for like 12 hours and then she would be up and bitching about food. That was the one thing about Alison. She could go like the proverbial Energizer Bunny but when she crashed, she crashed and only hunger would wake her up.

My room wasn't empty. I hadn't expected it to be. I hadn't expected it to have not just Michael and Katherine but Peter as well. Alicia must have been really burned out too because she was missing Peter's story telling of all the things that Alison had told plus a few things she hadn't.

"And I'm just strapping my seat belt on when Bam." Peter was saying as he slaps his hands together.

Michael is rolling and Katherine is trying very hard not to laugh too.

As Peter continued his story it didn't take me long to figure out that he had been much more amused by everything than Alison had. "You should have seen her eyes Michael. They were about this big. She had no clue that there was anything back there to hit. How can you possible miss a concrete pole, I ask you?"

"Well in her defense she did have a lot on her mind from what you told us." Katherine answered. "Maybe you should have offered to drive from the first, you having a clearer head and all."

"I did but Alison is stubborn and since Michael left her in charge she has been dead set on trying to do everything all by her lonesome. And I just thought you were a dictator. She even started wanting us to check-in when Leez and I were on the road. You never asked for that."

"Alison was just being cautious. With all the things going on I can't say I blame her." Michael told Peter. He was coming to the defense of his long time friend and I couldn't blame him. Besides he was right. There were a lot of people out there that didn't like me much and because of that those I left behind were in more danger than usual. That was why I hadn't let Peter take on the task of sole protector. He was a good guy and very capable but if the Aspanari wanted pay back for what had happened with Hans and Josef, then hitting my family would be a good way to do it.

Some people, like Peter, were just too damned happy and didn't see the darker things until they had to. It made for a great way to live most of the time but sort of caused rude awakenings from time to time when he had to take off the rose colored glasses.

"Well I think you can rest assured that Alison is not eager to drive that silver thing again anytime soon." I said as I went the rest of the way in the room and sat down on the bed next to where Michael was lounging.

Peter snorted and sort of chuckled too. "She is so darned short she has problems seeing over the dash board."

"All you see is knuckles and the top of her hair." Katherine chimed. I knew that if either of the two vertically challenged ladies were in the room nobody would have dared say anything like what was being bantered about. Alicia and Alison may be short but they could hold their own and would have been in somebody's face all too quickly.

"Hey for all you towering people just remember the higher you go the less air you have. Lack of oxygen causes the brain to malfunction." I said in defense because I wasn't six foot and change either.

"Did she just tell me I'm stupid?" Peter asked looking down at me and trying to glare and not succeeding worth a damn.

"Nope but if the shoe fits." I shot back at him.

"Shoes, oh heavens. Don't bring up shoes." Katherine groaned and threw herself back on the bed she had deposited herself on.

Peter lost all interest in our little battle of wits and immediately zeroed in on Katherine. "What, what about shoes? Don't tell me you went on a spending spree and have a closet full like Alison does?"

"No she likes to throw them." I said remembering just a few days ago and what that had brought about.

Katherine groaned again and blushed. Michael hadn't been around for any of this and had been busy himself.

"Katherine is a very good shot with high heels and platform shoes. There are some very sore wolves that will agree that she is pretty darned good at inflicting damage." I told both of them. Michael had known something happened but I'm not sure he put the possible concussions and my old joke presents that had been sticking up in the snow together.

"OH so that's what happened." Michael chuckled and gave Katherine an appraising look, which didn't lessen her embarrassment at all.

"Ok give." Peter said as he sat down in a chair that was way too small for his long legs but he didn't seem to mind that he was a little cramped.

Where to start? I had no idea. I guess when everything sort of went wrong all at once.

"We left the Center in sort of a rush." I began. "We tried for the southern route because we knew a nasty storm was on the way and hoped we could get ahead of it. We didn't make it exactly. Oh, we would have outrun the worst of it but we sort of had an accident too and ended up in ditch."

"No, I put us in the ditch." Michael clarified and I dismissed it with a wave of my hand.

"Anyway. What caused the problem was a stuck mini van that had Nohus in it. Pregnant lady, two kids, father all in this van in the middle of nowhere."

"No way. Michael don't tell me you had to deliver a baby in all of that?" Peter asked eyes getting all soft at the idea.

"He was magnificent." I answered before Michael could because he would just try and brush it off like he always did.

"I did my part but Maggie and Katherine discovered an independent that has telepathy with animals."

"Really. You know I heard about one a long time ago but she sort of just up and disappeared and nobody would really talk about it."

"Because everybody made fun of her." Katherine growled. "If I was constantly ridiculed for being the only female protector I wouldn't stay around either."

Peter nodded. How would anybody know how to answer that? I could understand a little how Katherine would have an almost instant feeling of sisterhood for Jerri. If Joshua had been any other type man the same could have easily happened to her. Maybe that was why she had never asked for a transfer to another house but had stayed where she was valued.

"So you guys had to deal with a pissed off independent that could control the local wildlife. Not good." Peter summarized but had come to the wrong conclusion.

"No, not really." Katherine said. "I know a lot of people that would have held a grudge for that kind of treatment for centuries but Jerri didn't. She was just trying to help what she thought was a bunch of stranded motorists. When Gabriella went for help she didn't want anyone else getting lost and had her animals sort of make sure that nobody else went anywhere and when Gabriella showed back up, she was rather forceful in making sure she didn't leave again."

Peter sort of understood that but he had no idea of what had actually happened and maybe later on we might sit down and all of us compare notes on what really took place. Right now Peter may have the stamina of a protector but nobody could keep going forever and I could tell by the slight circles under his eyes that he had been up and running for some time.

"We will have plenty of time to go into more detail later." I said getting up from the bed. "You need sleep as much as that pretty redhead does. Shooo."

He smiled and left. You rarely had to tell Peter twice, especially if it meant keeping near his wife.

It was barely nighttime and food was in order but I didn't think the others of our family would be interested. Still if they woke up in the middle of the night things might not be open. So trying to plan ahead I found the phone book and discovered that there were several places that sold cold cuts and the like, even salads that sounding appealing and would sit well with Alison. Alicia was more of a carnivore and liked her meat.

So after putting our heads together we placed an order and Katherine said she would go pick it up since it was just a block away. That left me with little to do but think about what I had found out.

I was worried that Rafael would continue to plague us. Of course what could I do about it? Maybe after we got Gabriel out of the pickle he was in I could get Peter to find that person too. I didn't think I would get any arguments from anybody with that extension to our mission. Something sure had to be done about him and nobody could find a missing person or thing better than the two people that had been doing it for a living for a few decades.

What then? What would I do when I found him? I knew what I wanted to do. Kill him but did that make it right? My heart said yes but my conscious wasn't in total agreement and PIB wasn't saying anything at all. I couldn't blame him really that should be my decision and later on if it turned out wrong then the only person or thing I could blame was me.

"Michael if I have to kill Rafael later on because there isn't another option how will you feel?" I knew it was my decision but what would my husband think if I had to kill him in front of Michael. We had sort of discussed this same thing months ago but that had been an abstract scenario and now it wasn't quite so abstract anymore.

He had known Rafael for years, decades. I know he was mad at him for all the things he had done but would he think me a murderer later on for taking his life. Granted he was a murderer too. For sure at least once and maybe many more times than that if what Daniel had found out proved true. Couldn't one argue that a protector had to kill sometimes to protect and playing the part of my own devil's advocate maybe Rafael had felt in the right.

Did that make what he did better or worse? In my eyes he had betrayed people that had loved him or at least depended on him. He had hurt and killed and would have done a lot worse if we hadn't figured it all out like we had. And he had accomplices too in other parts of the world that had done almost the same thing.

Was that what I was now involved in? A war? It sure felt like one even though I had never actually been in battle before.

Michael hadn't answered me yet and that worried me. When I finally looked in his eyes they didn't hold what I thought they would. If he didn't want to take action against Rafael I would have thought they would tell me that. Maybe even tell me that he was horrified that I spoke of taking a life so easily even though in my heart and mind it wasn't an easy decision.

His eyes were as cold as ice and he said exactly what I had thought just a moment before. "You will do what you have to Maggie. You always do. But this isn't something that any of us has been through before. We have taken pot shots at each other for centuries. The Aspanari more than us but I am sure we didn't always play fair either. When you are in a fight for what you believe in you rarely do."

"But are we in that type of fight? Are we really going to war with the Aspanari?" I hated to say the words out loud. It sounded so final like the ending of something and the bringing of destruction.

"They have manipulated and caused fear and death for who knows how long so I believe we have been at war for a rather long time. Nobody bothered to tell us is all. Now we have to do what we have to do." He said simply and it did sound simple. Somehow I knew that simple things rarely stayed that way.

So we were at war and there was nothing I could to do to stop it and after looking into my own heart I knew deep down part of me didn't want to. I knew I should but I didn't. I wanted them to pay for what they had done to us. Down to the last single little bastard of them. I wanted to leave a bloody trail as bad as what they had done to us. I wanted them to learn what it meant when the bully has somebody stand up and say no more and then shoved his face into the dirt for a change.

Anthony had said I should be all things as needed but I had been the one to stand up to bullies all my life and I didn't need any prompting to know what I had to do. Battle sounded really good about now I just had to have a little help finding the enemy and I didn't think I would have any trouble getting volunteers for that either.

So we were at war now. Three little letters that mean a whole lot of bad.

# Chapter 15

## GABRIEL'S TALE

I had always loved December. Even in Florida where the seasons didn't really change that much except to get hotter and stickier in the summer. I had loved December. Not this one. This one sucked. Even if the snow and cold of Michigan should have made me feel like it was almost Christmas I knew I wouldn't be enjoying this holiday.

Homesickness wasn't something I had ever really suffered from before. Of course home had never had so much meaning as it did now. I missed all my family back in Florida. My thoughts went once again to the one I missed more than all the others, Maggie. And I had stupidly thought that this Christmas, her first with us, would be so special. How could I have been so wrong?

How was she doing? Anya teased me with tidbits of information to try and get a rise from me from time to time. It was just so damned frustrating. She knew more than she was telling me. I knew it too, all the tells were there if you knew to look for them. Why I hadn't been able to get into her confidences better was another thing that frustrated me. After what I had gone through I should have been given the Aspanari keys to the city.

That thought had me going back to August. The day before Maggie's birthday everything had come to a roaring head. Nothing had gone as I had planned. Not a single damned thing.

First I had to practically kill Peter to get him out of the way. That man had proved a lot tougher than I thought he would. I had never really confronted my fellow protector before but thought with him being a second-class one he wouldn't be that strong. Well I must be getting old because it took me hitting him in the head with the hood of my truck to knock him out all the way.

I punched him in the stomach hard enough to knock him into the grill of the Ram and he barely flinched. At first he thought I was just horsing around with him because he sort of chuckled about it. That blow should have doubled him over but it hadn't and I knew I had to do a lot more than I had planned. Finally I had him out but I could tell he wouldn't stay that way long. For a supposed second-class protector he was a resilient man. I didn't want to kill him so I chained him up instead.

Then in the house, when I had wanted to drag Maggie with me everything had just gone to hell. First it was Anya in what I had thought was her paranoid imagination. But as it turned out Maggie was a lot more than even I had guessed. I knew there was more to her than met the eye. For one thing Anthony wouldn't have wasted so much time training her even if he had been totally in love with her. He was and he wasn't, it was more of a friendship thing but there was love there.

The second was Maggie herself. There were a lot of little things that made me question her. Things like her nails having something that would only be used against me or someone like me. What reason would a guide have for something like that? And then the way she had disappeared the night Michael had totally went nuts. The only reason my best friend still had his head on his shoulders at all was I had been trying to find her. I couldn't waste time pummeling him in the dirt like I wanted to and by the time I had the opportunity I knew that if I hurt him like I had wanted too, Maggie would have been hurt in the process. She loved him and to hurt him, even though he deserved it, would have hurt her too.

But she had run so fast and had eluded not just me but Peter as well. Something I didn't think anyone could do. She didn't want to be found and she had the ability to do it too. For so long I really was worried that she had just thrown herself into the sea, never to be found again. But I didn't even want to think that thought. If she had died I don't think anybody could have saved Michael and from the look on his face as we broke up in groups or alone to search for her, I didn't think he would want anybody to stop me.

The fact that Michael felt so horrible made me feel a tad better. At least he knew that he had messed up. He had been so unstable I was starting to wonder if he even knew reality any more. But Maggie disappearing on us had been the thing to snap him out of whatever had been plaguing him.

Now they were married. I was happy for them or at least that is what I kept trying to tell myself.

But Maggie had proved to be a lot more than anybody had thought. When she broke free of Josef's gift I had thought at first she had voice guide. That was the only thing that Josef had said would break his hold on a mind. But no simple little guide and trainer had ever had a voice guide before. The Powers That Be didn't waste a gift like that. Tracking guides had instincts that kept them from ending up in trouble but Maggie obviously was a lot more than just a guide and trainer. What was she really? At first nobody could figure it out.

Then that instant when I had almost blown everything, Josef had ordered Hans to kill her and she had drawn him away to fight him alone. I could see the confidence in her. She wasn't really even afraid of that giant man. The way she moved told me that Anthony had been doing a lot more than showing her how to just survive in the woods and swamps.

Before I knew what was going on Anya was on Michael tearing him up with a knife. It was all I could do to get her away from him and even give him a chance to live. As it was I had to wonder if I had reacted too slowly to save him?

Hans dying in the car on the way back to the warehouse had thrilled me to no end but I had to act appalled and mad even though all I wanted to do was cheer. Maggie was lethal with those pretty nails of hers and I didn't realize then that they could become living blades. When we got back all Josef wanted to do was get into the computer that didn't have as much information in as he thought it did.

Oh, Rafael had given me some really good ideas about how to get in to their local network of spies and agents. I had no idea how he knew what he knew but Phillip had contacts all over the world and I guess that he had let his trusted bodyguard in on a few things, tidbits really but enough to find Josef and arrange a meeting with him. But him showing up at my bar the very night all my family was there should have told me that things wouldn't go as planned with him, ever.

Now he was dead. Maggie had taken very nice care of him and I had to smile at her phrase for that evil man, ferret face. Yeah, that fit him really good. I knew Maggie was special but an infiltrator was not something I would have ever come up with. Of course I knew what that was. I had never met our last one. My human death had happened after Jacob had already gone to his final reward and I had nothing but the small bit I remembered from my training time with Joshua In Colorado to draw information.

But Josef had come to that conclusion very quickly. I never would have in a million years. He just knew that was why she could break his hold. He had used his power of auditory hypnosis to kill the last infiltrator so when The Power That Be sent a new one they made sure that this one wouldn't be as vulnerable. It made sense to everybody. Josef was many things but stupid or slow wasn't on the list.

I had tried to tell Maggie without saying the words as she had stood over Josef's dead body that I wasn't the horrible person that I had to pretend to be. It was so hard to see the accusation in her eyes, the hurt and betrayal. I almost couldn't go through with my orders. But I knew this was the best chance we had to find out what our enemies were up to. If only…….

Shaking myself to get away from what happened I wasn't able to completely. At least my body didn't scar but the injuries my love had given me went a lot further in my heart than her sharp nails ever could. I understood I had left her with no choice and just hoped that both her and Michael would forgive me and get me out of this hellhole I found myself in.

Two more months, that was all I had to wait before I knew. I don't know why I questioned that they would find me. I knew the type of people both Maggie and Michael were. Maggie loved and forgave and never held a grudge. Michael stood by those that he chose as friends against anyone. Loyal, you couldn't get much more loyal than those two were.

Still I had to ask myself quite a few questions. Did I really want them to find me to start with? Part of me yearned to end this charade as quickly as possible. Part of me hated to see them again. See the woman I loved happy with another man would hurt so much. But to live the rest of my life without her being in it would be the worst part of hell imaginable. So when they found me I would be happy to see her again, act the part of the loving brother she needed me to be. I could never let her know how I felt. It would hurt her too much and that I couldn't do. Besides having her as my loving sister was more than what I should get after what my duty made me do to her.

Then there was the other more important question for me at the moment. Well maybe not more important but definitely more urgent. Why didn't Anya and the rest of the Aspanari trust me enough to tell more than just a few things here and there? Why were we constantly moving from place to place?

Anya was clearly in charge of our little group. How in the world had fate made it so I had to deal with Michael's ex bond mate? I understood now why he had so many issues and was sort of surprised it wasn't worse. To be married to that witch, it was hard enough just to deal with her for the little time I had to spend with her. She was manipulative and loved to pull your strings just for the hell of it.

She tried to do that to me enough and I had to act like what she teased and taunted me with actually bothered. The one that did was when she 'accidentally' revealed something about Maggie. She knew little things about her that I just didn't understand how she knew.

First was her location. How did the Aspanari keep track of our people? The only answer I had was a spy or spies and that scared me to death. Then there were more than tidbits of Maggie and Michael being so very much in love. Again, how did she know what should have been impossible for her to know?

I heard a crunch of a footstep in the snow. "Aren't you cold Gabe?" Anya asked me. I had been standing outside in the dark cold for quite a while now. It was a stupid question really. Our kind didn't get cold unless we were exposed to freezing temperatures for a very long time without any protection at all. I was a protector and had even more ability to withstand the cold than most did and the decent coat I had provided more than enough of a barrier between elements and me.

"Not really." I answered out of pure courtesy. Even though I more or less hated her, Anya had been as nice to me as her personality allowed. I could see how different she treated me than the three others we had with us. Two assassins and another simple Aspanari were never treated with deference she paid me most of the time. I wasn't sure why. Did she still think that if she played with me enough I would end up in bed with her? That wasn't happening, ever.

"You should come in now. I think Alan is getting tired of watching you stare out into nothing." She said quietly. That was another thing I didn't get. Why wasn't I allowed out much on my own? It was like I was a prisoner or something. Other than for a few minutes right after we left Florida, I hadn't manage a single minute of real alone time. Oh, it would have seemed like it if I weren't so sensitive. If my hearing and sense of smell was just a little less I would probably never know how closely I was being guarded.

I was really starting to think that something more was going on than I knew. What I did know told me that something was up or going to come up soon. Some big plan as the tension level kept rising on an almost hourly basis. Well time for a few answers. Anya never liked it when anyone questioned her orders especially me. She didn't exactly show it except in her eyes. Now I would get evasive answers that really were no answers at all but I could read a lot from what she said and how she said and more importantly what she didn't say.

"Why? He doesn't have stand at the window and watch me. Where would I go?" I snorted. At least as far as they knew my entire family had thought I had defected to the Aspanari. Other than Maggie and I had to assume Michael nobody else could possibly know.

"Because I worry about you." Anya said. There was truth in her words and in her eyes when I looked at them. "You haven't assimilated to our group like I had hoped you would. You still hold yourself back so much. You don't try and make friends with anyone. You are aloof and almost cold."

Anya knew more about my personality than I wanted her to know. She knew I was usually a happy guy that cared about those around him. Well time for some truths of my own and some lies too.

"I am still very disappointed that things didn't work out like I had hoped they would." I said. That much was all too true but I knew exactly how she would take that.

Anya got mad. "Still mooning over that woman. I would have thought by now that you would have gotten over someone you hadn't even made love to." She huffed. "I mean really Gabe you could have your pick of any of the ladies you have met along the way but you just aren't interested. I have even made myself more than available but it's like you are a monk or something. What is wrong with two people enjoying each other? I understand you never had a problem with that before that little female came into your life. Is she really that special?"

Not only was she pissed that I had turned her down more times than I could count, I had also done the same for a very large number of women that Anya had parade around me. This week alone two more had come and gone like a never-ending harem line that I just couldn't stand the sight of. One had even had the nerve to show up naked in my bed in the middle of the night. I was glad I was very light sleeper but the lack of shame from that female was unbelievable. At least Anya had more restraint than that, not much but some.

"Special? Yes. Maggie is beyond special and I love her and it makes no difference if I can be with her or not it doesn't change my heart." For what had started out as an attempt to lie had turned into something a lot different. I was telling her the truth, a truth that hurt to just say out loud. But it did explain why I was acting the way I was, a very convenient excuse that just happened to be true.

I felt a small hand rub my shoulder. "I'm sorry." Anya said. "I did try and change what she felt but she was right there was nothing for me to tap into. Her feelings for Michael were too strong for me to change. I did try Gabriel but if it makes you feel any better she has changed her name to Gabriella. She wouldn't do that without a very good reason."

My start at the tidbit of information was a lot more than I should have allowed. That Maggie would do something like that surprised me completely. Maybe my heart hadn't chosen wrong but she had already told me she loved Michael. I knew they were bonded and that type of relationship wasn't dissolved easily. Anya had something up her sleeve and I should have realized it right away. Compassion wasn't a trait she had ever developed. Still that small amount of information just made me yearn for more and I should have known better.

"Do you know why?" I couldn't help but ask. It was beyond a curiosity just as Anya knew it would be.

"Because she said you had disgraced the arc angel's name and she wanted to bring honor back to it. I don't think she is very happy with you right now." She said sinking the barbs in all the way.

Ah, so that was what she told everybody. Or was that the truth and they wouldn't be coming for me after all? She had given me a chance to live but was that just because she couldn't kill me because her heart wouldn't let her admit to itself what a horrible person I turned out to be? Did she not get what I had tried to tell her that day and she had just had pity on me because of our history? Was that the reason I was still alive. If that were true, I was sunk. That was the one thing that Rafael had been sort of vague about. How was I to get out of this dilemma I found myself in?

I hadn't really thought about getting out of here, the getting in had been hard enough. Now that I was here I had managed to get some information about the Aspanari and how they worked. Almost like the small terrorist cells that plagued the world today. The Aspanari were exactly the same. Living and working in small groups that had one leader and a second in command they moved and changed locations frequently.

Changing people as needed to perform whatever bit of trouble they could figure out to do. From kidnappings and robberies to just plain destruction of important property, they were up for all of it.

The Aspanari were indeed our complete opposite or at least those in charge were. Some of those that had come and gone in the last few months weren't happy about the damage being done. I could see it in the hesitation but they had no one else to turn to and were made to think it was an obligation to do as instructed. Once in you were in and unlike the Resurrected organization you didn't really have the choice of leaving.

I heard a couple of them talking once when they didn't realize I was that close. Hearing them mention about another Aspanari that had been killed because he had tried to leave and live on his own, an assassin had taken care of the 'security breach' quickly. It wasn't security it was intimidation and almost slavery. I was appalled at all of this but something about what Anya said really bothered me.

"How do you know that she changed her name and why she did it? You are just trying to yank my chain Anya. Get me to forget about her. That is very manipulative of you."

I knew how to yank that chain back now or at least a bit. "You should forget about her Gabriel. She has forgotten all about you. Do you know how she spent one entire day? Sealed up in her room with her lover and being so loud and noisy about it that you could have heard them up the next floor. How she even finds him attractive at all is beyond me. When she could have chosen you, a real man and not some want to be. She isn't worth it Gabriel. She doesn't love you and never will."

Those words hit a lot closer to home than I wanted but I had to walk the tightrope for just a bit more. "She didn't kill me. Maybe she just wanted me to suffer more. I told her how I felt and it didn't seem to make a difference at all."

That was a complete lie. I had seen how much what I said to Maggie hurt her. How torn her heart was when she realized that she couldn't love me as anything but a friend and brother. I told her it was all right but it wasn't but I had to make it that way. For now it was a useful tool to keep Anya talking. The more she talked the more she revealed. Even if it was just what she knew and not how she knew it.

Anya just sort of nodded. "I suspected as much. She is selfish Gabriel. Thinks only of herself and what ever momentary pleasure she can get. You wouldn't believe how she has turned that old center of yours on its ear. Has everybody running around without a clue what they are doing and won't cooperate with anybody no matter who it is. She has even told Phillip and the rest of the council to jump in a lake more than once. One of us could never get away with something like that."

"They are a lot more disorganized than we are." I admitted. That was true but what the Aspanari failed to understand was that it left a lot more room for individual flexibility to respond to a problem. Did it always work like it should? No, but it was better than being ruled with an iron first. Maggie had chafed at our rules to start with so I really wasn't surprised that she had upset everything at her new home just like she had her old one. But it had turned out better because we relied on each as only family could do. If she could accomplish that for all the Resurrected, the Aspanari were in for a big surprise. No wonder Anya sounded almost worried about what Maggie was doing even though she tried to hide it her voice had given it away.

But I couldn't stand where this conversation was going any longer. To hear how Maggie was doing and have to agree that she was less than almost perfect was a ruse I could only do for so long. I had reached my limit now. "I really don't want to hear any more about her." I said putting as much of my present poor attitude into my voice as possible. It really wasn't that hard. Could February please just get here? Tomorrow was Christmas and I didn't feel like celebrating. I think that I would just spend the next few days in my room being the grumpy recluse that Michael had been. At least I had a good role model if I wanted to act the half crazed lovesick man I felt like I was.

Maybe if I could swallow the bile I could actually make Anya think I had finally decided to get over Maggie in the next month or two. Looking at her face and how it was almost gloating at my words I decided I wasn't nearly that dedicated to my mission. I thought I could when I started but being around her just turned my stomach when I remembered how she had smiled tearing into Michael like that. How could any woman treat a man she had supposedly loved to that type of torment? Anya hadn't just tried to kill him she had almost disemboweled him.

If I didn't know better I would think she had a split personality. Sometimes, like now she could be rather nice but then I would see something pass over her face and it was like somebody else was living inside her. I had never really considered possession before but dealing with her and a few of the other Aspanari I could see how one could mistake the insanity that sometimes griped them as being something not from this world.

Nobody sane would want to think that a human or even someone that used to be human could possibly be that evil, that crazy and tormented. But I had seen Anya fly into a rage before. First with Michael and then because of Hans dieing, I had taken her away to calm down. It had been Josef's idea to keep from totally venting her frustrations out on Anthony. Josef was a cunning man but mean he wasn't. However, he had no qualms in using those that enjoyed inflicting pain on others and when Anya was on a roll she did indeed enjoy that very much. Her little fists flailing away in Anthony's face until he passed out from the pain. Because of the low light level I don't think he even knew which one of us it had been that had hit him.

Every time it was bright enough to see, his eyes had never left my face. He had no qualms about me being a traitor, he believed every single lie I had told and bought the story hook, line and sinker. I had hoped more from him just as I had hoped and prayed more from Maggie.

If it did turn out that nobody was coming to get me. If February came and went and I discovered I was on my own I guess I would just have to try and escape and take my chances. Get back to either Alabama or Colorado on my own. I would never get through on any phone call to the Center and nobody at my old home would believe me. My hurting Peter and allowing Michael and Anthony to be hurt had pretty much sealed my fate with all the others. Alicia had the memory of an elephant and Peter would never do something to upset her. Alison had a vengeful streak in her too as I remembered her telling me once that the man that had killed her she had found sometime not too long after her resurrection and made sure he never hurt anybody again. How she had managed that I was never told, as Alison never really bragged about that sort of thing. I had no doubts that she would remember what I had done until she was only ash in jar sitting on a shelf. That was the type of women my two sisters were.

So I went back inside, went to my room and hid myself away. Listening and waiting for any information to sift its way into my room. I paid attention any time somebody moved. When Anya or Alan was on the phone I would try and be close enough to listen. If somebody new came in I would be there to sort of greet them even though I had no desire to get to know anybody. I did feel sorry for some of them that came with an escort like they might run away and the idea of being a slave was brought to mind again.

Our little cell caused trouble, so much trouble. Most of it small, like electrical outages that seemed to be Alan's specialty. He liked blowing things up, transformers and just about anything that would make a nice bang. My very large and sometimes jovial guard at least had a sense of humor. He enjoyed a lot of the same things I did so I couldn't really hate him. I don't think he was really evil, just misguided maybe. Having Anya around all the time and Claude didn't really help any. Alan was a prankster but Claude; he was the one I would have to watch out for. Claude was like a snake waiting to strike. He was the one that came and went frequently. That brought new people in and escorted them somewhere else. And nobody messed with Claude; even Alan wasn't that brave or maybe just plain foolish was a better word.

So now I was stuck in a jail of my own making. I had learned some but not nearly enough to make all of this worthwhile. Most of it I think Rafael already knew. If he and Phillip actually thought I would discover something they were in for a very serious disappointment. I was frustrated and disappointed and every day that past I knew it would just get worse.

I hated to disappoint my old charge like this. Phillip hadn't said a word to me because he knew I would do what needed doing. Yeah, that was me, loyal Gabriel. When this had all started Maggie hadn't even been in my life yet and all of this wasn't supposed to start until around now. When Anthony paid his bi-annual visit. But then things had been moved up when Phillip had insisted that Anthony visit early and I knew then that something was happening, something was going on that nobody else knew. Phillip didn't ask for people to make that sort of sacrifice without a damned good reason. I had wanted to ask more but Rafael had sealed everything top secret. Not to be mentioned by word or gesture because somebody else might figure it out and blow it all.

Dreading every single achievement that Maggie made I was torn between rejoicing at how happy she was and wanting to sabotage every single thing she did just to keep Anthony with us a little longer. Then I came on an inspired idea. If Maggie came instead of Anthony then a guide could get me out of any situation I might find myself in. That was the whole reason I had told Josef to take her instead of Anthony. It sure helped to say I wanted her for myself. He had seen her that night in the bar and he had more than expressed a desire for her himself. Maggie had been more than beautiful that night as I remembered how her face had looked up into mine when I danced with her. Held her close for those view brief seconds. I hadn't yearned for woman liked that in a very long time. Now I just hoped she didn't hate me.

Everything had worked out for the best more or less. I was in the Aspanari camp and I was finding out things. Small and not nearly as much as I had thought I would considering I had almost died to get here. You would think that Anya would recognize that fact. Maybe it was that I was former Resurrected and it took a long time and maybe a few missions before I was trusted with anything really important. Maybe I was rushing things. But if I had to stay here for years I didn't think I could mentally withstand it. From the way Rafael acted it shouldn't be taking this long. He hadn't exactly said it but he lead me to believe that there was something big coming soon. What he had no idea and maybe it was just a feeling that Phillip or one of the other council members had that was the catalysis for all of this. I had no idea and no way to find out.

So now I would wait. I hadn't been able to prove myself more than I already had because I was never given the chance. Every few weeks we would pack up and move someplace else. As far as I could see there was no rhyme or reason to it. I always hoped we would double back and I might get a familiar setting but every time it was someplace different. This time it was in the country but many times it was in the cities and then I was so closely guarded I could barely take a deep breath without somebody noticing.

It was just a lucky fluke that I had managed to get out and get my package to Maggie like I had. It had been at the beginning when Anya didn't realize yet how down right slippery I could be. It was right after that we got Claude as an extra little watchdog for me because Alan just wasn't good enough.

I had been both lucky and unlucky that day. Getting the picture sent off had been a close thing as I parted from Anya while at the grocery store. Alan had been just an isle away doing something and I had managed to move fast enough that they didn't even realize I wasn't there until they caught up with me about 15 minutes later. I had just made it back from the little mailbox place that most shopping centers sported now days.

They looked at me a little funny but didn't really ask why I was outside on a windy rainy Pennsylvania afternoon. I sort of looked sheepish, something I was rather good at doing when I choose, and said I just needed some fresh air. After that day I never went shopping, never got the chance to even go for a walk by myself. I always had a constant shadow. Something about that made me wonder if they knew this all was a lie, and that I was playing a role and didn't really want to be here at all.

But how could they know? There were only a hand full of people that knew of my mission. The two that sent me and the two that would help get me out of it. I had thought of contacting Phillip directly but didn't know if somebody at his house would intercept the message and find out. I was lucky that Phillip had asked Stephan to move back to New York during all of this. According to Rafael, he didn't want his old friend and confidant to go prying. Stephan couldn't help it, it was part of who he was and that many people were just too many.

Phillip must be really, really worried about information leaks or he wouldn't have gotten so paranoid. It would explain why he wouldn't even mention it to me but he knew that Rafael and I could get away and talk shop and nobody would think twice about it. And he had good reason to be worried. Anya would never tell me how she knew about Maggie, Michael and all the things there were going on in Colorado or Florida. Things she used to taunt me and get under my skin and they worked a lot better than I would like to admit.

So how did she know that Maggie had changed her name or why she had? Did we have a spy in our midst just like I was a spy in theirs? It would be silly to think we didn't, especially considering all that I had been told and overheard in the last few months. Yes, Phillip had very good reason to be worried. I just wish I knew what in the hell was happening or was going to be happening soon.

I had always been pretty sensitive to subtle things. Most protectors weren't as good as I was at reading body language and hearing slight things in the way something was said as I was. I knew beyond a doubt that things were getting more anxious around here. Like Anya too was getting ready for something. Maybe they had a big project that was going to be happening soon. Something I might finally get a chance to get involved in.

Well whatever it was it had better happen by February. That was it. I had made a commitment to myself that I would make it that long. Like the light at the end of a long, dark tunnel the month of February called to me. Told me just a little while longer for at the end of the tunnel was Maggie and even though I knew I could never be with her the way my heart wanted being by her side was more important than anything else in this world.

Gabriel you are pathetic. I was but what I didn't know then was just how gullible I was. And that mistake would cost quite a few people their lives and I would be really lucky if I wasn't one of them.

# Authors note:

There are always back-stories that could be told about the many characters I have created in my books. Some you will get as part of the story but for others there just never seems to be a way to work them in that makes sense. Not if I didn't want my novels to be 800 pages long anyway.

You have already had the story of how Maggie came to be what she is and her bond mate Michael too. Alison's will come along in due time but that left a few of the main characters without the chance to tell how they came to be what they are. How life had been sometimes cruel beyond belief to some and others it had been so very generous only to take it away in a second leaving them alone.

My one girlfriend that I have loosely based one of the characters on wanted a chance to tell her story or what she thought would be her story. So with a little tweaking on my part I give you the great story of Alicia Fitzgerald and how she started out life before she became a Resurrected. When she was just a little thief and always in trouble. The little red headed fire breather that has taken my heart away so many times that it should be impossible to surprise me but she still can.

So with great pleasure I give you Alicia's Story. I hope you enjoy it as much as I did.

# ALICIA S STORY

# Chapter I

## When Everything Goes to Hell What Do You Do Then?

I couldn't stop crying. Whenever I felt alone and abandoned I did the same thing. I would go sit at the park. Maybe I was a masochist because I couldn't keep myself from watching all of these happy families and loving couples. I hurt myself every day watching these people. I was so envious of them. Once I had been blessed like that.

I had been raised in a loving catholic family. My mother was a lovely little Irish woman. I used to get mad when I realized I wasn't ever going to get any taller than I was as 10. My mother was the reason I was so darn short, but I learned to use my height to my advantage.

My father was a very large Spanish man. I remember even now how dark his brown eyes had been. I had I inherited that too along with his huge laugh when I found something funny. Irish and Spanish blood combined is what gave me my auburn red hair. It wasn't that orange color most people consider to be red. My hair was actually the color of red flame.

As I watched a cute family playing tag, a small boy and his older sister along with mom and dad, I started to cry harder. My memory of my parents was suddenly all I could think about. It was a beautiful Sunday morning in February. It was warm for February even in Texas it was unusual. My parents had decided to go to town to get things for my birthday.

I went outside to lie under my favorite tree to read my favorite book. I didn't make it far, less than a chapter. That's when I saw the police car come up to my house. A tall officer with a goofy mustache got out of the driver's side. A short stocky officer got out from the other side; together they came up the walk. When they saw me, they changed direction and started what seemed like an endless journey towards me. Once they finally reached me the tall man tried to clear his voice like he wanted to say something but couldn't figure out how.

"Are you Alicia Canizales?" The tall man asked with a rough voice.

"Yes sir I am. What is wrong? Did I do something?"

"No Miss Canizales, it is about your parents. There was a bad accident in town. The car had flipped twice…" The tall officer just stopped talking to stare at the ground. It was like he couldn't finish what he started.

"We regret to inform you that your parents did not make it." The stocky man said cold-heartedly. He clearly had done this many times and didn't seem to care that he had just destroyed my whole world.

I couldn't move. I did not know what to say. I was literally in shock. I was only 15 years old; how was I going to live without them? Being an only child I had no one else to turn to, no one else to care. They had been my world. I had my whole life in front of me but now my parents would never see me grow up. I was so devastated they were gone. I was all alone.

The insensitive stocky officer cleared his voice to bring me out of my thoughts. "We are aware that you are an only child and have no other family. We have already called child services and they will have an agent out here this afternoon. So you need to start packing." I have never been so fueled by anger before. This insensitive jerk first tells me my parents were dead like this happened every day, well maybe so but not to me. Then he tells me I have to give up even the rest of my life and become an orphan. I wanted so badly to punch this guy in the face. I knew I could not attack him, he was an officer and my parents had taught respect for the law. Even if I could get around that ingrained respect, I wouldn't have, I was still too shocked to move.

Once the officers decided that they were done trying to talk to me they left but not before reminding me to be ready by noon. The poor tall officer gave me a look that said he at least felt horrible for me. Maybe he had children of his own?

The officers were gone and still I just stood there. It had always amazed me that when I cried from tragic news, it always rained so hard. It had been a beautiful day and now I could see the storm clouds rolling in, dark and ominous. It was like the angels were crying with me.

I was so afraid. What would I do now? I was not about to be sent to an orphanage where I would be treated like crap. I didn't want to be adopted either by somebody that would expect me to treat them with the same love I had for my mom and dad. How could I be expected to forget them like that? I had to at least pack, I knew no matter what happened this would no longer be my home.

Finally I got myself to move as I headed to the house. I went to my room and started to pack. I grabbed my backpack I used for school and stuffed some clothes into it as I pulled them almost randomly from my closet. Then I grabbed the book that I had been reading and put it in there too. At least I was going to have something to help me escape reality. After shoving everything down as hard as I could to give me as much space as possible I went to my nightstand.

On the nightstand, other than the lamp and more books, was a happy picture of my parents holding me at a zoo. I had loved that picture mainly because you could see a beautiful wolf in the background. Of course I loved it because it had my parents in it too, but for some reason that wolf was my focal point every time. I grabbed the picture, took it out of the frame and shoved it into my bag. I had room left for a few small things.

I went to the bathroom and grabbed my toothbrush and the toothpaste. I didn't know where I was going but I sure as heck knew I wouldn't have a smelly breath. My mom used to use baking soda and hydrogen peroxide to brush her teeth. I figured if I ran out I could use her method, although I hoped I never would run out of my toothpaste. I loved the winter fresh taste it had. I also grabbed some soap. I was not about to stink wherever life took me. I went back to my room and shoved what I believed were necessary essentials into my bag. I certainly had a lot to learn about what was 'the necessary essentials.'

Looking at the clock, I realized it was already 11:30 and I had to go. I grabbed my stuff as I went into my parents' room. The idea of leaving without my mother's beautiful Rosary was impossible. I also knew money would be important and I took as much money as I could find. Sadly the only emergency money my parents had was about fifty dollars. That wouldn't last me long at all. But I couldn't complain because it was better than nothing.

Shoving the money in my pocket, I held onto my mother's Rosary and said a silent prayer. Lord please protect me on my journey and guide my parents to heaven. Trying to look up through the ceiling to where I knew they now were, I crossed myself, put the Rosary around my neck and hid it under my shirt. I left the house to begin my new life, alone. I left and never really looked back. Soon I wouldn't have the time and then later I wouldn't want to.

By now I had sat in the park long enough for it to start to get dark. Most of the families were gone or in the process of leaving. I never even noticed that they had disappeared into a misty world my tears had changed everything too. I wiped my eyes as a woman and her two sons walked by. I noticed she slowed up to stare at me as she walked by where I was sitting on a bench by myself. If I were her I would be wondering why a small young girl was all alone in a dark park. She was probably the old fashion type of woman thinking a young girl should never be alone. I didn't bother to even stare back at her. She should have known I was a street kid. I probably looked more than a little rough. Thinking about how sad I looked brought another memory to me.

After I had escaped from home, I had walked for about a day and didn't get anywhere really. I had lived in a small beach town just outside of Galveston, Texas. I had no idea what my plan had been, I didn't think I even had one, not really. I just packed up and left. I knew my parents were probably not happy with me right now. At that moment I didn't care. I had to get away from that town. That had been my only plan, to get as far away as I could. Maybe I thought I could escape the pain that way; the pain of their death and my new loneliness. I knew I was acting very immature about everything but I didn't see any other options.

I finally just stopped walking and sat down on the ground. I had to think of a plan and quick. I needed to do something; I couldn't just walk around forever. Maybe I could get some type of job? Affording a house was out of the question, but maybe if I could get a job I could at least afford a motel every once in awhile. That sounded like an ok idea. So that was my plan, I would go to Galveston cause there was always job opportunities for anyone in a city. Now I had to figure out how to get to there, I didn't want to use up all of my money on a bus or a taxi. That left only one option besides walking; hitchhiking. Yup, my parents would be very disappointed in me.

People were very dangerous and I did know better but again I didn't seem to have a choice. I gave people my trust quite easily but in the back of my mind I always stayed cautious. My mother used to say I had a good sense of judgment. I denied that, I just used common sense. Never go walking over to a pond that you know gators hang around at. That was my dad's favorite saying when it came to common sense.

I took a deep breath before I stuck out my thumb waiting for my free ride to Galveston. When a car came passing by that just screamed out dangerous I quickly put my hand down and looked away. All the safe kind people were the smart ones that wouldn't pick me up. I knew this was a hopeless try. If every other family were like mine then no one would pick up a strange crazy looking girl. However, being the stubborn girl that I was, I did not give up on trying to hitch a ride.

It is amazing how being stubborn pays off. After about an hour or so a blue car came pulling up to me. Inside were two gorgeous ladies. One had pretty brown hair and looked a little less than average size from the way the driver's seat was pulled up. The woman in the passenger seat had beautiful blonde hair and had a much-aggravated look. When I saw her face I noticed her eyes. Well I actually noticed both of their eyes. They both had beautiful bright shining blue eyes. I had never seen anything like that before.

"Hey kid, aren't you a little young to be walking on a road by yourself?" asked the blonde.

"Well, it is a long story and I honestly don't care to talk about it at the moment." I mumbled and tried to look embarrassed about my situation, it wasn't hard.

It amazed me how quickly I felt so relaxed that they were the ones that stopped. I just felt a comfort that I could trust them. It also amazed me that without even giving them a good answer the one driving told me to get into the backseat. I could have been hiding that I was a serial killer, but they didn't even second-guess themselves. Since I felt like I could trust them I jumped into the back and asked them to take me to Galveston.

Once the brunette started driving the girls seemed to forget I was with them because the blonde resumed their interrupted conversation.

"What do you mean he isn't the one for me, we would be perfect together." The blonde said annoyed.

"Have you even noticed he doesn't pay attention to you? How can two people be meant for each other when one doesn't even notice the other? I just know he is not your soul mate, so please stop whining." The brunette huffed then stared at me from the rearview mirror. She had a look that seemed a little distant yet her eyes were connected to mine. As if she was looking right into my soul. She finally broke the connection by staring at the road. It looked like she smiled, but I wasn't sure.

"So, you never gave us a proper answer. We won't pressure you but it is hard not to worry about a kid walking and hitchhiking." The brunette said. She actually sounded a little worried for me.

"I will be fine." I tried to promise her, but deep down I just knew I wouldn't be.

"Well just in case, I will give you our number. If one day you need help don't hesitate to call." The brunette said with a determined voice. I didn't want to argue with her so I just nodded. The blonde still didn't say anything. She was probably mad that her love interest wasn't giving her the time of day. I felt bad for her.

We finally got to the outskirts of Galveston. I didn't want them to drive out of their way so I asked them to pull over. I didn't want them to think I wasn't grateful for driving me. But I felt terrible for them going out of their way to take a stranger to Galveston. Once the brunette pulled over she turned and looked at me. "I mean it, no matter when or where you are if you need anything just call us. Just ask for Alison." As she said the name she pointed to herself. Then she pointed towards the blonde and said, "Or you can ask for Melissa, she is a nurse so she has a lot of training." I couldn't help notice Alison's stare when she said that like she was annoyed with her friend. I couldn't figure out why a person would be mad at a nurse.

"My name is Alicia Canizales. Thank you so much for everything." After she gave me a plain business card with only a phone number on it, I said my thanks and goodbye, shut the door and walked away as they drove off. That was the last thing I could remember going my way.

Now so many years later, I was sitting in the park as the stars started to appear. They were beautiful. I have always loved stars. I laughed at the thought about how I believed I was going to succeed on my own. It was sad irony because I know my parents would be so disappointed in me. The two lovely ladies that had driven me to Galveston made me think of another memory. Since I had gotten to Galveston nothing went right. No one would give me a job; I was too inexperienced. Everything just kept going downhill.

It was about four months being on my own when I met the only person willing to give me a job. His name was Derrick. Needless to say this was not the person people chose to be around; but since he was the only one willing to give me a chance I didn't think I had a lot of options. He was not the nicest person and yelled at me every time I didn't do something the way he wanted it. My Job was a surprising one and it wasn't easy at all. I was now a petty thief. I, of course, started with easy missions such as taking wallets and purses.

I laughed at the thought of little me being some thief. When I first started I was 15, I wasn't good at it at all. Now, five years later, I had become very skilled at stealing. I wasn't proud of what I did but it was better than having nothing.

I watched the stars for a little longer then decided to go back to Derrick's apartment. Since I was working for him he let me stay at his place. I hated being there so I tried to stay away as much as possible. He was very mean and quite disgusting. If he and his girlfriend weren't doing drugs, they were doing each other or fighting. Crystal, his girlfriend, had a lovely jealous streak, so she was always trying to fight with me also. It was normally when she was high off her wits. It was ironic how I was a thief and hung out with terrible people, yet I hated druggies, alcoholics and everything they were. I didn't even have sex ever; then again even for being a thief I had my morals. I laughed a little at that thought.

I finally got up off the little bench and started my walk home. I always walked slowly when I headed over to the apartment. I always loved to walk and think. I had stolen a brand new Walkman from a popular music store, so I always went everywhere with it. I loved music, so when I would walk around I would listen to my music. I listened to every type of genre. Music just made life so much easier, plus it being the 80s most people were into music of some type. As I was walking and singing along to some Heart songs, I saw a woman who was out a little later than she should be. She was tipsy so an easy target to pick pocket. She had a beautiful pearl necklace on and a leopard fur shawl. She defiantly had money. This would be a perfect "present" to bring to Derrick so he would not get angry with me for being late. She tumbled over a little, which was my chance to collect some items. I ran over to her as a concern citizen.

"Are you ok ma'am?" I asked sounding concerned.

"I think I had a little too much!" She swayed back and forth as she spoke. "Would you please take my shoes? They are just so heavy."

"How about you keep your shoes and I go call a cab?"

"That is probably a good idea. Here, hold my purse so I can put my shoes on." She handed me her purse. It would have been so easy for me to just walk away with her whole purse. However, I never did anything the easy way. So while she was trying to balance herself I was going through her wallet grabbing money yet leaving enough to get her home safely. I put her wallet back and grabbed the diamond earrings that I saw shimmering in the bottom. Now those were a find that would make Derrick swallow his tongue a bit. She finally had her shoes on so I helped her up and gave her the purse back. As I was helping her up I managed to unhook her pearl necklace and snatched it away before she even noticed anything was missing. She smiled at me and then gave me a lazy hug, like she was about to fall asleep in my arms. I hugged her back then led her towards the bus stop; glad again I was a lot stronger than I looked because she wasn't exactly a skinny lady.

Once I knew she was safely on the bus I started walking towards the apartment again. I was finally a block away. In the beginning I had felt pretty bad for stealing, now I didn't feel much of anything. In order to save myself from the wrath of Derrick, I had to become immune to the feelings I caused people. I never took from people that looked like they needed the money no matter how much Derrick threatened me. I only took from filthy rich people that wouldn't even notice if their items were stolen.

I finally got to the apartment. I hated this place. It was filthy and old. Nothing worked right and the residents were not the best people. I heard one of the steps creak ominously as I walked slowly up the stairs. It was a constant worry that one day down I they would go and me with them. Reaching the second floor, I let out a sigh of relief. I turned left to reach the door to the pitiful excuse of an apartment I now lived in. When I opened it up I walked right in on Derrick and Crystal weighing some powdery substance. For living with criminals I never got into their drug business, so I never learned what drug was what. Derrick turned around and stared at me. Since I turned 20 he started noticing I had a body. Which made me very uncomfortable, but luckily Crystal was always there to preoccupy his mind. I grabbed the pearls and earrings out of my pocket and threw them into his lap.

"Hmm. Very nice, worth at least a couple hundred." He smiled with greed all over his face. Every time I saw that look I hated him even more. I didn't say anything to either of them. I just went into the tiny area that was my room. It had enough space for a small bed and a dresser. Once I got into my room I shut the door and made sure I locked it. Then I went to lie down. I could hear Derrick and Crystal start arguing about which piece of jewelry was theirs. When I managed to get cash I always hid it in a dictionary that I hollowed out. Neither of the people I lived with read let alone read a dictionary so I used it as my own emergency fund, now I had a small stash. Not great but better than nothing.

I heard them get off the couch and go to bed. They both were the noisiest people I have ever heard. Since they were so loud I always turned on the radio and just focused on the lyrics. Tonight my lullaby was by a rock legend, Dio, and the song was *Rainbow in the Dark*. It was one of my favorite songs since that was what I needed; a rainbow in this tragic darkness. As the song hit the chorus I started to doze…. Then everything went dark and I finally escaped reality.

# Chapter 2

## Diamond Ring

I woke up to a lovely stormy cold February day. I always hated when it was cold. The nice thought though was my birthday was in one day. I would be 21 years old. I was not really excited since I had no one who cared, but it was nice to know I survived another year. I sat in my bed for a little bit staring out of my window. I loved when it stormed yet I was still afraid of them.

I finally got out of bed. Derrick and Crystal were probably asleep so I snuck over to the kitchen. I couldn't cook anything to save my life, but I could make some awesome cereal! I giggled at that thought. Neither of these people knew how to cook either, so there was not much learning. Once I had my cereal all ready and I washed off a spoon I sat down and started to eat. While I ate Derrick came out of his room wearing nothing but jeans. He was not very attractive, but he thought he was the sexiest person on the planet. He was about 5'10 and was thin but had no muscle. He always had stubble, but he could never grow a full beard. In my eyes he looked very grotesque. His eyes were always red; I thought a good drug dealer wasn't supposed to use their own products.

As I took my fourth bite of food, Derrick's annoying voice started working, "Good morning gorgeous…" He only said that when he was giving me that disgusting look over or when he needed me to do a job. "What are you doing today? Let me guess… nothing?" He chuckled a little; he thought he was so hilarious. "Well, my dearest little kitty…" I hated when he said that, it was his version of saying cat burglar. I would rather be called a wolf because I wanted to rip him apart like a wolf with rabies. "I have a little job for you kitty cat. I need a diamond ring."

"Ha, what are you going to do propose to the woman that sleeps around as much as you do?" I rolled my eyes. I hated these people but if I said no to his jobs I got bruises all over.

"No kitty cat, the main man promised to pay me if I got him in a diamond ring and I imagine the earrings you got last night will be a nice addition. Now all I need is the ring." He came over and decided he had the right to touch me. He started to caress my cheek but I moved away. "When he pays me I will give you twenty percent and a bonus." He winked when he said bonus.

"I will get you a ring but I will pass on the twenty percent and your so called bonus." I said with an annoyed tone.

"You know you want me, Crystal wouldn't get so jealous when you are around if you didn't want me." He sounded so sure. He was more delusional than I thought.

"No, she is just an idiot who thinks that other girls would want you. I love how wrong she is. What she needs to worry about is you not knowing how to keep it in your pants. Now if you would stop staring down my shirt, I will go get you a ring." I grabbed my bowl and poured the rest of my cereal down the drain. I didn't eat much because living with these people made my stomach churn.

I couldn't get out the kitchen fast enough and fled to my room. I grabbed a pair of jeans and a white t-shirt and all the stuff that goes underneath and went to the bathroom. When I shut the door behind me I made sure it was locked as I jiggled the handle a few times. I wasn't about to have Derrick walk in while I was in the shower. I turned the water on before I got undressed. This place was so cheap it took the water forever to get warm and in the cold of February it never really made it beyond lukewarm. It really wasn't unusual that I never got even that and cold showers were just something I had had to get used to. At least I was clean and that was better than living on the street. Today was a good day as I felt the water actually make it to a decent temperature. I just knew it had to be because it was my birthday. Somebody up there must still like me. I got undressed then jumped in. I got all washed up then got out of the shower and grabbed a grungy towel. I dried my hair first and tossed it around a little. Then I dried the rest of myself off. Once I got dressed I grabbed the eyeliner and mascara that I hid in the drawer. I loved how Joan Jett did her eye make-up so that's how I started to do mine. Making the bottom eyelid darker made my eyes darker, which made me look a little more intimidating. Since I usually look so sweet and innocent I had to work on looking mean.

Once I was done getting dressed, brushing my teeth, and getting make-up on I went to my bedroom to get my shoes. I surprisingly knew how to walk in heels but I didn't own any. I thought it was pointless to wear heels when I didn't have anyone to impress. Converse shoes worked well enough for the idiots I had to deal with all the time. I put on my small leather jacket and I was ready to go.

I walked quickly out of the door before Derrick could call me "Kitty" or before Crystal called me a whore for Derrick talking to me. I hated her more than Derrick; she was the biggest slut I had ever seen. Yeah those two were a perfect match for each other I snickered a little. I looked forward to every second I could find away from that place and now I was in such a happy mood. Was it wrong of me to take an almost perverse joy when I managed a little extra time away from those horrible people? Once I was well away from the apartment I started walking towards the park. I had to think of the best place to get a stupid diamond ring for Derrick's boss. Diamond rings were one thing I would rather not steal. It wasn't because it was challenging or anything, I just didn't want to steal from a person that worked so hard to afford one ring to propose to the woman of his dreams. I guess you could call me a hopeless romantic because anything about true love I thought was beautiful and special.

Maybe, I could steal from a jewelry store. I did enjoy doing things the hard way but I thought this job was pointless. Why would a person need a diamond ring? This was such a pathetic job. As I kept walking I came across a poster on a window that was advertising a beautiful rare pink five-carat princess cut diamond ring. It was also known as a freakishly expensive ring and that would be my target. Derrick rarely appreciated how good I was. Maybe if I got something like that he would get off my case for quite a while. I couldn't help but smile at the challenge the ring brought.

I read the flyer for a location of where it was. But the flyer wasn't advertising it for sale; it was offering a reward for its return. Well shoot. How was I going to steal it if I didn't know where it was? It was a valuable ring so the award had to be pretty good. Well I could put my ear to ground around here and find out who had it. I wasn't the only thief in this city and there was nothing better to make my day than stealing from another thief.

I had a plan now. I could steal back the ring, get the reward and give that to the Jerk Off and his Sleaze Bag. It was a win-win situation. I just had to tell the lovely duo. Then get to the streets and find that ring. Something that important the thief wouldn't be able to keep to himself. Most thieves weren't like me. They were proud of what they did and bragged about their scores to each other and I knew where all my competition hung out. It was only a matter of time.

I tore the flyer down and folded it into my back pocket. I turned my happy little butt around and ran towards the apartment. This was a very rare occasion. I am pretty sure all the people walking past me were thinking I was some psychopath. I didn't care though because I was actually excited. For once I could steal something that would be helping instead of hurting. I would do something that my parents would be proud of. Well, the stealing part not so much, but returning a person's prized possession was defiantly a good deed. Once I was only a block away from the apartment I started to sprint. By the time I had gotten to the apartment I was worn out. I didn't want to go any farther but I had to get up the stairs to share my news. I finally made my climb to the second floor and got to our door. I opened up the door to see Derrick and Crystal sitting down while a man in a luxurious business suit was lecturing them. I assumed this was 'Mr. Boss Man' that Derrick mentioned a couple of times. He looked up at me and gave me a wicked smile.

"Good day darling. I am Robert Carson. You can call me Mr. Carson." He motioned for me to sit down. "So I am going to guess that you are the little thief that Derrick speaks so highly of." Crystal gave me a mean look when he said that. "Well, you are little that is for sure, but if you can get this job done then that would be wonderful."

"Well, yes sir I am Derrick's thief." Even though I hated saying that Derrick had any ownership over me I knew it was more than true.

I could not hesitate on telling my plan. I knew if I waited too long they would start giving me instructions of how to do some complicated heist that they didn't have a clue about. "I hate to interrupt your lecture sir but I just got done reading a flyer about a ring you that might be exactly what you want. When I read it a great idea occurred to me." I took a deep breath, "Instead of stealing just some ring we could return that one to the rightful owners. The flyers promised a cash prize and.."

Mr. Carson cut me off before I could say anything else, "Well you are smart thing but have come to the wrong conclusion. I know the person that stole that ring already. Made a deal with him for it even. There isn't much that goes on in this town that I don't control. Now that fucker has decided he wants more money before he turns it over. I have a buyer for the special ring and they are paying more than twice what it is worth but I won't have anybody playing me that way. He is going to learn not to double deal me but I can't do anything until I have that ring. Then he will get what is coming to him."

I honestly did not understand, well I didn't care to understand. Here I was giving them the chance to make some decent money by doing the right thing and it wasn't enough. Instead they went for the choice that gave them more money, which means more power. Power was an awful thing. It made people corrupt and selfish. Anyone with power always searched for higher power. I hated greedy, power hungry people like Mr. Carson, who conned and manipulated people at his will. When Mr. Carson stared at me with an impatient look I finally answered him, "Yes sir, I do understand you." After I said that, and not a moment too soon, Mr. Carson decided to leave. I refused to meet his eyes as he planted me with another wicked look that made my skin crawl. He couldn't get out the door fast enough to suit me as I heard the door close a few seconds later.

"Kitty, we have a plan to get that ring. The guy that is stupid enough to double cross Mr. Carson should know better, he used to work for him. I think he has decided to keep it for himself and is trying to sell it. Luckily for us Crystal has met this guy before. She thinks she can distract him." Derrick looked at Crystal and gave her a smile.

I couldn't help but laugh at how blind Derrick was. Crystal probably did things with our mystery man that Derrick would have only dreamed of doing. I didn't even have to know the whole plan to figure out what her 'distraction' would be. Poor Derrick, his stupidity was going to be his own downfall one day.

I finally came out of my thoughts to hear Derrick finish up the details of his plans. "Crystal will get with him tonight and you will sneak into his apartment and look for the diamond. Mr. Carson said this guy wasn't the craftiest person so that should help…"

I couldn't help but to sigh out loud. This job was quite ridiculous. It was more like a plan for Crystal to get out of the house and go whore around. Most likely Derrick was promised lies, like he will get a huge cut of the profit. And lucky little me got to be the one to do the work to fulfill their demented dreams. Before either of them could say anything else I escaped to my room.

Closing the door behind me, I just stood there for a moment. I knew that this ring was very valuable. I knew that no reward would be the same as the amount for the ring. I knew that this Carson guy needed the ring to make money. I also knew that if you crossed him, like the guy with the ring we are after, he would take you down and would probably take great delight in doing it. He thought he was some kind of godfather. I rolled my eyes at that thought.

It was time to turn over a leaf, because I was done helping these pathetic people. I was going to do my original plan except I would use the little method of false pretense. I would use their plans to get the ring then ditch them and return it. Maybe that would give me enough money to get out of this city for good. A couple of grand would go a long way and I'm sure I could use my skills in another city. I had never been to anywhere but Texas, and from what I had heard New Orleans sounded real promising.

Nightfall was finally among us so I figured it was time for us to get going. Once I came out of my room I noticed that Crystal was ready for the night. Crystal dressed in a black snakeskin mini-skirt and a small red tube top. She also had on red pumps to match her outfit. Her outfit made me mad in an envious type of way. She had a soft face with naturally curly light brown hair. Compared to her hair my long and straight red hair looked boring. It also made me jealous by how graceful she was. How could such a nasty vixen be so graceful? I was such a clumsy mess until I was concentrating on stealing something. I turned away before she could notice the green monster in me. I didn't need her to flaunt and brag about her stunning looks.

"Are you ready ladies?" Derrick asked as he walked to Crystal. His gaze was not on her face but down her shirt. She was also not lacking in the chest department. That however never made me jealous. I much preferred being a smaller size, which meant I wouldn't have back problems later on. Being petite also made it easier to sneak around and get into smaller areas with ease. It also didn't hurt to have flexibility on my side. Even with her pretty face she wouldn't last long trying to do the stuff I did.

"Let me just put on my lipstick then I will be ready." Crystal said as she batted her long eyelashes. I hated when she did that. She acted like she would get her way with just batting her eyelashes and showing off a little too much skin. When I first met her I wanted to kick her down a flight of stairs for being herself. Now that I knew her better I had changed my mind. A kick from the top of a ten-story building was more appropriate. Crystal finally had her lipstick on and was headed toward the door. When she turned to see if I was coming her voice got all snotty. "You coming or not!?"

I just nodded at her, and then followed her out of the door. She started getting irritated as I walked slowly down the stairs. When we were finally standing beside her car, Crystal gave me an odd look. At first I figured it was the irritated look she always gave me; although, this look was much different. Her eyes showed something I had never seen from her before; fear. I didn't understand what she would be afraid of. This mission should be pretty simple for her. I just acted like I didn't notice anything as she unlocked the door and walked to the driver's side.

"So, how is this plan going to work?" I asked trying to sound casual.

"I am going to drop you off at his place and then I am going to meet up with him for our date. While I preoccupy his mind you will search for the ring. He is pretty observant so when you break you can't make it obvious." I thought it was funny that this was the most Crystal ever said to me, without turning it into a fight. She normally avoided me or gave me death stares instead. As she went on with details on the plan I just nodded my head as I was thinking of the ways I would deceive them.

We finally pulled up to a beat up apartment complex. The best way to explain this guy's apartment is by saying it made ours look like a beach condo. It was no wonder that he wanted to keep the ring. I felt bad for him because I had a mission to take it from him, and when I was on a mission I never gave up. I looked at Crystal before I got out; she had the same odd look as before. However, this time it was more hidden. She then gave me a tiny smile and whispered good luck. I wished her luck also then got out of the car. Once the door shut with a thud, Crystal was burning rubber to leave. She was such a scary driver. Maybe she wouldn't have been so scared if she had let me drive.

Before I started doing anything I had to survey my surroundings. I had to know the best places to hide or make any quick exits. So I started turning slowly taking in all the scenery around me. I then turned to the apartments and studied that for a moment. There were only two stories to the complex and the windows on the first floor were all broken. It was defiantly an easy way in but I preferred to not get all cut up. Instead I walked over to the rusty fire escape. I was too small to just jump and climb up so I had to find something to stand on. I was in luck when I realized the dumpster was right beside the fire escape. It grossed me out a little knowing I had to climb on top of it, but then again being a thief was not a glamorous job.

I finally got myself to move over to the dumpster. I held my breath as I climbed up the side and reached for the ladder. I pulled myself up with a little struggle. I have never had great upper arm strength; all my strength was in my legs. Once I was finally on the fire escape I went to the first window. The lock for the window had been broken off. It was easy enough to slide the window up so I could step in. Now I was in the apartment I froze and held my breath. Listening for any movement, I had to be cautious since I didn't know what apartment was his. I did not hear anything but I still moved around silently.

I walked towards the front door. By the look of how dusty everything was and the almost total lack of useable furnishings, I could assume this one had been abandoned for a real long time. I opened up the front door and poked my head out to see my surroundings once again. The area was clear, so I crept out and down the hall to the right. There sure wasn't any other direction to go except back out the window. Now this door was locked as I tried to turn the knob. I gave a little smirk; this mission was testing all of my skills. I knelt down to get a better look at what type of doorknob I was dealing with. Amazingly it was just a simple turn-style lock. As I gave another little smirk I got up and put my hand in my right pocket. I had to wiggle my hand around to get it down my pocket since my hips and butt always made jeans a bit snug. Once I found the item I was after I managed to pull it from my pocket. The item was a little flat hair clip. I opened up the hair clip and turned it to its side. Then I inserted it into the keyhole and turned. I took out the clip and turned the knob. The doorknob turned with ease and the door opened slightly with a groan that made me wince.

It was amazing how well everything was going. Either I had gotten quite skilled at this occupation or luck was just on my side this evening.

I opened the door slowly and walked in quietly. As I put my first foot into the door I listened for any sign of movement. There was nothing to be heard. I was once again in luck. I looked around this apartment and noticed someone was recently in here. It had a musky smell and it was not the most organized. I figured a man must live here.

I walked all the way into the living room and took a quick look around. This room was darker than the first due to blinds on the window that filtered most of the streetlight from outside so I had to let my eyes adjust to the darkness. The living room was quite grotesque. There was old food lying all over the coffee table and something fuzzy was growing in drinks on top of the TV. I started to gag from the musky smell as it became stronger. I quickly snuck into the first door on my left. Once I entered into the room I took a quick breath then held it for a moment to judge whether this room was bearable or not. Once the decision to breath was made I began to open drawers and look through all of this gentleman's items. I did not have the slightest clue if this was the right person's apartment; I just figured it didn't hurt to look.

After looking through four drawers of underwear, shirts and condoms, I went over to the nightstand. I opened the little drawer there and found some lighters, smoking pipes, and a small bong. Maybe I found the right guy's apartment? I thought to myself. The way Crystal had described him it seemed this had to be the apartment. From her telling there weren't but a couple of people that lived in this run down place anyway, so I stubbornly kept at it. The gross part of searching through his more intimate items was knowing the type of girls he went for, young, very, very young. I shivered at the revolting image.

I finally turned toward his bed and knelt down to check underneath. All I saw was a pizza box, which probably had some food in it, and some playboy magazines. Other than being a druggie this guy looked like a normal college kid. Well no, even the college students probably had drugs everywhere. I looked over the bed for a moment and then grabbed his sheets and moved them over. There was still nothing important. I started to get a little annoyed since I really didn't want to go through his kitchen.

Irritably I picked up the pillows and then just stopped moving. There underneath his pillows was a small black box. I put down the pillows and gave a hopeful sigh. Once the pillows were out of the way I grabbed the box and opened the lid slowly. As the darkness from the lid faded away the beauty of a rare pink five-carat princess cut diamond ring began to show. I sighed again this time from excitement as a huge smile crept across my face. All I had to do now was get out of here unnoticed and contact the owners of the ring. Once I returned the ring and got a cash prize I could get out of this horrible life. Excitement was just radiating through my skin.

My excitement left me when I walked toward the door and I heard a sound that startled me. It was the sound of a man's voice.

"I thought I locked this door?" He said with a confused voice. I froze for a moment trying to figure out what to do. The only window in his room was more or less bordered up and I obviously couldn't walk out of the door. I had to hide and wait for a chance to get out.

"Don't you want to do something fun Shane?" I heard another voice say. It didn't take long to realize Crystal was trying to stall him.

"No, you dumb bitch! Something isn't right here; I know I locked that door." I heard him throw open the door and stomp into the apartment with high heels clicking right behind. I finally pulled out of my shocked state and slid myself under his bed just as a bright light flipped on in the other room. I just barely managed to fit. I didn't pay any attention that I was still holding the open box.

"Maybe your lock is broken? This is an old apartment. Everything breaks in old apartments."

"I guess you are right. I just feel paranoid like something is wrong. Where is the ice? I will be fine once I get some more." I didn't know many terms for different drugs but I knew ice was a term for Crystal Meth. I remembered that drug nickname real well because in school it had a far worse rep than any thing else around. I heard Shane's footsteps fade away a little. By the sound of his feet I guessed he was in the kitchen. I heard Crystal's heels click to where I remembered the couch being. I could tell when Shane brought over the drug and they began snorting the substance. It was quite disgusting hearing their loud snorts then their sighs of enjoyment. It wasn't long before laughing and moaning started. It didn't take a rocket scientist to figure out what those tweakers were doing now.

I was probably waiting there for about thirty minutes before the room finally got quiet. Hopefully they were asleep and I would be able to sneak out of the door. I heard footsteps once again but this time they grew louder. The feet sounded large so that meant Shane was coming to his bedroom. Crystal was probably stoned out of her mind so she wouldn't even think that I could be in here. I froze and sucked in my breath as the bedroom door opened and light poured in. From my spot underneath I could see his footsteps go to the dresser. He was probably getting some condoms for his hot date. I cringed at the thought. I kept wishing for my nerves to calm because I was afraid he would hear my heart pounding. His feet turned to the door and he took one step then stopped. I saw his feet turn slowly back towards the bed. I braced myself because I knew he wasn't stoned enough to notice his ring being gone.

"What the Hell!" He hollered. He raced towards the bed and I could feel it move above me. He was throwing blankets and pillows all around looking for the ring. I heard him then tug the bedside drawer out from its place. He threw that onto the ground and gave an angry growl. I saw his feet run back to the door and then disappear through the threshold into the living room. "I knew something was wrong! I have been robbed!"

"Don't worry I bet you just misplaced your ring…" My heart sank when I heard that last word. If he hadn't mentioned it to Crystal she had just given us all up and then my fear came home all too quickly.

"Did you just say my ring? I never told you about any ring." I heard Crystal get up but before she could say anything I heard a loud slap and then a body crumple to the ground. I bit my lips shut, I couldn't let him know I was here. I had heard that one side effect from meth was that users became violent. I saw the feet run into the room again and did a quick circle. Then they stopped at an angle that pointed straight at the bed. I froze. I knew he had just figured out the only place a person could hide in this room. "Hmm I wonder if anyone is here? Crystal could not have worked alone since she was with me all night. I bet it's you Derrick. I figured Mr. Carson would put you up to this."

The violent tone of his voice made me shiver in fear. I have never been caught during a theft so this was a new and frightful experience for me. It was mainly frightful because he was drugged up and very ready to hurt anyone. And for once I had absolutely no way out.

The feet shuffled the last few inches towards the bed and stopped. I quit breathing completely once they were right beside my arm. Before I could even blink I saw two fierce dilated eyes staring at me. His lips turned up into a cruel smile. His teeth were bearing like he was growling even though there was no sound. He grabbed my wrist and pulled me from under the bed.

"Well, you are a new addition to the club. You are a lot smaller than Derrick and braver than him too." Even in my fear I fought to have my arm back or maybe because I was scared but for what ever reason I was wiggling and squirming for all my worth. "Quit struggling you little bitch."

He then dragged me to the living room where Crystal was trying to get up. Once he let go of my arm he kicked Crystal in the stomach. She immediately curled herself into a ball. Shane wasn't very happy about that so he went to punch her in the face. Before he could strike her I dove in and covered her with my body. I ended up getting the fist into my back and I screamed as the pain hit. He was a lot stronger than he looked as he pried my arms from around Crystal and threw me away. Once again he balled up his fist and went for her face. This time he succeeded. When he finally turned to me he had the cruelest smile I had ever seen. "Derrick would have run away leaving this little slut behind. You are far braver than he is. I will enjoy killing you both." He said with a psychotic almost giggle in his voice.

He kicked me in the stomach so hard I about puked. "Now stay put or I will kick you again; or worse." Grabbing Crystal by the hair he drug her to the bathroom. I could hear her cry even harder telling him she loved him. If she thought this would stop him she was wrong. He began to fill the tub up as I heard it make a gurgling sound that scared me really bad.

Crystal screamed again as another brutal hit connected somewhere on her. When Shane came out of the bathroom he had a look of pure delight on his face. When he came back from the kitchen with two nasty looking knives I didn't know what he planned on doing with them but I knew it couldn't be anything good. I didn't cook much but to me they looked like some sort of butcher knives. My heart sank, I didn't like Crystal but she didn't deserve to die like this.

He walked back into the bathroom and I heard splashing noises that made me think he had thrown her into the tub. I felt sick at the gurgling and screaming. As I tried to block out the noise I looked around to find something that could help me. I couldn't get up because of my back and stomach hurt so much I could barely move. I had to find something nearby. That's when I noticed the phone on a side table by the couch.

Why did I crawl to the phone when it wouldn't do any good? My body and mind were not connecting at the moment and I guess some part of me figured it was the best shot I had. It was too far for me to reach so I yanked it by the chord and it fell right onto my stomach. I gasped painfully from even that small pressure landing where his fist had done so much damage. I took the phone off the hook and dialed the first number that came through my head. Once the phone started ringing someone quickly answered with a curious hello.

"This is Alicia Canizales…." I took a jagged breath and spoke slowly, "Alison or Melissa… I need help…" As I took another hard breath my brain picked up the horrible screams coming from the bathroom. He was torturing Crystal. I told the person on the phone my location then before I could say anything else I felt Shane grab my ankle and yank my leg hard.

"Why you little bitch! I told you to stay put. Oh well, whoever you called will get here too late, you will already be dead by then."

As he turned me towards him I tried to fight him. He laughed and drug me to the bathroom as well. I could see red water dripping from a limp hand that hung out of the tub. He dropped me and pulled Crystal's lifeless body out. I could see now how horribly he had hurt her. She had puncture holes all over her body that were still oozing. Her face was disfigured from his fist. On her chest he carved the word 'whore' into her skin. I began to shake violently because I knew I was next. He threw her body onto the floor like it was nothing. No remorse at all as he came back for me

It was my turn as he pushed my head into the bloody water. Shane got all excited as I struggled futilely. I could feel his penis get hard against my back as he got off on what he was doing. Once he pulled my head out of the water and slammed my face straight into the side of the tub. I never felt pain like that before. Before I could scream out he had shoved one knife straight into the side of my stomach. I wanted to scream from the pain but choked on my own blood. I didn't even have a chance to take a breath before the second knife found a home on my other side. I was close to passing out. All I could wish for was to die already. He knew I was almost gone but he wanted to delay my death and have as much fun as he could.

My gaze became tunnel vision as more burning pain erupted everywhere. I was not really sure about everything he was doing to me. The only thing I was coherent for was the feeling of him tearing open my shirt and carving something onto my chest. The movement of the blade against my skin began to spell out the word thief and I wanted to cry in my shame and humiliation. As if just murdering me wasn't enough he had to brand me too.

I felt so much pain yet I could not move or cry. I felt the carving stop. Through my blurred vision I saw him walk out of the bathroom. The pain was unbearable. I wanted to cry. I prayed to die. Dying seemed like the better option so I willed my body to quit fighting. Right before my eyes shut my vision cleared long enough for me to get a good look at the bloody knives right by my face. My body finally shut down as darkness fell upon me.

# Part 3 – Surprise – You're Alive

I had thought I had led a pretty good life. Not great but not bad enough to earn a trip to Hell. The pain I felt when I came to was just as bad as all those stories that had terrified me as a child in Mass at the Catholic Church I had gone to. And I had just thought what I had gone through before had hurt, this was so much worse.

It hurt, hurt so bad I was screaming on the inside but for some reason I couldn't make a sound. Maybe between the beating and stabbing something important had been broken. I had no idea how if I couldn't move and couldn't scream that I could hurt like I did. My brain tried to think but it really couldn't. At first I thought Shane was back stabbing me with a knife that had been dipped in acid. It burned so badly that maybe he had stuck the blade on the hot plate in the kitchen just to make the pain worse. He was sadistic enough to do something like that too.

But when I managed to actually listen I knew there was nobody there. Nobody but me and I was sure that even though I had managed to live through my assault, I couldn't live for very long.

Then it was cold, graveyard cold or at least that is what I thought and I knew then I was about to die for sure. It changed again and the searing pain was back, all over and in my head I writhed and screamed and beat my hands on the dirty bathroom floor. Even though that is what my head was doing my body wasn't doing a damned thing. It just lay on the floor like a limp dishrag and bled.

I could feel it when I managed to think around the awful burning and freezing. My hands were laying in something sticky and wet that had started out pretty warm but felt just like honey right now. And I had been around enough beatings and stabbings in my life to know what blood smelled like too and that overwhelming stink was shoved up my nose and I knew it would never go away.

There was a crash in the front of apartment and feet, a lot of running feet and voices not yelling but sort of heavy shouting. "Oh shit." I heard a man's voice say as a pair of feet came closer and a hand touched my throat. "Get a medic in here." He shouted out.

I had no idea who had called the cops and right now I didn't care. My only thought was even if this guy looked like a monster I would think he was an angel in disguise because he had saved my life.

The next few minutes were even more painful than before. How that was possible I had no idea. There was fussing and arguing and some of the men were extremely pissed off. Because of my small size they at first thought I was a child that had been attacked. It wasn't until I reached the ambulance and they were hooking up stuff that somebody realized I was just a very small woman.

It didn't change the attitude anyone had as one guy was grumbling about my condition. "I just don't see how anybody could do this to a little girl."

Another man answered him. "If the blues brothers ever get their hands on him he won't live long enough to make to trial."

My medic huffed a bit at that. "You know I don't like to hear things like that. I'm supposed to save lives not condone taking them."

The other guy snorted. "It wouldn't be like killing a human George. Whoever did this is just an animal that walks on two feet and we might just save a few lives in the long run."

"Yeah, maybe so but it should be up to the courts to punish." My medic argued back.

I understood how both guys felt, sort of. But if I ever got the chance my attacker would be dead. He had taken me by surprise this time but nobody would ever do that again, had cornered me where I had no escape. I didn't know how but I was determined that since I had survived all this I was going to change my life. I would surround myself with people that loved me and didn't just have me around to use me for what I could do. I had been trying to get out and waited just one day too long to do it.

Almost getting dead sure changed the way I looked at things. I wasn't going to take the easy way anymore. Not that it had been all that easy but many times I had taken the path of least resistance and done the wrong thing because of it. I had hurt people, maybe not physically but I had still hurt them by taking what wasn't mine to take.

The ambulance got to the hospital and I was rushed into the emergency room and then to the operating room. I didn't know anything about hospitals and such. It had been years since I had even been to the doctors.

A couple of times my eyes were shot with bright white lights but then I was in darkness once again. People talked around me but they used words I didn't understand at all and I just sort of tried not to think about anything. The painful heat was still there and each time it came upon me it seemed to focus on every stab wound I had. Like somebody was taking lighter fluid and pouring it in there then setting it ablaze. The cold I liked a lot better. It seemed to just numb everything and that was easier to deal with.

Then I had a mask thrown over my face and it felt like I couldn't breath and some really nasty tasting air was forced down my lungs. I felt like puking but nothing worked right.

If I had been able to move I would have been arching my back at the pain when something sliced into my stomach and then moved its way up my chest. The fire was back and burned and burned as the knife kept cutting and cutting and cutting. I was being skinned alive this time and nobody cared.

There were murmured words that I couldn't even listen to because the pain was so bad. Then the jabbing started and the pulling and that went on forever. It would have been nice to pass out from the pain but even that ability had been taken from me. I couldn't move, scream, puke or pass out. I was a frozen zombie that had no say so in what happened.

Now, I was sure that I really had died and this was Hell and the devil had just been teasing me, letting me think that I had survived. I hadn't and now I was paying the price for all the things I had done wrong.

The pain kept on and on but finally I was left alone to think about my sins. Contemplate all those that I had let down or hurt or turned a blind eye to. How long I lay in my pain filled limbo I didn't have a clue. It seemed that this lasted longer than my short life had. How long did you have to stay in Hell before you made up for the things you had done wrong? I hoped it wasn't true that you stayed there forever but it sure seemed like it.

Finally the pain and the burning faded to a really bad ache and I passed out into the cold sleep of nothingness. As my mind finally found someplace to retreat I wondered if this was it and I would just fade away into nothing. That didn't scare me. Nothing sure was better than what I had just been through. Yeah, nothing sounded just perfect.

Waking up a second time surprised me even more than the first. I was alive still and as my eyes flew open all on their own I saw I was still in the hospital. The second shock came so fast after the first it didn't really register right away.

"Hey." The pretty lady with the long wavy brown hair and bright blue happy eyes said to me.

It took me a minute to recognize her. Although it had been a few years she hadn't changed at all. Well maybe her hair was styled a bit different but Alison looked just the same as she did when I had caught a ride from her in what seemed a different life.

"Hi." I answered. My voice coming out as a hoarse whisper and sounded like a frog was there instead.

"Here." She said putting a straw to my mouth and the water tasted so good and cold. "I just got some fresh when you started stirring a bit. I thought you would be waking up for good soon and stale water tastes just gross."

I nodded to her as my stomach decided water wasn't the only thing it wanted. The growl was louder than my voice was and she smiled at the noise.

She picked up the phone on my table and started talking. I was still trying to figure out what in the world was going on, how I wasn't dead and in Hell and how did I rate a nice woman visiting me here. I was nobody, just a street rat and petty thief. Why would anybody waste their time with me?

Yeah, I know I had called her but as that terrifying and more than distorted memory came back to me I had known it wasn't her voice or Melissa's that had answered the phone. It had been late at night and I thought it was a business number she had given me. It really had been a desperate hope that I didn't think would accomplish anything. But a man had answered the phone. A man with a very deep voice that would have sent a shiver down my spine any other time.

When she hung up she smiled at me again. Her eyes were so sweet and understanding. She brushed away the hair that was in my eyes. "It's okay sweetie. We are here and you are home."

I had no idea what she meant but the idea of having a home instead of just a roof over my head sounded real good. But why?

"Confused a bit aren't you?" She said as she stared into my eyes. When she handed me a mirror I didn't understand why. As I looked at the person staring back at me I turned it around trying to see how the joke worked. "No it isn't a trick mirror." She said laughing. "That really is you."

As she stroked my face I could see her fingers moving down the image in the mirror so I knew if it was a magic trick it was the best one I had ever heard of. I still didn't understand it but I wasn't the most worldly person around and I had never even made it out of high school let alone college so I knew I wasn't that educated but even I knew that eye color didn't change this late in life.

But mine had. Mine were usually brown and now they were blue. The same exact color as Alison's were, a beautiful bright shiny blue.

"How?" Was all I could get out. My throat still hurt and as I rubbed it I noticed I had needles in my hand and grimaced at that.

"Sorry we have to let the doctors think they have worked a miracle in keeping you alive. It is just easier that way."

I didn't nod because I had no idea what in the heck she was talking about. If what I had been through was a miracle I think I would pass on anything more terrifying.

"I know you don't understand. But you will. You are coming home with me and a few friends and everything will be just fine."

I tried to move a bit and groaned with effort. Everything hurt. I swear even my toes did. With a little help from the electric bed Alison got going and her pulling as gently as she could I was soon sitting up and even though it ached to do I felt better afterwards because things looked a lot better when you weren't flat on your back.

"I have somebody bringing food for us." She said as she sat back down in the chair near the bed. I was surprised I didn't have a roommate but the bed on the other side of the curtain was empty.

"It will take me forever to pay off this bill." I groused. Then I wanted to bite my tongue. I should be happy to be alive and not worried about stupid things like money. But I hadn't had any in so long that it was all I could think about.

Hospital bills were expensive and I didn't have any of that fancy insurance that was now all the rage when I had the chance to watch TV or read advertisements. When I was a kid nobody had heard of anything like that. Now there was insurance for just about everything. Not that I had any idea of how much it was or how it worked or much of anything really.

Now that I was away from the day-to-day struggle to live I realized just how far I had really sunk. Well not any more. I may still have to work hard for money to eat and a place to stay but I would find a way to do it. That is what my parents would have wanted. And when I got better off in some very distant future I would try and help people like me. Be there for them and pull them off the streets and find them before they got as lost as I had been.

I had a mission in life now but I still had no way to do it but I came from very stubborn stock. My Mamma had shown me to never give up and I had. My Dad had told me to stand up for what I knew was right and I hadn't. By the grace of God I had been given a second chance and I wouldn't waste this one the way I had my first one.

Alison wasn't really the chatty type or maybe she knew I had a lot on my mind. She just sat over in her chair, read a book and would look up at me every once in a while and smile. The smile warmed my heart.

Even though my past should have had me hesitant to take a helping hand from anybody it didn't seem to think Alison fit it the group of don't trust. In fact that was all I wanted to do. Run to her and put my arms around her and cry until I ran out of tears.

I could feel them starting. Trying to fight them didn't seem to do any good as I sniffed loudly. Her head came up and she looked into my eyes.

She was sitting on the bed so fast I don't know how she did it. "It's okay. Most of us have that reaction when we finally make it through. Go ahead sweetie, cry." I had no idea really what she was talking about. But I couldn't hold back the tears any longer and I cried. No, I bawled and sobbed and probably slobbered some too. It felt really good to have somebody hold me. Even though she wasn't much bigger than me it was like she knew everything and nothing would hurt me as long as she was here. I was home.

When I had snuffled my last two things finally dawned on me. One she hadn't even said my name, did she remember me from so many years ago. I couldn't have made that big of an impression or at least not at much as she had to me.

"Do you remember me?" I blurted out. It would explain why she was willing to take in a stray cat like she was. She seemed to have offered me a way out, a place to stay. Who would do that to a perfect stranger?

Alison smiled. "Of course I do. You are family." And that statement made as little sense as the rest of the world did at the moment.

I shook my head. She must have me confused with somebody else because I knew I wasn't related to this marvelous, well-dressed, self-assured woman. I wish I was but I knew better. "No but we've met once before. Several years back you gave me a ride."

She kept smiling. "Of course. That explains the phone call we received. Scared the heck out of all of us. Simon knew we wouldn't make it to the address you gave him in time so he called the police. It took us forever to find out where you were after that. They had you listed as a Jane Doe until I told them differently. I'm sorry we didn't make it in time. But I think that a couple of our guys are taking care of your problem."

Some of that made sense and some of it didn't but it did explain why she was here. I just hoped that the guys she was talking about didn't get in over their heads. Mr. Carson was dangerous but Shane was crazy.

It seemed so strange to feel this comfortable with a person that I had only met once but I had trusted her the first time so why not now. She had come to see me for no reason other than I had bummed a ride from her. I doubted I was the first or the last to do that but she came. Her and some of her friends had responded to a desperate call late at night from someone that they didn't know.

This was the type of people I needed to know. Alison was nice. She hadn't asked me a single thing and had sat around for I don't know how long while I slept and waited. "I wish I had stayed with you when I met you the last time." I told her wistfully.

She chuckled. "And I wish I had been able to keep you. But you weren't a little kitten to be adopted. You had to make your own way in the world and I'm sorry things have been so rough on you. I should have done more than give you a business card and send you on your way."

I grimaced a bit at that. I wished she had done more than that too. But my life had been my choice and even though I had been pushed into things I could have chosen differently. I could have gone into foster care and been put into a home after my parents died. Things could have hardly been worse. But I had been stubborn at the wrong time in my life and hot headed and thought I knew everything.

Now I would take it slow, I promised myself. Ask questions and find out before I decided anything. That was a good plan but a few minutes later the door opened up and all my plans went right out the window.

Two men came in carrying bags of food that smelled great and should have made my stomach snarl worse than ever. But food was suddenly not real high on my list. One of the guys was black and big and had muscles upon muscles upon muscles. He was good looking in his way I guess but he could have been an ugly skinny kid for all I cared.

The second man in the door was the one that had all my attention. He had those same blue eyes that Alison did and long reddish brown hair and a full beard. It wasn't any of those things that made me stop and go wow. It was his voice and the way he looked at me. As soon as our eyes met it was like a bus had hit me.

"Hey, nice to you see are awake finally." He said and smiled. "I'm Peter." And that is when my life really started.